"I WISH YOU WOULD GIVE IT TO ME FOR MY BIRTH PLACE."

What Can.

The Works of E. P. Roe

VOLUME TEN

WHAT CAN SHE DO?

ILLUSTRATED

WILDSIDE PRESS

DEDICATION

IF I WERE
TO DEDICATE THIS
BOOK IT WOULD BE TO THOSE
GIRLS WHO RESOLVE THAT THEY WILL NOT
PLAY THE POOR ROLE OF MICAWBER, THEIR ONLY CHANCE FOR
LIFE BEING THAT SOME ONE WILL "TURN UP"
WHOM THEY MAY BURDEN WITH
THEIR HELPLESS
WEIGHT

PREFACE

THIS book was not written to amuse, to create purpose-less excitement, or to secure a little praise as a bit of artistic work. It would probably fail in all these things. It was written with a definite, earnest purpose, which I trust will be apparent to the reader.

As society in our land grows older, and departs from primitive simplicity, as many are becoming rich, but more poor, the changes that I have sought to warn against become more threatening. The ordinary avenues of industry are growing thronged, and it daily involves a more fearful risk for a woman to be thrown out upon the world with un-skilled hands, an untrained mind, and an unbraced moral nature. Impressed with this danger by some considerable observation, by a multitude of facts that might wring tears from stony eyes, I have tried to write earnestly if not wisely.

Of necessity, it touches somewhat on a subject delicate and difficult to treat—the "skeleton in the closet" of society. But the evil exists on every side, and at some time or other threatens every home and life. It is my belief that Christian teachers should not timidly or loftily ignore it, for, mark it well, the evil does not let us or ours alone. It is my belief that it should be dealt with in a plain, fear-

(5)

less, manly manner.   Those who differ with me have a right to their opinion.

There is one other thought that I wish to suggest. Much of the ˋfiction of our day, otherwise strong and admirable, is discouraging in this respect.   In the delineation of character, some are good, some are bad, and some indifferent.   We have a lovely heroine, a noble hero, developing seemingly in harmony with the inevitable laws of their natures.   Associated with them are those of the commoner or baser sort, also developing in accordance with the innate principles of their natures.   The first are presented as if created of finer clay than the others.   The first are the flowers in the garden of society, the latter the weeds. According to this theory of character, the heroine must grow as a moss-rose and the weed remain a weed.   Credit is not due to one; blame should not be visited on the other. Is this true?   Is not the choice between good and evil placed before every human soul, save where ignorance and mental feebleness destroy free agency?   In the field of the world which the angels of God are to reap, is it not even possible for the tares to become wheat?   And cannot the sweetest and most beautiful natural flowers of character borrow from the skies a fragrance and bloom not of earth? So God's inspired Word teaches me.

I have turned away from many an exquisite and artistic delineation of human life, sighing, God might as well never have spoken words of hope, warning, and strength for all there is in this book.   The Divine and human Friend might have remained in the Heavens, and never come to earth in human guise, that He might press His great heart of world-wide sympathy against the burdened, suffering heart of humanity.   He need not have died to open a way of life for all. There is nothing here but human motive, human strength, and earthly destiny. We protest against this narrowing down of life, though it be done with the faultless skill and taste of the most cultured genius. The children of men are not orphaned. Our Creator is still "Emmanuel —God with us." Earthly existence is but the prelude of our life, and even from this the Divine artist can take much of the discord, and give an earnest of the eternal harmonies.

We all are honored with the privilege of "co-working with Him."

If I in my little sphere can by this book lead one father to train his children to be more strong and self-reliant, one mother to teach her daughters a purer, more patient, more heroic womanhood—if I have placed one more barrier in the tempter's way, and inspired one more wholesome fear and principle in the heart of the tempted—if, by lifting the dark curtain a moment, I can reveal enough to keep one country girl from leaving her safe native village for unprotected life in some great city—if I can add one iota toward a public opinion that will honor useful labor, however humble, and condemn and render disgraceful idleness and helplessness, however gilded—if, chief of all, I lead one heavy-laden heart to the only source of rest, I shall be well rewarded, whatever is said of this volume.

CONTENTS

(9)

LIST OF ILLUSTRATIONS

WHAT CAN SHE DO?

WHAT CAN SHE DO?

CHAPTER I

THREE GIRLS

IT was a very cold blustering day in early January, and even brilliant thronged Broadway felt the influence of winter's harshest frown. There had been a heavy fall of snow which, though in the main cleared from the sidewalks, lay in the streets comparatively unsullied and unpacked. Fitful gusts of the passing gale caught it up and whirled it in every direction. From roof, ledges, and window-sills, miniature avalanches suddenly descended on the startled pedestrians, and the air was here and there loaded with falling flakes from wild hurrying masses of clouds, the rear-guard of the storm that the biting northwest wind was driving seaward.

It was early in the afternoon, and the great thoroughfare was almost deserted. Few indeed would be abroad for pleasure in such weather, and the great tide of humanity that must flow up and down this channel every working day of the year under all skies had not yet turned northward.

But surely this graceful figure coming up the street with quick, elastic steps has not the aspect of one driven forth by grave business cares, nor in the natural course of things would one expect so young a lady to know much of life's burdens and responsibilities. As she passes I am sure the reader would not turn away from so pleasant a vision, even if Broadway were presenting all its numberless attractions, but at such a time would make the most of the occasion, assured that nothing so agreeable would greet his eyes again that sombre day.

The fierce gusts make little impression on her heavy, close-fitting velvet dress, and in her progress against the wind she appears so trim and taut that a sailor's eye would be captivated. She bends her little turbaned head to the blast, and her foot strikes the pavement with a decision that suggests a naturally brave, resolute nature, and gives abundant proof of vigor and health. A trimming of silver fox fur caught and contrasted the snow crystals against the black velvet of her dress, in which the flakes catch and mingle, increasing the sense of lightness and airiness which her movements awaken, and were you seeking a fanciful embodiment of the spirit of the snow, you might rest satisfied with the first character that appears upon the scene of my story.

But on nearer view there was nothing spirit-like or even spirituelle in her aspect, save that an extremely transparent complexion was rendered positively dazzling by the keen air and the glow of exercise; and the face was much too full and blooming to suggest the shadowy and ethereal.

When near Twenty-first Street she entered a fruit store and seemed in search of some delicacy for an invalid. As her eye glanced around among the fragrant tropical fruits that suggested lands in wide contrast to the wintry scene without, she suddenly uttered a low exclamation of delight, as she turned from them to old friends, all the more welcome because so unexpected at that season. These were nothing less than a dozen strawberries, in dainty baskets, decked out, or more truly eked out, with a few green leaves. Three or four baskets constituted the fruiterer's entire stock, and probably the entire supply for the metropolis of America that day.

She had scarcely time to lift a basket and inhale its delicious aroma, before the proprietor of the store was in bowing attendance, quite as openly admiring her carnation

cheeks as she the ruby fruit. The man's tongue was, however, more decorous than his eyes, and to her question as
to price he replied:

"*Only* two dollars a basket, miss, and certainly they are
beauties for this season of the year. They are all I could
get, and I don't believe there is another strawberry in New
York."

"I will take them all," was the brief, decisive answer,
and from a costly portemonnaie she threw down the price,
a proceeding which the man noted in agreeable surprise,
again curiously scanning the fair face as he made up the
parcel with ostentatious zeal. But his customer was unconscious, or, more truly, indifferent to his admiration, and
seemed much more interested in the samples of choice fruit
arranged on every side. From one to another of these she
flitted with the delicate sensuousness of a butterfly, smell-
ing them and touching them lightly with the hand she had
ungloved (which was as white as the snow without), as if
they had for her a peculiar fascination.

"You seem very fond of fruit," said the merchant, his
amour propre pleased by her evident interest in his stock.

"I have ever had a passion for fine fruits and flowers,"
was the reply, spoken with that perfect frankness characteristic of American girls. "No, you need not send it; I prefer
to take it with me."

And with a slight smile, she passed out, leaving the
fruiterer chuckling over the thought that he had probably
had the pleasantest bit of trade on Broadway that dull day.

Plunging through the drifts, our nymph of the snow
resolutely crossed the street and passed down to a flower
store, but, instead of buying a bouquet, ordered several
pots of budding and blooming plants to be sent to her
address. She then made her way to Fifth Avenue and soon
mounted a broad flight of steps to one of its most stately
houses. The door yielded to her key, her thick walking
boots clattered for a moment on the marble floor, but could
not disguise the lightness of her step as she tripped up the

winding stair and pushed open a rosewood door leading into the upper hall.

"Mother, mother," she exclaimed, "here is a treat for you that will banish nerves, headache, and horrors generally. See what I have found for you out in the wintry snows. Now am I not a good fairy for once?"

"Oh, Edith, child, not so boisterous, please," responded a querulous voice from a great easy-chair by the glowing grate, and a middle-aged lady turned a white, faded face toward her daughter.

"Forgive me, mother, but my tramp in the January storm has made me feel rampantly well. I wish you could go out and take a run every day as I do. You would then look younger and prettier than your daughters, as you used to."

The invalid shivered and drew her shawl closer around her, complaining:

"I think you have brought the whole month of January in with you. You really must show more consideration, my dear, for if I should take cold—" and the lady ended with a weary, suggestive sigh.

In fact, Edith had entered the dim heavily-perfumed room like a gust of wholesome air, her young blood tingling and electric with exercise, and her heart buoyant with the thought of the surprise and pleasure she had in store for her mother. But the manner in which she had been received had already chilled her more than the biting blasts on Broadway. She therefore opened her bundle and set out the little baskets before her mother very quietly. The lady glanced at them for a moment and then said, indifferently:

"It is very good of you to think of me, my dear; they look very pretty. I am sorry I cannot eat them, but their acid would only increase my dyspepsia. Those raised in winter must be very sour. Ugh! the thought of it sets my teeth on edge," and the poor, nervous creature shrank deeper into her wrappings.

"I am very sorry, mother, I thought they would be a

great treat for you," said Edith, quite crestfallen. "Never mind; I got some flowers, and they will be here soon."

"Thank you, dear, but the doctor says they are not healthy in a room—Oh, dear—that child! what shall I do!"

The front door banged, there was a step on the stairs, but not so light as Edith's had been, and a moment later the door burst open, and "the child" rushed in like a mild whirlwind, exclaiming:

"Hurrah! hurrah! school to the shades. No more teachers and tyrants for me," and down went an armful of books with a bang on the table.

"Oh, Zell!" cried Edith, "please be quiet; mother has a headache."

"There, there, your baby will kiss it all away," and the irrepressible young creature threw her arms around the bundle that Mrs. Allen had made herself into by her many wrappings, and before she ceased, the red pouting lips left the faintest tinge of their own color on the faded cheeks of the mother.

The lady endured the boisterous embrace with a martyr-like expression. Zell was evidently a privileged character, the spoiled pet of the household. But a new voice was now heard that was sharper than the "pet" was accustomed to.

"Zell, you are a perfect bear. One would think you had learned your manners at a boys' boarding school."

Zell's great black eyes blazed for a moment toward the speaker, who was a young lady reclining on a lounge near the window, and who in appearance must have been the counterpart of Mrs. Allen herself as she had looked twenty-three years before. In contrast with her sharp, annoyed tone, her cheeks and eyes were wet with tears.

"What are you crying about?" was Zell's brusque response. "Oh, I see; a novel. What a ridiculous old thing you are. I never saw you shed a tear over real trouble, and yet every few days you are dissolved in brine over Adolph Moonshine's agonies, and Seraphina's sentiment, which any sensible person can see is caused by dyspepsia. No such whipped syllabub for me, but real life."

"And what does 'real life' mean for you, I would like to know, but eating, dressing, and flirting?" was the acid retort.

"Though you call me 'child,' I have lived long enough to learn that eating, dressing, and flirting, and while you are about it you might as well add drinking, is the 'real life' of most of the ladies of our set. Indeed, if my poor memory does not fail me, I have seen you myself take a turn at these things sufficiently often to make the sublime scorn of your tone a little inconsistent."

As these barbed arrows flew, the tears rapidly exhaled from the hot cheeks of the young lady on the sofa. Her elegant languor vanished, and she started up; but Mrs. Allen now interfered, and in tones harsh and high, very different from the previous delicate murmurs, exclaimed:

"Children, you drive me wild. Zell, leave the room, and don't show yourself again till you can behave yourself."

Zell was now sobbing, partly in sorrow and partly in anger, but she let fly a few more Parthian arrows over her shoulder as she passed out.

"This is a pretty way to treat one on their birthday. I came home with heart as light as the snowflakes around me, and now you have spoiled everything. I don't know how it is, but I always have a good time everywhere else, but there is something in this house that often sets one's teeth on edge," and the door banged appropriately with a spiteful emphasis as the last word was spoken.

"Poor child," said Edith, "it *is* too bad that she should be so dashed with cold water on her birthday."

"She isn't a child," said the eldest sister, rising from the sofa and sweeping from the room, "though she often acts like one, and a very bad one too. Her birthday should remind her that if she is ever to be a woman, it is time to commence," and the stately young lady passed coldly away.

Edith went to the window and looked dejectedly out into
the early gloom of the declining winter day. Mrs. Allen
sighed and looked more nervous and uncomfortable than
usual.

The upholsterer had done his part in that elegant home.
The feet sank into the carpets as in moss. Luxurious chairs
seemed to embrace the form that sank into them. Everything was padded, rounded, and softened, except tongues
and tempers. If wealth could remove the asperities from
these as from material things, it might well be coveted.
But this is beyond the upholsterer's art, and Mrs. Allen
knew little of the Divine art that can wrap up words and
deeds with a kindness softer than eider-down.

"Mother's room," instead of being a refuge and a favorite haunt of these three girls, was a place where, as we have
seen, their "teeth were set on edge."

Naturally they shunned the place, visiting the invalid
rather than living with her; their reluctant feet impelled
across the threshold by a sense of duty rather than drawn
by the cords of love. The mother felt this in a vague, uncomfortable way, for mother love was there, only it had
seemingly turned sour, and instead of attracting her children by sweetness and sympathy, she querulously complained to them and to her husband of their neglect. He
would sometimes laugh it off, sometimes shrug his shoulders indifferently, and again harshly chide the girls, according to his mood, for he varied much in this respect. After
being cool and wary all day in Wall Street, he took off the
curb at home; therefore the variations that never could be
counted on. How he would be at dinner did not depend
on himself or any principle, but on circumstances. In the
main he was indulgent and kind, though quick and passionate, brooking no opposition; and the girls were really more
attached to him and found more pleasure in his society than
in their mother's. Zelica, the youngest, was his special
favorite, and he humored and petted her at a ruinous rate,
though often storming at some of her follies.

Mrs. Allen saw this preference of her husband, and was weak enough to feel and show jealousy. But her complainings were ineffectual, for we can no more scold people into loving us than nature could make buds blossom by daily nipping them with frost. And yet she made her children uncomfortable by causing them to feel that it was unnatural and wrong that they did not care more for their mother. This was especially true of Edith, who tried to satisfy her conscience, as we have seen, by bringing costly presents and delicacies that were seldom needed or appreciated.

Edith soon became so oppressed by her mother's sighs and silence and the heavy perfumed air, that she sprang up, and pressing a remorseful kiss on the white thin face, said:

"I must dress for dinner, mamma: I will send your maid," and vanished also.

CHAPTER II

A FUTURE OF HUMAN DESIGNING

THE dining-room at six o'clock wore a far more cheerful aspect than the invalid's room upstairs. It was furnished in a costly manner, but more ostentatiously than good taste would dictate. You instinctively felt that it was a sacred place to the master of the house, in which he daily sacrificed to one of his chosen deities.

The portly colored waiter, in dress coat and white vest, has just placed the soup on the table, and Mr. Allen enters, supporting his wife. He had sort of manly toleration for all her whims and weaknesses. He had never indulged in any lofty ideas of womanhood, nor had any special longings for her sympathy and companionship. Business was the one engrossing thing of his life, and this he honestly believed woman incapable of, from her very nature. It was true of his wife, but due to a false education rather than to any innate difficulties, and he no more expected her to comprehend and sympathize intelligently with his business operations, than to see her go down to Wall Street with him wearing his hat and coat.

She had been the leading belle in his set years ago. He had admired her immensely as a stylish, beautiful woman, and carried her off from dozens of competitors, who were fortunate in their failure. He always maintained a show of gallantry and deference; which, though but veneer, was certainly better than open disregard and brutal neglect.

So now, with a good-natured tolerance and politeness, he seated the feeble creature in a cushioned chair at the table, treating her more like a spoiled child than as a friend and companion. The girls immediately appeared also, for they knew their father's weakness too well to keep him waiting for his dinner.

Zell bounded into his arms in her usual impulsive style, and the father caressed her in a way that showed that his heart was very tender toward his youngest child.

"And so my baby is seventeen to-day," he said. "Well, well, how fast we are growing old."

The girl laughed; the man sighed. The one was on the threshold of what she deemed the richest pleasures of life; the other had well-nigh exhausted them, and for a moment realized it.

Still he was in excellent spirits, for he had been unusually fortunate that day, and had seen his way to an "operation" that promised a golden future. He sat down therefore to the good cheer with not a little of the spirit of the man in the parable, whose complacent exhortation to his soul has ever been the language of false security and prosperity.

The father's open favoritism for Zell was another source of jealousy, her sisters naturally feeling injured by it. Thus in this household even human love was discordant and perverted, and the Divine love unknown. What chance had character, that thing of slow growth, in such an atmosphere?

The popping of a champagne cork took the place of grace at the opening of the meal, and the glasses were filled all around. In honor of Zell's birthday they drank to her health and happiness. By no better form or more suggestive ceremony could this Christian (?) family wish their youngest member "God-speed" on entering the vicissitudes of a new year of life. But what they did was done heartily, and every glass was drained. To them it seemed very appropriate, and her father said, glancing admiringly at her flaming cheeks and dancing eyes—

"This is just the thing to drink Zell's health in, for she is as full of sparkle and effervescence as the champagne itself."

Had he been a wiser and more thoughtful man, he would have carried the simile further and remembered the fate of champagne when exposed. However piquant and pleasing Zell's sparkle might be, it would hardly secure success and safety for life. But in his creed a girl's first duty was to be pretty and fascinating, and he was extremely proud of the beauty of his daughters. It was his plan to marry them to rich men who would maintain them in the irresponsible luxury that their mother had enjoyed.

Circumstances seemed to justify his security. The son of a rich man, he had also inherited a taste for business and the art of making money. Years of prosperity had confirmed his confidence, and he looked complacently around upon his family and talked of the future in sanguine tones.

He was a man considerably past his prime, and his florid face and portly form indicated that he was in the habit of doing ample justice to the good cheer before him. Intense application to business in early years and indulgence of appetite in later life had seriously impaired a constitution naturally good. He reminded you of a flower fully blown or of fruit overripe.

"Since you have permitted Zell to leave school, I suppose she must make her début soon," said Mrs. Allen with more animation than usual in her tone.

"Oh, certainly," cried Zell, "on Edith's birthday, in February. We have arranged it all, haven't we, Edith?"

"Heigho! then I am to have no part in the matter," said her father.

"Yes, indeed, papa," cried the saucy girl, "you are to have no end of kisses, and a very long bill."

This sally pleased him immensely, for it expressed his ideal of womanly return for masculine affection, at least the bills had never been wanting in his experience. But, mellowed by wine and elated by the success of the day, he now prepared to give the coup that would make a far greater sensation in the family circle than even a début or a birthday party. So, glancing from one eager face to another (for between the wine and the excitement even Mrs. Allen was no longer a colorless, languid creature, ready to faint at the embrace of her child), he said with a twinkle in his eye—

"Well, go to your mother about the party. She is a veteran in such matters. But let there be some limit to the length of the bill, or I can't carry out another plan I have in view for you."

Chorus—"What is that?"

Coolly filling his glass, he commenced leisurely sipping, while glancing humorously from one to another, enjoying their impatient expectancy.

"If you don't tell us right away," cried Zell, bouncing up, "I'll pull your whiskers without mercy."

"Papa, you will throw mother into a fever. See how flushed her face is!" said Laura, the eldest daughter, speaking at the same time two words for herself.

The face of Edith, with dazzling complexion all aglow, and large dark eyes lustrous with excitement, was more eloquent than words could have been, and the bon vivant drank in her expression with as much zest as he sipped his wine. Perhaps it was well for him to make the most of that little keen-edged moment of bright anticipation and bewildering hope, for what he was about to propose would cost him many thousands, and exile him from business, which to him was the very breath of life.

But Mrs. Allen's matter-of-fact voice brought things to a crisis, for with an injured air she said:

"How can you, George, when you know the state of my nerves?"

"What I propose, mamma, will cure your nerves and everything else, for it is nothing less than a tour through Europe."

There was a shriek of delight from the girls, in which even the exquisite Laura joined, and Mrs. Allen trembled with excitement. Apart from the trip itself, they considered it a sort of disgrace that a family of their social position and wealth had never been abroad. Therefore the announcement was doubly welcome. Hitherto Mr. Allen's devotion to business had made it impossible, and he had given them no hints of the near consummation of their wishes. But he had begun to feel the need of change and rest himself, and this weighed more with him than all their entreaties.

In a moment Zell had her arms about his neck, and her sisters were throwing him kisses across the table. His wife, looking unusually gratified, said:

"You are a sensible man at last," which was a great deal for Mrs. Allen to say.

"Why, mamma," exclaimed her husband, elevating his eyebrows in comic surprise, "that I should live to hear you say that!"

"Now don't be silly," she replied, joining slightly in the laugh at her expense, "or we shall think that you have taken too much champagne, and that this Europe business is all a hoax."

"Wait till you have been outside of Sandy Hook an hour, and you will find everything real enough then. I think I see the elegant ladies of my household about that time."

"For shame, papa! what an uncomfortable suggestion over a dinner table!" said the fastidious Laura. "Picture the ladies of your household in the salons of Paris. I promise we will do you credit there."

"I hope so, for I fear I shall have need of *credit* when you all reach that Mecca of women."

"It's no more the Mecca of women than Wall Street is the Jerusalem of men. What you are all going to do in Heaven without Wall Street, I don't see."

Mr. Allen gave his significant shrug and said, "I don't meet notes till they are due," which was his way of saying: "Sufficient unto the day is the evil thereof."

"The salons of Paris!" said Edith, with some disdain. "Think of the scenery, the orange-groves, and vineyards that we shall see, the Alpine flowers—"

"I declare," interrupted Zell, "I believe that Edith

would rather see a grape-vine and orange-tree than all the toilets of Paris."

"I shall enjoy seeing both," was the reply, "and so have the advantage of you in having two strings to my bow."

"By the way, that reminds me to ask how many beaux you now have on the string," said the father.

Edith tossed her head with a pretty blush and said: "Pity me, my father; you know I am always poor at arithmetic."

"You will take up with a crooked stick after all. Now Laura is a sensible girl, like her mother, and has picked out one of the richest, longest-headed fellows on the street."

"Indeed!" said his wife. "I do not see but you are paying yourself a greater compliment than either Laura or me."

"Oh, no, a mere business statement. Laura means business, and so does Mr. Goulden."

Laura looked annoyed and said:

"Pa, I thought you never talked business at home."

"Oh, this is a feminine phase that women understand. I want your sisters to profit by your good example."

"I shall marry an Italian count," cried Zell.

"Who will turn out a fourth-rate Italian barber, and I shall have to support you both. But I won't do it. You would have to help him shave."

"No, I should transform him into a leader of banditti, and we would live in princely state in the Apennines. Then we would capture you, papa, and carry you off to the mountains, and I would be your jailer, and give you nothing but turtle-soup, champagne, and kisses till you paid a ransom that would break Wall Street."

"I would not pay a cent, but stay and eat you out of house and home."

"I never expect to marry," said Edith, "but some day I am going to commence saving my money—now don't laugh, papa, for I could be economical if I once made up my mind"—and the pretty head gave a decisive little nod.

"I am going to save my money and buy a beautiful place in the country and make it as near like the garden of Eden as possible."

"Snakes will get into it as of old," was Mrs. Allen's cynical remark.

"Yes, that is woman's experience with a garden," said her husband with a mock sigh.

Popping off the cork of another bottle, he added, "I have got ahead of you, Edith. I own a place in the country, much as I dislike that kind of property. I had to take it to-day in a trade, and so am a landholder in Pushton—prospect, you see, of my becoming a rural gentleman (Squire is the title, I believe), and of exchanging stock in Wall Street for the stock of a farm. Here's to my estate of three acres with a story and a half mansion upon it! Perhaps you would rather go up there this summer than to Paris, my dear?" to his wife.

Mrs. Allen gave a contemptuous shrug as if the jest were too preposterous to be answered, but Edith cried:

"Fill my glass; I will drink to your country place. I know the cottage is a sweet rustic little box, all smothered with vines and roses like one I saw last June." Then she added in sport, "I wish you would give it to me for my birthday present. It would make such a nice porter's lodge at the entrance to my future Eden."

"Are you in earnest?" asked the father suddenly.

Both were excited by the wine they had drunk. She glanced at her father, and saw that he was in a mood to say yes to anything, and, quick as thought, she determined to get the place if possible.

"Of course I am. I would rather have it than all the jewelry in New York." She was over-supplied with that style of gift.

"You shall have it then, for I am sure I don't want it, and am devoutly thankful to be rid of it."

Edith clapped her hands with a delight scarcely less demonstrative than that of Zell in her wildest moods.

"Nonsense!" said Mrs. Allen; "the idea of giving a young lady such an elephant!"

"But remember," continued her father, "you must manage it yourself, pay the taxes, keep it repaired, insured, etc. There is a first-class summer hotel near it. Next year, after we get back from Europe, we will go up there and stay awhile. You shall then take possession, employ an agent to take care of it, who by the way will cheat you to your heart's content. I will wager you a box of gloves that, before a year passes, you will try to sell the ivy-twined cottage for anything you can get, and will be thoroughly cured of your mania for country life."

"I'll take you up," said Edith, in great excitement, "but remember, I want my deed on my birthday."

"All right," said Mr. Allen, laughing. "I will transfer it to you to-morrow, while I think of it. But don't try to trade it off to me before next month for a new dress."

Edith was half wild over her present. Many and varied were her questions, but her father only said:

"I don't know much about it. I did not listen to half the man said, but I remember he stated there was a good deal of fruit on the place, for it made me think of you at the time. Bless you, I could not stop for such small game. I am negotiating a large and promising operation which you understand about as well as farming. It will take some time to carry it through, but when finished we will start for the 'salons of Paris.'"

"I half believe," said Laura, with a covert sneer, "that Edith would rather go up to her farm of three acres."

"I am well satisfied as papa has arranged it," said the practical girl. "Everything in its place, and get all out of life you can, is my creed."

"That means, get all out of me you can, don't it, sly puss?" laughed the father, well pleased, though, with the worldly wisdom of the speech.

"Kisses, kisses, unlimited kisses, and consider yourself well repaid," was the arch rejoinder; and not a few, looking at her as she then appeared, would have coveted such bargains. So her father seemed to think as he gazed admiringly at her.

But something in Zell's pouting lips and vexed expression caught his eye, and he said good-naturedly:

"Heigho, youngster, what has brought a thunder-cloud across your saucy face?"

"In providing for birthdays to come, I guess you have forgotten your baby's birthday present."

"Come here, you envious elf," said her father, taking something from his pocket. Like light she flashed out from under the cloud and was at his side in an instant, dimpling, smiling, and twinkling with expectation, her black eyes as quick and restless as her father was deliberate and slow in undoing a dainty parcel.

"Oh, George, do be quick about it, or Zell will explode. You both make me nervous," said Mrs. Allen fretfully.

Suddenly pressing open a velvet casket, Mr. Allen hung a jewelled watch with a long gold chain about his favorite's neck, while she improvised a hornpipe around his chair.

"There," said he, "is something that is worth more than Edith's farm, tumble-down cottage, roses, and all. So remember that those lips were made to kiss, not to pout with."

Zell put her lips to proper uses to that extent that Mrs. Allen began to grow jealous, nervous, and out of sorts generally, and having finished her chocolate, rose feeoly from the table. Her husband offered his arm and the family dinner party broke up.

And yet, take it altogether, each one was in higher spirits than usual, and Zell and Edith were in a state of positive delight. They had received costly gifts that specially gratified their peculiar tastes, and these, with the promise of a grand party and a trip to Europe, youthful buoyancy, and champagne, so dilated their little feminine souls that Mrs. Allen's fears of an explosion of some kind were scarcely groundless. They dragged their stately sister Laura, now unwontedly bland and affable, to the piano, and called for the quickest and most brilliant of waltzes, and a moment later their lithe figures flowed away in a rhythm of motion, that from their exuberance of feeling, was as fantastic as it was graceful.

Mr. Allen assisted his wife to her room and soon left her in an unusually contented frame of mind to develop strategy for the coming party. Mrs. Allen's nerves utterly incapacitated her for the care of her household, attendance upon church, and such humdrum matters, but in view of a great occasion like a "grand crush ball," where among the luminaries of fashion she could become the refulgent centre of a constellation which her fair daughters would make around her, her spirit rose to the emergency. When it came to dress and dressmakers and all the complications of the campaign now opening, notwithstanding her nerves, she could be quite Napoleonic.

Her husband retired to the library, lighted a choice Havana, skimmed his evening papers, and then as usual went to his club.

This, as a general thing, was the extent of the library's literary uses. The best authors in gold and Russia smiled down from the black walnut shelves, but the books were present rather as furniture than from any intrinsic value in themselves to the family. They were given prominence on the same principle that led Mrs. Allen to give a certain tone to her entertainments by inviting many literary and scientific men. She might be unable to appreciate the works of the *savants*, but as they appreciated the labors of her masterly French cook, many compromised the matter by eating the *petits soupers* and shrugging their shoulders over the entertainers.

And yet the Allens were anything but vulgar upstarts. Both husband and wife were descended from old and wealthy New York families. They had all the polish which life-long association with the fashionable world bestows. What was more, they were highly intelligent, and, in their own sphere, gifted people. Mr. Allen was a leader in business in one of the chief commercial centres, and to lead in legitimate business in our day requires as much ability, indeed we may say genius, as to lead in any order department of life. He would have shown no more ignorance in the study, studio, and laboratory, than their occupants would have shown in the counting-room. That to which he devoted his energies he had become a master in. It is true he had narrowed down his life to little else than business. He had never acquired a taste for art and literature, nor had he given himself time for broad culture. But we meet narrow artists, narrow clergymen, narrow scientists just as truly. If you do not get on their hobby and ride with them, they seem disposed to ride over you. Indeed, in our brief life with its fierce competitions, few other than what are known as "one idea" men have time to succeed. Even genius must drive with tremendous and concentrated energy, to distance competitors. Mr. Allen was quite as great in his department as any of the lions that his wife lured into her parlors were in theirs.

Mrs. Allen was also a leader in her own chosen sphere, or rather in the one to which she had been educated. Given *carte-blanche* in the way of expense, she would produce a brilliant entertainment which few could surpass. The coloring and decorations of her rooms would not be more rich, varied, or in better taste, than the diversity, and yet harmony of the people she would bring together by her adroit selections. She had studied society, and for it she lived, not to make it better, not to elevate its character, and tone down its extravagances, but simply to shine in it, to be talked about and envied.

Both husband and wife had achieved no small success, and to succeed in such a city as New York in their chosen departments required a certain amount of genius. The *savants* had a general admiration for Mrs. Allen's style and taste, but found that she had nothing to offer on the social exchange of her parlors but fashion's smallest chit-chat. They had a certain respect for Mr. Allen's wealth and business power, but, having discussed the news of the day, they would pass on, and the people during the intervals of dancing drifted into congenial schools and shoals, like fish in a lake. Mr. and Mrs. Allen had a vague admiration for the learning of the scholars and the culture of the artists, but would infinitely prefer marrying their daughters to downtown merchant princes.

Take the world over, perhaps all classes of people are despising others quite as much as they are despised themselves.

But when the French cook appeared upon the scene, then was produced your true democracy. Then was shown a phase of life into which all entered with a zest that proved the common tie of humanity.

CHAPTER III

THREE MEN

WHILE Mrs. Allen was planning the social pyro-
technics that should dazzle the fashionable world,
Edith and Zell were working off their exuberant
spirits in the manner described in the last chapter, which
was as natural to their city-bred feet as a wild romp is to
a country girl.

The brilliant notes of the piano and the rustle of their
silks had rendered them oblivious to the fact that the door-
bell had rung twice, and that three gentlemen were peering
curiously through the half-open door. They were evidently
frequent and favored visitors, and had motioned the old
colored waiter not to announce them, and he reluctantly
obeyed.

For a moment they feasted their eyes on the scene, as
the two girls, with twining arms and many innovations on
the regular step, whirled through the rooms, and then Zell's
quick eye detected them.

Pouncing upon the eldest gentleman of the party, she
dragged him from his ambush, while the others also entered.
The youngest approached the blushing, panting Edith with
an almost boyish confidence of manner, as if assured of a
welcome, while the remaining gentleman, who was verging
toward middle age, quietly glided to the piano and gave
his hand to Laura, who greeted him with a cordiality
scarcely to be expected from so stately a young lady.

The laws of affinity and selection were evidently in force

here, and as the reader must surmise, long acquaintance had led to the present easy and intimate relations.

"What do you mean," cried Zell, dragging under the gaslight her cavalier, who assumed much penitence and fear, "by thus rudely and abruptly breaking in upon the retirement of three secluded young ladies?"

"At their devotions," added the cynical voice of the gentleman at the piano, who was no other than Mr. Goulden, Laura's admirer.

Zell's attendant threw himself in the attitude of a suppliant and said deprecatingly:

"Nay, but we are astronomers."

"That's a fib, and not a very white one either," she retorted. "I don't believe you ever look toward heaven for anything."

"What need of looking thither for heavenly bodies?" he replied in a low, meaning tone, regarding with undisguised admiration her glowing cheeks. "Moreover, I don't like telescopic distances," he continued, with a half-made motion to put his arm around her waist.

"Come," she said, pirouetting out of his reach, "remember I am no longer a child, I am seventeen to-day."

"Would that you might never be a day older in appearance and feelings!"

"Are you willing to leave me so far behind?" she asked with some maliciousness.

"No, but you would make me a boy again. If old Ponce de Leon had met a Miss Zell, he would soon have forsaken the swamps and alligators of Florida."

"Oh, what a watery, scaly compliment! Preferred to swamps and alligators! Who would have believed it?"

"I am not blind to your pretty, wilful blindness. You know I likened you to something too divine and precious to be found on earth."

"Which is still true in the carrying out of your marvellously mixed metaphors. I must lend you my rhetoric book. But as your meaning dawns on me, I see that you are symbolized by old Ponce. I shall look in the history for the age of the ancient Spaniard to-morrow, and then I shall know how old you are, a thing I could never find out."

As with little jets of silvery laughter and with butterfly motion she hovered round him, the very embodiment of life and beautiful youth, she would have made, to an artist's eye, a very true realization of the far-famed mythical fountain.

And yet, as a moment later she confidingly took his arm and strolled toward the library, it was evident that all her flutter and hesitancy, her seeming freedom and mimic show of war, were like those of some bright tropical bird fascinated by a remorseless serpent whose intent eyes and deadly purpose are creating a spell that cannot be resisted.

Mr. Van Dam, upon whose arm she was leaning, was one of the worst products of artificial metropolitan life. He had inherited a name which ancestry had rendered honorable, but which he to the utmost dishonored, and yet so adroitly, so shrewdly respecting fashion's code, though shunning nothing wrong, that he did not lose the *entrée* of the gilded homes of those who called themselves "the best society."

True, it was whispered that he was rather fast, that he played heavily and a trifle too successfully, and that he lived the life of anything but a saint at his luxurious rooms. "But then," continued society, openly and complacently, "he is so fine-looking, so courtly and polished, so well connected, and what is still more to the point, my dear, he is reputed to be immensely wealthy, so we must not heed these rumors. After all, it is the way of these young men of the world."

Thus "the best society" that would have politely frozen out of its parlors the Chevalier Bayard, *sans peur et sans reproche*, had he not appeared in the latest style, with golden fame rather than golden spurs, welcomed Mr. Van Dam. Indeed, not a few forced exotic belles, who had prematurely developed in the hothouse atmosphere of wealth and extravagance, regarded him as a sort of social lion; and his reticence, with a certain mystery in which he shrouded his evil life, made him all the more fascinating. He was past the prime of life, though exceedingly well preserved, for he was one of those cool, deliberate votaries of pleasure that reduce amusement to a science, and carefully shun all injurious excess. While exceedingly deferential toward the sex in general, and bestowing compliments and attentions as adroitly as a financier would place his money, he at the same time permitted the impression to grow that he was extremely fastidious in his taste, and had never married because it had never been his fortune to meet the faultless being who could satisfy his exacting eyes. Any special and continued admiration on his part therefore made its recipient an object of distinction and envy to very many in the unreal world in which he glided serpent-like, rather than moved as a man. To morbid minds his rumored evil deeds became piquant eccentricities, and the whispers of the oriental orgies that were said to take place in his bachelor apartments made him an object of a curious interest, and many sighed for the opportunity of reforming so distinguished a sybarite.

On Edith's entrance into society he had been much impressed by her beauty, and had gradually grown quite attentive, equally attracted by her father's wealth. But she, though with no clear perception of his character, and with no higher moral standard than that of her set, instinctively shrank from the man. Indeed, in some respects, they were too much alike for that mysterious attraction that so often occurs between opposites. Not that she had his unnatural depravity, but like him she was shrewd, practical, resolute, and was controlled by her judgment rather than by her impulses. Her vanity, of which she had no little share, led her to accept his attentions to a certain point, but the keen man of the world soon saw that his "little game," as in his own vernacular he styled it, would not be successful, and he was the last one to sigh in vain or mope an hour in lovelorn melancholy. While ceasing to press his suit, he con-

tinued to be a frequent and familiar visitor at the house,
and thus his attention was drawn to Zell, who, though
young, had developed early in the stimulating atmosphere
in which she lived. At first he petted and played with her
as a child, as she wilfully flitted in and out of the parlors,
whether her sisters wanted her or not. He continually
brought her *bon-bons* and like fanciful trifles, till at last, in
jest, the family called him Zell's "ancient beau."

But during the past year it had dawned on him that the
child he petted on account of her beauty and sprightliness,
was rapidly becoming a brilliant woman, who would make
a wife far more to his taste than her equally beautiful but
matter-of-fact sister. Therefore he warily, so as not to
alarm the jealous father, but with all the subtle skill of
which he was master, sought to win her affections, knowing
that she would have her own way when she knew what way
she wanted.

For Zell this unscrupulous man had a peculiar fascination. He petted and flattered her to her heart's content,
and thus made her the envy of her young acquaintances,
which was incense indeed to her vain little soul. He never
lectured or preached to her on account of her follies and
nonsense, as her elderly friends usually did, but gave to
her wild, impulsive moods free rein. Where a true friend
would have cautioned and curbed, he applauded and in-
cited, causing Zell to mistake extravagance in language and
boldness in manner for spirit and brilliancy. Laura and
Edith often remonstrated with her, but she did not heed
them. Indeed, she feared no one save her father, and Mr.
Van Dam was propriety itself when he was present, which
was but seldom. What with his business, and club, and
Mrs. Allen's nerves, the girls were left mainly to themselves.

What wonder that there are so many shipwrecks, when
young, heedless, inexperienced hands must steer, unguided,
through the most perilous and treacherous of seas?

Mr. Allen's elegant, costly home was literally an unguarded fold, many a laborer, living in a tenement house, doing more to shield his daughters from the evil of the world.

To Mr. Van Dam, Zell was a perfect prize. Though he had sipped at the cup of pleasure so leisurely and system-atically, he was getting down to the dregs. His taste was becoming palled, and satiety was burdening him with its leaden weight. But as the child he petted developed daily toward womanhood, he became interested, then fascinated by the process. Her beauty was so brilliant, her excessive sprightliness so contagious, that he felt his sluggish pulses stir and tingle with excitement the moment he came into her presence. Her wild, varying moods kept him con-stantly on the *qui vive*, and he would say in confidence to one of his intimate cronies:

. "The point is, Hal, she is such a spicy, piquant contrast to the insipid society girls, who have no more individuality than fashion blocks in Broadway windows."

He liked the kittenish young creature all the more be-cause her repartee was often a little cutting. If she had al-ways struck him with a velvet paw, the thing would have grown monotonous, but he occasionally got a scratch that made him wince, cool and brazen as he was. But, after all, he daily saw that he was gaining power over her, and the manner in which the frank-hearted girl took his arm and leaned upon it spoke volumes to the experienced man. While he habitually wore a mask, Zell could conceal nothing, and across her April face flitted her innermost thoughts.

If she had had a *mother*, she might, even in the wilder-ness of earth, have become a blossom fit for heavenly gar-dens, but as it was, her wayward nature, so full of danger-ous beauty, was left to run wild.'

Edith was beginning to be troubled at Zell's intimacy with Mr. Van Dam, and to conceive a growing dislike for him mingled with suspicion. As for Laura, the eldest, she was like her mother, too much wrapped up in herself to

have many thoughts for any one else, and they all regarded
Zell as a mere child still. Mr. Allen, who would have been
very anxious had Zell been receiving the attentions of some
penniless young clerk or artist, laughed at her "flirtation
with old Van Dam" as an eminently safe proceeding.

But on the present evening her sisters were too much
occupied with their own friends to give Zell or her dangerous admirer much attention. As yet no formal engagement
had bound any of them, but an intimacy and mutual liking,
tending to such a result, was rapidly growing.

In Edith's case the attraction of contrasts was again
shown. Augustus Elliot, the youth who had approached
her with such confidence and grace, was quite as stylish a
personage as herself, and that was saying a great deal. But
every line of his full handsome face, as well as the expression of his light blue eyes, showed that he had less decision
in the whole of his luxurious nature than she in her little
finger. Self-indulgence and good-natured vanity were un-
mistakably his characteristics. To yield, not for the good
of others, but because not strong enough to stand sturdily
alone, was the law of his being. If he could ever have been
kept under the influence of good and stronger natures, who
would have developed his naturally kind heart and good impulses into something like principle, he might have had a
safe and creditable career. But he was the idol of a foolish, fashionable mother, and the pet of two or three sisters
who were empty-brained enough to think their handsome
brother the perfection of mankind; and by eye, manner,
and often the plainest words, they told him as much, and
he had at last come to believe them. Why should they
not? He was faultless in his own dress, faultless in his
criticism of a lady's dress, taking the prevailing fashion as
the standard. He was perfectly versed in the polite slang
of the day. He scented afar off and announced the slightest change in the mode, so that his elegant sisters could appear on the avenue in advance of the other fashion-plates.
As they sailed away on a sunny afternoon in their gorgeous

plumage, the envy of many a competing belle, they would say:

"Isn't he a duck of a brother to give us a hint of a change so early? After all there is no eye or taste like that of man when once perfected."

And then they knew him to be equally *au fait* on the flavor of wines, the points of horses, the merits of every watering-place, and all the other lore which in their world gave pre-eminence. They had been educated to have no other ideal of manhood, and if an earnest, straightforward man, with a purpose, had spoken out before them, they would have regarded him as an uncouth monster.

Notwithstanding all his vanity, "Gus," as he was familiarly called, was a very weak man, and though he would not acknowledge it, even to himself, instinctively recognized the fact. He continually attached himself to strong, resolute natures, by whom, if they were adroit, he could easily be made a tool of. He took a great fancy to Edith from the first hour of their acquaintance, and she soon obtained a strong influence over him. She instinctively detected his yielding disposition, and liked him the better for it, while his good-nature and abundant supply of society talk made him a general favorite.

When every one whispered, "What a handsome couple they would make!" and she found him so looked up to and quoted in the fashionable world, she began to entertain quite an admiration as well as liking for him, though she saw more and more clearly that there was nothing in him that she could lean upon.

Gus's parents, who knew that the Allens were immensely wealthy, urged on the match, but Mr. Allen, aware that the Elliots were living to the extent of their means, discouraged it, plainly telling Edith his reasons.

"But," said Edith, at the same time showing her heart in the practical suggestion, "could not Gus go into business himself?"

"The worst thing he could do," said the keen Mr. Allen.

"He has tried it a few times, I have learned, but has not one business qualification. He could not keep himself in toothpicks. His mother and sisters have spoiled him. He is nothing but a society man. Mr. Elliot has not a word to say at home. His business is to make money for them to spend, and a tough time he has to keep up with them. You girls must marry men who can take care of you, unless you wish to support your husbands."

Mr. Allen's verdict was true, and Edith felt that it was. When a boy, Gus could get out of lessons by running to his mother with a plea of headache or any trifle, and in youth he had escaped business in like manner. His father had tried him a few times in his office, but was soon glad to fall in with his wife's opinion, that *her* son "had too much spirit and refinement for plodding humdrum business, that he was a born gentleman and suited only to elegant leisure," and as his gentleman son only did mischief downtown, the poor over-worked father was glad to have him out of the way, for he with difficulty made both ends meet, as it was. Hoping he would do better with strangers, he had, by personal influence, procured him situations elsewhere, but between the mother's weakness and the young man's confirmed habits of idleness, it always ended by Gus saying to his employers:

"I'm going off on a little trip—by-by," at which they gave a sigh of relief. It had at last become a recognized fact that Gus must marry an heiress, this being about the only way for so fine a gentleman to achieve the fortune that he could not stoop to toil for. As he admired himself complacently in the gilded mirror that ornamented his dressing-room, he felt that a wise selection would be his only difficulty, and though an heiress is something of a *rara avis*, he sternly resolved to cage one with such heavy golden plumage that even his mother, whom no one satisfied save himself, would give a sigh of perfect content. When at last he met Edith Allen, it seemed as if inclination might happily blend with his lofty sense of duty, and he soon became Edith's devoted and favored attendant. And yet, as we have seen, our heroine was not the sentimental style of girl that falls hopelessly and helplessly in love with a man for some occult reason, not even known to herself, and who mopes and pines till she is permitted to marry him, be he fool, villain, or saint. Edith was fully capable of appreciating and weighing her father's words, and under their influence nearly decided to chill her handsome but helpless admirer into a mere passing acquaintance; but when he next appeared before her in his uniform, as an officer in one of the "crack" city regiments, her eyes, taste, and vanity, and somehow her heart, so pleaded for him that, so far from being an icicle, she smiled on him like a July sun.

But whenever he sought to press his suit into something definite, she evaded and shunned the point, as only a feminine diplomatist can. In fact, Gus, on account of his vanity, was not a very urgent suitor, as the idea of final refusal was preposterous. He regarded himself as virtually accepted already. Meanwhile Edith for once in her life was playing the rôle of Micawber, and "waiting for something to turn up." And something had, for this trip to Europe would put time and space between them, and gently cure both of their folly, as she deemed it. Folly! She did not realize that Gus regarded himself as acting on sound business principles and a strong sense of duty, as well as obeying the impulses of what heart he had. The sweet approval of conscience and judgment attended his action, while both condemned her.

As Gus approached this evening, she felt a pang of commiseration that not only were they separated by her father's and her own disapproval, but that soon the briny ocean would also be between them, and she was unusually kind. She decided to play with her poor little mouse till the last, and then let absence remedy all. Her mind was quick, if not very profound.

As Mr. Goulden leaned across the corner of the piano, and paid the blushing Laura some delicate compliments, one could not but think of an adroit financier, skilfully placing some money. There was nothing ardent, nothing incoherent and lover-like, in his carefully modulated tones, and nicely selected words that meant much or little, as he might afterward decide. Mr. Goulden always knew what he was about, as truly in a lady's boudoir as in Wall Street. The stately, elegant Laura suited his tastes; her father's financial status *had* suited him also. But he, who through his agents knew all that was going on in Wall Street, was aware that Mr. Allen had engaged in a very heavy speculation, which, though promising well at the time, might, by some unexpected turn of the wheel, wear a very different aspect. He would see the game through before proceeding with his own, and in the meantime, by judicious attention, hold Laura well in hand.

In that brilliantly lighted parlor none of these currents and counter currents were apparent on the surface. That was like the ripple and sparkle of a summer sea in the sunlight. Every year teaches us something of what is hidden under the fair but treacherous seeming of life.

The young ladies were now satisfied with the company they had, and the gentlemen, as can well be understood, wished no further additions. Therefore they agreed to retire to the library for a game of cards.

"Hannibal," said Edith, summoning the portentous colored butler who presided over the front door and dining-room, "if any one calls, say we are out or engaged."

That solemn dignitary bowed as low as his stiff white collar would permit, but soliloquized:

"I guess I is sumpen too black to tell a white lie, so I'se say dey is engaged."

As the ladies swept away, leaning heavily on the arms of their favored gallants, he added, with a slight grin illumining the gravity of his face, "It looks mighty like it."

CHAPTER IV

THE SKIES DARKENING

THE game of cards fared indifferently, for they were all too intent on little games of their own to give close attention. Mr. Van Dam won when he chose, and gave the game away when he chose, but made Zell think the skill was mainly hers.

Still, in common parlance, they had a "good time." From such clever men the jests and compliments were rather better than the average, and repartee from the ruby lips that smiled upon them could not seem other than brilliant.

Edith soon added to the sources of enjoyment by ordering cake and wine, for though not the eldest she seemed naturally to take the lead.

Mr. Goulden drank sparingly. He meant that not a film should come across his judgment. Mr. Van Dam drank freely, but he was seasoned to more fiery potations than sherry. Not so poor Gus, who, while he could never resist the wine, soon felt its influence. But he had sufficient control never to go beyond the point of tipsiness that fashion allows in the drawing-room.

Of course through Zell's unrestrained chatter the recently made plans soon came out.

Adroit Mr. Van Dam turned to Zell with an expression of much pleased surprise, exclaiming:

"How fortunate I am! I had completed my plans to go abroad some little time since."

Zell clapped her hands with delight, but an involuntary shadow darkened Edith's face.

Gus looked nonplussed. He knew that his father and mother with difficulty kept pace with his home expenses and that a Continental tour was impossible for him. Mr. Goulden looked a little thoughtful, as if a new element had entered into the problem.

"Oh, come," laughed Zell. "Let us all be good, and go on a pilgrimage together to Paris—I mean Jerusalem."

"I will worship devoutly with you at either shrine," said Mr. Van Dam.

"And with equal sincerity, I suppose," said Edith, rather coldly.

"I sadly fear, Miss Edith, that my sincerity will not be superior to that of the other devotees," was the keen retort, in blandest tones.

Edith bit her lip, but said gayly, "Count me out of your pilgrim band. I want no shrine with relics of the past. I wish no incense rising about me obscuring the view. I like the present, and wish to see what is beyond."

"But suppose you are both shrine and divinity yourself?" said Gus, with what he meant for a killing look.

"Do you mean that compliment for me?" asked Edith, all sweetness.

Between wine and love Gus was inclined to be sentimental, and so in a low, meaning tone answered:

"Who more deserving?"

Edith's eyes twinkled a moment, but with a half sigh she replied:

"I fear you read my character rightly. A shrine suggests many offerings, and a divinity many worshippers."

Zell laughed outright, and said, "In that respect all women would be shrines and divinities if they could."

Van Dam and Goulden could not suppress a smile at the unfortunate issue of Elliot's sentiment, while the latter glanced keenly to see how much truth was hinted in the badinage.

"For my part," said Laura, looking fixedly at nothing, "I would rather have one true devotee than a thousand pilgrims who were *gushing* at every shrine they met."

"Brava!" cried Mr. Goulden. "That was the keenest arrow yet flown;" for the other two men were notorious flirts.

"I do not think so. Its point was much too broad," said Zell, with a meaning look at Mr. Goulden, that brought a faint color into his imperturbable face, and an angry flush to Laura's.

A disconcerted manner had shown that even Gus's vanity had not been impervious to Edith's barb, but he had now recovered himself, and ventured again:

"I would have my divinity a patron saint sufficiently human to pity human weakness, and so come at last to listen to no other prayer than mine."

⁕ "Surely, Mr. Elliot, you would wish your saint to listen for some other reason than your weakness only," said Edith.

"Come, ladies and gentlemen, I move this party breaks up, or some one will get hurt," said Gus, with a half-vexed laugh.

"What is the matter?" asked Edith innocently.

"Yes," echoed Zell, rising, "what is the matter with *you*, Mr. Van Dam? Are you asleep, that you are so quiet? Tell us about your divinity."

"I am an astronomer and fire-worshipper, somewhat dazzled at present by the nearness and brilliancy of my bright luminary."

"Nonsense! your sight is failing, and you have mistaken a will-o'-the-wisp for the sun.

" 'Dancing here, dancing there,
Catch it if you can and dare,' "

and she flitted away before him.

He followed with his intent eyes and graceful, serpent-like gliding, knowing her to be under a spell that would soon bring her fluttering back.

After circling round him a few moments she took his arm and he commenced breathing into her ear the poison of his passion.

No woman could remain the same after being with Mr. Van Dam. Out of the evil abundance of his heart he spoke, but the venom of his words and manner were all the more deadly because so subtle, so minutely and delicately distributed, that it was like a pestilential atmosphere, in which truth and purity withered.

No parent should permit to his daughters the companionship of a thoroughly bad man, whatever his social standing. His very tone and glance are unconsciously demoralizing, and, even if he tries, he cannot prevent the bitter waters overflowing from their bad source, his heart.

Mr. Van Dam did not try. He meant to secure Zell, with or without her father's approval, believing that when the marriage was once consummated Mr. Allen's consent and money would follow eventually.

For some little time longer the young ladies and their favored attendants strolled about the room in quiet tête-à-tête, and then the gentlemen bowed themselves out.

The door-bell had rung several times during the evening, but Hannibal, with the solemnity of a funeral, had quenched each comer by saying with the decision of the voice of fate:

"De ladies am engaged, sah," and no Cerberus at the door, or mailed warder of the middle ages, could have proved such an effectual barrier against all intruders as this old negro in his white waistcoat and stiff necktie, backed by the usage of modern society. Indeed, in some respects he was a greater potentate than old King Canute, for he could say to the human passions, inclinations, and desires that surged up to Mr. Allen's front door, "Thus far and no farther."

But upon this evening there was a caller who looked with cool, undaunted eyes upon the stiff necktie and solemn visage rising above it, and to Hannibal's reiterated state-

3—ROE—X

ment, "Dey *am* engaged," replied in a quiet tone of command:

"Take that card to Miss Edith."

Even Hannibal's sovereignty broke down before this persistent, imperturbable visitor, and scratching his head with a perplexed grin he half soliloquized, half replied:

"Miss Edith mighty 'ticlar to hab her orders obeyed."

"I am the best judge in this case," was the decisive response. "You take the card and I will be responsible."

Hannibal came to the conclusion that for some occult reason the gentleman, who was well known to him, had a right to pronounce the "open sesame" where the portal had been remained closed to all others, and, being a diplomatist, resolved to know more fully the quarter of the wind before assuming too much. But his statecraft was sorely puzzled to know why one of Mr. Allen's under-clerks should suddenly appear in the rôle of social caller upon the young ladies, for Mr. Fox, the gentleman in question, ostensibly had no higher position. His appearance and manner indicated a mystery. Old Hannibal's wool had not grown white for nothing, and he was the last man in the world to go through a mystery as a blundering bumblebee would through a spider's web. He was for leaving the web all intact till he knew who spun it and whom it was to catch. If it was Mr. Allen's work or Miss Edith's, it *must* stand; if not, he could play bumblebee with a vengeance, and carry off the gossamer of intrigue with one sweep.

So, showing Mr. Fox into a small reception room, he made his way to the library door with a motion that would have reminded you of a great, stealthy cat, and called in a loud, impressive whisper:

"Miss Edith!"

Edith at once rose and went to him, knowing that her prime minister had some important question of state to present when summoning her in that tone.

Screened by the library door, Hannibal commenced in a deprecating way:

"I told Mr. Fox you'se engaged, but he say I must give you dis card. He kinder acted as if he own dis niggar and de whole establishment."

A sudden heavy frown drew Edith's dark eyebrows together and she said loud enough for Mr. Fox in his ambush to hear:

"Was there ever such impudence!" and straightway the frown passed to the listener, intensified, like a flying cloud darkening one spot now and another a moment later.

"Return the card, and say I am engaged," she said haughtily. "Stay," she added thoughtfully. "Perhaps he wished to see papa, or there is some important business matter which needs immediate attention. If not, dismiss him," and Edith returned to the library quite as much puzzled as Hannibal had been. Two or three times recently she had found Mr. Fox's card on returning from evenings out. Why had he called? She had only a cool, bowing acquaintance with him, formed by his coming occasionally to see her father on business, and her father had not thought it worth while to formally introduce Mr. Fox to any of his family at such times, but had treated him as a sort of upper servant. Her certainly was putting on strange airs, as her old grand-vizier had intimated. But in the game of cards, and her other little game with Gus, she soon forgot his existence.

Meantime Hannibal, reassured, was regal again, and marched down the marble hall with something like the feeling and bearing of his great namesake. If there were a web here, the Allens were not spinning it, and he owed Mr. Fox nothing but a slight grudge for his "airs."

Therefore with the manner of one feeling himself master of the situation he said:

"Hab you a message for Mr. Allen?"

"No," replied Mr. Fox quietly.

"Den I tell you again Miss Edith *am* engaged."

Looking straight into Hannibal's eyes, without a muscle changing in his impassive face, Mr. Fox said in the steady tone of command:

"Say to Miss Edith I will call again," and he passed out of the door as if *he* were master of the situation.

Hannibal rolled up his eyes till nothing but the whites were seen, and muttered:

"Brass ain't no name for it."

Mr. Fox's action can soon be explained. Mr. Allen, while accustomed to operate largely in Wall Street through his brokers, was also the head of a cloth-importing firm. This in fact had been his regular and legitimate business, but like so many others he had been drawn into the vortex of speculation, and after many lucky hits had acquired that overweening confidence that prepares the way for a fall. He came to believe that he had only to put his hand to a thing to give it the needful impulse to success. In his larger and more exciting operations in Wall Street he had left the cloth business mainly to his junior partners and dependants, they employing his capital. Mr. Fox was merely a clerk in this establishment, and not in very high standing either. He was also another unwholesome product of metropolitan life. As office boy among the lawyers, as a hanger-on of the criminal courts, he had scrambled into a certain kind of legal knowledge and had gained a small pettifogging practice when an opening in Mr. Allen's business led to his present connection. Mr. Allen felt that in his varied and extended business he needed a man of Mr. Fox's stamp to deal with the legal questions that came up, look after the intricacies of the revenue laws, and manage the immaculate saints of the custom-house. As far as the firm had dirty, disagreeable, perplexing work to do, Mr. Fox was to do it. Whenever it came in contact with the majesty (?) of the law and government, Mr. Fox was to represent it. Whenever some Israelite in whom *was* guile sought, on varied pretext, to wriggle out of the whole or part of a bill, the wary Mr. Fox met him on his own plane and with his own weapons, skirmished with him, and won the little fight.

I would not for a moment give the impression that Mr.

Allen was in favor of sharp practice. He merely wished to conduct his business on the business principles and practice of the day, and it was not his purpose, and certainly not his policy, to pass beyond the law. But even the judges disagree as to what the law is, and he was dealing with many who thrived by evading it; therefore the need of a nimble Mr. Fox who could burrow and double on his tracks with the best of them. All went well for years, and the firm was saved many an annoyance, many a loss, and if this guerilla of the house, as perhaps we may term him, had been as devoted to Mr. Allen's interests as to his own, all might have gone well to the end. But these very sharp tools are apt to cut both ways, and so it turned out in this case. The astute Mr. Fox determined to serve Mr. Allen faithfully as long as he could faithfully and pre-eminently serve himself. If he who had scrambled from the streets to his present place of power could reach a higher position by stepping on the great rich merchant, such power would have additional satisfaction. He was as keen-scented after money as Mr. Allen, only the latter hunted like a lion, and the former like a fox. He mastered Mr. Allen's business thoroughly in all its details. Until recently no opportunity had occurred save work which, though useful, caused him to be half-despised by the others who would not or could not do it. But of late he had gained a strong vantage point. He watched with intense interest Mr. Allen's attraction toward, and entrance upon, a speculation that he knew to be as uncertain of issue as it was large in proportions, for, if the case ever became critical, he was conscious of the power of introducing a very important element into the problem.

In his care of the custom-house business he had discovered technical violations of the revenue laws which already involved the loss to the firm of a million dollars, and, with his peculiar loyalty to himself, thought this knowledge ought to be worth a great deal. As Mr. Allen went down into the deep waters of Wall Street, he saw that it might be. In saving his employer from wreck he might virtually become captain of the ship.

After this brief delineation of character, it would strike the reader as very incongruous to say that Mr. Fox had fallen in love with Edith. Mr. Fox never stumbled or fell. He could slide down and scramble up to any extent, and when cornered could take a flying leap like that of a cat. But he had been greatly impressed by Edith's beauty, and to win her also would be an additional and piquant feature in the game. He had absolute confidence in money, much of which he might have gained from Mr. Allen himself. He knew a million of her father's money was in his power, and this, in a certain sense, placed him in the position of a suitor worth a million, and such he knew to be almost omnipotent on the avenue. If this money could also be the means of causing Mr. Allen's ruin, or saving him from it, he believed that Edith would be his as truly as the bonds and certificates of stock that he often counted and gloated over. Even before Mr. Allen entered on what he called his great and final operation for the present, Mr. Fox was half inclined to show his hand and make the most of it, but within the last few days he had learned that perhaps a greater opportunity was opening before him. Meantime in the full consciousness of power he had begun to call on Edith, as we have seen, something as a cat plays around and watches a caged bird, which it expects to have in its claws before long.

The next morning at breakfast Edith mentioned Mr. Fox's recent calls.

"What is he coming here for?" growled Mr. Allen, looking with a frown at his daughter.

"I'm sure I don't know."

"I hope you don't see him."

"Certainly not. I was out the first two times, and last night sent word that I was engaged. But he insisted on his card being given to me and put on airs generally, so Hannibal seems to think."

That dignitary gave a confirming and indignant grunt.
"He said he would call again, didn't he, Hannibal?"

"Yes'm," blurted Hannibal, "and he looked as if de next time he'd put us all in his breeches pocket and carry us off."

"What's Fox up to now?" muttered Mr. Allen, knitting his brows. "I must look into this."

But even within a few hours the cloud land of Wall Street had changed some of its aspects. The serenity of the preceding day was giving place to indications of a disturbance in the finanical atmosphere. He had to buy more stock to keep the control he was gaining on the market, and things were not shaping favorably for its rise. He was already carrying a tremendous load, and even his herculean shoulders began to feel the burden. In the press and rush of business he forgot about Fox's social ambition in venturing to call where such men as Van Dam and Gus Elliot had undisputed rights.

Those upon whom society lays its hands are orthodox of course.

The wary Fox was watching the stock market as closely as Mr. Allen, and chuckled over the aspect of affairs; and he concluded to keep quietly out of the way a little longer, and await further developments.

Things moved rapidly as they usually do in the maelstrom of speculation. Though Mr. Allen was a trained athlete in business, the strain upon him grew greater day by day. But true to his promise, and in accordance with his habit of promptness, he transferred the deed for the little place in the country to Edith, who gloated over its dry technicalities as if they were full of romantic hope and suggestion to her.

One day when alone with Laura, Mr. Allen asked her suddenly:

"Has Mr. Goulden made any formal proposal yet?"

With rising color Laura answered:

"No."

"Why not? He seems very slow about it."

"I hardly know how you expect me to reply to such a question," said Laura, a little haughtily.

"Is he as attentive as ever?"

"Yes, I suppose so, though he has not called quite so often of late."

"Humph!" ejaculated Mr. Allen meditatively, adding after a moment, "Can't you make him speak out?"

"You certainly don't mean me to propose to him?" asked Laura, reddening.

"No, no, no!" said her father with some irritation, "but any clever woman can make a man who has gone as far as Mr. Goulden commit himself whenever she chooses. Your mother would have had the thing settled long ago, or else would have enjoyed the pleasure of refusing him."

"I am not mistress of that kind of finesse," said Laura coldly.

"You are a woman," replied her father coolly, "and don't need any lessons. It would be well for us both if you would exert your native power in this case."

Laura glanced keenly at her father and asked quickly:

"What do you mean?"

"Just what I say. A word to the wise is sufficient."

Having thus indicated to his daughter that phase of Wall Street tactics and principles that could be developed on the avenue, he took himself off to the central point of operations.

CHAPTER V

THE STORM THREATENING

L AURA had a better motive than that suggested by her father for wishing to lead Mr. Goulden to commit himself, for as far as she could love any one beyond herself she loved him, and she also realized fully that he could continue to her all that her elegant and expensive tastes craved. Notwithstanding her show of maidenly pride and reserve, she was ready enough to do as she had been bidden. Mr. Allen guessed as much. Indeed, as was quite natural, his wife was the type of the average woman to his mind, only he believed that she was a little cleverer in these matters than the majority. The manner in which she had "hooked" him made a deep and lasting impression on his memory.

But Mr. Goulden was a wary fish. He had no objection to being hooked if the conditions were all right, and until satisfied as to these he would play around at a safe distance. As he saw Mr. Allen daily getting into deeper water, he grew more cautious. His calls were not quite so frequent. He managed never to be with Laura except in company with others, and while his manner was very complimentary it was never exactly lover-like. Therefore, all Laura's feminine diplomacy was in vain, and that which a woman can say frankly the moment a man speaks, she could scarcely hint. Moreover, Mr. Goulden was adroit enough to chill her heart while he flattered her vanity. There was something about his manner she could not understand, but it was impossible to take offence at the polished gentleman.

Her father understood him better. He saw that Mr.
Goulden had resolved to settle the question on financial
principles only.

As the chances diminished of securing him indirectly
through Laura as a prop to his tottering fortunes, he at
last came to the conclusion to try to interest him directly
in his speculation, feeling sure if he could control only a
part of Mr. Goulden's large means and credit, he could
carry his operation through successfully.

Mr. Goulden warily listened to the scheme, warily
weighed it, and concluded within the brief compass of Mr.
Allen's explanation to have nothing to do with it. But his
outward manner was all deference and courteous attention.

At the end of Mr. Allen's rather eager and rose-colored
statements, he replied in politest and most regretful tones
that he "was very sorry he could not avail himself of so
promising an opening, but in fact, he was 'in deep' himself
—carrying all he could stand up under very well, and was
rather in the borrowing than in the lending line at present."

Keen Mr. Allen saw through all this in a moment, and
his face flushed angrily in spite of his efforts at self-control.
Muttering something to the effect:

"I thought I would give you a chance to make a good
thing," he bade a rather abrupt "good-morning."

As the pressure grew heavier upon him he was led to do
a thing the suggestion of which a few weeks previously he
would have regarded as an insult. Mrs. Allen had a snug
little property of her own, which had been secured to her
on first mortgages, and in bonds that were quiet and safe.
These her husband held in trust for her, and now pledged
them as collateral on which to borrow money to carry
through his gigantic operation. In respect to part of this
transaction, Mrs. Allen was obliged to sign a paper which
might have revealed to her the danger involved, but she
languidly took the pen, yawned, and signed away the result of her father's long years of toil without reading a line.

"There," she said, "I hope you will not bother me about

business again. Now in regard to this party—'' and she was about to enter into an eager discussion of all the complicated details, when her husband, interrupting, said:

"Another time, my dear—I am very much pressed by business at present."

"Oh, business, nothing but business," whined his wife. "You never have time to attend to me or your family."

But Mr. Allen was out of hearing of the querulous tones before the sentence was finished.

Of course he never meant that his wife should lose a cent, and to satisfy his conscience, and impressed by his danger, he resolved that as soon as he was out of this quaking morass of speculation he would settle on his wife and each daughter enough to secure them in wealth through life, and arrange it in such a way that no one could touch the principal.

The large sum that he now secured eased up matters and helped him greatly, and affairs began to wear a brightening aspect. He felt sure that the stock he had invested in was destined to rise in time, and indeed it already gave evidences of buoyancy. He noticed with an inward chuckle that Mr. Goulden began to call a little oftener. He was the best financial barometer in Wall Street.

But the case would require the most adroit and delicate management for weeks still, and this Mr. Allen could have given. Success also depended on a favorable state of the money market, and a good degree of stability and quietness throughout the financial world. Political changes in Europe, a war in Asia, heavy failures in Liverpool, London, or Paris, might easily spoil all. Reducing Mr. Allen's vast complicated operation to its final analysis, he had simply bet several millions—all he had—that nothing would happen throughout the world that could interfere with a scheme so problematical that the chances could scarcely be called even.

But gambling is occasionally successful, and it began to look as if Mr. Allen would win his bet; and so he might

had nothing happened.   The world was quiet enough, re-
markably quiet, considering the superabundance of explo-
sive elements everywhere.

The financial centres seethed on as usual, like a witch's
caldron, but there were no infernal ebullitions in the form
of "Black Fridays."   The storm that threatened to wreck
Mr. Allen was no wide, sweeping tempest, but rather one
of those little local whirlwinds that sometimes in the west
destroy a farm or township.

For the last few weeks Mr. Fox had quietly watched the
game, matured his plans, and secured his proof in the best
legal form.   He now concluded it was time to act, as he believed Mr. Allen to be in his power.   So one morning he
coolly walked into that gentleman's office, closed the door,
and took a seat.   Mr. Allen looked up with an expression
of surprise and annoyance on his face.   He instinctively
disliked Mr. Fox, as a lion might be irritated by a cat, and
the instinctive enmity was all the stronger because of a certain family likeness.   But Mr. Allen's astuteness had nothing mean or cringing in it, while Mr. Fox heretofore had
been a sort of Uriah Heep to him.   Therefore his surprise
and annoyance at his new rôle of cool confidence.

"Well, sir," said he, rather impatiently, returning to his
writing, as a broad hint that communications must be brief
if made at all.

"Mr. Allen," said Mr. Fox, in that clear-cut, decisive
tone, that betokens resolute purpose, and a little anger
also "I must request you to give me your undivided attention for a little time, and surely what I am about to say
is important enough to make it worth the while."

Though Mr. Allen flushed angrily, he knew that his
clerk would not employ such a tone and manner without
reason, so he raised his head and looked steadily at his unwelcome visitor and again said briefly:

"Well, sir ?"

"I wish, in the first place," said Mr. Fox, thinking to
begin with the least important exaction, and gradually

reach a climax in his extortion, "I wish permission to pay my addresses to your daughter Miss Edith."

Knowing nothing of a father's pride and affection, he had unwittingly brought in the climax first.

The angry flush deepened on Mr. Allen's face, but he still managed to control himself, and to remember that the father of three pretty daughters must expect some scenes like these, and that the only thing to do was to get rid of the objectionable suitors as civilly as possible. He was also too much of an American to put on any of the high-stepping airs of the European aristocracy. Here it is simply one sovereign proposing for the daughter of another, and generally the young people practically arrange it all before asking any consent in the case. After all, Mr. Fox had only paid his daughter the highest compliment in his power, and if any other of his clerks had made a similar request he would probably have given as kind and delicate a refusal as possible. It was because he disliked Mr. Fox, and instinctively gauged his character, that he said with a short, dry laugh:

"Come, Mr. Fox, you are forgetting yourself. You have been a useful employé in my store. If you feel that you should have more salary, name what will satisfy you, and I will consult my partners, and try and arrange it."— "There," thought he, "if he can't take that hint as to his place, I shall have to give him a kick." But both surprise and anger began to get the better of him when Mr. Fox replied:

"I must really beg your closer attention; I said nothing of increased salary. You will soon see that is no object with me now. I asked your permission to pay my addresses to your daughter."

"I decline to give it," said Mr. Allen, harshly, "and if I hear any more of this nonsense I will discharge you from my employ."

"Why?" was the quiet response, yet spoken with the intensity of passion.

"Because I never would permit my daughter to marry a man in your circumstances, and, if you will have it, you are not the style of a man I would wish to take into my family."

"If a man who was worth a million asked for your daughter's hand would you answer him in this manner?"

"Perhaps not," said Mr. Allen, with another of his short, dry laughs, which expressed little save irritation, "but you have my answer as respects yourself."

"I am not so sure of that," was the bold retort. "I am practically worth a million—indeed several millions to you, as you are now situated. You have talked long enough in the dark, Mr. Allen. For some time back there have been in your importations violations of the revenue laws. I have only to give the facts in my possession to the proper authorities and the government would legally claim from you a million of dollars, of which I should get half. So you see that I am positively worth five hundred thousand, and to you I am worth a million with respect to this item alone."

Mr. Allen sprang excitedly to his feet. Mr. Fox coolly got up and edged toward the door, which he had purposely left unlatched.

"Moreover," continued Mr. Fox, in his hard metallic voice, "in view of your other operations in Wall Street, which I know all about, the loss of a million would involve the loss of all you have."

Mr. Fox now had his hand on the door-knob, and Mr. Allen was glaring at him as if purposing to rush upon him and rend him to pieces.

Standing in the passageway, Mr. Fox concluded, in a low, meaning tone:

"You had better make terms with me within twenty-four hours."

And the door closed sharply, reminding one of the shutting of a steel trap.

Mr. Allen sank suddenly back in his chair and stared at

the closed door, looking as if he were a prisoner and all escape cut off.

He seemed to be in a lethargy or under a partial paralysis; he slowly and weakly rubbed his head with his hand, as if vaguely conscious that the trouble was there.

Gradually the stupor began to pass off, his blood to circulate, and his mind to realize the situation.

Rising feebly, as if a sudden age had fallen on him, he went to the door and gave orders that he must not be disturbed, and then sat down to think. Half an hour later he sent for his lawyer, stated the case to him, enjoined secrecy, and asked him to see Fox, hoping that it might be a case of mere blackmailing bravado. Keen as Mr. Allen's lawyer was, he had more than his match in the astute Mr. Fox. Moreover the latter had everything in his favor. There had been a slight infringement of the revenue laws, and though involving but small loss to the government, the consequences were the same. The invoice would be confiscated as soon as the facts were known. Mr. Fox had secured ample proof of this.

Mr. Allen might be able to prove that there was no intention to violate the law, as indeed there had not been. In fact, he had left those matters to his subordinates, and they had been a little careless, averaging matters, contenting themselves with complying with the general intent of the law, rather than, with painstaking care, conforming to its letter. But the law is very matter-of-fact, and can be excessively literal when money is to be made by those who live by enforcing or evading it, as may suit them. Mr. Fox could carry his case, if he pressed it, and secure his share of the plunder. On account of a very slight loss, Mr. Allen might be compelled to lose a million.

Before the day's decline the lawyer had asked Mr. Fox to take no further steps, stating vaguely that Mr. Allen would look into the matter, and would not be unreasonable.

A sardonic grin gave a momentary lurid hue to Mr. Fox's sallow face. Knowing the game to be in his own hands, he could quietly bide his time; so, assuming a tone of much moderation and dignity, he replied, he had no wish to be hard, and could be reasonable also. "But," added he, in a meaning tone, "there must be no double work in this matter. Mr. Allen must see what I am worth to him—nothing could be plainer. His best policy now is to act promptly and liberally toward me, for I pledge you my word that if I see any disposition to evade my requirements I will blow out the bottom of everything," and a snaky glitter in his small black eyes showed how remorselessly he could scuttle the ship bearing Mr. Allen's fortunes.

A speedy investigation showed Mr. Fox's fatal power, and Mr. Allen's partners were for paying him off, but when they found that he exacted an interest in the business that quite threw them into the background, they were indignant and inclined to fight it out. Mr. Allen could not tell them that he was in no condition to fight. If his financial status had been the same as some weeks previously, he would rather have lost the million than have listened one moment to Mr. Fox's repulsive conditions, but now to risk litigation and commercial reputation on one hand, and total ruin on the other, was an abyss from which he shrank back appalled.

His only resource was to temporize, both with his partners and Mr. Fox, and so gain time, hoping that the Wall Street scheme, that had caused so much evil, might also cure it. Of course he could not tell his partners how he was situated. The slightest breath of suspicion might cause the evenly balanced scales in which hung all chances to hopelessly decline. The speculation now promised well. If he could only keep things quiet a little longer—

Edith must help him. Calling her into the library after dinner, he asked:

"Has Mr. Fox called lately?"

"No, sir, not for some little time."

"Will you oblige me by seeing him and being civil if he calls again?"

"Why, papa, I thought you did not wish me to see him."

"Circumstances have altered since then. Is he very disagreeable to you?"

"Well, papa, I have scarcely thought of him, but to tell
you the truth when he has been here on business I have in-
voluntarily thought of a mousing cat, or the animal he is
named after on the scent of a hen-roost. But of course
I can be civil or even polite to him if you wish it."

A spasm of pain crossed her father's face and he put his
hand hastily to his head, a frequent act of late. He rose
and took a few turns up and down the room, muttering:

"Curse it all, I must tell her. Half knowledge is always
dangerous, and is sure to lead to blunders, and there must
be no blunders now."

Stopping abruptly before his daughter, he said, "He has
proposed for your hand."

An expression of disgust flitted across Edith's face, and
she replied quickly:

"We both have surely but one answer to such a proposition from *him*."

"Edith, you seem to have more sense in regard to business and such matters than most young ladies. I must now
test you, and it is for you to show whether you are a woman
or a shallow-brained girl. I am sorry to tell you these
things. They are not suited to your age or sex, but there
is no help for it," and he explained how he was situated.

Edith listened with paling cheek, dilating eyes, and parting lips, but still with rising courage and a growing purpose
to help her father.

"I do not wish you to marry this villain," he continued.
"Heaven forbid!" (Not that Mr. Allen referred this or any
other matter to Heaven; it was only a strong way of ex-
pressing his own disapproval.) "But we must manage to
temporize and keep this man at bay till I can extricate
myself from my difficulties. As soon as I stand on firm
ground I will defy him."

To Edith, with her standard of morality, the course indicated by her father seemed eminently filial and praisewor-

thy. The thought of marrying Mr. Fox made her flesh creep, but a brief flirtation was another affair. She had flirted not a little in her day for the mere amusement of the thing, and with the motives her father had presented she could do it in this case as if it were an act of devotion. Of the pure and lofty morality of the Bible she had as little idea as a Persian houri, and rugged Roman virtue could not develop in the social atmosphere in which the Allens lived. It was with a clear conscience that she resolved to beguile Mr. Fox, and signified as much to her father.

"Play him off," said this model father, "as Mr. Goulden does Laura. Curse him!—how I would like to slam the front door in his face. But my time may come yet," he added with set teeth.

That morning Mr. Allen sent for Mr. Fox, as he dared brave him no longer without some definite show of yielding, in order to keep back his fatal disclosures. With a dignity and formality scarcely in keeping with his fear and the import of his words, he said:

"I have considered your statements, sir, and admit their weight. As I informed you through my lawyer, I wish to be reasonable and hope you intend to be the same, for these are very grave matters. In regard to my daughter, you have my permission to call upon her as do her other gentleman friends, and she will receive you. In this land, that is all the vantage-ground a *gentleman* asks, as indeed it is all that can be granted. I am not the King of Dahomey or the Shah of Persia, and able to give my daughters where interest may dictate. A lady's inclination must be consulted. But I give you the permission you ask; you may pay your addresses to my daughter. You could scarcely ask a father to say more."

"It matters little to me what you or others say, but much what they do. My action shall be based upon yours and Miss Edith's. I have learned in your employ the value of promptness in all business matters. I hope you understand me."

"I do, sir, but there can be no indecent haste in these matters. In gaining the important position—in assuming the relations you desire—there should be some show of dignity, otherwise society would be disgusted, and you would lose the respect which should follow such vast acquirements."

"Where I can secure the whole cloth, I shall not worry about the selvage of etiquette and passing opinion," was Mr. Fox's cynical reply.

Mr. Allen could not prevent an expression of intense disgust from coming out upon his face, and he replied with some heat:

"Well, sir, something is due to my own position, and I cannot treat my daughter like a bale of cloth, as you suggest in your figurative speech. However," he added, warily, "I will take the necessary steps as soon as possible, and will trespass upon your time no longer."

As Mr. Fox glided out of the office with his sardonic smile, Mr. Allen felt for the moment that he would rather become bankrupt than make terms with him.

Meanwhile the month of February was rapidly passing, though each day was an age of anxiety and suspense to Mr. Allen. The tension was too much for him, and he evidently aged and failed under it. He drank more than he ate, and his temper was very variable. From his wife he only received chidings and complaints that in his horrid "mania for business" he was neglecting her and his family in general. She could never get him to sit down and talk sensibly of the birthday and début party that was now so near. He would always say, testily, "Manage it to suit yourselves."

Laura and Zell were too much wrapped up in their own affairs to give much thought to anything else. But Edith, of late, understood her father and felt deeply for him. One evening finding him sitting dejectedly alone in the library after dinner, she said:

"Why go on with this party, papa? I am sure I am ready to give it up if it will be any relief to you."

The heart of this strong, confident man of the world was sore and lonely. For perhaps the first time he felt the need of support and sympathy. He drew his beautiful daughter, whom thus far he had scarcely more than admired, down upon his lap and buried his face upon her shoulder. A breath of divine impulse swept aside for a moment the stifling curtains of his sordid life, and he caught a glimpse of the large happy realm of love.

"And would you really give up anything for the sake of your old father?" he asked in a low tone.

"Everything," cried Edith, much moved by the unusual display of affection and feeling on the part of her father.

"The others would not," said he bitterly.

"Indeed, papa, I think they would if they only knew. We would all do anything to see you your old jovial self again. Give up this wretched struggle; tell Mr. Fox to do his worst. I am not afraid of being poor; I am sure we could work up again."

"You know nothing about poverty," sighed her father. "When you are down, the world that bowed at your feet will run over and trample on you. I have seen it so often, but never thought of danger to me and mine."

"But this party," said the practical Edith, "why not give this up? It will cost a great deal."

"By no means give it up," said her father. "It may help me very much. My credit is everything now. The appearance of wealth which such a display insures will do much to secure the wealth. I am watched day and night, and must show no sign of weakness. Go on with the party and make it as brilliant as possible. If I fail, two or three thousand will make no difference, and it may help me to succeed. Whatever strengthens my credit for the next few days is everything to me. My stock is rising, only it is too slow. Things look better—if I could only gain time. But I am very uneasy—my head troubles me," and he put his hand to his head, and Edith remembered how often she had seen him do that of late.

"By the way," said he, abruptly, "tell me how you get on with Mr. Fox."

"Oh, never mind about that now; do rest a little, mind and body."

"No, tell me," said her father sharply, showing how little control he had over himself.

"Well, I think I have beaten him so far. He is very demonstrative, and acts as if I belonged to him. Did I not manage to always meet him in company with others, he would come at once to an open declaration. As it is, I cannot prevent it much longer. He is coming this evening, and I fear he will press matters. He seems to think that the asking is a mere form, and that our extremity will leave no choice."

"You must avoid him a little longer. Come, we will go to the theatre, and then you might be sick for a few days."

In a few minutes they were off, and were scarcely well away when Mr. Fox, dressed in more style than he could carry gracefully, appeared.

"Miss Edith am out," said Hannibal loftily.

"I half believe you lie," muttered Mr. Fox, looking very black.

"Sarch de house, sah. It am a berry gentlemanly proceeding."

"Where has she gone? and whom did she go with?"

"I hab no orders to say," said Hannibal, looking fixedly at the ceiling of the vestibule.

The knightly suitor turned on his heel, muttering, "They are playing me false."

'Twas a pity, and he so true.

The next day Edith was sick and Mr. Allen's stock was rising. Hannibal again sent Mr. Fox baffled away, but with a dangerous gleam in his eyes.

On the following morning Mr. Allen found a note on his desk. His face grew livid as he read it, and he often put his hand to his head. He sat down and wrote to this effect, however:

"I am arranging the partnership matter as rapidly as possible. In regard to my daughter you will ruin all if you show no more discretion. I cannot compel her to marry you. You may make it impossible to influence her in your favor. You have been well received. What more can you ask? A matter of this kind must be arranged delicately."

Mr. Fox pondered over this with a peculiarly foxy expression. "It sounds plausible. If I only thought he was true," soliloquized this embodiment of truth.

Mr. Allen's stock was higher, and Mr. Fox watched the rise grimly, but he saw Edith, who was all smiles and graciousness, and gave him a verbal invitation to her birthday-party which was to take place early in the following week.

The fellow had not a little vanity, and was insnared, his suspicions quieted for the time. Valuing money himself supremely, it seemed most rational that father and daughter should regard him as the most eligible young man in the city.

Edith's friends, and Gus in particular, were rather astonished at the new-comer. Laura was frigid and remonstrant, Zell and Mr. Van Dam satirical, but Edith wilfully tossed her head and said he was clever and well off, and she liked him well enough to talk to him a little. Society had made her a good actress. Meanwhile on the Tuesday following (and this was Friday) the long expected party would take place.

CHAPTER VI

THE WRECK

O N Saturday Mr. Allen's stock was rising, and he
ventured to sell a little in a quiet way. If he "un-
loaded" rapidly and openly, he would break down
the market.

Mr. Fox watched events uneasily. Mr. Goulden grew
genial and more pronounced in his attentions. Gus, on
Saturday, showed almost as much solicitude for a decisively
favorable answer as did Mr. Fox, if the language of his eyes
meant anything; but Edith played him and Mr. Fox off
against each other so adroitly that they were learning to
hate each other as cordially as they agreed in admiring her.
Though she inclined in her favor to Mr. Fox, he was suspicious from nature, and annoyed at never being able to
see her alone.

As before, they were at cards together in the library,
and Edith went for a moment into the parlor to get something. With the excuse of obtaining it for her, Mr. Fox
followed, and the moment they were alone he seized her
hand and pressed a kiss upon it. An angry flush came into
her face, but by a great effort she so far controlled herself
as to put her finger to her lips and point to the library, as
if her chief anxiety was that the attention of its occupants
should not be excited. Mr. Fox was delighted, though the
angry flush was a little puzzling. But if Edith permitted
that she would permit more, and if her only shrinking was
lest others should see and know at present, that could soon
be overcome. These thoughts passed through his mind

while the incensed girl hastily obtained what she wished.
But she, feeling that her cheeks were too hot to return immediately to the critical eyes in the library, passed out
through the front parlor, that she might have time to be
herself again when she appeared.   On what little links
destiny sometimes hangs!

That which changed all her future and that of others—
that involving life and death—occurred in the half moment
occupied in her passing out of the front parlor.   The consequences she would feel most keenly, terribly indeed at
times, though she might never guess the cause.   Her act
was a simple, natural one under the circumstances, and yet
it told Mr. Fox, in his cat-like watchfulness, that with all
his cunning he was being made a fool of.   The moment
Edith had passed around the sliding door and thought herself unobserved, an expression of intense disgust came out
upon her expressive face, and with her lace handkerchief
she rubbed the hand he had kissed, as if removing the slime
of a reptile; and the large mirror at the further end of the
room had faithfully reflected the suggestive little panto-
mime.   He saw and understood all in a flash.

. No words could have so plainly told her feeling toward
him, and he was one of those reptiles that could sting remorselessly in revenge.   The nature of the imposition practiced upon him, and the fact that it was partially successful
and might have been wholly so, cut him in the sorest spot.
He who thought himself able to cope with the shrewdest
and most artful had been overreached by a girl, and he
saw at that moment that her purpose to beguile him long
enough for Mr. Allen to extricate himself from his difficulties might have been successful.   He had had before an
uneasy consciousness that he ought to act decisively, and
now he knew it.

"I'm a fool—a cursed fool," he muttered, speaking the
truth for once, "but it's not too late yet."

His resolution was taken instantly, but when Edith appeared after a moment in the library, smiling and affable

again, he seemed in good spirits also, but there was a steely, serpent-like glitter in his eyes, that made him more repulsive than ever. But he stayed as late as the others, knowing that it might be his last evening at the Allens'. For Edith had said as part of her plan for avoiding Mr. Fox:

"We shall be too busy to see any company till Tuesday evening, and then we hope to see you all."

Her sisters had assented, expecting that it would be the case.

With a refinement of malice, Mr. Fox sought to give general annoyance, by a polite insolence toward the others, which they with difficulty ignored, and a lover-like gallantry toward Edith, which was like nettles to Gus, and nauseating to her; but she did not dare resent it. He could at least torment her a little longer.

At last all were gone, and her father coming in from his club said, drawing her aside:

"All right yet?"

"Yes, but I hope the ordeal will be over soon, or I shall die with disgust, or, like some I have read of in fairy stories, be killed by a poisonous breath."

"Keep it up a little longer, that is a good, brave girl. I think that by another week we shall be able to defy him," said her father in cheerful tones. "If my stock rises as much in the next few days as of late, I shall soon be on *terra firma.*"

If he had known that the mine beneath his feet was loaded, and the fuse fired, his full face would have become as pale as it was florid with wine and the dissipation of the evening.

Monday morning came—all seemed quiet. His stock was rising so rapidly that he determined to hold on a little longer.

Goulden met and congratulated him, saying that he had bought a little himself, and would take more if Mr. Allen would sell, as now he was easier in funds than when spoken to before on the subject.

Mr. Allen replied rather coldly that he would not sell any stock that day.

Mr. Fox kept out of the way, and quietly attended to his routine as usual, but there was a sardonic smile on his face, as if he were gloating over some secret evil.

Tuesday, the long-expected day that the Allens believed would make one of the most brilliant epochs in their history, dawned in appropriate brightness. The sun dissipated the few opposing clouds and declined in undimmed splendor, and Edith, who alone had fears and forebodings, took the day as an omen that the storm had passed, and that better days than ever were coming.

Invitations by the hundred, with imposing monogram and coat-of-arms, had gone out, and acceptances had flowed back in full current. All that lavish expenditure could secure in one of the most luxurious social centres of the world had been obtained without stint to make the entertainment perfect.

But one knew that it might become like Belshazzar's feast.

The avalanche often hangs over the Alpine passes so that a loud word will bring it whirling down upon the hapless traveller. The avalanche of ruin, impending over Mr. Allen, was so delicately poised that a whisper could precipitate its crushing weight, and that whisper had been spoken.

All the morning of Tuesday his stock was rising, and he resolved that on the morning after the party he would commence selling rapidly, and, so far from being bankrupt, he would realize much of the profit that he had expected.

But a rumor was floating through the afternoon papers that a well-known merchant, eminent in financial and social circles, had been detected in violating the revenue laws, and that the losses which such violation would involve to him would be immense. The stock market, more sensitive than a belle's vanity, paused to see what it meant. One of Mr. Allen's partners of the cloth house brought a paper to him. He grew pale as he read it, put his hand suddenly

SHE EXTENDED HER WHITE ROUNDED ARM TOWARDS HIM.

What Can.

Page 78.

to his head, but after a moment seemingly found his voice and said:

"Could Fox have been so dastardly?"

His partner shrugged his shoulder as much as to say, "Fox could do anything in that line."

Mr. Allen sent for Fox, but he could not be found. In the meantime the stock market closed and the rise of his stock was evidently checked for the moment.

By reason of the party, Mr. Allen had to return uptown, but he arranged with his partner to remain and if anything new developed to send word by special messenger.

By eight o'clock the Allen mansion on Fifth Avenue was all aglow with light. By nine, carriages began to roll up to the awning that stretched from the heavy arched doorway across the sidewalk, and ladies that would soon glide through the spacious rooms in elegant drapery, now seemed misshapen bundles in their wrapping, and gathered up dresses as they hurried out of the publicity of the street. The dressing-rooms where the spheroidal bundles were undergoing metamorphose became buzzing centres of life.

Before the long pier glasses there was a marshalling of every charm, real or borrowed (more correctly bought), in view of the hoped-for conquests of the evening, and it would seem that not a few went on the military maxim that success is often secured by putting on as bold a front, and making as great and startling display, as possible. But as fragrant, modest flowers usually bloom in the garden with gaudy, scentless ones, so those inclined to be *bizarre* made an excellent foil for the refined and elegant, and thus had their uses. There is little in the world that is not of value, looking at it from some point of view.

In another apartment the opposing forces, if we may so style them, were almost as eagerly investing themselves in—shall we say charms also? or rather with the attributes of manhood? At any rate the glasses seem quite as anxiously consulted in that room as in the other. One might almost imagine them the magic mirrors of prophecy in which

anxious eyes caught a glimpse of coming fate. There were
certain youthful belles and beaux who turned away with
open complacent smiles, vanity whispering plainly to them
of noble achievement in the parlors below. There were
others, perhaps not young, who turned away with faces
composed in the rigid and habitual lines of pride. They
were past learning anything from the mirror, or from any
other source that might reflect disparagingly upon them.
Prejudice in their own favor surrounded their minds as with
a Chinese wall. Conceit had become a disease with them,
and those faculties that might have let in wholesome, though
unwelcome, truth were paralyzed.

But the majority turned away not quite satisfied—with
an inward foreboding that all was not as well as it might
be—that critical eyes would see ground for criticism.
Especially was this true of those whom Time's interfering
fingers had pulled somewhat awry, even beyond the remedy
of art, and of those whose bank account, jewels, silks, etc.,
were not quite up to the standard of some others who might
jostle them in the crush. Realize, my reader, the anguish
of a lady compelled to stand by another lady wearing larger
diamonds than her own, or more point lace, or a longer
train. What *will* the world think, as under the chandelier
this painful contrast comes out? Such moments of deep
humiliation cause sleepless nights, and the next day result
in bills that become as crushing as criminal indictments to
poor overworked men. Under the impulse of such trying
scenes as these, many a matron has gone forth on Broadway with firm lips and eyes in which glowed inexorable
purpose, and placed the gems that would be mill-stones
about her husband's neck on the fat arms or fingers that
might have helped him forward. There are many phases
of heroism, but if you want your breath quite taken away,
go to Tiffany's, and see some large-souled woman, who will
not even count the cost or realize the dire consequences—
see her, like some martyr of the past, who would show to
the world the object of his faith though the heavens fell,

march to the counter, select the costliest, and say in tones
of majesty:

"Send the bill to my husband!"

"Oh, acme of faith! The martyrs knew that the Al-
mighty was equal to the occasion. She knows that her
husband is not; yet she trusts, or, what is the same thing
here, gets trusted. Men allied to such women are soon
lifted up to—attics. It is still true that great deeds bring
humanity nearer heaven!

Therefore, my reader, deem it not trivial that I have
paused so long over the Allens' party. It is philosophical
to trace great events and phenomenal human action to their
hidden causes.

There were also diffident men and maidens who descended into the social arena of Mrs. Allen's parlors, as
awkward swimmers venture into deep water, but this is
fleeting experience in fashionable life. And we sincerely
hope that some believed that the old divine paradox, "It
is more blessed to give than to receive," is as true in the
drawing-room as when the contribution-box goes round,
and proposed to enjoy themselves by contributing to the
enjoyment of others, and to see nothing that would tempt
to heroic conduct at Tiffany's the next day.

When the last finishing touches had been given, and
maids and hairdressers stood around in rapt politic breath-
lessness, and were beginning to pass into that stage in which
they might be regarded as exclamation points, Mrs. Allen
and her daughters swept away to take their places at the
head of the parlors in order to receive. They liked the
prelude of applause upstairs well enough, but then it was
only like the tuning of the instruments before the orchestra
fairly opens.

Mrs. Allen, as she majestically took her position, evidently belonged to that class whom pride petrifies. Her
self-complacency on such an occasion was habitual, her
coolness and repose those of a veteran. A nervous creature upstairs with her family, excitement made her, under

the eye of society, so steady and self-controlled that she was like one of the old French marshals who could plan a campaign under the hottest fire. Her blue eyes grew quite brilliant and seemed to take in everything. Some natural color shone where the cosmetics permitted, and her form seemed to dilate with something more than the mysteries of French modistes. Her manner and expression said:

"I am Mrs. Allen. We are of an old New York family. We are very, very rich. This entertainment is immensely expensive and perfect in kind. I defy criticism. I expect applause."

Of course this was all veiled by society's completest polish; but still by a close observer it could be seen, just as a skilful sculptor drapes a form, but leaves its outlines perfect.

Laura was the echo of her mother, modified by the element of youth.

Zell fairly blazed. What with sparkling jewelry, flaming cheeks, flashing eyes, and words thrown off like scintillating sparks, she suggested an exquisite July firework, burning longer than usual and surprising every one. Admiration followed her like a torrent, and her vanity dilated without measure as attention and compliments were almost forced upon her, and yet it was frank, good-natured vanity, as naturally to be expected in her case as a throng of gaudy poppies where a handful of seed had been dropped. Zell's nature was a soil where good or bad seed would grow vigorously.

Mr. Van Dam was never far off, and watched her with intent, gloating eyes, saying in self-congratulation:

"What a delicious morsel she will make!" and adding his mite to the general chorus of flattery by mild assertions like the following:

"Do you know that there is not a lady present that for a moment can compare with you?"

"How delightfully frank he is!" thought Zell of her distinguished admirer, who was as open as a quicksand that can swallow up anything and leave not a trace on its surface.

Edith was quite as beautiful as Zell, but far less brilliant and pronounced. Though quiet and graceful, she was not stately like Laura. Her full dark eyes were lustrous rather than sparkling, and they dwelt shrewdly and comprehendingly on all that was passing, and conveyed their intelligence to a brain that was judging quite accurately of men and things at a time when so many people "lose their heads."

Zell was intoxicated by the incense she received. Laura offered herself so much that she was enshrouded in a thick cloud of complacency all the time. Edith was told by the eyes and manner of those around her that she was beautiful and highly favored by wealth and position generally. But she knew this, as a matter of fact, before, and did not mean to make a fool of herself on account of it. These points thoroughly settled and quietly realized, she was in a condition to go out of herself and enjoy all that was going on.

She was specially elated at this time also, as she had gathered from her father's words that his danger was nearly over and that before the week was out they could defy Mr. Fox, look forward to Europe and bright voyaging generally.

Mr. Allen did not tell her his terrible fear that Mr. Fox had been a little too prompt, and that crushing disaster might still be impending. He had said to himself, "Let her and all of them make the most of this evening. It may be the last of the kind that they will enjoy."

The spacious parlors filled rapidly. If lavish expenditure and a large brilliant attendance could insure their enjoyment, it was not wanting. Flowers in fanciful baskets on the tables and in great banks on the mantels and in the fireplaces deservedly attracted much attention and praise, though the sum expended on their transient beauty was appalling. Their delicious fragrance mingling with perfumes of artificial origin suggested a like intermingling of the more delicate, subtile, but genuine manifestations of character, and the graces of mind and manner borrowed for the occasion.

The scene was very brilliant. There were marvellous toilets—dresses not beginning as promptly as they should, perhaps, but seemingly seeking to make up for this deficiency by elegance and costliness, having once commenced. There was no economy in the train, if there had been in the waist. Therefore gleaming shoulders, glittering diamonds, the soft radiance of pearls, the sheen of gold, and lustrous eyse aglow with excitement, and later in the evening, with wine, gave a general phosphorescent effect to the parlors that Mrs. Allen recognized, from long experience, as the sparkling crown of success. So much elegance on the part of the ladies present would make the party the gem of the season, and the gentlemen in dark dress made a good black enamel setting.

There was a confused rustle of silks and a hum of voices, and now and then a silvery laugh would ring out above these like the trill of a bird in a breezy grove. Later, light airy music floated through the rooms, followed by the rhythmic cadence of feet. A thinly clad shivering little match-girl stopped on her weary tramp to her cellar and caught glimpses of the scene through the oft-opening door and between the curtains of the windows. It seemed to her that those glancing forms were in heaven. Alas for this earthly paradise!

Mr. Fox, with characteristic malice, had managed that Mr. Allen and perhaps the family should have, as his contribution to the entertainment, the sickening dread which the news in the afternoon papers would occasion. As the evening advanced he determined to accept the invitation and watch the effect. He avoided Mr. Allen, and soon gathered that Edith and the rest knew nothing of the impending blow. Edith smiled graciously on him; she felt that, like the sun, she could shine on all that night. But as, in his insolence, his attentions grew marked, she soon shook him off by permitting Gus Elliot to claim her for a waltz.

Mr. Fox glided around, Mephistopheles-like, gloating on the sinister changes that he would soon occasion. He was to succeed even better than he dreamed.

The evening went forward with music and dancing, dis-
cussing, disparaging, flirting, and skirmishing, culminating
in numbers and brilliancy as some gorgeous flower might
expand; and seemingly it would have ended by the gay
company's rustling departure like the flower, as the varied
colored petals drop away from the stem, had not an event
occurred which was like a rude hand plucking the flower in
its fullest bloom and tearing the petals away in mass.

The magnificent supper had just been demolished. Champagne had foamed without stint, cause and symbol of the increasing but transient excitement of the occasion. More po-
tent wines and liquors, suggestive of the stronger and deeper
passions that were swaying the mingled throng, had done
their work, and all, save the utterly *blasé*, had secured that
noble elevation which it is the province of these grand social
combinations to create. Even Mr. Allen regained his habitual confidence and elevation as his waist-coat expanded
under, or rather over, those means of cheer and consolation which he had so long regarded as the best panacea for
earthly ills. The oppressive sense of danger gave place to
a consciousness of the warm, rosy present. Mr. Fox and the
custom-house seemed but the ugly phantoms of a past dream.
Was he not the rich Mr. Allen, the owner of this magnificent
mansion, the cornerstone of this superb entertainment? If
by reason of wine he saw a little double, he only saw double
homage on every side. He heard in men's tones, and saw
in woman's glances, that any one who could pay for his
surroundings that night was no ordinary person. His wife
looked majestic as she swept through the parlors on the arm
of one of his most distinguished fellow-citizens. Through
the library door he could see Mr. Goulden leaning toward
Laura and saying something that made even her pale face
quite peony-like. Edith, exquisite as a moss-rose, was
about to lead off in the German in the large front parlor.
Zell was near him, the sparkling centre of a breezy, merry
little throng that had gathered round her. It seemed that
all that he loved and valued most was grouped around him

in the guise most attractive to his worldly eyes.   In this
moment of unnatural elation hope whispered, "To-morrow
you can sell your stock, and, instead of failing, increase
your vast fortune, and then away to new scenes, new pleasures, free from the burden of care and fear."   It was at that
moment of false confidence and pride, when in suggestive
words descriptive of the ancient tragedy of Belshazzar he
"had drank wine and praised the gods of gold and of silver"
which he had so long worshipped, and which had secured to
him all that so dilated his soul with exultation, that he saw
the handwriting, not of shadowy fingers "upon the wall,"
but of his partner, sent, as agreed, by a special messenger.
With revulsion and chill of fear he tore open the envelope
and read:

"Fox has done his worst.   We are out for a million—
All will be in the morning papers."

Even his florid, wine-inflamed cheeks grew pale, and he
raised his hand tremblingly to his head, and slowly lifted
his eyes like a man who dreads seeing something, but is impelled to look.   The first object they rested on was the sardonic, mocking face of Mr. Fox, who, ever on the alert, had
seen the messenger enter, and guessed his errand.   The moment Mr. Allen saw this hated visage, a sudden fury took
possession of him.   He crushed the missive in his clenched
fist, and took a hasty stride of wrath toward his tormentor,
stopped, put his hand again to his head, a film came over
his eyes, he reeled a second, and then fell like a stone to
the floor.   The heavy thud of the fall, the clash of the
chandelier overhead, could be heard throughout the rooms
above the music and hum of voices, and all were startled.
Edith in the very act of leading off in the dance stood a
second like an exquisite statue of awed expectancy, and
then Zell's shriek of fear and agony, "Father!" brought her
to the spot, and with wild, frightened eyes, and blanched
faces, the two girls knelt above the unconscious man, while
the startled guests gathered round in helpless curiosity.

The usual paralysis following sudden accident was brief

on this occasion, for there were two skilful physicians present, one of them having long been the family attendant.
Mrs. Allen and Laura, in a half-hysterical state, stood
clinging to each other, supported by Mr. Goulden, as the
medical gentlemen made a slight examination and applied
restoratives. After a moment they lifted their heads and
looked gravely and significantly at each other; then the
family adviser said:

"Mr. Allen had better be carried at once to his room,
and the house become quiet."

An injudicious guest asked in a loud whisper, "Is it
apoplexy?"

Mrs. Allen caught the word, and with a stifled cry fainted
dead away, and was borne to her apartment in an unconscious state. Laura, who had inherited Mrs. Allen's nervous nature, was also conveyed to her room, laughing and
crying in turns beyond control. Zell still knelt over her
father, sobbing passionately, while Edith, with her large
eyes dilated with fear, and her cheeks in wan contrast with
the sunset glow they had worn all the evening, maintained
her presence of mind, and asked Mr. Goulden, Mr. Van
Dam, and Gus Elliot, to carry her father to his room.
They, much pleased in thus being singled out as special
friends of the family, officiously obeyed.

Poor Mr. Allen was borne away from the pinnacle of his
imaginary triumph as if dead, Zell following, wringing her
hands, and with streaming eyes; but Edith reminded one of
some wild, timid creature of the woods, which, though in
an extremity of danger and fear, is alert and watchful, as
if looking for some avenue of escape. Her searching eyes
turned almost constantly toward the family physician, and
he as persistently avoided meeting them.

CHAPTER VII

AFTER another brief but fuller examination of Mr.
Allen in the privacy of his own room, Dr. Mark
went down to the parlors. The guests were gathered in little groups, talking in low, excited whispers;
those who had seen the reading of the note and Mr.
Allen's strange action gaining brief eminence by their repeated statements of what they had witnessed and their
varied surmises. The rôle of commentator, if mysterious
human action be the text, is always popular, and as this
explanatory class are proverbially gifted in conjecture,
there were many theories of explanation. Some of the
guests had already the good taste to prepare for departure, and when Dr. Mark appeared from the sick room,
and said:

"Mr. Allen and the family will be unable to appear
again this evening. I am under the painful necessity of
saying that this occasion, which opened so brilliantly, must
now come to a sad and sudden end. I will convey your
adieux and expressions of sympathy to the family"—there
was a general move to the dressing-rooms. The doctor was
overwhelmed for a moment with expressions of sympathy,
that in the main were felt, and well questioned by eager and
genuine curiosity, for Fox had dropped some mysterious
hints during the evening, which had been quietly circulat-
ing. But Dr. Mark was professionally non-committal, and
soon excused himself that he might attend to his patient.

The house, that seemingly a moment before was ablaze

with light and resounding with fashionable revelry, suddenly became still, and grew darker and darker, as if the shadowing wings of the dreaded angel were drawing very near. In the large, elegant rooms, where so short a time before gems and eyes had vied in brightness, old Hannibal now walked alone with silent tread and a peculiarly awed and solemn visage. One by one he extinguished the lights, leaving but faint glimmers here and there, that were like a few forlorn hopes struggling against the increasing darkness of disaster. Under his breath he kept repeating fervently, "De Lord hab mercy," and this, perhaps, was the only intelligent prayer that went up from the stricken household in this hour of sudden danger and alarm. Though we believe the Divine Father sees the dumb agony of His creatures, and pities them, and often when they, like the drowning, are grasping at straws of human help and cheer, puts out His strong hand and holds them up; still it is in accordance with His just law that those who seek and value His friendship find it and possess it in adversity. The height of the storm is a poor time and the middle of the angry Atlantic a poor place in which to provide life-boats.

The Allens had never looked to Heaven, save as a matter of form. They had a pew in a fashionable church, but did not very regularly occupy it, and such attendance had done scarcely anything to awaken or quicken their spiritual life. They came home and gossiped about the appearance of their "set," and perhaps criticised the music, but one would never have dreamed from manner or conversation that they had gone to a sacred place to worship God in humility. Indeed, scarcely a thought of Him seemed to have dwelt in their minds. Religious faith had never been of any practical help, and now in their extremity it seemed utterly intangible, and in no sense to be depended on.

When Mrs. Allen recovered from her swoon, and Laura had gained some self-control, they sent for Dr. Mark, and eagerly suggested both their hope and fear.

"It's only a fainting fit, doctor, is it not? Will he not soon be better?" .   •

"My dear madam, we will do all we can," said the doctor, with that professional solemnity which might accompany the reading of a death warrant, "but it is my painful duty to tell you to prepare for the worst. Your husband has an attack of apoplexy."

He had scarcely uttered the words before she was again in a swoon, and Laura also lost her transient quietness. Leaving his assistant and Mrs. Allen's maid to take care of them, he went back to his graver charge.

Mr. Allen lay insensible on his bed, and one could hardly realize that he was a dying man. His face was as flushed and full as it often appeared on his return from his club. To the girls' unpracticed ears, his loud, stertorous breathing only indicated heavy sleep. But neither they nor the doctor could arouse him, and at last the physician met Edith's questioning eyes, and gravely and significantly shook his head. Though she had borne up so steadily and quietly, he felt more for her than for any of the others.

"Oh, doctor! can't you save him?" she pleaded.

"You must save him," cried Zell, her eyes flashing through her tears, "I would be ashamed, if I were a physician, to stand over a strong man, and say helplessly, 'I can do nothing.' Is this all your boasted skill amounts to? Either do something at once or let us get some one who will."

"Your feelings to-night, Miss Zell," said the doctor quietly, "will excuse anything you say, however wild and irrational. I am doing all—"

"I am not wild or unreasonable," cried Zell. "I only demand that my father's life be saved." Then starting up she threw off a shawl and stood before Dr. Mark in the dress she had worn in the evening, that seemed a sad mockery in that room of death. Her neck and arms were bare, and even the cool, experienced physician was startled by her wonderful beauty and strange manner. Her white throat was convulsed, her bosom heaved tumultuously, and on her face was the expression that might have rested on the face of a maiden like herself centuries before, when shown the rack and dungeon, and told to choose between her faith and her life.

But after a moment she extended her white rounded arm toward him and said steadily:

"I have read that if the blood of a young, vigorous person is infused into another who is feeble and old, it will give renewed strength and health. Open a vein in my arm. Save his life if you take mine."

"You are a brave, noble girl," said Dr. Mark, with much emotion, taking the extended hand and pressing it tenderly, "but you are asking what is impossible in this case. Do you not remember that I am an old friend of your father's? It grieves me to the heart that his attack is so severe that I fear all within the reach of human skill is vain."

Zell, who was a creature of impulse, and often of noblest impulse, as we have seen, now reacted into a passion of weeping, and sank helplessly on the floor. She was capable of heroic action, but she had no strength for woman's lot, which is so often that of patient endurance.

Edith came and put her arms around her, and with gentle, soothing words, as if speaking to a child, half carried her to her room, where she at last sobbed herself asleep.

For another hour Edith and the doctor watched alone, and the dying man sank rapidly, going down into the darkness of death without word or sign.

"Oh that he would speak once more!" moaned Edith.

"I fear he will not, my dear," said the doctor, pitifully.

A little later Mr. Allen was motionless, like one who has been touched in unquiet sleep and becomes still. Death had touched him, and a deeper sleep had fallen upon him.

.   .   .   .

One of the great daily bulletins will go to press in an hour. A reporter jumps into a waiting hack and is driven rapidly uptown.

While the city sleeps preparations must go on in the markets for breakfast, and in printing rooms for that equal necessity in our day, the latest news. Therefore all night long there are dusky figures flitting hither and thither, seeing to it that when we come down in gown and slippers, our steak and the world's gossip be ready.

The breakfast of the Gothamites was furnished abundantly with *sauce piquante* on the morning of the last day of February, for Hannibal had shaken his head ominously, and wiped away a few honest tears, before he could tremulously say to the eager reporter:

"Mr. Allen—hab—just—died."

Gathering what few particulars he could, and imagining many more, the reporter was driven back even more rapidly, full of the elation of a man who has found a good thing and means to make the most of it. Mr. Allen himself was not of importance to him, but news about him was. And this fact crowning the story of his violation of the revenue law and his prospective loss of a million, would make a brisk breeze in the paper to which he was attached, and might waft him a little further on as an enterprising news-gatherer.

It certainly would be the topic of the day on all lips, and poor Mr. Allen might have plumed himself on this if he had known it, for few people, unless they commit a crime, are of sufficient importance to be talked of all day in large, busy New York. In the world's eyes Mr. Allen had committed a crime. Not that they regarded his stock gambling as such. Multitudes of church members in good and regular standing were openly engaged in this. Nor could the slight and unintentional violation of the revenue law be regarded as such, though so grave in its consequences. But he had faltered and died when he should not have given way. What the world demands is success: and sometimes a devil may secure this where a true man cannot. The world regarded Mr. Van Dam and Mr. Goulden as very successful men.

Mr. Fox also had secured success by one adroit wriggle —we can describe his mode of achieving greatness by no better phrase. He was destined to receive half a million for his treachery to his employers. During the war, when United States securities were at their worst; when men, pledged to take them, forfeited money rather than do so, Mr. Allen had lent the government millions, because he believed in it, loved it, and was resolved to sustain it. That same government now rewards him by putting it in the power of a dishonest clerk to ruin him, and gives him $500,000 for doing so. Thus it resulted; for we are compelled to pass hastily over the events immediately following Mr. Allen's death. His partners made a good fight, showed that there was no intention to violate the law, and that it was often difficult to comply with it literally—that the sum claimed to be lost to the government was ridiculously disproportionate to the amount confiscated. But it was all in vain. There was the letter of the law, and there were Mr. Fox and his associates in the custom-house, "all honorable men," with hands itching to clutch the plunder.

But before this question was settled the fate of the stock operation in Wall Street was most effectually disposed of. As soon as Mr. Goulden heard of Mr. Allen's death, he sold at a slight loss all he had; but his action awakened suspicion, and it was. speedily learned that the rise was due mainly to Mr. Allen's strong pushing, and the inevitable results followed. As poor Mr. Allen's remains were lowered into the vault, his stock in Wall Street was also going down with a run.

In brief, in the absence of the master's hand, and by reason of his embarrassments, there were general wreck and ruin in his affairs; and Mrs. Allen was soon compelled to face the fact, even more awful to her than her husband's death, that not a penny remained of his colossal fortune, and that she had yawningly signed away all of her own means. But she could only wring her hands in view of these blighting truths, and indulge in half-uttered com-

plaints against her husband's "folly," as she termed it.
From the first her grief had been more emotional than deep,
and her mind, recovering in part its usual poise, had begun
to be much occupied with preparations for a grand funeral,
which was carried out to her taste.   Then arose deeply interesting questions as to various styles of mourning cos-
tume, and an exciting vista of dressmaking opened before
her. She was growing into quite a serene and hopeful frame
when the miserable and blighting facts all broke upon her.
When there was little of seeming necessity to do, and there
were multitudes to do for her, Mrs. Allen's nerves permitted
no small degree of activity.   But now, as it became certain
that she and her daughters must do all themselves, her
hands grew helpless.   The idea of being poor was to her like
dying.   It was entering on an experience so utterly foreign
and unknown that it seemed like going to another world
and phase of existence, and she shrank in pitiable dread
from it.

Laura had all her mother's helpless shrinking from poverty, but with another and even bitterer ingredient added.
Mr. Goulden was extremely polite, exquisitely sympathetic,
and in terms as vague as elegantly expressed had offered to
do anything (but nothing in particular) in his power to show
his regard for the family and his esteem for his departed
friend.   He was very sorry that business would compel him
to leave town for some little time—

Laura had the spirit to interrupt him saying, "It matters
little, sir.   There are no further Wall Street operations to
be carried on here.   Invest your time and friendship where
it will pay."

Mr. Goulden, who plumed himself that he would slip out
of this bad matrimonial speculation with such polished skill
that he would leave only flattering regret and sighs behind,
under the biting satire of Laura's words suddenly saw what
a contemptible creature is the man whom selfish policy,
rather than honor and principle, governs.   He had brains
enough to comprehend himself and lose his self-respect then

and there, as he went away tingling with shame from the girl whom he had wronged, but who had detected his sordid meanness. Sigh after him! She would ever despise him, and that hurt Mr. Goulden's vanity severely. He had come very near loving Laura Allen, about as near perhaps as he ever would come to loving any one, and it had cost him a little more to give her up than to choose between a good and a bad venture on the Street. With compressed lips he had said to himself—"No gushing sentiment. In carrying out your purpose to be rich you must marry wealth." Therefore he had gone to make what he meant to be his final call, feeling quite heroic in his steadfastness—his loyalty to purpose, that is, himself. But as he recalled during his homeward walk her glad welcome, her wistful, pleading looks, and then, as she realized the truth, her pain, her contempt, and her meaning words of scorn, his miserable egotism was swept aside, and for the first time the selfish man saw the question from her standpoint, and as we have said he was not so shallow but that he saw and loathed himself. He lost his self-respect as he never had done before, and therefore to a certain extent his power ever to be happy again.

Small men, full of petty conceit, can recover from any wounds upon their vanity, but proud and large-minded men have a self-respect, even though based upon questionable foundation. It is essential to them, and losing it they are inwardly wretched. As soldiers carry the painful scars of some wounds through life, so Mr. Goulden would find that Laura's words had left a sore place while memory lasted.

Mr. Van Dam quite disarmed Edith's suspicions and prejudices by being more friendly and intimate with Zell than ever, and the latter was happy and exultant in the fact, saying, with much elation, that her friend was "not a mercenary wretch, like Mr. Goulden, but remained just as true and kind as ever."

It was evident that this attention and show of kindness

to the warm-hearted girl made a deep impression and greatly increased Mr. Van Dam's power over her. But Edith's suspicion and dislike began to return as she saw more of the manner and spirit of the man. She instinctively felt that he was bad and designing.

One day she quite incensed Zell, who was chanting his praises, by saying:

"I haven't any faith in him. What has he done to show real friendship for us? He comes here only to amuse himself with you; Gus Elliot is the only one who has been of any help."

But Edith had her misgivings about Gus also. Now, in her trouble and poverty, his weakness began to reveal itself in a new and repulsive light. In fact, that exquisitely fine young gentleman loved Edith well enough to marry her, but not to work for her. That was a sacrifice that he could not make for any woman. Though out of his natural kindness and good-nature he felt very sorry for her, and wanted to help and pet her, he had been shown his danger so clearly that he was constrained and awkward when with her, for, to tell the truth, his father had taken him aside and said:

"Look here, Gus. See to it that you don't entangle yourself with Miss Allen, now her father has failed. She couldn't support you now, and you never can support even yourself. If you would go to work like a man—but one has got to be a man to do that. It seems true, as your mother says, that you are of too fine clay for common uses. Therefore, don't make a fool of yourself. You can't keep up your style on a pretty face, and you must not wrong the girl by making her think you can take care of her. I tell you plainly, I can't bear another ounce added to my burden, and how long I shall stand up under it as it is, I can't tell."

Gus listened with a sulky, injured air. He felt that his father never appreciated him as did his mother and sisters, and indeed society at large. Society to Gus was the ultra-fashionable world of which he was one of the shining lights.

The ladies of the family quite restored his equanimity by saying:

"Now see here, Gus, don't dream of throwing yourself away on Edith Allen. You can marry any girl you please in the city. So, for Heaven's sake" (though what Heaven had to do with their advice it is hard to say), "don't let her lead you on to say what you would wish unsaid. Remember they are no more now than any other poor people, except that they are refined, etc., but this will only make poverty harder for them. Of course we are sorry for them, but in this world people have got to take care of themselves. So we must be on the lookout for some one who has money which can't be sunk in a stock operation as if thrown into the sea."

After all this sound reason, poor, weak Gus, vaguely conscious of his helplessness, as stated by his father, and quite believing his mother's assurance that "he could marry any girl he pleased," was in no mood to urge the penniless Edith to give him her empty hand, while before the party, when he believed it full, he was doing his best to bring her to this point, though in fact she gave him little opportunity.

Edith detected the change, and before very long surmised the cause. It made the young girl curl her lip, and say, in a tone of scorn that would have done Gus good to hear:

"The idea of a *man* acting in this style."

But she did not care enough about him to receive a wound of any depth, and with a good-natured tolerance recognized his weakness, and his genuine liking for her, and determined to make him useful.

Edith was very practical, and possessed of a brave, resolute nature. She was capable of strong feelings, but Gus Elliot was not the man to awaken such in any woman. She liked his company, and proposed to use him in certain ways. Under her easy manner Gus also became at ease, and, finding that he was not expected to propose and be sentimental, was all the more inclined to be friendly.

"I want you to find me books, and papers also, if there

are any, that tell how to raise fruit," she said to him one
day.

"What a funny request! I should as soon expect you
would ask for instruction how to drive four-in-hand."

"Nothing of that style, henceforth. I must learn something useful now. Only the rich can afford to be good-for-
nothing, and we are not rich now."

"For which I am very sorry," said Gus, with some
feeling.

"Thank you. Such disinterested sympathy is beautiful," said Edith dryly.

Gus looked a little red and awkward, but hastened to
say, "I will hunt up what you wish, and bring it as soon as
possible."

"You are very good. That is all at present," said Edith,
in a tone that made Gus feel that it was indeed all that it
was in his power to do for her at that time, and he went
away with a dim perception that he was scarcely more than
her errand boy. It made him very uncomfortable. Though
he wished her to understand he could not marry her now, he
wished her to sigh a little after him. Gus's vanity rather
resented that, instead of pining for him, she should with a
little quiet satire set him to work. He had never read a
romance that ended so queerly. He had expected that they
might have a little tender scene over the inexorable fate
that parted them, give and take a memento, gasp, appeal
to the moon, and see each other's face no more, she going to
the work and poverty that he could never stoop to from the
innate refinement and elegance of his being, and he to hunt
up the heiress to whom he would give the honor of main-
taining him in his true sphere.

But his little melodrama was entirely spoiled by her
matter-of-fact way, and what was worse still he felt in her
presence as if he did not amount to much, and that she
knew it; and yet, like the poor moth that singes its wings
around the lamp, he could not keep away.

The prominent trait of Gus's character, as of so many

others in our luxurious age of self-pleasing, was weakness; and yet one must be insane with vanity to be at ease if he can do nothing resolutely and dare nothing great. He is a cripple, and, if not a fool, knows it.

During the eventful month that followed Mr. Allen's death, Mrs. Allen and her daughters led what seemed to them a very strange life. While in one sense it was real and intensely painful, in another the experiences were so new and strange that it all seemed an unreal dream, a distressing nightmare of trouble and danger, from which they might awaken to their old life.

Mrs. Allen, from her large circle of acquaintances, had numerous callers, many coming from mere morbid curiosity, more from mingled motives, and not a few from genuine tearful sympathy. To these "her friends," as she emphatically called them, she found a melancholy pleasure in recounting all the recent woes, in which she ever appeared as chief sufferer and chief mourner, though her husband seemed among the minor losses, and thus most of her time was spent during the last few weeks at her old home. Her friends appeared to find a melancholy pleasure in listening to these details and then in recounting them again to other "friends" with a running commentary of their own, until that little fraction of the feminine world acquainted with the Allens had sighed, surmised, and perhaps gossiped over the "afflicted family" so exhaustively that it was really time for something new. The men and the papers downtown also had their say, and perhaps all tried, as far as human nature would permit, to say nothing but good of the dead and unfortunate.

Laura, after the stinging pain of each successive blow to her happiness, sank into a dreary apathy, and did mechanically the few things Edith asked of her.

Zell lived in varied moods and conditions, now weeping bitterly for her father, again resenting with impotent passion the change in their fortunes, but ending usually by comforting herself with the thought that Mr. Van Dam was true to her. He was as true and faithful as an insidious, incurable disease when once infused into the system. His infernal policy now was to gradually alienate her interest from her family and centre it in him. Though promising nothing in an open, manly way, he adroitly made her believe that only through him could she now hope to reach brighter days again, and to Zell he seemed the one means of escape from a detested life of poverty and privation. She became more infatuated with him than ever, and cherished a secret resentment against Edith because of her distrust and dislike of him.

The Allens had but few near relatives in the city at this time, and with these they were not on very good terms, nor were they the people to be helpful in adversity. Mr. Allen's partners were men of the world like himself, and they were also incensed that he should have been carrying on private speculations in Wall Street to the extent of risking all his capital. His fatal stock operation, together with the government confiscation, had involved them also in ruin; and they had enough to do to look after themselves. They were far more eager to secure something out of the general wreck than to see that anything remained for the family. The Allens were left very much to themselves in their struggle with disaster, securing help and advice chiefly as they paid for it.

Mr. Allen was accustomed to say that women were incapable of business, and yet here are the ladies of his own household compelled to grapple with the most perplexing forms of business or suffer aggravated losses. Though all of his family were of mature years, and thousands had been spent on their education, they were as helpless as four children in dealing with the practical questions that daily came to them for decision. At first all matters were naturally referred to the widow, but she would only wring her hands and say:

"I don't know anything about these horrid things. Can't I be left alone with my sorrow in peace a few days? Go to Edith."

And to Edith at last all came till the poor girl was almost distracted. It was of no use to go to Laura for advice, for she would only say in dreary apathy:

"Just as you think best. Anything you say."

She was indulging in unrestrained wretchedness to the utmost. Luxurious despair is so much easier than painful perplexing action.

Zell was still "the child" and entirely occupied with Mr. Van Dam. So Edith had to bear the brunt of everything. She did not do this in uncomplaining sweetness, like an angel, but scolded the others soundly for leaving all to her. They whined back that they "couldn't do anything, and didn't know how to do anything."

"You know as much as I do," retorted Edith.

And this was true. Had not Edith possessed a practical resolute nature, that preferred any kind of action to apathetic inaction and futile grieving, she would have been as helpless as the rest.

Do you say then that it was a mere matter of chance that Edith should be superior to the others, and that she deserved no credit, and they no blame? Why should such all-important conditions of character be the mere result of chance and circumstance? Would not Christian education and principle have vastly improved the Edith that existed? Would they not have made the others helpful, self-forgetting, and sympathetic? Why should the world be full of people so deformed, or morally feeble, or so ignorant, as to be helpless? Why should the naturally strong work with only contempt and condemnation for the weak? While many say, "Stand aside, I am holier than thou," perhaps more say, "Stand aside, I am wiser—stronger than thou," and the weak are made more hopelessly discouraged. This helplessness on one hand, and arrogant fault-finding strength on the other, are not the result of chance, but of an imperfect education. They come from the neglect and wrong-doing of those whose province it was to train and educate.

5—ROE—X

If we find among a family of children reaching maturity one helpless from deformity, and another from feebleness, and are told that the parents, by employing surgical skill, might have removed the deformity, and overcome the weakness by tonic treatment, but had neglected to do so, we should not have much to say about chance. I know of a poor man who spent nearly all that he had in the world to have his boy's leg straightened, and he was called a "good father." What are these physical defects compared with the graver defects of character?

Even though Mr. Allen is dead, we cannot say that he was a good father, though he spent so many thousands on his daughters. We certainly cannot call Mrs. Allen a good mother, and the proof of this is that Laura is feeble and selfish, Zell deformed through lack of self-control, and Edith hard and pitiless in her comparative strength. They were unable to cope with the practical questions of their situation. They had been launched upon the perilous, uncertain voyage of life without the compass of a true faith or the charts of principle to guide them, and they had been provided with no life-boats of knowledge to save them in case of disaster. They are now tossing among the breakers of misfortune, almost utterly the sport of the winds and waves of circumstances. If these girls never reached the shore of happiness and safety, could we wonder?

How would your daughter fare, my reader, if you were gone and she were poor, with her hands and brain to depend on for bread, and her heart culture for happiness? In spite of all your providence and foresight, such may be her situation. Such becomes the condition of many men's daughters every day.

But time and events swept the Allens forward, as the shipwrecked are borne on the crest of a wave, and we must follow their fortunes. Hungry creditors, especially the petty ones uptown, stripped them of everything they could lay their hands on, and they were soon compelled to leave their Fifth Avenue mansion. The little place in the country,

given to Edith partly in jest by her father as a birthday
present, was now their only refuge, and to this they prepared to go on the first of April. Edith, as usual, took the
lead, and was to go in advance of the others with such furniture as they had been able to keep, and prepare for their
coming. Old Hannibal, who had grown gray in the service
of the family, and now declined to leave it, was to accompany her. On a dark, lowering day, symbolic of their fortunes, some loaded drays took down to the boat that with
which they would commence the meagre housekeeping of
their poverty. Edith went slowly down the broad steps
leading from her elegant home, and before she entered the
carriage turned for one lingering, tearful look, such as Eve
may have bent upon the gate of Paradise closing behind
her, then sprang into the carriage, drew the curtains, and
sobbed all the way to the boat. Scarcely once before, during that long, hard month, had she so given way to her feelings. But she was alone now and none could see her tears
and call her weak. Hannibal took his seat on the box with
the driver, and looked and felt very much as he did when
following his master to Greenwood.

CHAPTER VIII

WARPED

IT is the early breakfast hour at a small frame house, situated about a mile from the staid but thriving village of Pushton. But the indications around the house do not denote thrift. Quite the reverse. As the neighbors expressed it, "there was a screw loose with Lacey," the owner of this place. It was going down hill like its master. A general air of neglect and growing dilapidation impressed the most casual observer. The front gate hung on one hinge; boards were off the shackly barn, and the house had grown dingy and weather-stained from lack of paint. But as you entered and passed from the province of the master to that of the mistress a new element was apparent, struggling with, but unable to overcome, the predominant tendency to unthrift and seediness. But everything that Mrs. Lacey controlled was as neat as the poor overworked woman could keep it.

At the time our story becomes interested in her fortunes, Mrs. Lacey was a middle-aged woman, but appeared older than her years warranted, from the long-continued strain of incessant toil, and from that which wears much faster still, the depression of an unhappy, ill-mated life. Her face wore the pathetic expression of confirmed discouragement. She reminded one of soldiers fighting when they know that it is of no use, and that defeat will be the only result, but who fight on mechanically, in obedience to orders.

She is now placing a very plain but wholesome and well-prepared breakfast on the table, and it would seem that both the eating and cooking were carried on in the same large living-room. Her daughter, a rosy-cheeked, half-grown girl of fourteen, was assisting her, and both mother and daughter seemed in a nervous state of expectancy, as if hoping and fearing the result of a near event. A moment's glance showed that this event related to a lad of about seventeen, who was walking about the room, vainly trying to control the agitation which is natural even to the cool and experienced when feeling that they are at one of the crises of life.

It could not be expected of Arden Lacey at his age to be cool and experienced. Indeed his light curling hair, blue eyes, and a mobile sensitive mouth, suggested the reverse of a stolid self-poise, or cheerful endurance. Any one accustomed to observe character could see that he was possessed of a nervous, fine-fibred nature capable of noble achievement under right influences, but also easily warped and susceptible to sad injury under brutal wrong. He was like those delicate and somewhat complicated musical instruments that produce the sweetest harmonies when in tune and well played upon, but the most jangling discords when unstrung and in rough, ignorant hands. He had inherited his nervous temperament, his tendency to irritation and excess, from the diseased, over-stimulated system of his father, who was fast becoming a confirmed inebriate, and who had been poisoning himself with bad liquors all his life. From his mother he had obtained what balance he had in temperament, but he owed more to her daily influence and training. It was the one struggle of the poor woman's life to shield her children from the evil consequences of their father's life. For her son she had special anxiety, knowing his sensitive, high-strung nature, and his tendency to go headlong into evil if his self-respect and self-control were once lost. His passionate love for her had been the boy's best trait, and through this she had controlled him thus far. But she had thought that it might be best for him to be away from his father's presence and influence if she could only find

something that accorded with his bent.   And this eventually proved to be a college education.   The boy was of a
quick and studious mind.   From earliest years he had been
fond of books, and as time advanced, the passion for study
and reading grew upon him.   He had a strong imagination,
and his favorite styles of reading were such as appealed to
this.   In the scenes of history and romance he escaped from
the sordid life of toil and shame to which his father condemned him, into a large realm that seemed rich and glorified in contrast.   When he was but fourteen the thought
of a liberal education fired his ambition and became the
dream of his life.   He made the very most of the district
school to which he was sent in winter.   The teacher happened to be a well-educated man, and took pride in his apt,
eager scholar.   Between the boy's and the mother's savings
they had obtained enough to secure private lessons in Latin
and Greek, and now at the age of seventeen he was tolerably
well pepared for college.

But the father had no sympathy at all with these tastes,
and from the incessant labor he required of his son, and the
constant interruptions he occasioned in his studies even in
winter, he had been a perpetual bar to all progress.

On the day previous to the scene described in the opening of this chapter, the winter term had closed, and Mr. Rule,
the teacher, had declared that Arden could enter college,
and with natural pride in his own work as instructor, intimated that he would lead his class if he did.

Both mother and son were so elated at this that they determined at once to state the fact to the father, thinking that
if he had any of the natural feelings of a parent he would take
some pride in his boy, and be willing to help him obtain the
education he longed for.

But there is little to be hoped from a man who is completely under the influence of ignorance and rum.   Mr. Lacey
was the son of a small farmer like himself, and never had
anything to recommend him but his fine looks, which had
captivated poor Mrs. Lacey to her cost.   Unlike the ma-

jority of his class, who are fast becoming a very intelligent part of the community, and are glad to educate their children, he boasted that he liked the "old ways," and by these he meant the worst ways of his father's day, when books and schools were scarce, and few newspapers found their way to rural homes. He was, like his father before him, a graduate of the village tavern, and had imbibed bad liquor and his ideas of life at the same time from that objectionable source. With the narrow-mindedness of his class, he had a prejudice against all learning that went beyond the three R's, and had watched with growing disapprobation his son's taste for books, believing that it would spoil him as a farm hand, and make him an idle dreamer. He was less and less inclined to work himself as his frame became diseased and enfeebled from intemperance, and he determined now to get as much work as possible out of that "great hulk of a boy," as he called Arden. He had picked up some hints of the college hopes, and the very thought angered him. He determined that when the boy broached the subject he would give him such a "jawing" (to use his own vernacular) "as would put an end to that nonsense." Therefore both Arden and his mother, who were waiting as we have described in such a perturbed anxious state for his entrance, were doomed to bitter disappointment. At last a heavy red-faced man entered the kitchen, stalking in on the white floor out of the drizzling rain with his muddy boots leaving tracks and blotches in keeping with his character. But he had the grace to wash his grimy hands before sitting down to the table. He was always in a bad humor in the morning, and the chilly rain had not improved it. A glance around showed him that something was on hand, and he surmised that it was the college business. He at once thought within himself:

"I'll squelch the thing now, once for all."

Turning to his son, he said, "Look here, youngster, why hain't you been out doing your chores? D'ye expect me to do your work and mine, too?"

"Father," said the impulsive boy with a voice of trembling eagerness, "if you will let me go to college next fall, I'll do my work and yours too. I'll work night and day—"

"What cussed nonsense is this?" demanded the man harshly, clashing down his knife and fork and turning frowningly toward his son.

"No, but father, listen to me before you refuse. Mr. Rule says I'm fit to enter college and that I can lead my class too. I've been studying for this three years. I've set my heart upon it," and in his earnestness, tears gathered in his eyes.

"The more fool you, and old Rule is another," was the coarse answer.

The boy's eyes flashed angrily, but the mother here spoke.

"You ought to be proud of your son, John; if you were a true father you would be. If you'd encourage and help him now, he'd make a man that—"

"Shut up! little you know about it. He'd make one of your snivelling white-fingered loafers that's too proud to get a living by hard work. Perhaps you'd like to make a parson out of him. Now look here, old woman, and you, too, my young cock, I've suspicioned that something of this kind was up, but I tell you once for all it won't go. Just as this hulk of a boy is gettin' of some use to me, you want to spoil him by sending him to college. I'll see him hanged first," and the man turned to his breakfast as if he had settled it. But he was startled by his son's exclaiming passionately:

"I will go."

"Look here, what do *you* mean?" said the father, rising with a black ugly look.

"I mean I've set my heart on going to college and I will go. You and all the world shan't hinder me. I won't stay here and be a farm drudge all my life."

The man's face was livid with anger, and in a low, hissing tone he said:

"I guess you want taking down a peg, my college gentleman. Perhaps you don't know I'm master till you're twenty-one," and he reached down a large leather strap.

"You strike me if you dare," shouted the boy.

"If I dare! haw! haw! If I don't cut the cussed nonsense out of yer this morning, then I never did," and he took an angry stride toward his son, who sprang behind the stove.

The wife and mother had stood by growing whiter and whiter, and with lips pressed closely together. At this critical moment she stepped before her infuriated husband and seized his arm, exclaiming:

"John, take care. You have reached the end."

"Stand aside," snarled the man, raising the strap, "or I'll give you a taste of it, too."

The woman's grasp tightened on his arm, and in a voice that made him pause and look fixedly at her, she said:

"If you strike me or that boy I'll take my children and we will leave your roof this hateful day never to return."

"Hain't I to be master in my own house?" said the husband sullenly.

"You are not to be a brute in your own house. I know you've struck me before, but I endured it and said nothing about it because you were drunk, but you are not drunk now, and if you lay a finger on me or my son to-day, I will never darken your doors again."

The unnatural father saw that he had gone too far. He had not expected such an issue. He had long been accustomed to follow the lead of his brutal passions, but had now reached a point where he felt he must stop, as his wife said. Turning on his heel, he sullenly took his place at the table, muttering:

"It's a pretty pass when there's mutiny in a man's own house." Then to his son, "You won't get a d—n cent out of me for your college business, mind that."

Rose, the daughter, who had been crying and wringing her hands on the door-step, now came timidly in, and at a sign from her mother she and her brother went into another room.

The man ate for a while in dogged silence, but at last in a tone that was meant to be somewhat conciliatory said:

"What the devil did you mean by putting the boy up to such foolishness?"

"Hush!" said his wife imperiously, "I'm in no mood to talk with you now."

"Oh, ah, indeed, a man can't even speak in his own house, eh? I guess I'll take myself off to where I can have a little more liberty," and he went out, harnessed his old white horse, and started for his favorite groggery in the village.

His father had no sooner gone than Arden came out and said passionately:

"It's no use, mother, I can't stand it; I must leave home to-day. I guess I can make a living; at any rate I'd rather starve than pass through such scenes."

The poor, overwrought woman threw herself down in a low chair and sobbed, rocking herself back and forth.

"Wait till I die, Arden, wait till I die. I feel it won't be long. What have I to live for but you and Rosy? And if you, my pride and joy, go away after what has happened, it will be worse than death," and a tempest of grief shook her gaunt frame.

Arden was deeply moved. Boylike he had been thinking only of himself, but now as never before he realized her hard lot, and in his warm, impulsive heart there came a yearning tenderness for her such as he had never felt before. He took her in his arms and kissed and comforted her, till even her sore heart felt the healing balm of love and ceased its bitter aching. At last she dried her eyes and said with a faint smile:

"With such a boy to pet me, the world isn't all flint and thorns yet."

And Rosy came and kissed her too, for she was an affectionate child, though a little inclined to be giddy and vain.

"Don't worry, mother," said Arden. "I will stay and take such good care of you that you will have many years yet, and happier ones, too, I hope," and he resolved to keep this promise, cost what it might.

"I hardly think I ought to ask it of you, though even the thought of your going away breaks my heart."

"I will stay," said the boy, almost as passionately as he had said, "I will go." "I now see how much you need a protector."

That night the father came home so stupidly drunk that they had to half carry him to bed where he slept heavily till morning, and rose considerably shaken and depressed from his debauch. The breakfast was as silent as it had been stormy on the previous day. After it was over, Arden followed his father to the door and said:

"I was a boy yesterday morning, but you made me a man, and a rather ugly one too. I learned then for the first time that you occasionally strike my mother. Don't you ever do it again, or it will be worse for you, drunk or sober. I am not going to college, but will stay at home and take care of her. Do we understand each other?"

The man was in such a low, shattered condition that his son's bearing cowed him, and he walked off muttering:

"Young cocks crow mighty loud," but from that time forward he never offered violence to his wife or children.

Still his father's conduct and character had a most disastrous effect upon the young man. He was soured, because disappointed in his most cherished purpose at an age when most youths scarcely have definite plans. Many have a strong natural bent, and if turned aside from this, they are more or less unhappy, and their duties, instead of being wings to help life forward, become a galling yoke.

This was the case with Arden. Farm work, as he had learned it from his father, was coarse, heavy drudgery, with small and uncertain returns, and these were largely spent at the village rum shops in purchasing slow perdition for the husband, and misery and shame for his wife and children.

In respectable Pushton, a drunkard's family, especially
if poor, had a very low social status. Mrs. Lacey and her
children would not accept of bad associations, so they had
scarcely any. This ostracism, within certain limits, is perhaps right. •The preventive penalties of vice can scarcely
be too great, and men and women must be made to feel that
wrong-doing is certain to be followed by terrible consequences. The fire is merciful in that it always burns, and
sin and suffering are inseparably linked. But the consequences of one person's sin often blight the innocent. The
necessity of this from our various ties should be a motive,
a hostage against sinning, and doubtless restrains many a
one who would go headlong under evil impulses. But multitudes do slip off the paths of virtue, and helpless wives,
and often helpless husbands and children, writhe from
wounds made by those under sacred obligations to shield
them. Upon the families of criminals, society visits a mil-
dew of coldness and scorn that blights nearly all chance of
good fruit. But society is very unjust in its discrimina-
tions, and some of the most heinous sins in God's sight are
treated as mere eccentricities, or condemned in the poor,
but winked at in the rich. Gentlemen will admit to their
parlors men about whom they know facts which if true of
a woman would close every respectable door against her,
and God frowns on the Christian (?) society that makes such
arbitrary and unjust distinctions. Cast both out, till they
bring forth fruits meet for repentance.

But we hope for little of a reformative tendency from
the selfish society of the world. Changing human fashion
rules it, rather than the eternal truth of the God of love.
The saddest feature of all is that the shifting code of fashion
is coming more and more to govern the church. Doctrine
may remain the same, profession and intellectual belief the
same, while practical action drifts far astray. There are
multitudes of wealthy churches, that will no more admit
associations with that class among which our Lord lived
and worked, than will select society. They seem designed

to help only respectable, well-connected sinners, toward heaven.

This tendency has two phases. In the cities the poor are practically excluded from worshipping with the rich, and missions are established for them as if they were heathen. There can be no objection to costly, magnificent churches. Nothing is too good to be the expression of our honor and love of God. But they should be like the cathedrals of Europe, where prince and peasant may bow together on the same level they have in the Divine presence. Christ made no distinction between the rich and poor regarding their spiritual value and need, nor should the Christianity named after Him. To the degree that it does, it is not Christianity. The meek and lowly Nazarene is not its inspiration. Perhaps the personage He told to get behind Him when promising the "kingdoms of the world and the glory of them" has more to do with it.

The second phase of this tendency as seen in the country, is kindred but unlike. Poverty may not be so great a bar, but moral delinquencies are more severely visited; and the family under a cloud, through the wrong-doing of one or more of its members, is treated very much as if it had a perpetual pestilence. The highly respectable keep aloof. Too often the quiet country church is not a sanctuary and place of refuge for the victims either of their own or another's sin, a place where the grasp of sympathy and words of encouragement are given; but rather a place where they meet the cold critical gaze of those who are hedged about with virtues and good connections. I hope I am wrong, but how is it where you live, my reader? If a well-to-do thriving man of integrity takes a fine place in your community, we all know how church people will treat him. And what they do is all right. But society—the world— will do the same. Is Christianity—are the followers of the "Friend of publicans and sinners"—to do no more?

If in contrast a drunken wretch like Lacey with his wife and children come in town on top of a wagon-load of shattered furniture, and all are dumped down in a back alley to scramble into the shelter of a tenement house as best they can, do you call upon them? Do you invite them to your pew? Do you ever urge and encourage them to enter your church? and do you make even one of its corners homelike and inviting?

I hope so; but, alas! that was not the general custom in Pushton, and poor Mrs. Lacey had acquired the habit of staying at home, her neighbors had become accustomed to call her husband a "dreadful man," and the family "very irreligious," and as the years passed they seemed to be more and more left to themselves. Mr. Lacey had brought his wife from a distant town where he had met and married her. She was a timid, retiring woman, and time and kindness were needed to draw her out. But no one had seemingly thought it worth while, and at the time our story takes an interest in their affairs, there was a growing isolation.

All this had a very bad effect upon Arden. As he grew out of the democracy of boyhood he met a certain social coldness and distance which he learned to understand only too early, and soon returned this treatment with increased coldness and aversion. Had it not been for the influence of his mother and the books he read, he would have inevitably fallen into low company. But he had promised his mother to shun it. He saw its result in his father's conduct, and as he read, and his mind matured, the narrow coarseness of such company became repugnant. From time to time he was sorely tempted to leave the home which his father made hateful in many respects, and try his fortunes among strangers who would not associate him with a sot; but his love for his mother kept him at her side, for he saw that her life was bound up in him, and that he alone could protect her and his sister and keep some sort of a shelter for them. In his unselfish devotion to them his character was noble. In his harsh cynicism toward the world and especially the church people, for whom he had no charity whatever—in his utter hatred and detestation of his father—it was faulty, though allowance must be made for him. He was also peculiar in other respects, for his unguided reading was of a nature that fed his imagination at the expense of his reasoning faculties. Though he drudged in a narrow round, and his life was as hard and real as poverty and his father's intemperance could make it, he mentally lived and found his solace in a world as large and unreal as an uncurbed fancy could create. Therefore his work was hurried through mechanically in the old slovenly methods to which he had been educated, he caring little for the results, as his father squandered these; and when the necessary toil was over, he would lose all sense of the sordid present in the pages of some book obtained from the village library. As he drove his milk cart to and from town he would sit in the chill drizzling rain, utterly oblivious of discomfort, with a half smile upon his lips, as he pictured to himself some scene of sunny aspect or gloomy castellated grandeur of which his own imagination was the architect. The famous in history, the heroes and heroines of fiction, and especially the characters of Shakespeare were more familiar to him than the people among whom he lived. From the latter he stood more and more aloof, while with the former he held constant intercourse. He had little in common even with his sister, who was of a very different temperament. But his tenderness toward his mother never failed, and she loved him with the passionate intensity of a nature to which love was all, but which had found little to satisfy it on earth, and was ignorant of the love of God.

And so the years dragged on to Arden, and his twenty-first birthday made him free from his father's control as he practically long had been, but it also found him bound more strongly than ever by his mother's love and need to his old home life.

CHAPTER IX

A DESERT ISLAND

THE good cry that Edith indulged in on her way to the boat was a relief to her heart, which had long been overburdened. But the necessity of controlling her feelings, and the natural buoyancy of youth, enabled her by the time they reached the wharf to see that the furniture and baggage were properly taken care of. No one could detect the traces of grief through her thick veil, or guess from her firm, quiet tones, that she felt somewhat as Columbus might when going in search of a new world. And yet Edith had a hope from her country life which the others did not share at all.

When she was quite a child her feeble health had induced her father to let her spend an entire summer in a farmhouse of the better class, whose owner had some taste for flowers and fruit. These she had enjoyed and luxuriated in as much as any butterfly of the season, and as she romped with the farmer's children, roamed the fields and woods in search of berries, and tumbled in the fragrant hay, health came tingling back with a fullness and vigor that had never been lost. With all her subsequent enjoyment, that summer still dwelt in her memory as the halcyon period of her life, and it was with the country she associated it. Every year she had longed for July, for then her father would break away from business for a couple of months and take them to a place of resort. But the fashionable watering-places were not at all to her taste as compared with that old farmhouse, and whenever it was possible she would wander off and make "disreputable acquaintances," as Mrs. Allen termed them, among the farmers' and laborers' families in the vicinity of the hotel. But by this means she often obtained a basket of fruit or bunch of flowers that the others were glad to share in.

In accordance with her practical nature she asked questions as to the habits, growth, and culture of trees and fruits, so that few city girls situated as she had been knew as much about the products of the garden. She had also haunted conservatories and green-houses as much as her sisters had frequented the costly Broadway temples of fashion, where counters are the altars to which the women of the city bring their daily offerings; and as we have seen, a fruit store was a place of delight to her.

The thought that she could now raise without limit fruit, flowers, and vegetables on her own place was some compensation even for the trouble they had passed through and the change in their fortunes.

Moreover she knew that because of their poverty she would have to secure from her ground substantial returns, and that her gardening must be no amateur trifling, but earnest work. Therefore, having found a seat in the saloon of the boat, she drew out of her leather bag one of her garden-books and some agricultural papers, and commenced studying over for the twentieth time the labors proper for April. After reading a while, she leaned back and closed her eyes and tried to form such crude plans as were possible in her inexperience and her ignorance of a place that she had not even seen.

Opening her eyes suddenly she saw old Hannibal sitting near and regarding her wistfully.

"You are a foolish old fellow to stay with us," she said to him. "You could have obtained plenty of nice places in the city. What made you do it?"

"I'se couldn't gib any good reason to de world, Miss Edie, but de one I hab kinder satisfies my ole black heart."

"Your heart isn't black, Hannibal."

"How you know dat?" he asked quickly.

"Because I've seen it often and often. Sometimes I think it is whiter than mine. I now and then feel so desperate and wicked, that I am afraid of myself."

"Dere now, you'se worried and worn-out and you tinks dat's bein' wicked."

"No, I'm satisfied it is something worse than that. I wonder if God does care about people who are in trouble, I mean practically, so as to help them any?"

"Well, I specs he does," said Hannibal vaguely. "But den dere's so many in trouble dat I'm afeard some hab to kinder look after demselves." Then as if a bright thought struck him, he added, "I specs he sorter lumps 'em jes as Massa Allen did when he said he was sorry for de people burned up in Chicago. He sent 'em a big lot ob money and den seemed to forget all about 'em."

Hannibal had never given much attention to religion, and perhaps was not the best authority that Edith could have consulted. But his conclusion seemed to secure her consent, for she leaned back wearily and again closed her eyes, saying:

"Yes, we are mere human atoms, lost sight of in the multitude."

Soon her deep regular breathing showed that she was asleep, and Hannibal muttered softly:

"Bress de child, dat will do her a heap more good dan askin' dem deep questions," and he watched beside her like a large faithful Newfoundland dog.

At last he touched her elbow and said, "We get off at de next landin', and I guess we mus' be pretty nigh dere."

Edith started up much refreshed and asked, "What sort of an evening is it?"

"Well, I'se sorry to say it's rainin' hard and berry dark."

To her dismay she also found that it was nearly nine o'clock. The boat had been late in starting, and was so heavily laden as to make slow progress against wind and tide. Edith's heart sank within her at the thought of landing alone in a strange place that dismal night. It was indeed a new experience to her. But she donned her waterproof, and the moment the boat touched the wharf, hurried ashore, and stood under her small umbrella, while her household gods were being hustled out into the drenching rain. She knew the injury that must result to them unless they could speedily be carried into the boat-house near. At first there seemed no one to do this save Hannibal, who at once set to work, but she soon observed a man with a lantern gathering up some butter-tubs that the boat was landing, and she immediately appealed to him for help.

"I'm not the dock-master," was the gruff reply.

"You are a man, are you not? and one that will not turn away from a lady in distress. If my things stand long in this rain they will be greatly injured."

The man thus adjured turned his lantern on the speaker, and while we recognize the features of our acquaintance, Arden Lacey, he sees a face on the old dock that quite startles him. If Edith had dropped down with the rain, she could not have been more unexpected, and with her large dark eyes flashing suddenly on him, and her appealing yet half-indignant voice breaking in upon the waking dream with which he was beguiling the outward misery of the night, it seemed as if one of the characters of his fancy had suddenly become real. He who would have passed Edith in surly unnoting indifference on the open street in the garish light of day, now took the keenest interest in her. He had actually been appealed to, as an ancient knight might have been, by a damsel in distress, and he turned and helped her with a will, which, backed by his powerful strength, soon placed her goods under shelter. The lagging dock-master politicly kept out of the way till the work was almost done and then bustled up and made some show of assisting in time for any fees, if they should be offered, but Arden told him that since he had kept out of sight so long, he might remain invisible, which was the unpopular way the young man had.

When the last article had been placed under shelter Edith said:

"I appreciate your help exceedingly. How much am I to pay you for your trouble?"

"Nothing," was the rather curt reply.

The appearance of a lady like Edith, with a beauty that seemed weird and strange as he caught glimpses of her face by the fitful rays of his lantern, had made a sudden and strong impression on his morbid fancy and fitted the wild imaginings with which he had occupied the dreary hour of waiting for the boat. The presence of her sable attendant had increased these impressions. But when she took out her purse to pay him his illusions vanished. Therefore the abrupt tone in which he said "Nothing," and which was mainly caused by vexation at the matter-of-fact world that continually mocked his unreal one.

"I don't quite understand you," said Edith. "I had no intention of employing your time and strength without remuneration."

"I told you I was not the dock-master," said Arden rather coldly. "He'll take all the fees you will give him. You appealed to me as a man, and said you were in distress. I helped you as a man. Good-evening."

"Stay," said Edith hastily. "You seem not only a man, but a gentleman, and I am tempted, in view of my situation, to trespass still further on your kindness," but she hesitated a moment.

It perhaps had never been intimated to Arden before that he was a gentleman, certainly never in the tone with which Edith spoke, and his fanciful, chivalric nature responded at once to the touch of that chord. With the accent of voice he ever used toward his mother, he said:

"I am at your service."

"We are strangers here," continued Edith. "Is there

any place near the landing where we can get safe, comfortable lodging ?''

"I am sorry to say there is not. The village is a mile away."

"How can we get there ?''

"Isn't the stage down?" asked Arden of the dockmaster.

"No!" was the gruff response.

"The night is so bad I suppose they didn't come. . I would take you myself in a minute if I had a suitable wagon."

"Necessity knows no choice," said Edith quickly. "I will go with you in any kind of a wagon, and I surely hope you won't leave me on this lonely dock in the rain."

"Certainly not," said Arden, reddening in the darkness that he could be thought capable of such an act. "But I thought I could drive to the village and send a carriage for you."

"I would rather go with you now, if you will let me," said Edith decidedly.

"The best I have is at your service, but I fear you will be sorry for your choice. I've only a board for a seat, and my wagon has no springs. Perhaps I could get a low box for you to sit on."

"Hannibal can sit on the box. With your permission I will sit with you, for I wish to ask you some questions."

Arden hung his lantern on a hook in front of his wagon, and helped or partly lifted Edith over the wheel to the seat, which was simply a board resting on the sides of the box. He turned a butter-tub upside down for Hannibal, and then they jogged out from behind the boat-house where he had sheltered his horses.

This was all a new experience to Arden. He had, from his surly misanthropy, little familiarity with society of any kind, and since as a boy he had romped with the girls at school he had been almost a total stranger to all women save those in his own home. Most young men would have

been awkward louts under the circumstances. But this was
not true of Arden, for he had daily been holding converse
in the books he dreamed over with women of finer clay than
he could have found at Pushton. He would have been excessively awkward in a drawing-room or any place of conventional resort, or rather he would have been sullen and
bearish, but the place and manner in which he had met
Edith accorded with his romantic fancy, and the darkness
shielded his rough exterior from observation.

Moreover, the presence of this flesh-and-blood woman at
his side gave him different sensations from the stately dames,
or even the most piquant maidens that had smiled upon him
in the shadowy scenes of his imagination; and when at times,
as the wagon jolted heavily, she grasped his arm for a second
to steady herself, it seemed as if the dusky little figure at
his side was a sort of human electric battery charged with
that subtile fluid which some believe to be the material life
of the universe. Every now and then as they bounced over
a stone, the lantern would bob up and throw a ray on a face
like those that had looked out upon him from those plays of
Shakespeare the scenes of which are laid in Italy.

Thus the dark, chilly, rainy night was becoming the most
luminous period of his life. Reason and judgment act slowly,
but imagination takes fire.

But to poor Edith all was real and dismal enough, and
she often sighed heavily. To Arden each sigh was an appeal for sympathy. He had driven as rapidly as he dared
in the darkness to get her out of the rain, but at last she
said, clinging to his arm:

"Won't you drive slowly? The jolting has given me a
pain in my side."

He was conscious of a new and peculiar sensation there
also, though not from jolting. He had been used to that in
many ways all his life, but thereafter they jogged forward
on a walk through the drizzling rain, and Edith, recovering
her breath, and a sense of security, began to asked the questions.

"Do you know where the cottage is that was formerly owned by Mr. Jenks?"

"Oh, yes, it's not far from our house—between our house and the village." Then as if a sudden thought struck him he added quickly, "I heard it was sold; are you the owner?"

"Yes," said Edith a little coolly. She had expected to question and not to be questioned. And yet she was very glad she had met one who knew about her place. But she resolved to be non-committal till she knew more about him.

"What sort of a house is it?" she asked after a moment. "I have never seen it."

"Well, it's not very large, and I fear it is somewhat out of repair—at least it looks so, and I should think a new roof was needed."

Edith could not help saying pathetically, "Oh, dear! I'm so sorry."

Arden then added hastily, "But it's a kind of a pretty place too—a great many fruit-trees and grapevines on it."

"So I've been told," said Edith. "And that will be its chief attraction to me."

"Then you are going to live there?"

"Yes."

Arden's heart gave a sudden throb. Then he would see this mysterious stranger often. But he smiled half bitterly in the darkness as he queried, "What will she appear like in the daylight?"

Her next question broke the spell he was under utterly. They were passing through the village and the little hotel was near, and she naturally asked:

"To whom am I indebted for all this kindness? I am glad to know so much as that you are my neighbor."

Suddenly and painfully conscious of his outward life and surroundings, he answered briefly:

"My name is Arden Lacey. We have a small farm a little beyond your cottage."

Wondering at his change of tone and manner, Edith still ventured to ask:

"And do you know of any one who could bring my furniture and things up to-morrow?"

As he sometimes did that kind of work, an impulse to see more of her impelled him to say:

"I suppose I can do it. I work for a living."

"I am sure that is nothing against you," said Edith kindly.

"You will not live long in Pushton before learning that there is something against us," was the bitter reply. "But that need not prevent my working for you, as I do for others. If you wish, I will make a fire in your house early, to take off the chill and dampness, and then go for your furniture. The people here will send you out in a carriage."

"I shall be greatly obliged if you will do so and let me pay you."

"Oh, certainly, I will charge the usual rates."

"Well, then, how much for to-night?" said Edith as she stood in the hotel door.

"To-night is another affair," and he jumped into his wagon and rattled away in the darkness, his lantern looking like a "will-o'-the-wisp" that might vanish altogether.

The landlord received Edith and her attendant with a gruff civility, and gave her in charge of his wife, who was a bustling red-faced woman with a sort of motherly kindness about her.

"Why, you poor child," she said to Edith, turning her round before the light, "you're half drowned. You must have something hot right away, or you'll take your death o' cold," and with something of her husband's faith in whiskey, she soon brought Edith a hot punch that for a few moments seemed to make the girl's head spin, but as it was followed by strong tea and toast, she felt none the worse, and danger from the chill and wet was effectually disposed of.

As she sat sipping her tea before a red-hot stove, she

told, in answer to the landlady's questions, how she had got up from the boat.

"Who is this Lacey, and what is there against them?" she asked suddenly.

The hostess went across the hall, opened the bar-room door, and beckoned Edith to follow her.

In a chair by the stove sat a miserable bloated wreck of a man, drivelling and mumbling in a drunken lethargy.

"That's his father," said the woman in a whisper. "When he gets as bad as that he comes here because he knows my husband is the only one as won't turn him out of doors."

An expression of intense disgust flitted across Edith's face, and by the necessary law of association poor Arden sank in her estimation through the foulness of his father's vice.

"Is there anything against the son?" asked Edith in some alarm. "I've engaged him to bring up my furniture and trunks. I hope he's honest."

"Oh, yes, he's honest enough, and he'd be mighty mad if anybody questioned that, but he's kind o' soured and ugly, and don't notice nobody nor nothing. The son and Mrs. Lacey keep to themselves, the man does as you see, but the daughter, who's a smart, pretty girl, tries to rise above it all, and make her way among the rest of the girls; but she has a hard time of it, I guess, poor child."

"I don't wonder," said Edith, "with such a father."

But between the punch and fatigue, she was glad to take refuge from the landlady's garrulousness, and all her troubles in quiet sleep.

The next morning the storm was passing away in broken masses of cloud, through which the sun occasionally shone in April-like uncertainty.

After an early breakfast she and Hannibal were driven in an open wagon to what was to be her future home—the scene of unknown joys and sorrows.

The most memorable places, where the mightiest events

6—ROE—X

of the world have transpired, can never have for us the interest of that humble spot where the little drama of our own
life will pass from act to act till our exit.

Most eagerly did Edith note everything as revealed by
the broad light of day. The village, though irregular, had
a general air of thriftiness and respectability. The street
through which she was riding gradually fringed off, from
stores and offices, into neat homes, farmhouses, and here
and there the abodes of the poor, till at last, three-quarters
of a mile out, she saw a rather quaint little cottage with a
roof steeply sloping and a long low porch.

"That's your place, miss," said the driver.

Edith's intent eyes took in the general effect with something of the practiced rapidity with which she mastered a
lady's toilet on the avenue.

In spite of her predisposition to be pleased, the prospect
was depressing. The season was late and patches of discolored snow lay here and there, and were piled up along
the fences. The garden and trees had a neglected look.
The vines that clambered up the porch had been untrimmed
of the last year's growth, and sprawled in every direction.
The gate hung from one hinge, and many palings were off
the fence, and all had a sodden, dingy appearance from the
recent rains. The house itself looked so dilapidated and
small, in contrast with their stately mansion on Fifth Avenue,
that irrepressible tears came into her eyes, as she murmured:

"It will kill mother just to see it."

Old Hannibal said in a low, encouraging tone, "It'll look
a heap better next June, Miss Edie."

But Edith dropped her veil to hide her feelings, and
shook her head.

They got down before the rickety gate, took out the
basket of provisions which Hannibal had secured, paid the
driver, who splashed away through the mud as a boat might
that had landed and left two people on a desert island.
They walked up the oozy path with hearts about as chill
and empty as the unfurnished cottage before them.

But utter repulsiveness had been taken away by a bright fire that Arden had kindled on the hearth of the largest room; and when lighting it he had been so romantic as to dream of the possibility of kindling a more sacred fire in a heart that he knew now to be as cold to him as the chilly room in which he shivered.

Poor Arden! If he could have seen the expression on Edith's face the night previous, as she looked on his besotted father, he would have cursed more bitterly than ever what he termed the blight of his life.

CHAPTER X

EDITH BECOMES A "DIVINITY"

AS the wrecked would hasten up the strand and explore eagerly in various directions in order to gain some idea of the nature and resources of the place where they might spend months and even years, so Edith hurriedly passed from one room to another, looking the house over first, as their place of refuge and centre of life, and then went out to a spot from which she could obtain a view of the garden, the little orchard, and the pasture field.

The house had three rooms on the first floor, as many on the second, and a very small attic. There was also a pretty good cellar, though it looked to Edith like a black, dismal hole, and was full of rubbish and old boxes.

The entrance of the house was at the commencement of the porch, which ran along under the windows of the large front room. Back of this was one much smaller, and doors opened from both the apartments named into a long and rather narrow room running the full depth of the house, and which had been designed as the kitchen. With the families that would naturally occupy a house of this character, it would have been the general living-room. To Edith's eyes, accustomed to magnificent spaces and lofty ceilings, these apartments seemed stifling dingy cells. The walls were broken in places and discolored by smoke. With the exception of the large room there were no places for open fires, but only holes for stovepipes.

"How can such a place as this ever look homelike?"

The muddy garden, with its patches of snow, its forlorn

and neglected air, its spreading vines and the thickly standing stalks of last year's weeds, was even less inviting.
Edith had never seen the country in winter, and the gar-
dens of her experience were full of green, beautiful life.
The orchard looked not only gaunt and bare, but very
untidy. The previous year had been most abundant in
fruit, and the trees were left to bear at will. Therefore
many of the limbs were wholly or partly broken off, and
lay scattered where they fell, or still hung by a little of the
woody fibre and bark.

Edith came back to the fire from the survey of her future
home, not only chilled in body by the raw April winds, but
more chilled in heart. Though she had not expected summer greenness and a sweet inviting home, yet the reality
was so dreary and forbidding, from its necessary contrast
with the past, that she sank down on the floor, and buried
her head in her lap in an uncontrollable passion of grief.
Hannibal was out gathering wood to replenish the fire, and
it was a luxury to be alone a few minutes with her sorrow.

But soon she had the consciousness that she was not
alone, and looking up, saw Arden in the door, with a grave
troubled face. Hastily turning from him, and wiping away
her tears, she said rather coldly:

"You should have knocked. The house is my home, if
it is empty."

His face changed instantly to its usua' hard sullen aspect,
and he said briefly:

"I did knock."

"The landlady has told her all about us," he thought,
"and she rejects sympathy and fellowship from such as we
are."

But Edith's feeling had only been annoyance that a
stranger had seen her emotion, so she said quickly, "I beg
your pardon. We have had trouble, but I don't give way
in this manner often. Have you brought a load?"

"Yes. If your servant will help me I will bring the
things in."

As he and Hannibal carried in heavy rolls of carpet and other articles, Edith removed as far as possible the traces of her grief, and soon began to scan by the light of day with some curiosity her acquaintance of the previous evening. He was the very opposite to herself in appearance. Her eyes were large and dark. He had a rather small but piercing blue eye. His locks were light and curly, and his beard sandy. Her hair was brown and straight. He was fully six feet tall, while she was only of medium height. And yet Edith was not a brunette, but possessed a complexion of transparent delicacy which gave her the fragile appearance characteristic of so many American girls. His face was much tamed by exposure to March winds, but his brow was as white as hers. In his morbid tendency to shun every one, he usually kept his eyes fixed on the ground so as to appear not to see people, and this, with his habitual frown, gave a rather heavy and repelling expression to his face.

"He would make a very good representative of the laboring classes," she thought, "if he hadn't so disagreeable an expression."

It had only dimly dawned upon poor Edith as yet that she now belonged to the "laboring classes."

But her energetic nature soon reacted against idle grieving, and her pale cheeks grew rosy, and her face full of eager life as she assisted and directed.

"If I only had one or two women to help me we could soon get things settled," she said, "and I have so little time before the rest come."

Then she added suddenly to Arden, "Haven't you sisters?"

"My sister does not go out to service," said Arden proudly.

"Neither do I," said the shrewd Edith, "but I would be willing to help any one in such an emergency as I am in," and she glanced keenly to see the effect of this speech, while she thought, "What airs these people put on!"

Arden's face changed instantly. Her words seemed like
a ray of sunlight falling on a place before shadowed, for the
sullen frowning expression passed into one almost of gentle-
ness, as he said:

"That puts things in a different light. I am sure Rose
and mother both will be willing to help you as neighbors,"
and he started for another load, going around by the way
of his home and readily obtaining from his mother and sister
a promise to assist Edith after dinner.

Edith smiled to herself and said, "I have found the key
to his surly nature already." She had, and to many other
natures also. Kindness and human fellowship will unbar
and unbolt where all other forces may clamor in vain.

Arden went away in a maze of new sensations. This one
woman of all the world beside his mother and sister that he
had come to know somewhat was to him a strange, beautiful
mystery. Edith was in many respects conventional, as all
society girls are, but it was the conventionality of a sphere
of life that Arden knew only through books, and she seemed
to him utterly different from the ladies of Pushton as he
understood them from his slight acquaintance. This difference was all in her favor, for he cherished a bitter and
unreasonable prejudice against the young girls of his neighborhood as vain, shallow creatures who never read, and
thought of nothing save dress and beaux. His own sister
in fact had helped to confirm these impressions, for while
he was fond of her and kind, he had no great admiration
for her, saying in his sweeping cynicism, "She is like the
rest of them." If he had met Edith only in the street and
in conventional ways, stylishly dressed, he would scarcely
have noticed her. But her half-indignant, half-pathetic appeal to him on the dock, the lonely ride in which she had
clung to his arm for safety, her tears, and the manner in
which she had last spoken to him, had all combined to
pierce thoroughly his shell of sullen reserve; and, as we
have said, his vivid imagination had taken fire.

Edith and Hannibal worked hard the rest of the forenoon, and her experienced old attendant was invaluable. Edith herself, though having little practical knowledge of work of any kind, had vigor and natural judgment, and her small white hands accomplished more than one would suppose.

So Arden wonderingly thought on his return with a second load, as he saw her lift and handle things that he knew to be heavy. Her short, close-fitting working-dress outlined her fine figure to advantage, and with complexion bright and dazzling with exercise, she seemed to him some frail fairylike creature doomed by a cruel fate to unsuited toil and sorrows. But Edith was very matter-of-fact, and had never in all her life thought of herself as a fairy.

Arden went home to dinner, and by one o'clock Edith said to Hannibal:

"There is one good thing about the place if no other. It gives one a savage appetite. What have you got in the basket?"

"A scrumptious lunch, Miss Edie. I told de landlady you'se used to havin' things mighty nice, and den I found a hen's nest in de barn dis mornin'."

"I hope you didn't take the eggs, Hannibal," said Edith slyly.

"Sartin I did, Miss Edie, cause if I didn't de rats would."

"Perhaps the landlady would also if you had shown them to her."

"Miss Edie," said Hannibal solemnly, "findin' a hen's nest is like findin' a gold mine. It belongs to de one dat finds it."

"I am afraid that wouldn't stand in law. Suppose we were arrested for robbing hens' nests. That wouldn't be a good introduction to our new neighbors."

"Now, Miss Edie," said Hannibal, with an injured air, "you don't spec I do a job like dat so bungly as to get cotched at it?"

"Oh, very well," said Edith, laughing, "since you have conformed to the morality of the age, it must be all right,

and a fresh egg would be a rich treat now that it can be
eaten with a clear conscience. But, Hannibal, I wish you
would find a gold mine out in the garden.''

"I guess you'se find dat with all your readin' about
strawberries and other yarbs.''

"I hope so,'' said Edith with a sigh, "for I don't see how
we are going to live here year after year.''

"You'se be rich again. De men wid de long pusses ain't
agoin' to look at your black eyes for nothin','' and Hannibal chuckled knowingly.

The color faintly deepened in Edith's cheeks, but she
said with some scorn, "Men with long purses want girls
with the same. But who are these?''

Coming up the path they saw a tall middle-aged woman,
and by her side a young girl of about eighteen who was a
marked contrast to her in appearance.

"Dey's his moder and sister. You will drive tings dis
arternoon.''

Mrs. Lacey and her daughter entered with some little
hesitancy and embarrassment, but Edith, with the poise of
an accomplished lady, at once put them at ease by saying:

"It is exceedingly kind of you to come and help, and I
appreciate it very much.''

"No one should refuse to be neighborly,'' said Mrs.
Lacey quietly.

"And to tell the truth I was delighted to come,'' said
Rose, "the winter has been so long and dull.''

"Oh, dear!'' thought Edith, "if you find them so, what
will be our fate?''

Mrs. Lacey undid a bundle and took out a teapot from
which the steam yet oozed faintly, and Rose undid another
containing some warm buttered biscuits, Mrs. Lacey saying,
"I thought your lunch might seem a little cold and cheerless,
so I brought these along.''

"Now that *is* kind,'' said Edith, so cordially that their
faces flushed with that natural pleasure which we all feel
when our ltitle efforts for others are appreciated. To them

it was intensified, for Edith was a grand city lady, and the inroads that she made on the biscuits, and the zest with which she sipped her tea, showed that her words had the ring of truth.

"Do sit down and eat, while things are nice and warm," she said to Hannibal. "There's no use in our putting on airs now," but Hannibal insisted on waiting upon her as when he was butler in the great dining-room on the avenue, and when she was through, carried the things off to the empty kitchen, and took his "bite" on a packing box, prefacing it as his nearest approach to grace by an indignant grunt and profession of his faith.

"Dis ole niggah eat before her? Not much! She's quality now as much as eber."

But the world and Hannibal were at variance on account of a sum of subtraction which had taken away from Edith's name the dollar symbol.

Edith set to work, her helpers now increased to three, with renewed zest, and from time to time stole glances at the mother and daughter to see what the natives were like.

They were very different in appearance: the mother looking prematurely old, and she also seemed bent and stooping under the heavy burdens of life. Her dark blue eyes had a weary, pathetic look, as if some sorrow was ever before them. Her cheek bones were prominent and her cheeks sunken, and the thin hair, brushed plainly under her cap, was streaked with gray. Her quietness and reserve seemed rather the result of a crushed, sad heart than of natural lack of feeling.

The daughter was in the freshest bloom of youth, and was not unlike the flower she was named after, when, as a dewy bud, it begins to develop under the morning sun. Though not a beautiful girl, there was a prettiness, a rural breeziness about her, that would cause any one to look twice as she passed. The wind ever seemed to be in her light flaxen curls, and her full rounded figure suggested superabundant vitality, an impression increased by her quick, restless motions. Her complexion reminded you of strawberries and cream, and her blue eyes had a slightly bold and defiant expression. She felt the blight of her father's course also, but it acted differently on her tempera-. ment. Instead of timidly shrinking from the world like her mother, or sullenly ignoring it like her brother, she was for going into society and compelling it to recognize and respect her.

"I have done nothing wrong," she said; "I insist on people treating me in view of what I am myself," and in the sanguine spirit of youth she hoped to carry her point. Therefore her manner was a little self-asserting, which would not have been the case had she not felt that she had prejudice to overcome. Unlike her brother, she cared little for books, and had no ideal world, but lived vividly in her immediate surroundings. The older she grew, the duller and more monotonous did her home life seem. She had little sympathy from her brother; her mother was a sad, silent woman, and her father a daily source of trouble and shame. Her education was very imperfect, and she had no resource in this, while her daily work seemed a tiresome round that brought little return. Her mother attended to the more important duties and gave to her the lighter tasks, which left her a good deal of leisure. She had no work that stimulated her, no training that made her thorough in any department of labor, however humble. From a friend, a dressmaker in the village, she obtained a little fancy work and sewing, and the proceeds resulting, and all her brother gave her, she spent in dress. The sums were small enough in all truth, and yet with the marvellous ingenuity that some girls, fond of dress, acquire, she made a very little go a great way, and she would often appear in toilets that were quite effective. With those of her own age and sex in her narrow little circle, she was not a special favorite, but she was with the young men, for she was bright, chatty, and had the knack of putting awkward fellows at ease. She kept her little parlor as pretty and inviting as her limited ma-

terials permitted, and with a growing imperiousness gave
the rest of the family, and especially her father, to understand that this parlor was her domain, and that she would
permit no intrusion.   Clerks from the village and farmers'
sons would occasionally drop in of an evening, though they
preferred taking her out to ride where they could see her
away from her home.   But the more respectable young
men, with anxious mothers and sisters, were rather shy of
poor Rose, and none seemed to care to go beyond a mild
flirtation with a girl whose father was "on the rampage,"
as they expressed it, most of the time.   On one occasion,
when she had two young friends spending the evening, her
father came home reckless and wild with drink, and his
language toward the young men was so shocking, and his
manner in general so outrageous, that they were glad to
get away.   If Arden had not come home and collared his
father, carrying him off to his room by his almost irresistible strength, Rose's parlor might have become a sad wreck,
literally as well as socially.   As it was, it seemed deserted
for a long time, and she felt very bitter about it.   In her
fearless frankness, her determination not to succumb to her
sinister surroundings (and perhaps from the lack of a sensitive delicacy), she reproached the same young men when
she met them for staying away, saying, "It's a shame to
treat a girl as if she were to blame for what she can't help."

But Rose's ambition had put on a phase against which
circumstances were too strong, and she was made to feel in
her struggle to gain a social footing that her father's leprosy
had tainted her, and her brother's "ugly, sullen disposition," as it was termed, was a hindrance also.   She had an
increasing desire to get away among strangers, where she
could make her own way on her own merits, and the city of
New York seemed to her a great Eldorado, where she might
find her true career.   Some very showily dressed, knowing-
looking girls, that she had met at a picnic, had increased
this longing for the city.   Her mother and brother thought
her restless, vain, and giddy, but she was as good and hon-

est a girl at heart as breathed, only her vigorous nature chafed at repression, wanted outlets, and could not settle down for life to cook, wash, and sew for a drunken father, a taciturn brother, or even a mother whose companionship was depressing, much as she was loved.

Rose welcomed the request of her brother, as helping Edith would cause a ripple in the current of her dull life, and give her a chance of seeing one of the grand city ladies, without the dimness and vagueness of distance, and she scanned Edith with a stronger curiosity than was bestowed upon herself. The result was rather depressing to poor Rose, for, having studied with her quick nice eye Edith's exquisite manner and movements, she sighed to herself:

"I'm not such a lady as this girl, and perhaps never can be."

While Edith was very kind and cordial to the Laceys, she felt, and made them feel, that there was a vast social distance between them. Even practical Edith had not yet realized her poverty, and it would take her some time to doff the manner of the condescending lady.

They accomplished a great deal that afternoon, but it takes much time and labor to make even a small empty house look home-like. Edith had taken the smallest room upstairs, and by evening it was quite in order for her occupation, she meaning to take Zell in with her. Work had progressed in the largest upper room, which she designed for her mother and Laura. Mrs. Lacey and Hannibal were in the kitchen getting that arranged, they very rightly concluding that this was the mainspring in the mechanism of material living, and should be put in readiness at once. Arden had been instructed to purchase and bring from the village a cooking-stove, and Hannibal's face shone with something like delight, as by five o'clock he had a wood fire crackling underneath a pot of water, feeling that the *terra firma* of comfort was at last reached. He could now *soak* in his favorite beverage of tea, and make Miss Edie quite "pertlike" too when she was tired.

Mrs. Lacey worked silently. Rose was inclined to be chatty and draw Edith out in regard to city life. She responded good-naturedly as long as Rose confined herself to generalities, but was inclined to be reticent on their own affairs.

Before dark the Laceys prepared to return, the mother saying gravely:

"You may feel it too lonely to stay by yourself. Our house is not very inviting, and my husband's manner is not always what I could wish, but such as it is, you will be welcome in it till the rest of your family comes."

"You are very kind to a stranger," said Edith, heartily, "but I am not a bit afraid to stay here since I have Hannibal as protector," and Hannibal, elated by this compliment, looked as if he might be a very dragon to all intruders. "Moreover," continued Edith, "you have helped me so *splendidly* that I shall be very comfortable, and they will be here to-morrow night."

Mrs. Lacey bowed silently, but Rose said in her sprightly voice, from the doorway:

"I'll come and help you all day to-morrow."

Arden was still to bring one more load. The setting sun, with the consistency of an April day, had passed into a dark cloud which soon came driving on with wind and rain, and the thick drops dashed against the windows as if thrown from a vast syringe, while the gutter gurgled and groaned with the sudden rush of water.

"Oh, dear! how dismal!" sighed Edith, looking out in the gathering darkness. Then she saw that the loaded wagon had just stopped at the gate, and in dim outline Arden sat in the storm as if he had been a post. "It's too bad," she said impatiently, "my things will all get wet." After a moment she added: "Why don't he come in? Don't he know enough to come in out of the rain?"

"Well, Miss Edie, he's kind o' quar," said Hannibal, "I'se jes done satisfied he's quar."

But the shower ceased suddenly, and Arden dismounted,

secured his horses, and soon appeared at the door with a piece of furniture.

"Why, it's not wet," said Edith with surprise.

"I saw appearances of rain, and so borrowed a piece of canvas at the dock."

"But you didn't put the canvas over yourself," said Edith, looking at his dripping form, grateful enough now to bestow a little kindness without the idea of policy. "As soon as you have brought in the load I insist on your staying and taking a cup of tea."

He gave his shoulders an indifferent shrug, saying, "A little cold water is the least of my troubles." Then he added, stealing a timid glance at her, "But you are very kind. People seldom think of their teamsters."

"The more shame to them then," said Edith. "I at least can feel a kindness if I can't make much return. It was very good of you to protect my furniture, and I appreciate your care. Besides your mother and sister have been helping me all the afternoon, and I am oppressed by my obligations to you all."

"I am sorry you feel that way," he said briefly, and vanished in the darkness after another load.

Soon all was safely housed, and he said, about to depart, "There is one more load; I will bring that to-morrow."

From the kitchen she called, "Stay, your tea will be ready in a moment."

"Do not put yourself to that truble," he answered, at the same time longing to stay. "Mother will have supper ready for me." He was so diffident that he needed much encouragement, and moreover he was morbidly sensitive.

But as she turned she caught his wistful glance, and thought to herself, "Poor fellow! he's cold and hungry." With feminine shrewdness she said, "Now, Mr. Lacey, I shall feel slighted if you don't take a cup of my tea, for see, I have made it myself. It's the one thing about housekeeping that I understand. Your mother brought me a nice cup at noon, and I enjoyed it very much. I am going to pay that debt now to you.''

''Well—if you really wish it''—said Arden hesitatingly, with another of his bright looks, and color even deeper than the ruddy firelight warranted.

''My conscience!'' thought Edith, ''how suddenly his face changes. ''He is 'quar,' as Hannibal says.'' But she settled matters by saying, ''I shall feel hurt if you don't. You must let there be at least some show of kindness on my part, as well as on yours and your friends'.''

There came in again a delicate touch of that human fellowship which he had never found in the world, and had seemingly repelled, but which his soul was thirsting for with an intensity never so realized before, and this faintest semblance of human companionship and sympathy seemed inexpressibly sweet to his sore and lonely heart.

He took the cup from her as if it had been a sacrament, and was about to drink it standing, but she placed a chair at the table and said:

''No, sir, you must sit down there in comfort by the fire.''

He did so as if in a dream. The whole scene was taking a powerful hold on his imagination.

''Hannibal,'' she cried, raising her voice in a soft, bird-like call, and from the dim kitchen whence certain spluttering sounds had preceded him, Hannibal appeared with a heaping plate of buttered toast.

''With your permission,'' she said, ''I will sit down and take a cup of tea with you, in a neighborly way, for I wish to ask you some more questions, and tea, you know, is a great incentive to talk,'' and she took a chair on the opposite side of the table, while Hannibal stood a little in the background to wait on them with all the formality of the olden time.

The wood fire blazed and crackled, and threw its flicker-

ing light over Edith's fair face, and intensified her beauty,
as her features gleamed out, or faded, as the flames rose and
fell. Hannibal stood motionless behind her chair as if he
might have been an Ethiopian slave attendant on a young
sultana. To Arden's aroused imagination, it seemed like
one of the scenes of his fancy, and he was almost afraid to
move or speak, lest all should vanish, and he find himself
plodding along the dark muddy road.

"What is the matter?" she asked curiously. "Why
don't you drink your tea?"

"It all seems as strange and beautiful as a fairy tale," he
said, looking at her earnestly.

Her hearty laugh and matter-of-fact tone dispelled his il-
lusion, as she said:

"It's all dreadfully real to me. I feel as if I had done
more work to-day than in all my life before, and we have
only made a beginning. I want to ask you about the place
and the garden, and how to get things done," and she plied
him well with the most practical questions.

Sometimes he answered a little incoherently, for through
them all he saw a face full of strange weird beauty, as the
firelight flickered upon it, and gave a star-like lustre to the
large dark eyes.

Hannibal, in the background, grinned and chuckled
silently, as he saw Arden's dazed, wondering admiration,
saying to himself, "Dey ain't used to such young ladies as
mine, up here—it kind o' dazzles 'em."

At last, as if breaking away from the influence of a spell,
Arden suddenly rose, turning upon Edith one of those warm,
bright looks that he sometimes gave his mother, and said,
"You have been very kind; good-night," and was gone in
a moment. But the night was luminous about him. Along
the muddy road, in the old barn as he cared for his horses,
in his poor little room at home, to which he soon retired,
he saw only the fair face of Edith, with the firelight
playing upon it, with the vividness of one looking directly upon an exquisite cabinet picture, and before that

picture his heart was inclined to bow, in the most devoted homage.

Edith's only comment was, "He is 'quar,' Hannibal, as you said."

Wearied with the long day's work, she soon found welcome and dreamless rest.

CHAPTER XI

MRS. ALLEN'S POLICY

TRUE to her promise, Rose helped Edith all the next day, and while she worked, the frank-hearted girl poured out the story of her troubles, and Edith came to have a greater respect and sympathy for her "kind and humble neighbors" as she characterized them in her own mind. Still with her familiarity with the farming class, kept up since her summer in the country as a child, she made a broad distinction between them and the mere laborer. Moreover, the practical girl wished to conciliate the Laceys and every one else she could, for she had a presentiment that there were many trials before them, and that they would need friends. She said in answer to Rose:

"I never realized before that the world was so full of trouble. We have seen plenty of late."

"One can bear any kind of trouble better than a daily shame," said Rose bitterly.

For some unexplained reason Edith thought of Zell and Mr. Van Dam with a sudden pang.

Arden brought his last load and watched eagerly for her appearance, fearing that there might be some great falling off in the vision of the past evening.

But to his eyes the girl he was learning to glorify presented as fair an exterior in the garish day, and the reality of her beauty became a fixed fact in his consciousness, and his fancy had already begun to endow her with angelic qualities. With all her vanity, even sorrowful Edith would have laughed heartily at his ideal of her. It was one of the hardest ordeals of his life to take the money she paid him, and she saw and wondered at his repugnance.

"You will never get rich," she said, "if you are so prodigal in work, and so spare in your charges."

"I would rather not take anything," he said dubiously, holding the money, as if it were a coal of fire, between his thumb and finger.

"Then I must find some one who will do business on business principles," she said coldly. "If the fellow has any sentimental nonsense about him, I'll soon cure that," she thought.

Arden colored, thrust his money carelessly into his pocket as if it were of no account, and said briefly, "Good-morning."

But when alone he put the money in the innermost part of his pocketbook, and when his father asked him for some of it, he sternly answered:

"No, sir, not a cent." Nor did he spend it himself; why he kept it could scarcely have been explained. He was simply acting according to the impulses of a morbid romantic nature that had been suddenly and deeply impressed. The mother's quick eye detected a change in him and she asked:

"What do you think of our new neighbor?"

"Mother," said he fervently, "she is an angel."

"My poor boy," said she anxiously, "take care. Don't let your fancy run away with you."

"Oh," said he with assumed indifference, "one can have a decided opinion of a good thing as well as a bad thing, without making a fool of one's self."

But the mother saw with a half-jealous pang that her son's heart was awaking to a new and stronger love than her own.

Mrs. Allen with Zell and Laura was to come by the boat that evening, and Edith's heart yearned after them as her kindred. Now that she had had a little experience of lone-

liness and isolation, she deeply regretted her former harshness and impatience, saying to herself, "It is harder for
them than for me. They don't like the country, and don't
care anything about a garden," and she purposed to be very
gentle and long-suffering.

If good resolutions were only accomplished certainties as
soon as made, how different life would be!

Arden had ordered a close carriage that she might go
down and meet them, and had agreed to bring up their
trunks and boxes in his large wagon.

The boat fortunately landed under the clear starlight on
this occasion, and feeble Mrs. Allen was soon seated comfortably in the carriage. But her every breath was a sigh,
and she regarded the martyrs as a favored class in compari-
son with herself. Laura still had her look of dreary apathy;
but Zell's face wore an expression of interest in the new
scenes and experiences, and she plied Edith with many
questions as she rode homeward. Mrs. Allen brought a
servant up with her who was condemned to ride with
Arden, much to their mutual disgust.

"Oh, dear!" sighed Edith as they rode along. "It's a
dreadful come-down for us all and I don't know how you
are going to stand it, mother."

Mrs. Allen's answer was a long inarticulate sigh.

When she reached the house and entered the room where
supper was awaiting them, she glanced around as a prisoner
might on being thrust into a cell in which years must be
spent, and then she dropped into a chair, sobbing—

"How different—how different from all my past!" and
for a few moments they all cried together. As with Edith
at first, so now again the new home was baptized with tears
as if dedicated to sorrow and trouble.

Edith then led them upstairs to take off their things, and
Mrs. Allen had a fresh outburst of sorrow as she recognized
the contrast between this bare little chamber and her luxurious sleeping-apartment and dressing-room in the city.
Laura soon regained her air of weary indifference, but Zell,

hastily throwing off her wraps, came down to explore, and
to question Hannibal.

"Bress you, chile, it does my eyes good to see you all,
ony you'se musn't take on as if we'se all dyin' with slow
'sumption.''

Zell put her hand on the black's shoulder and looked up
into his face with a wonderfully gentle and grateful expression, saying:

"You are as good as gold Hannibal. I am so glad you
stayed with us, for you seem like one of the best bits of our
old home. Never mind, I'll have a grander house again
soon, and you shall have a stiffer necktie and higher collar
than ever.''

"Bress you,'' said Hannibal with moist eyes, "it does
my ole black heart good to hear you. But, Miss Zell, I
say,'' he added in a loud whisper, "when is it gwine
to be?''

"Oh!'' said poor Zell, asked for definiteness, "some
day,'' and she passed into the large room where Arden
was just setting down a trunk.

"Don't leave it there in the middle of the floor," she
said sharply. "Take it upstairs.''

Arden suddenly straightened himself as if he had received a slight cut from a whip, and turned his sullen face
full on Zell, and it seemed very repulsive to the imperious
little lady.

"Don't you hear me?'' she asked sharply.

"Perhaps it would be well for you not to ask favors of
your neighbors in that tone,'' he replied curtly.

Edith, coming down, saw the situation and said with oil
in her voice, "You must excuse my sister, Mr. Lacey. She
does not know who you are. Hannibal will assist with the
trunks if you will be so kind as to take them upstairs.''

"She is different from the rest,'' thought Arden, readily
complying with her request.

But Zell said as she turned away, loud enough for him
to hear, "What airs these common country people do put

on!'' Zell might have loaded Arden's wagon with gold, and he would not have lifted a finger for her after that. If he had known that Edith's kindness had been half policy, his face would have been more sullen and forbidding than ever. But she dwelt glorified and apart in his consciousness, and if she could only maintain that ideal supremacy, he would be her slave. But in his morbid sensitiveness she would have to be very careful. The practical girl at this time did not dream of his fanciful imagining about her, but she was bent on securing friends and helpers, however humble might be their station, and she had shrewdly and quickly learned how to manage Arden.

The next day was spent by the family in getting settled in their narrow quarters, and a dreary time they had of it. It was a long rainy day, the roof leaked badly, and every element of discomfort seemed let loose upon them.

Mrs. Allen had a nervous headache, and one of her worst touches of dyspepsia, and Zell and Laura were so weary and out of sorts that little could be accomplished. Between the tears and sighs within, and the dripping rain without, Edith looked back on the first two days, when the Laceys were helping her, as bright in contrast. But Mrs. Allen was already worrying over the Laceys' connection with their settlement in the neighborhood.

"We shall be associated with these low people," said she to Edith querulously. "Your first acquaintances in a new place are of great importance."

Edith was not ready any such association, and she felt that there was force in her mother's words. She had thought of the Laceys chiefly in the light of their usefulness.

She was glad when the long miserable day came to a close, and she welcomed the bright sunshine of the following morning, hoping it would dispel some of the gloom that seemed gathering round them more thickly than ever.

After partaking of a rather meagre breakfast, for Hannibal's materials were running low, Edith pushed back her chair, and said:

"I move we hold a council of war, and look the situation in the face. We are here, and we've got to live here. Now what shall we do? I suppose we must go to work at something that will bring in money."

"Go to work, and for money!" said Mrs. Allen sharply from her cushioned arm-chair. "I hope we haven't ceased to be ladies."

"But, mother, we can't live forever on the title. The 'butchers, bakers, and candlestick-makers' won't supply us long on that ground. What did the lawyer, who settled father's estate, say before you left?"

"Well," replied Mrs. Allen vaguely, "he said he had placed to our credit in—— Bank, what there was left, and he gave me a check-book and talked economy as men always do. Your poor father, after losing hundreds at the club, would talk economy the next morning, in the most edifying way. He also said that there was some of that hateful stock remaining that ruined your father, but that it was of uncertain value, and he could not tell how much it would realize, but he would sell it and place the proceeds also to our credit. It will amount to considerable, I think, and it may rise.

"Now, girls," continued Mrs. Allen, settling herself back among the cushions, and resting the forefinger of her right hand impressively on the palm of the left, "this is the proper line of policy for us to pursue. I hope in all these strange changes I am still mistress of my own family. You certainly don't think that I expect to stay in this miserable hovel all my life. If you two girls, Laura and Edith, had made the matches you might, we should still be living on the avenue. But I certainly cannot permit you now to spoil every chance of getting out of this slough. You may not be able to do as well as you could have done, but if you are once called working-girls, what can you do?

"In the first place we must go into the best society of this town. Our position warrants it of course. Therefore,

for heaven's sake don't let it get abroad that we are asso-
ciating with these drunken Laceys." (Mrs. Allen in her
rapid generalization gave the impression that the entire
family were habitually "on the rampage," and Edith remembered with misgivings that she had drunk tea with
Arden Lacey on that very spot.) "Moreover," continued
Mrs. Allen, "there is a large summer hotel near here, and
'my friends' have promised to come and see me this summer. We must try to present an air of pretty, rural elegance, and your young gentleman friends from the city will
soon be dropping in. Then Gus Elliot and Mr. Van Dam
continue very kind and cordial, I am sure. Zell, though
so young, may soon become engaged to Mr. Van Dam, and
it's said he is very rich—"

"I can't get up much faith in these two men," interrupted Edith, "and as for Gus, he can't support himself."

"I hope you don't put Gus Elliot and my friend on the
same level," said Zell indignantly.

"I don't know where to put 'your friend,'" said Edith
curtly. "Why doesn't he speak out? Why doesn't he do
something open, manly, and decided? It seems as if he
can see nothing and think of nothing but your pretty face.
If he would become engaged to you and frankly take the
place of lover and brother, he might be of the greatest help
to us. But what has he done since father's death but pet
and flatter you like an infatuated old—"

"Hush!" cried Zell, blazing with anger and starting up;
"no one shall speak so of him. What more has Gus Elliot
done?"

"He has been useful as my errand boy," said Edith contemptuously, "and that's all he amounts to as far as I'm
concerned. I am disgusted with men. Who in all our
trouble has been noble and knightly toward us?—"

"Be still, children; stop your quarrelling," broke in
Mrs. Allen. "You have got to take the world as you find
it. Men of our day don't act like knights any more than
they dress like them. The point I wish you to understand

is that we must keep every hold we have on our old life
and society.   Next winter some of my friends will invite
you to visit them in the city and then who knows what
may happen?''—and she nodded significantly.   Then she
added, with a regretful sigh, ''What chances you girls have
had!   There's Cheatem, Argent, Livingston, Pamby, and
last and best, Goulden, who might have been secured if
Laura had been more prompt, and a host of others.   Edith
had better have taken Mr. Fox, even, than have had all
this happen.''

An expression of disgust came out on Edith's face, and
she said, ''It seems to me that I would rather go to work
than take any of them.''

''You don't know anything about work,'' said Mrs.
Allen.   ''It's a great deal easier to marry a fortune than
to make one, and a woman can't make a fortune.   Marrying
well is the only chance you girls have now, and it's my
only chance to live again as a lady ought, and I want to see
to it that nothing is done to spoil these chances.''

Laura listened with a dull assent, conscious that she
would marry any man *now* who would give her an establishment and enable her to sweep past Mr. Goulden in
elegant scorn.   Zell listened, purposing to marry Mr. Van
Dam, though Edith's words raised a vague uneasiness in
her mind, and she longed to see him again, meaning to
make him more explicit.   Edith listened with a cooling
adherence to this familiar faith and doctrine of the world
in which the mother had brought up her children.   She had
a glimmering perception that the course indicated was not
sound in general, or best for them in particular.

''And now,'' continued Mrs. Allen, becoming more definite, ''we must have a new roof put on the house right
away, or we shall all be drowned out, and the house must
be painted, a door-bell put in, and fences and things generally put in order.   We must fit this room up as a parlor,
and we can use the little room there as a dining and sitting-
room.   Laura and I will take the chamber over the kitchen,

and the one over this can be kept as a spare room, so that if any of our city friends come out to see us, they can stay all night."

"Oh, mother, the proposed arrangements will make us all uncomfortable, you especially," remonstrated Edith.

"No matter, I've set my heart on our getting back to the old life, and we must not stop at trifles."

"But are you sure we have money to spare for all these improvements?" continued Edith anxiously.

"Oh, yes, I think so," said Mrs. Allen indefinitely. "And as your poor father used to say, to spend money is often the best way to get money."

"Well, mother," said Edith dubiously, "I suppose you know best, but it doesn't look very clear to me. There seems nothing definite or certain that we can depend on."

"Perhaps not to-day, but leave all to me. Some one will turn up, who will fill your eye and fill your hand, and what more could you ask in a husband? But you must not be too fastidious. These difficult girls are sure to take up with 'crooked sticks' at last." (Mrs. Allen's views as to straight ones were not original.) "Leave all to me. I will tell you when the right ones turn up."

CHAPTER XII

WAITING FOR SOME ONE TO TURN UP

A ND so the girls were condemned to idleness and ennui,
and they all came to suffer from these as from a dull
toothache, especially Laura and Zell.   Edith had
great hopes from her garden, and saw the snow finally
disappear and the mud dry up, as the imprisoned inmates
of the ark might have watched the abatement of the waters.

On the afternoon of the council wherein Mrs. Allen had
marked out the family policy, Edith and Zell walked to
the village, and going to one of the leading stores, made
arrangements with the proprietor to have his wagon stop
daily at their house for orders.   They also asked him to
send them a carpenter.   They made these requests with the
manner of olden time, when money seemed to flow from
a full fountain, and the man was very polite, thinking he
had gained profitable customers.

While they were absent, Rose stepped in to see if she
could be of any further help.   Mrs. Allen surmised who
she was and resolved to snub her effectually.   To Rose's
question as to their need of assistance, she replied frigidly,
that they had two servants now, and did not wish to employ any more help.

Rose colored, bit her lip, then said with an open smile:

"You are under mistake.   I am Miss Lacey, and helped
your daughter the first two days after she came."

"Oh! ah! Miss Lacey.   I beg your pardon," said Mrs.
Allen, still more distantly.   "My daughter Edith is out.
Did she not pay you?"

Rose's face became scarlet, and rising hastily she said,

"Either I misunderstand, or am greatly misunderstood. Good-afternoon."

Mrs. Allen slightly inclined her head, while Laura took no notice of her at all. When she was gone, Mrs. Allen said complacently, "I think we will see no more of that bold-faced fly-away creature. The idea of her thinking that we would live on terms of social equality with them!"

Laura's only reply was a yawn, but at last she got up, put on her hat and shawl and went out to walk a little on the porch. Arden, who was returning home with his team, stopped a moment to inquire if there was anything further that he could do. He hoped the lady he saw on the porch was Edith, and the wish to see her again led him to think of any excuse that would take him to the house.

As Laura turned to come toward him, he surmised that it was another sister, and was disappointed and embarrassed, but it was too late to turn back, though she scarcely appeared to heed him.

"I called to ask Miss Edith if I could do anything more that would be of help to her," he said diffidently.

Giving him a cold, careless glance, Laura said, "I believe my sister wants some work done around the house before long. I will tell her that you were here looking for employment, and I have no doubt she will send for you if she needs your services," and Laura turned her back on him and continued her walk.

He whirled about on his heel as if she had struck him, and when he got home his mother noted that his face looked more black and sullen than she had ever seen it before. Rose was open and strong in her indignation, saying:

"Fine neighbors you have introduced us to! Nice return they make for all our kindness; not that I begrudge it. But I hate to see people get all out of you they can, and then about the same as slap your face and show you the door."

"Did you see Miss Edith?" asked Arden quickly.

"No, I saw the old lady and a proud pale-faced girl who

took no more notice of me than if I had come for cold victuals.''

"I suppose they have heard," said Arden dejectedly.

"They have heard nothing against me, nor you, nor mother," said Rose hotly. "If I ever see that Miss Edith again, I will give her a piece of my mind."

"You will please do nothing of the kind," said her brother. "She has not turned her back on you. Wait till she does. We are the last people to condemn one for the sake of another."

"I guess they are all alike; but, as you say, it's fair to give her a chance," answered Rose quietly.

With his habit of reticence he said nothing about his own experience. But it was a cruel shock that those connected with the one who was becoming the inspiration of his dreams should be so contemptible, as he regarded them, and as we are all apt to regard those who treat us with contempt. His faith in her was also shaken, and he resolved that she must "send for him," feeling her need, before he would go near her again. But, after all, his ardent fancy began to paint her more gentle and human on the background of the narrow pride shown by the others. He longed for some absolute proof that she was what he believed her, but was too proud to put himself in the way of receiving it.

When Edith heard how the Lacey acquaintance had been nipped in the bud, she said with honest shame, "It's too bad, after all their kindness."

"It was the only thing to be done," said Mrs. Allen. "It is better for such people to talk against you than to be claiming you as neighbors, and all that. It would give us a very bad flavor with the best people of the town."

"I only wish then," said Edith, "that I had never let them do anything for me. I shall hate to meet them again," and she sedulously avoided them.

The next day a carpenter appeared after breakfast, and seemed the most affably suggestive man in the world. "Of course he would carry out Mrs. Allen's wishes immediately,'' and he showed her several other improvements that might be made at the same time, and which would cost but little more while they were about it.

"But how much *will* it cost?" asked Edith directly.

"Oh, well," said the man vaguely, "it's hard to estimate on this kind of jobbing work." Then turning to Mrs. Allen, he said with great deference, "I assure you, madam, I will do it well, and be just as reasonable as possible."

"Certainly, certainly," said Mrs. Allen majestically, pleased with the deference, "I suppose that is all we ought to ask."

"I think there ought to be something more definite as to price and time of completing the work," still urged Edith.

"My dear," said Mrs. Allen with depressing dignity, "pray leave these matters to me. It is not expected that a young lady like yourself should understand them."

Mrs. Allen had become impressed with the idea that if they ever reached the haven of Fifth Avenue again, she must take the helm and steer their storm-tossed bark. As we have seen before, she was capable of no small degree of exertion when the motive was to attain position and supremacy in the fashionable world. She was great in one direction only—the one to which she had been educated, and to which she devoted her energies.

The man chuckled as he went away. "Lucky I had to deal with the old fool rather than that sharp black-eyed girl. By Jove! but they are a handsome lot though; only they look like the houses we build nowadays—more paint and finish than solid timber."

The next day there were three or four mechanics at work, and the job was secured. The day following there were only two, and the next day none. Edith sent word by the grocer, asking what was the matter. The following day one man appeared, and on being questioned, said "the boss was very busy, lots of jobs on hand."

"Why did he take our work then?" asked Edith indignantly.

"Oh, as to that, the boss takes every job he can get," said the man with a grin.

"Well, tell the boss I want to see him," she replied sharply.

The man chuckled and went on with his work in a snail-like manner, as if that were the only job "the boss" had, or was like to have, and he must make the most of it.

The house was hers, and Edith felt anxious about it, and indeed it seemed that they were going to great expense with no certain return in view. That night one corner of the roof was left open and rain came in and did not a little damage.

Loud and bitter were the complaints of the family, but Edith said little. She was too incensed to talk about it. The next day it threatened rain and no mechanics appeared. Donning her waterproof and thick shoes, she was soon in the village, and by inquiry found the man's shop. He saw her coming and dodged out.

"Very well, I will wait," said Edith, sitting down on a box.

The man, finding she would not go away, soon after bustled in, and was about to be very polite, but Edith interrupted him with a question that was like a blow between the eyes:

"What do you mean, sir, by breaking your word?"

"Great press of work just now, Miss Allen—"

"That is not the question," interrupted Edith. "You said you would do our work immediately. You took it with that distinct understanding; and, because you have been false to your word, we have suffered much loss. You knew the roof was not all covered. You knew it when it rained last night, but the rain did not fall on you, so I suppose you did not care. But is a person who breaks his word in that style a gentleman? Is he even a man, when he breaks it to a lady, who has no brother or husband to protect her interests?"

The man became very red. He was accustomed, as his

workman said, to secure every job he could, then divide
and scatter his men so as to keep everything going, but at
a slow, provoking rate, that wore out every one's patience
save his own. He was used to the annual fault-finding and
grumbling of the busy season, and bore it as he would a
northeast storm as a disagreeable necessity, and quite prided
himself on the good-natured equanimity with which he could
stand his customers' scoldings; and the latter had become
so accustomed to being put off that they endured it also as
they would a northeaster, and went into improvements and
building as they might visit a dentist.

But when Edith turned her scornful face and large indignant eyes full upon him, and asked practically what
he meant by lying to her, and said that to treat a woman
so proved him less than a man, he saw his habit of "putting
off" in a new light. At first he was a little inclined to blus-
ter, but Edith interrupted him sharply:

"I wish to know in a word what you will do. If that
roof is not completed and made tight to-day, I will put the
matter in a lawyer's hands and make you pay damages."

This would place the man in an unpleasant business
aspect, so he said gruffly:

"I will send some men right up."

"And I will take no action till I see whether they come,"
said Edith significantly.

They came, and in a few days the work was finished.
But a bill double the amount they expected came promptly
also. They paid no attention to it.

In the meantime Edith had asked the village merchant,
who supplied them with provisions, and who had also become a sort of agent for them, to send a man to plow the
garden. The next day a slouchy old fellow, with two melancholy shacks of horses that might well tremble at the caw
of a crow, was scratching the garden with a worn-out plow
when she came down to breakfast. He had already made
havoc in the flower borders, and Edith was disgusted with
the outward aspect of himself and team to begin with. But

when in her morning slippers she had picked her way dain-
tily to a point from which she could look into the shallow
furrows, her vexation knew no bounds. She had been reading about gardening of late, and she had carefully noted
how all the writers insisted on deep plowing and the thorough loosening of the soil. This man's furrows did not
average six inches, and with a frowning brow, and dress
gathered up, she stood perched on a little stone, like a bird
that had just alighted with ruffled plumage, while Zell was
on the porch laughing at her. The man with his gaunt
team soon came round again opposite her, with slow auto-
matic motion as if the whole thing were one crazy piece of
mechanism. The man's head was down, and he paid no
heed to Edith. The rim of his old hat flapped over his
face, the horses jogged on with dropping head and ears,
as if unable to hold them up, and all seemed going down,
save the plow. This light affair skimmed and scratched
along the ground like the sharpened sticks of oriental
tillage.

"Stop!" cried Edith sharply.

"Whoa!" shouted the man, and he turned toward Edith
a pair of watery eyes, and a face that suggested nothing but
snuff.

"Who sent you here?" asked Edith in the same tone.

"Mr. Hard, mum." (Mr. Hard was the merchant who
was acting as their agent.)

"Am I to pay you for this work, or Mr. Hard?"

"I guess you be, mum."

"Who's to be suited with this work, you, Mr. Hard,
or I?"

"I hain't thought nothin' about that."

"Do you mean to say that it makes no difference whether
I am suited or not?"

"What yer got agin the work?"

"I want my garden plowed, not scratched. You don't
plow half deep enough, and you are injuring the shrubs
and flowers in the borders."

"I guess I know more about plowin' than you do. Gee up thar!" to the horses, that seemed inclined to be Edith's allies by not moving.

"Stop!" she cried, "I will not pay you a cent for this work, and wish you to leave this garden instantly."

"Mr. Hard told me to plow this garding and I'm a-goin' to plow it. I never seed the day's work I didn't git paid for yit, and you'll pay for this. Git up thar, you cussed old critters," and the man struck the horses sharply with a lump of dirt. Away went the crazy rattling old automaton round and round the garden in spite of all she could do.

She was half beside herself with vexation, which was increased by Zell's convulsed laughter on the porch, but she stormed at the old plowman as vainly as a robin might remonstrate with a windmill.

"Mr. Hard told me to plow it, and I'm a-goin' to plow it," said the human part of the mechanism as it again passed, without stopping, the place where Edith stood.

Utterly baffled, Edith rushed into the house and hastily swallowed a cup of coffee. She was too angry to eat a mouthful.

Zell followed with her hand upon her side, which was aching from laughter, and as soon as she found her voice said:

"It was one of the most touchingly beautiful rural scenes I ever looked upon. I never had so close and inspiring a view of one of the 'sons of the soil' before."

"Yes," snapped Edith, "he is literally a clod."

"I can readily see," continued Zell, in a mock-sentimental tone, "how noble and refining a sphere the 'garding' (as your friend, out there, terms it) must be, even for women. In the first place there are your associates in labor—"

"Stop!" interrupted Edith sharply. "You all leave everything for me to do, but I won't be teased and tormented in the bargain."

"But really," continued the incorrigible Zell, "I have

been so much impressed by the first scene in the creation of your Eden, which I have just witnessed, that I am quite impatient for the second. It may be that our sole acquaintances in this delightful rural retreat, the 'drunken Laceys,' as mother calls them, will soon insist on becoming inspired with the spirit of the corn they raise in our arbor."

Edith sprang up from the table and went to her room.

"Shame on you, Zell," said Mrs. Allen sharply, but Laura was too apathetic to scold.

Impulsive Zell soon relented, and when Edith came down a few moments later in walking trim, and with eyes swollen with unshed tears, Zell threw her arms around her neck and said:

"Forgive your naughty little sister."

But Edith repulsed her angrily, and started toward the village.

"I do hate to see people sullenly hoard up things," said Zell snappishly. Then she dawdled about the house, yawning and saying fretfully, "I do wish I knew what to do with myself."

Laura reclined on the sofa with a novel, but Zell was not fond of reading. Her restless nature craved continual activity and excitement, but it was part of Mrs. Allen's policy that they should do nothing.   •

"Some one may call," she said, "and we must be ready to receive them," but at that season of the year, when roads were muddy, there was but little social visiting in the country.

So, consumed with ennui, Zell listened to the pounding of the carpenters overhead, and watched the dogged old plowman go round the small garden till it was all scratched over, and then the whole crazy mechanism rattled off to parts unknown. The two servants did not leave her even the recourse of housework, of which she was naturally fond.

Edith went straight to Mr. Hard, and was so provoked that she scarcely avoided the puddles in her determined haste.

Mr. Hard looked out upon his customers with cold, hard little eyes that changed their expression only in growing more cold and hard. The rest of his person seemed all bows, smirks, and smiles, but it was noticed that these latter diminished and his eyes grew harder as he wished to remind some lagging patron that his little account needed settling. This thrifty citizen of Pushton was soon in polite attendance on Edith, but was rather taken back when she asked sharply what he meant by sending such a good-for-nothing man to plow her garden.

"Well, Miss Allen," he said, his eyes growing harder but his manner more polite, "old Gideon does such little jobs around, and I thought he was just the one."

"Does he plow your garden?" asked Edith abruptly.

"I keep a gardener," said Mr. Hard with some dignity.

"I believe it would pay me to do the same," said Edith, "if I could find one on whom I could depend. The man you sent was very impudent. I told him the work didn't suit me—that he didn't plow half deep enough, and that he must leave. But he just kept right on, saying you sent him, and he would plow it, and he injured my flower borders besides. Therefore he must look to you for payment." (Mr. Hard's eyes grew very hard at this.) "Because I am a woman I am not going to be imposed upon. Now do you know of a man who can really plow my garden? If not, I must look elsewhere. I had hoped when you took our business you would have some interest in seeing that we were well served."

Mr. Hard, with eyes like two flint pebbles, made a low bow and said with impressive dignity:

"It is my purpose to do so. There is Mr. Skinner, he does plowing."

"I don't want Mr. Skinner," said Edith impatiently, "I don't like his name in reference to plowing."

"Oh! ah! excellent reason; very good, Miss Allen. Well, there's Mr. McTrump, a Scotchman, who has a small greenhouse and nursery, he looks after gardens for some people.''

"I will go and see him," said Edith, taking his address.

As she plodded off to find his place, she sighed, "Oh, dear! it's dreadful to have no men in the family. That Arden Lacey might have helped me so much, if mother was not so particular. I fear we are all on the wrong track, throwing away substantial and present good for uncertainties.''

Mr. McTrump was a little man with a heavy sandy beard and such bushy eyebrows and hair that he reminded Edith of a Scotch terrier. But her first glance around convinced her that he was a gardener. Neatness, order, thrift, impressed her the moment she opened his gate, and she perceived that he was already quite advanced in his spring work. Smooth seed-sown beds were emerging from winter's chaos. Crocuses and hyacinths were in bloom, tulips were budding, and on a sunny slope in the distance she saw long green rows of what seemed some growing crop. She determined if possible to make this man her ally, or by stratagem to gain his secret of success.

The little man stood in the door of his greenhouse with a transplanting trowel in his hand. He was dressed in clay-colored nankeen, and could get down in the dirt without seeming to get dirty. His small eyes twinkled shrewdly, but not unkindly, as she advanced toward him. He was fond of flowers, and she looked like one herself that spring morning.

"I was directed to call upon you," she said, with conciliatory politeness, "understanding that you sometimes assist people with their gardens.''

"Weel, noo and then I do, but I canna give mooch time with a' my ain work.''

"But you would help a lady who has no one else to help her, wouldn't you?" said Edith sweetly.

Old Malcom was not to be caught with a sugar-plum, so he said with a little Scotch caution:

"I canna vera weel say till I hear mair aboot it."

Edith told him how she was situated, and in view of her perplexity and trouble, her voice had a little appealing pathos in it. Malcom's eyes twinkled more and more kindly, and as he explained afterward to his wife, "Her face was sae like a pink hyacinth beent doon by the storm and a wantin' proppin'. oop," that by the time she was done he was ready to accede to her wishes.

"Weel," said he, "I canna refuse a blithe young leddy like yoursel, but ye must let me have my ain way."

Edith was inclined to demur at this, for she had been reading up and had many plans and theories to carry out. But she concluded to accept the condition, thinking that with her feminine tact she would have her own way after all. She did not realize that she was dealing with a Scotchman.

"I'll send ye a mon as will plow the garden, and not scratch it, the morrow, God willin'," for Mr. McTrump was a very pious man, his only fault being that he would take a drop too much occasionally.

"May I stay here a while and watch you work, and look at things?" asked Edith. "I don't want to go back till that hateful old fellow has done his mischief and is gone."

"Why not?" said Malcom, "an ye don't tech anything. The woman folk from the village as come here do pick and pull much awry."

"I promise you I will be good," said Edith eagerly.

"That's mair than ony on us can say of oursel," said Malcom, showing the doctrinal bias of his mind, "but I ken fra' yer bonnie face ye mean weel."

"Oh, Mr. McTrump, that is the first compliment I have received in Pushton," laughed Edith.

"I'm a thinkin' it'll not be the last. But I hope ye mind the Scripter where it says, 'We do all fade as a flower,' and ye will not be puffed oop."

But Edith, far more intent on horticultural than on scriptural knowledge, asked quickly:

"What were you going to set out with that trowel?"

"A new strawberry-bed. I ha' more plants the spring than I can sell, sae I thought to put oot a new bed, though I ha' a good mony."

"I am so glad. I wish to set out a large bed and can get the plants of you."

"How mony do ye want?" said Malcom, with a quick eye to business.

"I shall leave that to you when you see my ground. Now see how I trust you, Mr. McTrump."

"An' ye'll not lose by it, though I would na like a' my coostomers to put me sae strictly on my honesty."

Edith spent the next hour in looking around the garden and greenhouses and watching the old man put out his plants.

"These plants are to be cooltivated after the hill seestem," he said. "They are to stand one foot apart in the row, and the rows two feet apart, and not a rooner or weed to grow on or near them, and it would do your bright eyes good to see the great red berries they'll bear."

"Shall I raise mine that way?" said Edith.

"Weel, ye might soom, but the narrow row coolture will be best for ye, I'm thinkin'."

"What's that?"

"Weel, just let the plants run togither and make a thick close row a foot wide, an' two feet between the rows. That'll be the easiest for ye, but I'll show ye."

"I'm so glad I found you out!" said Edith, heartily; "and if you will let me, I want to come here often and see how you do everything, for to tell you the truth, between ourselves, we are poor, and may have to earn our living out of the garden, or some other way, and I would rather do it out of the garden."

"Weel, noo, ye're a canny lass to coom and filch all old Malcom's secrets to set oop opposition to him. But then sin' ye do it sae openly I'll tell ye all I know. The big wourld ought to be wide enough for a bonnie lassie like yoursel to ha' a chance in it, and though I'm a little mon, I would na be sae mean a one as to hinder ye. Mairover the gardener's craft be a gentle one, and I see na reason why, if a white lily like yoursel must toil and spin, it should na be oot in God's sunshine, where the flowers bloom, instead o' pricking the bluid oot o' yer body, and the hope oot o' yer heart, wi' the needle's point, as I ha' seen sae mony o' my ain coontry lassies do. Gude-by, and may the roses in yer cheeks bloom a' the year round.''

Edith felt as if his last words were a blessing, and started with her heart cheered and hopeful; and yet beyond her garden, with its spring promise, its summer and autumn possibilities, there was little inspiring or hopeful in her new home.

In accordance with their mother's policy, they were waiting for something to turn up—waiting, in utter uncertainty, and with dubious prospects, to achieve by marriage the security and competence which they must not work for, or they would utterly lose caste in the old social world in which they had lived.

Be not too hasty in condemning Mrs. Allen, my reader, for you may, at the same time, condemn yourself. Have you no part in sustaining that public sentiment which turns the cold shoulder of society toward the woman who works? Many are growing rich every year, but more are growing poor. What does the ''best society,'' in the world's estimation, say to the daughters in these families?

''Keep your little hands white, my dears, as long as you can, because as soon as the traces of toil are seen on them you become a working-woman, and our daughters can't associate with you, and our sons can't think of you, that is for wives. No other than little and white hands can enter our heaven.''

So multitudes struggle to keep their hands white, though thereby the risk that their souls will become stained and black increases daily. A host of fair girls find their way every year to darker stains than ever labor left, because they know how coldly society will ignore them the moment they enlist in the army of honest workers. But you, respectable men and women in your safe pleasant homes, to the extent that you hold and sustain this false sentiment, to the extent that you make the paths of labor hard and thorny, and darken them from the approving smile of the world, you are guilty of these girls' ruin.

Christian matron, with your husband one of the pillars of church and state, do you shrink with disgust from that poor creature who comes flaunting down Broadway? None but the white-handed enter your parlors, and the men (?) who are hunting such poor girls to perdition will sit on the sofa with your daughters this evening. Be not too confident. Your child, or one in whom your blood flows at a little later remove, may stand just where honor to toil would save, but the practical dishonoring of it, which you sustain, eventually blot out the light of earth and heaven.

Mrs. Allen knew that even if her daughters commenced teaching, which, with all the thousands spent on their education, they were incapable of doing, their old sphere on Fifth Avenue would be as unapproachable as the pearly gates, between which and the lost a "great gulf is fixed."

But Mrs. Allen knew also of a very respectable way, having the full approval of society, by which they might regain their place in the heaven from which they had fallen. Besides it was such a simple way, requiring no labor whatever, though a little scheming perhaps, no amount of brains or culture worth mentioning, no heart or love, and least of all a noble nature. A woman may sell herself, or if of a waxy disposition, having little force, may be sold at the altar to a man who will give wealth and luxury in return. This, society, in full dress, smiles upon, and civil law and sacred ceremony sanction.

With the forefinger of her right hand resting impressively on the palm of her left, Mrs. Allen had indicated this back door into the paradise, the gates of which were guarded against poor working-women by the flaming sword of public opinion, turning every way.

And the girls were waiting yawningly, wearily, as the long unoccupied days passed. Laura's cheek grew paler than even her delicate style of beauty demanded. She seemed not only a hot-house plant, but a sickly one. The light was fading from her eye as well as the color from her cheek, and all vigor vanishing from her languid soul and body. The resemblance to her mother grew more striking daily. She was a melancholy result of that artificial luxurious life by which the whole nature is so enervated that there seems no stamina left to resist the first cold blast of adversity. Instead of being like a well-rooted hardy native of the soil she seemed a tender exotic that would wither even in the honest sunlight. As a gardener would say, she needed "hardening off." This would require the bracing of principle and the development of work. But Mrs. Allen could not lead the way to the former, and the latter she forbade, so poor Laura grew more sickly and morbid every day of her weary idle waiting.

Mrs. Allen's policy bore even more heavily on Zell. We have all thought something perhaps of the cruelty of imprisoning a vigorous young person, abounding in animal life and spirits, in a narrow cell, which forbids all action and stifles hope. It gives the unhappy victim the sensation of being buried alive. There comes at last to be one passionate desire to get out and away. Impulsive, restless, excitable Zell, with every vein filled with hot young blood, was shut out from what seemed to her the world, and no other world of activity was shown to her. Her hands were tied by her mother's policy, and she sat moping and chafing like a chained captive, waiting till Mr. Van Dam should come and deliver her from as vile durance as was ever suffered in the moss-grown castles of the old world. The hope of his coming was all that sustained her. Her sad situation was the result of acting on a false view of life from beginning to end. Any true parent would have shuddered at the thought of a daughter marrying such a man as Van Dam, but Zell was forbidden to do one useful

thing, lest it should mar her chance of union with this
résumé of all vice and uncleanness; and though she had
heard the many reports of his evil life, her moral sense was
so perverted that he seemed a lion rather than a reptile to
her.   It is true, she looked upon him only in the light
of her future husband, but that she did not shrink from
any relationship with such a man shows how false and
defective her education had been.

Edith had employment for mind and hand, therefore she
was happier and safer than either of her sisters.   Malcom
had her garden thoroughly plowed, and helped her plant
it.   He gave her many flower roots and sold others at very
low prices.   In the lower part of the garden, where the
ground was rather heavy and moist, he put out a large
number of raspberries; and along a stone fence, where
weeds and bushes had been usurping the ground, he planted
two or three varieties of blackcaps.   He also lined another
fence with Kittatinny blackberries.   There were already
many currants and gooseberries on the place.   These he
trimmed, and put in cuttings for new bushes.   He pruned
the grapevines also somewhat, but not to any great extent,
on account of the lateness of the season, meaning to get
them into shape by summer cutting.   The orchard also was
made to look clean and trim, with the dead wood and interfering branches cut away.   Edith watched these operations
with the deepest interest, and when she could, without
danger of being observed from the road, assisted, though
in a very dainty, amateur way.   But Malcom did not aim
to put in as many hours as possible, but seemed to do everything with a sleight of hand that made his visits appear too
brief, even though she had to pay for them.   As a refuge
from long idle hours, she would often go up to Malcom's
little place, and watch him and his assistant as they deftly
dealt with nature in accordance with her moods, making
the most of the soil, sunlight, and rain.   Thus Malcom came
to take a great interest in her, and shrewd Edith was not
slow in fostering so useful a friendship.   But in spite of all

this, there were many rainy idle days that hung like lead
upon her hands, and upon these especially, it seemed impossible to carry out her purpose to be gentle and forbear-
ing, and it often occurred that the dull apathy of the household was changed into positive pain by sharp words and
angry retorts that should never have been spoken.

About the last Sabbath of April, Mrs. Allen sent for a
carriage and was driven with her daughters to the most
fashionable church of Pushton. Marshalled by the sexton,
they rustled in toilets more suitable for one of the gorgeous
temples of Fifth Avenue than for even the most ambitious
of country churches. Mrs. Allen hoped to make a profound
impression on the country people, and by this one dress
parade to secure standing and cordial recognition among
the foremost families. But she overshot the mark. The
failure of Mr. Allen was known. The costly mourning
suits and the little house did not accord, the solid, sensible
people were unfavorably impressed, and those of fashionable and aristocratic tendencies felt that investigation was
needed before the strangers could be admitted within their
exclusive circles. So, though it was not a Methodist church
that they attended, the Allens were put on longer probation by all classes, when if they had appeared in a simple
unassuming manner, rating themselves at their true worth
and position, many would have been inclined to take them
by the hand.

CHAPTER XIII

THEY TURN UP

ONE morning, a month after the Allens had gone into poverty's exile, Gus Elliot lounged into Mr. Van Dam's luxurious apartments. There was everything around him to gratify the eye of sense, that is, such sense as Gus Elliot had cultivated, though an angel might have hidden his face. We will not describe these rooms—we had better not. It is sufficient to say that in their decorations, pictures, bacchanalian ornaments, and general suggestion, they were a reflex of Mr. Van Dam's character, in the more refined and æsthetic phase which he presented to society. Indeed, in the name of art, whose mantle, if at times rather flimsy, is broader than that of charity, not a few would have admired the exhibitions of Mr. Van Dam's taste.

But concerning Gus Elliot, no doubt exists in our mind. The atmosphere of Mr. Van Dam's room was entirely adapted to his chosen direction of development. He was a young man of leisure and fashion, and was therefore what even the fashionable would be horrified at their daughters ever becoming. This nice distinction between son and daughter does not result well. It leaves men in the midst of society unbranded as vile, unmarked so that good women may shrink in disgust from them. It gives them a chance to prey upon the weak, as Mr. Van Dam purposed to do, and as he intended to induce Gus Elliot to do, and as multitudes of exquisitely dressed scoundrels are doing daily.

If Mr. and Mrs. Allen had done their duty as parents, they would have kept the wolf (I beg the wolf's pardon) the jackal, Mr. Van Dam, with his thin disguise of society polish, from entering their fold. Gus Elliot was one of those mean curs that never lead, and could always be drawn into any evil that satisfied the one question of his life, "Will it give me what *I* want?"

Gus was such an exquisite that the smell of garlic made him ill, and the sight of blood made him faint, and the thought of coarse working hands was an abomination, but in worse than idleness he could see his old father wearing himself out, he could get "gentlemanly drunk," and commit any wrong in vogue among the fast young men with whom he associated. And now Mephistopheles Van Dam easily induces him to seek to drag down beautiful Edith Allen, the woman he had meant to marry, to a life compared with which the city gutters are cleanly.

Van Dam in slippers and silken robe was smoking his meerschaum after a late breakfast and reading a French novel.

"What is the matter?" he said, noting Gus's expression of ennui and discontent.

"There is not another girl left in the city to be mentioned the same day with Edith Allen," said Gus, with the pettishness of a child from whom something had been taken.

"Well, spooney, what are you going to do about it?" asked Mr. Van Dam coolly.

"What is there to do about it? you know well enough that I can't afford to marry her. I suppose it's the best thing for me that she has gone off to the backwoods somewhere, for while she was here I could not help seeing her, and after all it was only an aggravation."

"I can't afford to marry Zell," replied Van Dam, "but I am going up to see her to-morrow. After being out there by themselves for a month, I think they will be glad to see some one from the civilized world." The most honest thing about Van Dam was his sincere commiseration for those compelled to live in quiet country places, without experience in the highly spiced pleasures and excitements of the metropolis. In his mind they were associated with oxen—innocent, rural, and heavy, these terms being almost synonymous to him, and suggestive of such a forlorn tame condition that it seemed only vegetating, not living. Mr. Van Dam believed in a life, like his favorite dishes, that abounded in cayenne. Zell's letters had confirmed this opinion, and he saw that she was half desperate with ennui and disgust at their loneliness.

"I imagine we have stayed away long enough," he continued. "They have had sufficient of the miseries of mud, rain, and exile, not to be very nice about the conditions of return to old haunts and life. Of course I can't afford to marry Zell any more than you can Edith, but for all that I expect to have her here with me before many months pass, and perhaps weeks."

"Look here, Van Dam, you are going too far. Remember how high the Allens once stood in society," said Gus, a little startled.

" 'Once stood;' where do they stand now? Who in society has lifted, or will lift a finger for them, and they seem to have no near relatives to stand by them. I tell you they are at our mercy. Luxury is a necessity, and yet they are not able to earn their bare bread.

"Let me inform you," he continued, speaking with the confidence of a hunter, who from long experience knows just where the game is most easily captured, "that there is no class more helpless than the very rich when reduced to sudden poverty. They are usually too proud to work, in the first place, and in the second, they don't know how to do anything. What does a fashionable education fit a girl for, I would like to know, if, as often occurs, she has to make her own way in the world?—a smattering of everything, mistress of nothing."

"Well, Van Dam," said Gus, "according to your showing, it fits them for little schemes like the one you are broaching."

"Precisely. Girls who know how to work and who are accustomed to it, will snap their fingers in your face, and tell you they can take care of themselves, but the class to which the Allens belong, unless kept up by some rich relations, are soon almost desperate from want. I have kept up a correspondence with Zell. They seem to have no near relatives or friends who are doing much for them. They are doing nothing for themselves, save spend what little there is left, and their monotonous country life has half-murdered them already. So I conclude I have waited long enough and will go up to-morrow. Instead of pouting like a spoiled child over your lost Edith, you had better go up and get her. It may take a little time and management. Of course they must be made to think we intend to marry them, but if they once elope with us, we can find a priest at our leisure."

"I will go up to-morrow with you any way," said Gus, who, like so many others, never made a square bargain with the devil, but was easily "led captive" from one wrong and villany to another.

It was the last day of April—one on which the rawness and harshness of early spring were melting into the mildness of May. The buds on the trees had perceptibly swollen. The flowering maple was still aflame, the sweet centre of attraction to innumerable bees, the hum of whose industry rose and fell on the languid breeze. The grass had the delicate green and exquisite odor belonging to its first growth, and was rapidly turning the brown, withered sward of winter into emerald. The sun shone through a slight haze, but shone warmly. The birds had opened the day with full orchestra, but at noon there was little more than chirp and twitter, they seeming to feel something of Edith's languor, as she leaned on the railing of the porch, and watched for the coming of Malcom. She sighed as she looked at the bare brown earth of the large space that she purposed for strawberries, and work there and everywhere seemed repulsive. The sudden heat was enervating and

8—ROE—X

gave her the feeling of luxurious languor that she longed
to enjoy with a sense of security and freedom from care.
But even as her eyelids drooped with momentary drowsi-
ness, there was a consciousness, like a dull, half-recognized
pain, of insecurity, of impending trouble and danger, and
of a need for exertion that would lead to something more
certain than anything her mother's policy promised.

She was startled from her heaviness by the sharp click
of the gate latch, and Malcom entered with two large
baskets of strawberry-plants. He had said to her:

"Wait a bit. The plants will do weel, put oot the last
o' the moonth. An ye wait I'll gie ye the plants I ha' left
oover and canna sell the season. But dinna be troobled,
I'll keepit enoof for ye ony way."

By this means Edith obtained half her plants without
cost, save for Malcom's labor of transplanting them.

The weather had little influence on Malcom's wiry frame,
and his spirit of energetic, cheerful industry was contagious.
Once aroused and interested, Edith lost all sense of time,
and the afternoon passed happily away.

At her request Malcom had brought her a pair of prun-
ing nippers, such as she had seen him use, and she kept up
a delicate show of work, trimming the rose-bushes and
shrubs, while she watched him. She could not bring her
mind to anything that looked like real work as yet, but she
had a feeling that it must come. She saw that it would
help Malcom very much if she went before and dropped the
plants for him, but some one might see her, and speak of
her doing useful work. The aristocratically inclined in
Pushton would frown on the young lady so employed,
but she could snip at roses and twine vines, and that
would look pretty and rural from the road.

But it so happened that the one who caught a glimpse
of her spring-day beauty, and saw the pretty rural scene
she crowned, was not the critical occupant of some family
carriage; for when, while near the road, she was reaching
up to clip off the topmost spray of a bush, her attention was

What Can.

"WHY, MR. ELLIOT, WERE DID YOU DROP FROM?"

Page 171.

drawn by the rattle of a wagon, and in this picturesque attitude her eyes met those of Arden Lacey. The sudden remembrance of the unkind return made to him, and the fact that she had therefore dreaded meeting him, caused her to blush deeply. Her feminine quickness caught his expression, a timid questioning look, that seemed to ask if she would act the part of the others. Edith was a society and city girl, and her confusion lasted but a second. Policy whispered, "You can still keep him as a useful friend, though you must keep him at a distance, and you may need him." Some sense of gratitude and of the wrong done him and his also mingled with these thoughts, passing with the marvellous rapidity with which a lady's mind acts in social emergencies. She also remembered that they were alone, and that none of the Pushton notables could see that she was acquainted with the "drunken Laceys." Therefore before the diffident Arden could turn away, she bowed and smiled to him in a genial, conciliatory manner. His face brightened into instant sunshine, and to her surprise he lifted his old weather-stained felt hat like a gentleman. Though he had received no lessons in etiquette, he was inclined to be a little courtly and stately in manner, when he noticed a lady at all, from unconscious imitation of the high-bred characters in the romances he read. He said to himself in glad exultation:

"She is different from the rest. She is as divinely good as she is divinely beautiful," and away he rattled toward Pushton as happy as if his old box wagon were a golden chariot, and he a caliph of Arabian story on whom had just shone the lustrous eyes of the Queen of the East. Then as the tumult in his mind subsided, questioning thoughts as to the cause of her blush came trooping through his mind, and at once there arose a long vista of airy castles tipped with hope as with sunlight. Poor Arden! What a wild, uncurbed imagination had mastered his morbid nature, as he lived a hermit's life among the practical people of Pushton! If he had known that Edith, had she seen him in the village, would have crossed the street rather than have met or recognized him, it would have plunged him into still bitterer misanthropy. She and his mother only stood between him and utter contempt and hatred of his kind, as they existed in reality, and not in his books and dreams.

She forgot all about him before his wagon turned the corner of the road, and chatted away to Malcom, questioning and nipping with increasing zest. As the day grew cooler, her spirits rose under the best of all stimulants, agreeable occupation. The birds ceased at last their nest-building, and from orchard and grove came many an inspiring song. Edith listened with keen enjoyment, and country life and work looked no longer as they had done in the sultry noon. She saw with deep satisfaction the long rows of strawberry-vines increasing under Malcom's labors. In the still humid air the plants scarcely wilted and stood up with the bright look of those well started in life.

As evening approached, and no carriage of note had passed, Edith ventured to get her transplanting trowel, doff her gloves, and commence dividing her flower roots, that she might put them elsewhere. She became so interested in her work that she was positively happy, and soft-hearted Malcom, with his eye for the beauties of nature, was getting his rows crooked, because of so many admiring glances toward her as she went to and fro.

The sun was low in the west and shone in crimson through the soft haze. But the color in her cheeks was richer as she rose from the ground, her little right hand lost in the scraggly earth-covered roots of some hardy phlox, and turned to meet exquisite Gus Elliot, dressed with finished care, his hands incased in immaculate gloves. Her broad-rimmed hat was pushed back, her dress looped up, and she made a picture in the evening glow that would have driven a true artist half wild with admiration; but poor Gus was quite shocked. The idea of Edith Allen, the girl he had meant to marry, grubbing in the dirt and soiling her hands in that style! It was his impression that only Dutch women worked in a garden; and for all he knew of its products she might be setting out a potato plant. Quick Edith caught his expression, and while she crimsoned with vexation at her plight, felt a new and sudden sense of contempt for the semblance of a man before her.

But with the readiness of a society girl she smoothed her way out of the dilemma, saying with vivacity:

"Why, Mr. Elliot, where did you drop from? You have surprised me among my flowers, you see."

"Indeed, Miss Edith," said Gus, in rather unhappily phrased gallantry, "to see you thus employed makes me feel as if we both had dropped into some new and strange sphere. You seem the lovely shepherdess of this rural scene, but where is your flock?"

Shrewd Malcom, near by, watched this scene as the terrier he resembled might have done, and took instant and instinctive dislike to the new-comer. With a contemptuous sniff he thought to himself, "There's mateerial enoof in ye for so mooch toward a flock as a calf and a donkey."

"A truce to your lame compliments," she said, concealing her vexation under badinage. "I do not live by hook and crook yet, whatever I may come to, and I remember that you only appreciate artificial flowers made by pretty shop girls, and these are not in the country. But come in. Mother and my sisters will be glad to see you."

Gus was not blind to her beauty, and while the idea of marriage seemed more impossible than ever, now that he had seen her hands soiled, the evil suggestion of Van Dam gained attractiveness with every glance.

Edith found Mr. Van Dam on the porch with Zell, who had welcomed him in a manner that meant much to the wily man. He saw how necessary he was to her, and how she had been living on the hope of seeing him, and the baseness of his nature was such that instead of being stirred to one noble kindly impulse toward her, he simply exulted in his power.

"Oh," said she, as with both hands she greeted him, her

eyes half filling with tears, "we have been living like poor
exiles in a distant land, and you seem as if just from home,
bringing the best part of it with you."

"And I shall carry you back to it ere long," he whispered.

Her face grew bright and rosy with the deepest happiness she had ever know. He had never spoken so plainly
before. "Edith can never taunt me again with his silence,"
she thought. Though sounding well enough to the ear,
how false were his words! Zell was giving the best love
of which her heart was capable in view of her defective
education and character. In a sincere and deep affection
there are great possibilities of good. Her passion, so frank
and strong, in the hands of a true man, was a lever that
might have lifted her to the noblest life. Van Dam sought
to use it only to force her down. He purposed to cause one
of God's little ones to offend.

Edith soon appeared, dressed with the taste and style of
a Fifth Avenue belle of the more sensible sort, and Gus was
comforted. Her picturesque natural beauty in the garden
was quite lost on him, but now that he saw the familiar
touches of the artificial in her general aspect, she seemed to
him the peerless Edith of old. And yet his nice eye noted
that even a month of absence from the fashionable centre
had left her ignorant of some of the shadings off of one
mode into another, and the thought passed over the polished
surface of his mind (all Gus's thoughts were on the surface,
there being no other accommodation for them), "Why, a
year in this out-of-the-world life, and she would be only
a country girl."

But all detracting thoughts of each other, all mean, vile,
and deadly purposes, were hidden under smiling exteriors.
Mrs. Allen was the gracious, elegant matron who would not
for the world let her daughters soil their hands, but schemed
to marry one to a weak apology for a man, and another to a
villain out and out, and the fashionable world would cordially approve and sustain Mrs. Allen's tactics if she
succeeded.

Laura brightened up more than she had done since her father's death. Anything that gave hope of return to the city, and the possibility of again meeting and withering Mr. Goulden with her scorn, was welcome.

And Edith, while she half despised Gus, found it very pleasant to meet those of her old set again, and repeat a bit of the past. The young crave companionship, and in spite of all his weakness she half liked Elliot. With youth's hopefulness she believed that he might become a man if he only would. At any rate, she half-consciously formed the reckless purpose to shut her eyes to all presentiments of coming trouble and enjoy the evening to the utmost.

Hannibal was enjoined to get up as fine a supper as possible, regardless of cost, with Mrs. Allen's maid to assist.

In the long purple twilight, Edith and Zell, on the arms of their pseudo lovers, strolled up and down the paths of the little garden and dooryard. As Edith and Gus were passing along the walk that skirted the road, she heard the heavy rumble of a wagon that she knew to be Arden Lacey's. She did not look up or recognize him, but appeared so intent on what Gus was saying as to be oblivious of all else, and yet through her long lashes she glanced toward him in a rapid flash, as he sat in his rough working garb on the old board where she, on the rainy night of her advent to Pushton, had clung to his arm in the jolting wagon. Momentary as the glance was, the pained, startled expression of his face as he bent his eyes full upon her caught her attention and remained with her.

His manner and appearance secured the attention of Gus also, and with a contemptuous laugh he said loud enough for Arden to hear partially:

"That native comes from pretty far back, I imagine. He looks as if he never saw a lady and gentleman before. The idea of living like such a cabbage-head as that!"

If Gus had not been with Edith, his good clothes and

good looks would have been spoiled within the next five
minutes.

Edith glanced the other way and pointed to her strawberry-bed as if not noticing his remark or its object, saying:

"If you will come and see us a year from next June,
I can give you a dainty treat from these plants."

"You will not be here next June," said Gus tenderly.
"Do you imagine we can spare you from New York? The
city has seemed dull since robbed of the light of your bright
eyes."

Edith rather liked sugar-plums of such make, even from
Gus, and she, as it were, held out her hand again by the
rather sentimental remark:

"Absent ones are soon forgotten."

Gus, from much experience, knew how to flirt beau-
tifully, and so with some aptness and show of feeling,
replied:

"From my thoughts you are never absent."

Edith gave him a quick questioning look. What did he
mean? He had avided everything tending to commit him
to a penniless girl after her father's death. Was this mere
flirtation? Or had he, in absence, learned his need of her
for happiness? and was he now willing to marry her even
though poor?

"If he is man enough to do this, he is capable of doing
more," she thought quickly, and circumstances pleaded for
him.. She felt so troubled about the future, so helpless and
lonely, and he seemed so inseparably associated with her
old bright life, that she was tempted to lean on such a
swaying reed as she knew Gus to be. She did not reply,
but he could see the color deepen in her cheeks even in the
fading twilight, her bosom rose and fell more quickly, and
her hand rested upon his arm with a more confiding pressure.
What more could he ask? and he exulted.

But before he could speak again they were summoned to
supper. Van Dam touched Gus's elbow as they passed in
and whispered:

"Don't be precipitate. Say nothing definite to-night. I gather from Zell that a little more of their country purgatory will render them wholly desperate."

Edith noticed the momentary detention and whispering, and the thought that there was some understanding between the two occurred to her. For some undefined reason she was always inclined to be suspicious and on the alert when Mr. Van Dam was present. And yet it was but a passing thought, soon forgotten in the enjoyment of the evening, after so long and dull an experience. Zell was radiant, and there was a glimmer of color in Laura's pale cheeks.

After supper they sat down to cards. The decanter was placed on the side table, and heavy inroads were made on Mrs. Allen's limited stock of wine, for the gentlemen, feeling that they were off on a lark, were little inclined to self-control. They also insisted on the ladies drinking health with them, which foolish Zell, and more foolish Mrs. Allen were too ready to do, and for the first time since their coming the little cottage resounded with laughter that was too loud and frequent to be inspired by happiness only.

If guardian angels watched there, as we believe they do everywhere, they may well have veiled their faces in sadness and shame.

But the face of poor innocent Hannibal shone with delight, and nodding his head toward Mr. Allen's maid with the complacency of a prophet who saw his predictions fulfilled, he said:

"I told you my young ladies wasn't gwine to stay long in Bushtown" (as Hannibal persisted in calling the place).

To Arden Lacey, the sight of Edith listening with glowing cheeks and intent manner to a stranger with her hand within his arm—a stranger too that seemed the embodiment of that conventionality of the world which he despised and hated, was a vision that pierced like a sword. And then Gus's contemptuous words and Edith's non-recognition, though he tried to believe she had not seen him, were like vitriol to a wound. At first there was a mad impulse of anger toward Elliot, and, as we have intimated, only Edith's presence prevented Arden from demanding instant apology. He knew enough of his fiery nature to feel that he must get away as fast as possible, or he might forever disgrace himself in Edith's eyes.

As he rode home his mind was in a sad chaos. He was conscious that his airy castles were falling about him with a crash, which, though unheard by all the world, shook his soul to the centre.

Too utterly miserable to face his mother, loathing the thought of food, he put up his horses and rushed out into the night.

In his first impulse he vowed never to look toward Edith again, but, before two hours of fruitless wandering had passed, a fascination drew him toward Edith's cottage, only to hear that detested voice again, only to hear even Edith's laugh ring out too loud and reckless to come from the lips of the exquisite ideal of his dreams. Though the others had spoken in thunder tones, he would have had ears for these two voices only. He rushed away from the spot, as one might from some torturing vision, exclaiming:

"The real world is a worse mockery than the one of my dreams. Would to heaven I had never been born!"

CHAPTER XIV

WE CAN'T WORK

THE gentlemen agreed to meet the ladies the next day at church. Mrs. Allen insisted upon it, as she wished to show the natives of Pushton that they were visited by people of style from the city. As yet they had not received many calls, and those venturing had come in a reconnoitring kind of way. She knew so little of solid country people as to suppose that two young men, like Gus Elliot and Van Dam, would make a favorable impression. The latter, with a shrug and grimace at Zell, which she, poor child, thought funny, promised to do so, and then they took leave with great cordiality.

So they were ready to hand the Allens out of their carriage the next morning, and were, with the ladies, who were dressed even more elaborately than on the previous Sabbath, shown to a prominent pew, the centre of many admiring eyes, as they supposed. But where one admired, ten criticised. The summer hotel at Pushton had brought New York too near and made it too familiar for Mrs. Allen's tactics. Visits to town were easily made and frequent, and by brief diversions of their attention from the service, the good church people soon satisfied themselves that the young men belonged to the bold fast type, an impression strengthened by the parties themselves, who had devotion only for Zell and Edith, and a bold stare for any pretty girl that caught their eyes.

After church they parted with the understanding that

the gentlemen should come out toward night and spend the
evening.

Mr. Van Dam and Gus Elliot dined at the village hotel,
having ordered the best dinner that the landlord was
capable of serving, and a couple of bottles of wine. Over
this they became so exhilarated as to attract a good deal
of attention. A village tavern is always haunted by idle
clerks, and a motley crowd of gossips, on the Sabbath, and
to these the irruption of two young bloods from the city
was a slight break in the monotony of their slow shuffling
jog toward perdition; and when the fine gentlemen began
to get drunk and noisy it was really quite interesting. A
group gathered round the bar, and through the open door
could see into the dining-room. Soon with unsteady step,
Van Dam and Elliot joined them, the latter brandishing an
empty bottle, and calling in a thick loud voice:

"Here landlord (hic) open a bottle (hic) of wine, for these
poor (hic) suckers. (hic) I don't suppose (hic) they ever
tasted (hic) anything better than corn-whiskey. (hic) But
I'll moisten (hic) their gullets to-day (hic) with a gentleman's drink."

The crowd was mean enough, as the loafers about a
tavern usually are, to give a faint cheer at the prospect
of a treat, even though accompanied by words equivalent
to a kick. But one big raw-boned fellow, who looked equal
to any amount of corn-whiskey or anything else, could not
swallow Gus's insolence, and stepped up saying:

"Look here, Cap'n, I'm ready enough to drink with a
chap when he asks me like a gentleman, but I feel more
like puttin' a head on you than drinkin' with yer."

Gus had the false courage of wine and prided himself on
his boxing. In the headlong fury of drunkenness he flung
the bottle at the man's head, just grazing it, and sprang
toward him, but stumbled and fell. The man, with a certain rude sense of chivalry, waited for him to get up, but
the mean loafers who had cheered were about to manifest
their change of sentiment toward Gus by kicking him in his

prostrate condition. Van Dam, who also had drunk too much to be his cool careful self, now drew a pistol, and with a savage volley of oaths swore he would shoot the first man who touched his friend. Then, helping Gus up, he carried him off to a private room, and with the skill of an old experienced hand set about righting himself and Elliot, so that they might be in a presentable condition for their visit at the Allens'.

"Curse it all, Gus, why can you not keep within bounds? If this gets to the girls' ears it may spoil everything."

By five o'clock Gus had so far recovered as to venture to drive to the Allens', and the fresh air restored him rapidly. Before leaving, the landlord said to Van Dam:

"You had better stay out there all night. From what I hear the boys are going to lay for you when you come home to-night. I don't want any rows connected with my house. I'd rather you wouldn't come back."

Van Dam muttered an oath, and told the driver to go on.

As a matter of course they were received very cordially. Gus was quite himself again. He only seemed a little more inclined than usual to be sentimental and in high spirits.

They walked again in the twilight through the garden and under the budding trees of the orchard. Gus assumed a caressing tone and manner, which Edith half received and half resented. She felt that she did not know her own mind and did not understand him altogether, and so she took a diplomatic middle course that would leave her free to go forward or retreat. Zell, under the influence of Mr. Van Dam's flattering manner, walked in a beautiful but lurid dream. At last they all gathered in the parlor and chatted and laughed over old times.

On this Sabbath evening one of the officers of the church, seeing that the Allens had twice worshipped with them, felt that perhaps he ought to call and give them some encouragement. As he came up the path he was surprised at the confused sound of voices. With his hand on the door-bell he paused, and through an opening between the curtains saw the young men of whose bar-room performance he had happened to hear. Not caring to meet any of their sort he went silently away, shaking his head with ill-omened significance. Of course one good man told his wife what sort of company their new neighbors kept, and whom didn't she tell?

The evening grew late, but no carriage came from the village.

"It's very strange," said Van Dam.

"If it doesn't come you must stay all night," said Mrs. Allen graciously. "We can make you quite comfortable even if we have a little house."

Mr. Van Dam, and Gus also, were profuse in their thanks. Edith bit her lip with vexation. She felt that she and Zell were being placed in a false position since the gentlemen who to the world would seem so intimate with the family in reality held no relation to them. But no scruples of prudence occurred to thoughtless Zell. With an arch look toward her lover she said:

"I think it threatens rain, so of course you cannot go."

"Let us go out and see," he said.

In the darkness of the porch he put his arm around the unresisting girl and drew her to him, but he did not say like a true man:

"Zell, be my wife."

But poor Zell thought that was what all his attention and show of affection meant.

Edith and Gus joined them, and the latter thought also to put his regard in the form of caressing action, rather than in honest outspoken words, but she turned and said a little sharply:

"You have no right."

"Give me the right then," he whispered.

"Whether I shall ever do that I cannot say. It depends somewhat on yourself. But I cannot now and here."

The warning hand of Van Dam was reached through the darkness and touched Gus's arm.

The next morning they walked back to the village, were driven two or three miles to the nearest railway station, and took the train to the city, having promised to come again soon.

The week following their departure was an eventful one to the inmates of the little cottage, and all unknown the most unfavorable influences were at work against them. The Sunday hangers-on of a tavern have their points of contact with the better classes, and gossip is a commodity always in demand, whatever brings it to market. Therefore the scenes in the dining and bar rooms, in which Mrs. Allen's "friends" had played so prominent a part, were soon portrayed in hovel and mansion alike, with such exaggerations and distortions as a story inevitably suffers as passed along. The part acted by the young men was certainly bad enough, but rumor made it much worse. Then this stream of gossip was met by another coming from the wife of the good man who had called with the best intentions on Sunday evening, but, pained at the nature of the Allen's associations, had gone lamenting to his wife, and she had gone lamenting to the majority of the elder ladies of the church. These two streams uniting, quite a tidal wave of "I want to knows," and "painful surprises," swept over Pushton, and the Allens suffered wofully through their friends. They had already received some reconnoitering calls, and a few from people who wanted to be neighborly. But the truth was the people of Pushton had been somewhat perplexed. They did not know where to place the Allens. The fact that Mr. Allen had been a rich merchant, and lived on Fifth Avenue, counted for something. But then even the natives of Pushton knew that all kinds of people lived on Fifth Avenue, as elsewhere, and that some of the most disreputable were the richest. A clearer testimonial than that was therefore needed. Then again there was another puzzle. The fact that Mr. Allen had failed, and that they lived in a little house, indicated poverty. But their style of dressing and ordering from the store also suggested not a little property left. The humbler portion of the community doubted whether they were the style of people for them to call on, and the rumor of Rose Lacey's treatment, getting abroad in spite of Arden's injunction to the contrary, confirmed these doubts, and alienated this class. The more wealthy and fashionably inclined doubted the grounds for their calling, having by no means made up their minds whether they could take the Allens into their exclusive circle. So thus far Mrs. Allen and her daughters had given audience to a sort of middle class of skirmishers and scouts representing no one in particular save themselves, who from a *penchant* in that direction went out and obtained information, so that the more solid ranks behind could know what to do. In addition, as we have intimated, there were a few good kindly people who said:

"These strangers have come to live among us, and we must give them a neighborly welcome."

But there was something in their homely honest heartiness that did not suit Mrs. Allen's artificial taste, and she rather snubbed them.

"Heaven deliver us soon from Pushton," she said, "if the best people have no more air of quality than these outlandish tribes. They all look and act as if they had come out of the ark."

If the Allens had frankly and patiently accepted their poverty and misfortunes, and by close economy and some form of labor had sought to maintain an honest independence, they could soon, through this latter class, have become *en rapport* with, not the wealthy and fashionable, but the finest people of the community; people having the refinement, intelligence, and heart to make the best friends we can possess. It might take some little time. It ought to. Social recognition and esteem should be earned. Unless strangers bring clear letters of credit, or established reputation, they must expect to be put on probation. But if they adopt a course of simple sincerity and dignity, and especially one of great prudence, they are sure to find the right sort of friends, and win the social position to which they are justly entitled. But let the finger of scandal and doubt be pointed toward them, and all having sons and daughters will stand aloof on the ground of self-protection, if nothing else. The taint of scandal, like the taint of leprosy, causes a general shrinking away.

The finger of doubt and scandal in Pushton was now most decidedly pointed toward the Allens. It was reported around:

"Their father was a Wall Street gambler who lost all in a big speculation and died suddenly or committed suicide. They belonged to the ultra-fast fashionable set in New York, and the events of the past Sabbath show that they are not the persons for self-respecting people to associate with."

Some of the rather dissipated clerks and semi-loafers of the village were inclined to make the acquaintance of such stylish handsome girls, but the Allens received the least advance from them with ineffable scorn.

Thus within the short space of a month Mrs. Allen had, by her policy, contrived to isolate her family as completely as if they had had a pestilence.

Even Mrs. Lacey and Rose were inclined to pass from indignation to contempt; for Mr. Lacey was present at the scene in the bar-room, and reported that the "two young bucks were friends of their new neighbors, the Allens, and had stayed there all Sunday night because they darsn't go back to town."

"Well," said Rose, "with all their airs, I haven't got to keeping company with that style of men yet."

"Cease to call yourself my sister if you ever do knowingly," said Arden sternly. "I don't believe Edith Allen knows the character of these men. They would not report themselves, and who is to do it?"

"Perhaps you had better," said Rose maliciously.

Arden's only answer was a dark frowning look. A severe conflict was progressing in his mind. One impulse was to regard Edith as unworthy of another thought. But his heart pleaded for her, and the thought that she was different from the rest, and capable of developing a character as beautiful as her person, grew stronger as he dwelt upon it.

"Like myself, she is related to others that drag her down," he thought, "and she seems to have no friend or brother to protect or warn her. Even if this over-dressed young fool is her lover, if she could have seen him prostrate on the bar-room floor, she would never look at him again. If she would I would never look at her."

His romantic nature became impressed with the idea that he might become in some sense her unknown knight and protector, and keep her from marrying a man that would sink to what his father was. Therefore he passed the house as often as he could in hope that there might be some opportunity of seeing her.

To poor Edith troubles thickened fast, for, as we have seen, the brunt of everything came on her. Early on the forenoon of Monday the carpenter appeared, asking with a hard, determined tone for his money, adding with satire:

"I suppose it's all right of course. People who want everything done at once must expect to pay promptly."

"Your bill is much too large—much larger than you gave us any reason to suppose it would be," said Edith.

"I've only charged you regular rates, miss, and you put me to no little inconvenience besides."

"That's not the point. It's double the amount you gave us to understand it would be, and if you should deduct the damage caused by your delay it would greatly reduce it. I do not feel willing that this bill should be paid as it stands."

"Very well then," said the man, coolly rising. "You threatened me with a lawyer; I'll let my lawyer settle with you."

"Edith," said Mrs. Allen majestically, "bring my check-book."

"Don't pay it, mother. He can't make us pay such a bill in view of the fact that he left our roof open in the rain."

"Do as I bid you," said Mrs. Allen impressively.

"There," she said to the chuckling builder, in lofty scorn, throwing toward him a check as if it were dirt. "Now leave the presence of ladies whom you don't seem to know much about."

The man reddened and went out muttering that "he had seen quite as good ladies before."

Two days later a letter from Mrs. Allen's bank brought dismay by stating that she had overdrawn her account.

The next day there came a letter from their lawyer saying that a messenger from the bank had called upon him—that he was sorry they had spent all their money—that he could not sell the stock he held at any price now—and they had better sell their house in the country and board.

This Mrs. Allen was inclined to do, but Edith said almost fiercely:

"I won't sell it. I am bound to have some place of refuge in this hard, pitiless world. I hold the deed of this property, and we certainly can get something to eat off of it, and if we must starve, no one at least can disturb us."

"What can we do?" said Mrs. Allen, crying and wringing her hands.

"We ought to have saved our money and gone to work at something," answered Edith sternly.

"I am not able to work," whined Laura.

"I don't know how to work, and I won't starve either," cried Zell passionately. "I shall write to Mr. Van Dam this very day and tell him all about it."

"I would rather work my fingers off," retorted Edith scornfully, "than have a man come and marry me out of charity, finding me as helpless as if I were picked up off the street, and on the street we should soon be, without shelter or friends, if we sold this place."

And so the blow fell upon them, and such was the spirit with which they bore it.

CHAPTER XV

THE TEMPTATION

THE same mail brought them a long bill from Mr. Hard, accompanied with a very polite but decisive note saying that it was his custom to have a monthly settlement with his customers.

The rest of the family looked with new dismay and help-lessness at this, and Edith added bitterly:

"There are half a dozen other bills also."

"What can we do?" again Mrs. Allen cried piteously. "If you girls had only accepted some of your splendid offers—"

"Hush, mother," said Edith imperiously. "I have heard that refrain too often already," and the resolute practical girl went to her room and shut herself up to think.

Two hours later she came down to lunch with the determined air of one who had come to a conclusion.

"These bills must be met, in part at least," she said, "and the sooner the better. After that we must buy no more than we can pay for, if it's only a crust of bread. I shall take the first train to-morrow and dispose of some of my jewelry. Who of you will contribute some also? We all have more than we shall ever need."

"Pawn our jewelry!" they all shrieked.

"No, sell it," said Edith firmly.

"You hateful creature!" sobbed Zell. "If Mr. Van Dam heard it he would never come near me again."

"If he's that kind of a man, he had better not," was the sharp retort.

"I'll never forgive you if you do it. You shall not spoil all my chances and your own too. He as good as offered himself to me, and I insist on your giving me a chance to write to him before you take one of your mad steps."

They all clamored against her purpose so strongly that Edith was borne down and reluctantly gave way. Zell wrote immediately a touching, pathetic letter that would have moved a man of one knightly instinct to come to her rescue. Van Dam read it with a look of fiendish exultation, and calling on Gus said:

"We will go up to-morrow. The right time has come. They won't be nice as to terms any longer."

It was an unfortunate thing for Edith that she had yielded at this time to the policy of waiting one hour longer. In the two days that intervened before the young men appeared there was time for that kind of thought that tempts and weakens. She was in that most dangerous attitude of irresolution. The toilsome path of independent labor looked very hard and thorny—more than that, it looked lonely. This latter aspect causes multitudes to shrink, where the work would not. She knew enough of society to feel sure that her mother was right, and that the moment she entered on bread-winning by any form of honest labor, her old fashionable world was lost to her forever. And she knew of no other world, she had no other friends save those of the gilded past. She did not, with her healthful frame and energetic spirit, shrink so much from labor as from association with the laboring classes. She had been educated to think of them only as coarse and common, and to make no distinctions.

"Even if a few are good and intelligent as these Laceys seem, they can't understand my feelings and past life, so there will be no congeniality, and I shall have to work practically alone. Perhaps in time I shall become coarse and common like the rest," she said with a half-shudder at the thought of old-fashioned garb, slipshod dressing, and long monotonous hours at one employment. All these were inseparable in her mind from poverty and labor.

Then after a long silence, during which she had sat with her chin resting on her hands, she continued:

"I believe I could stand it if I could earn a support out of the garden with such a man as Malcom to help me. There are variety and beauty there, and scope for constant improvement. But I fear a woman can't make a livelihood by such out-of-door, man-like work. Good heavens! what would my Fifth Avenue friends say if it should get to their ears that Edith Allen was raising cabbages for market?"

Then in contrast, as the alternative to labor, Gus Elliot continually presented himself.

"If he were only more of a man!" she thought. "But if he loves me so well as to marry me in view of my poverty, he must have some true manhood about him. I suppose I could learn to love him after a fashion, and I certainly like him as well as any one I know. Perhaps if I were with him to cheer, incite, and scold, he might become a fair business man after all."

And so Edith in her helplessness and fear of work was tempted to enter on that forlorn experiment which so many energetic women of decided character have made—that of marrying a man who can't stand alone, or do anything but dawdle, in the hope that they may be able to infuse in him some of their own moral and intellectual backbone.

But Gus Elliot was not man enough, had not sense enough, to give her this poor chance of matrimonial escape from labor that seemed to her like a giant taskmaster, waiting with grimy, horny hand to claim her as another of his innumerable slaves. Though a life of lonely, ill-paid toil would have been better for Edith than marriage to Gus, he was missing the one golden opportunity of his life, when he thought of Edith Allen in other character than his wife. God uses instruments, and she alone could give him a chance of being a man among men. In his meditated baseness toward her, he aimed a fatal blow at his own life.

And this is ever true of sins against the human brotherhood. The recoil of a blow struck at another's interests has often the retributive wrath of heaven in it, and the selfish soul that would destroy a fellow-creature for its own pleasure is itself destroyed.

False pride, false education, helpless, unskilled hands, an untaught, unbraced moral nature, made strong, resolute, beautiful Edith Allen so weak, so untrue to herself, that she was ready to throw herself away on so thin a shadow of a man as Gus Elliot. She might have known, indeed she half feared, that wretchedness would follow such a union. It is torment to a large strong-souled woman to despise utterly the man to whom she is chained. She revolts at his weakness and irresolution, and the probabilities are that she will sink into that worst phase of feminine drudgery, the supporting of a husband, who, though able, will not work, and that she will become that social monster of whom it is said with a significant laugh:

"She is the man of the house."

The only thing that reconciled her to the thought of marrying Gus was the hope that she could inspire him to better things; and he seemed the only refuge from the pressing troubles that environed her, and from a lonely life of labor; for the thought that she could bring herself to marry among the laboring classes had never occurred to her.

So she came to the miserable conclusion on the afternoon of the second day:

"I'll take him if he will me, knowing how I am situated."

If Gus could have been true and manly one evening, he might have secured a prop that would have kept him up, though it would have been at sad cost to Edith.

On the afternoon of Friday, Zell returned from the village with radiant face, and, waving a letter before Edith who sat moping in her room, exclaimed with a thrill of ecstasy in her tone:

"They are coming.   Help make me irresistible."

Edith felt the influence of Zell's excitement, and the mysteries of the toilet began.   Nature had done much for these girls, and they knew how to enhance every charm by art.   Edith good-naturedly helped her sister, weaving pure shimmering pearls in the heavy braids of her hair, whose raven hue made the fair face seem more fair.   The toilet-table of a queen had not the secrets of Zell's beauty, for the most skilful art must deal with the surface, while Zell's loveliness glowed from within.   Her rich young blood mantled her cheek with a color that came and went with her passing thoughts, and was as unlike the flaming, unchanging red of a painted face as sunlight that flickers through a breezy grove is to a gas-jet.   Her eyes shone with the deep excitement of a passionate love, and the feeling that the crisis of her life was near.   Even Edith gazed with wondering admiration at her beauty, as she gave the finishing touches to her toilet, before she commenced her own.

Discarded Laura had a sorry part in the poor little play. She was to be ill and unable to appear, and so resigned herself to a novel and solitude.   Mrs. Allen was to discreetly have a headache and retire early, and thus all embarrassing third parties should be kept out of the way.

The late afternoon of Friday (unlucky day for once) brought the gentlemen, dressed as exquisitely as ever, but the vision on the rustic little porch almost dazzled even their experienced eyes.   They had seen these girls more richly dressed before and more radiant.   There was, however, a delicious pensiveness hanging over them now, like those delicate veils that enhance beauty and conceal nothing.   And there was a deep undertone of excitement that gave them a magnetic power that they could not have in quieter moods.

Their appearance and manner of greeting caused secret exultation in the black hearts that they expected would be offered to them that night, but Edith looked so noble as well as beautiful that Gus rather trembled in view of his part in the proposed tragedy. As warm and gentle as had been her greeting, she did not appear like a girl that could be safely trifled with. However, Gus knew his one source of courage and kept up on brandy all day, and he proposed a heavier onslaught than ever on poor Mrs. Allen's wine. But Edith did not bring it out. She meant that all that was said that night should be spoken in sober earnest.

They sat down to cards for a while after tea, during which conversation was rather forced, consisting mainly of extravagant compliments from the gentlemen, and tender, meaning glances which the girls did not resent. Mrs. Allen languidly joined them for a while, and excused herself saying:

"My poor head has been too heavily taxed of late," though how, save as a small distillery of helpless tears, we do not remember.

The regret of the young men at being deprived of her society was quite affecting in view of the fact that they had often wished her dead and out of the way.

"Why should we shut ourselves up within walls this lovely spring evening, this delicious earnest of the coming summer?" said Mr. Van Dam to Zell. "Come, put on your shawl and show me your garden by moonlight."

Zell exultingly complied, believing that now she would show him, not their poor little garden, but the paradise of requited love. A moment later her graceful form, bending like a willow toward him, vanished in the dusky light of the rising moon, down the garden path which led to the little arbor.

Gus, having the parlor to himself, went over to the sofa, seated himself by the side of Edith and sought to pass his arm around her waist.

"You have no right," again said Edith with dignity, shrinking away.

"But will you not give the right? Behold me a suppliant at your feet," said Gus tenderly, but comfortably keeping his seat.

9—Roe—X

"Mr. Elliot," said Edith earnestly, "do you realize that you are asking a poor girl to marry you?"

"Your own beautiful self is beyond all gold," said Gus gushingly.

"You did not think so a month ago," retorted Edith bitterly.

"I was a fool. My friends discouraged it, but I find I cannot live without you."

This sounded well to poor Edith, but she said half sadly:

"Perhaps your friends are right. You cannot afford to marry me."

"But I cannot give you up," said Gus with much show of feeling. "What would my life be without you? I admit to you that my friends are opposed to my marriage, but am I to blight my life for them? Am I, who have seen the best of New York for years, to give up the loveliest girl I have ever seen in it? I cannot and I will not," concluded Gus tragically.

"And are you willing to give up all for me?" said Edith feelingly, her glorious eyes becoming gentle and tender.

"Yes, if you will give up all for me," said Gus languishingly, taking her hand and drawing her toward him.

Edith did not resist now, but leaned her head on his shoulder with the blessed sense of rest and at least partial security. Her cruelly harassed heart and burdened, threatened life could welcome even such poor shelter as Gus Elliot offered. The spring evening was mild and breathless, and its hush and peace seemed to accord with her feelings. There was no ecstatic thrilling of her heart in the divine rapture of mutual and open recognition of love, for no such love existed on her part. It was only a languid feeling of contentment—moon-lighted with sentiment, not sun-lighted with joy—that she had found some one who would not leave her to labor and struggle alone.

"Gus," she said pathetically, "we are very poor; we have nothing. We are almost desperate from want. Think twice ere you engage yourself to a girl so situated. Are you able to thus burden yourself?''

Gus thought these words led the way to the carrying out of Van Dam's instructions, for he said eagerly:

''I know how you are situated. I learned all from Zell's letter to Van Dam, but our hearts only cling the closer to you, and you must let me take care of you at once. If you will only consent to a secret marriage I can manage it.''

Edith slowly raised her head from his shoulder. Gus could not meet her eyes, but felt them fixed searchingly on his face. There was a distant mutter of thunder like a warning voice. He continued hurriedly:

''I think you will agree with me, when you think of it, that such a marriage would be best. It would be hard for me to break with my family at once. Indeed I could not afford to anger my father now. But I would soon get established in business myself, and I would work so hard if I knew that you were dependent on me!''

''Then you would wish me to remain here in obscurity your wife,'' said Edith in a low constrained tone that Gus did not quite like.

''Oh, no, not for the world,'' replied Gus hurriedly. ''It is because I so long for your daily and hourly presence that I urge you to come to the city at once.''

''What is your plan then?'' asked Edith in the same low tone.

''Go with me to the city, on the boat that passes here in the evening. I will see that you are lodged where you will have every comfort, yes luxury. We can there be quietly married, and when the right time comes we can openly acknowledge it.''

There was a tremble in Edith's voice when she again spoke, it might be from mere excitement or anger. At any rate Gus grew more and more uncomfortable. He had a vague feeling that Edith suspected his falseness, and that her seeming calmness might presage a storm, and he found it impossible to meet her full searching gaze, fearing that his face would betray him. He was bad enough for his project, but not quite brazen enough.

She detached herself from his encircling arm, went to a book-stand near and took from it a richly bound Bible. With this she came and stood before Gus, who was half trembling with fear and perplexity, and said in a tone so grave and solemn that his weak impressible nature was deeply moved:

"Mr. Elliot, perhaps I do not understand you. I have received several offers before, but never one like yours this evening. Indeed I need not remind you that you have spoken to me in a different vein. I know circumstances have greatly altered with me. That I am no longer the daughter of a millionaire, I am learning to my sorrow, but I am the same Edith Allen that you knew of old. I would not like to misjudge you, one of my oldest, most intimate friends of the happy past. And yet, as I have said, I do not quite understand your offer. Place your hand on this sacred book with me, and, as you hope for God's mercy, answer me this truly. Would you wish your own sister to accept such an offer, if she were situated like myself? Look me, an honest girl with all my faults and poverty, in the face, and tell me as a true brother."

Gus felt himself in an awful dilemma. Something in Edith's solemn tone and look convinced him that both he and Van Dam had misjudged her. His knees trembled so that he could scarcely rise. A fascination that he could not resist drew his face, stamped with guilt, toward her, and slowly he raised his fearful eyes and for a moment met Edith's searching, questioning gaze, then dropped them in confusion.

"Why do you not put your hand on the book and speak?" she asked in the low, concentrated voice of passion.

Again he looked hurriedly at her. A flash of lightning illumined her features, and he quailed before an expression such as he had never seen before on any woman's face.

"I—I—cannot," he faltered.

The Bible dropped from her hands, they clasped, and for a moment she seemed to writhe in agony, and in a low, shuddering tone she said:

"There are none to trust—not one."

Then, as if possessed by a sudden fury, she seized him roughly by the arm and said hoarsely:

"Speak, man! what then did you mean? What have all your tender speeches and caressing actions meant?"

Her face grew livid with rage and shame as the truth dawned upon her, while poor feeble Gus lost his poise utterly and stood like a detected criminal before her.

"You asked me to marry you," she hissed. "Must no one ask your immaculate sisters to do this, that you could not answer my simple question? Or, did you mean something else? How dare you exist longer in the semblance of a man? You have broken the sacred law of hospitality, and here, in my little home that has sheltered you, you purpose my destruction. You take mean advantage of my poverty and trouble, and like a cowardly hunter must seek out a wounded doe as your game. My grief and misfortune should have made a sanctuary about me, but the orphaned and unfortunate, God's trust to all true men, only invite your evil designs, because defenceless. Wretch, would you have made me this offer if my father had lived, or if I had a brother?"

"It's all Van Dam's work, curse him," groaned Gus, white as a ghost.

"Van Dam's work!" shrieked Edith, "and he's with Zell! So this is a conspiracy. You both are the flower of chivalry," and her mocking, half-hysterical laugh curdled Gus's blood, as her dress fluttered down the path that led to the arbor.

She appeared in the doorway like a sudden, supernatural vision. Zell's head rested on Mr. Van Dam's shoulder, and he was portraying in low, ardent tones the pleasures of city life, which would be hers as his wife.

"It is true," he had said, "our marriage must be secret

for the present. You must learn to trust me. But the time will soon come when I can acknowledge you as my peerless bride.''

Foolish little Zell was too eager to escape present miseries to be nice and critical as to the conditions, and too much in love, too young and unsuspecting, to doubt the man who had petted her from a child. She agreed to do anything he thought best.

Then Edith's entrance and terrible words broke her pretty dream in fragments.

Snatching her sister from Van Dam's embrace, she cried passionately:

''Leave this place. Your villany is discovered.''

''Really, Miss Edith''—began Van Dam with a poor show of dignity.

''Leave instantly!'' cried Edith imperiously. ''Do you wish me to strike you?''

''Edith, are you mad?'' cried Zell.

''Your sister must have lost her reason,'' said Van Dam, approaching Zell.

''Stand back,'' cried Edith sternly. ''I may go mad before this hateful night passes, but while I have strength and reason left, I will drive the wolves from our fold. Answer me this: have you not been proposing secret marriage to my sister?''

Her face looked spirit-like in the pale moonlight, and her eyes blazed like coals of fire. As she stood there with her arm around her bewildered, trembling sister, she seemed a guardian angel holding a baffled fiend at bay.

This was literally true, for even hardened Van Dam quailed before her, and took refuge in the usual resource of his satanic ally—lies.

''I assure you, Miss Edith, you do me great injustice. I have only asked your sister that our marriage be private for a time—''

''The same wretched bait—the same transparent falsehood,'' Edith cried. ''We cannot be married openly at our own home, but must go away with you, two spotless knights, to New York. Do you take us for silly fools? You know well what the world would say of ladies that so compromised themselves, and no true man would ask this of a woman he meant to make his wife. These premises are mine. Leave them.''

Van Dam was an old villain who had lived all his life in the atmosphere of brawls and intrigue, therefore he said brazenly:

''There is no use in wasting words on an angry woman. Zell, my darling, do me justice. Don't give me up, as I never shall you,'' and he vanished on the road toward the village, where Gus was skulking on before him.

''You weak, unmitigated fool,'' said he savagely, ''why did I bring you?''

''Look here, Van Dam,'' whined Gus, ''that isn't the way to speak to a gentleman.''

''Gentleman! ha, ha,'' laughed Van Dam bitterly.

''I be hanged if I feel like one to-night. A pretty scrape you have got me into,'' snarled Gus.

''Well,'' said Van Dam cynically. ''I thought I was too old to learn much more, but you may shoot me if I ever go on a lark again with one of your weak villains who is bad enough for anything, but has brains enough only to get found out. If it hadn't been for you I would have carried my point. And I will yet,'' he added with an oath. ''I never give up a game I have once started.''

And so they plodded on with mutual revilings and profanity, till Gus became afraid of Van Dam, and was silent.

The dark cloud that had risen unnoted in the south, like the slowly gathering and impending wrath of God, now broke upon them in sudden gusts, and then chased them, with pelting torrents of rain and stinging hail, into the village. The sin-wrought chaos—the hellish discord of their evil natures—seemed to have infected the peaceful spring evening, for now the very spirit of the storm appeared abroad. The rush and roar of the wind was so strong, the lightning so vivid, and the crashing thunder peals overhead so terrific, that even hardened Van Dam was awed, and Gus was so frightened and conscience-smitten that he could scarcely keep up with his companion, but shuddered at the thought of being left alone.

At last they reached the tavern, roused the startled landlord, and obtained welcome shelter.

"What!" he said, "are the boys after you?"

"No, no," said Van Dam impatiently; "the devil is after us in this infernal storm. Give us two rooms, a fire, and some brandy as soon as possible, and charge what you please."

When Gus viewed himself in the mirror, as he at once did from long habit, his haggard face, drenched, mud-splashed form, awakened sincere self-commiseration; and his stained, bedraggled clothes troubled him more than his soiled character. He did not remember the time when he had not been well dressed, and to be so was his religion —the sacred instinct of his life. Therefore he was inexpressibly shocked, and almost ready to cry, as he saw his forlorn reflection in the glass. And he had no change with him. What should he do? All other phases of the disastrous night were lost in this.

"There is nothing to be bought in this mean little town, and how can I go to the city in this plight?" he anxiously queried.

"Go to the devil then," and the sympathetic Van Dam wrapped himself up and went to sleep.

Gus worked fussily at his clothes till a late hour, devoutly hoping he should meet no one whom he knew before reaching his dressing-room in New York.

CHAPTER XVI

BLACK HANNIBAL'S WHITE HEART

EDITH half led, half carried her sobbing sister to the parlor. Mrs. Allen, no longer languid, and Laura from her exile, were already there, and with dismayed faces drew near the sofa where Zell had been placed.

"What has happened?" asked Mrs. Allen tremblingly.

Edith's self-control, now that her enemies were gone, gave way utterly, and sinking on the floor, she swayed back and forth, sobbing even more hysterically than Zell, and her mother and Laura, oppressed with the sense of some new impending disaster, caught the contagion of their bitter grief, and wept and wrung their hands also.

The frightened maid stood in one door, with white questioning face, and old gray-haired Hannibal in another, with streaming eyes of honest sympathy.

"Speak, speak, what is the matter?" almost shrieked Mrs. Allen.

Edith could not speak, but Zell sobbed, "I—don't—know. Edith—seems to have—gone—mad."

At last, after the application of restoratives, Edith so far recovered herself as to say brokenly:

"We've been betrayed—they're—villains. They never —meant—marriage at all."

"That's false!" screamed Zell. "I won't believe it of my lover, whatever may have been true of your mean little Gus Elliot. He promised to marry me, and you have spoiled everything by your mad folly. I'll never forgive you."—

When Zell's wild fury would have ceased, cannot be said,

but a new voice startled and awed them into silence. In the storm of sorrow and passion that raged within, the outer storm had risen unnoted, but now an awful peal of thunder broke over their heads and rolled away among the hills in deep reverberations. Another and a louder crash soon followed, and a solemn, expectant silence fell upon them akin to that when the noisy passionate world will suddenly cease its clamor as the trump of God proclaims the end.

"Merciful heaven! we shall be struck," said Mrs. Allen shudderingly.

"What's the use of living?" said Zell in a hard, reckless tone.

"What is there to live for?" sighed Edith, deep in her heart. "There are none to be trusted—not one."

Instead of congratulations received with blushing happiness, and solitaire engagement rings, thus is shown the first result of Mrs. Allen's policy, and of society's injunction:

"Keep your hands white, my dears."

The storm passed away, and they crept off to such poor rest as they could get, too miserable to speak, and too worn to renew the threatened quarrel that a voice seemingly from heaven had interrupted.

The next morning they gathered at a late breakfast-table with haggard faces and swollen eyes. Zell looked hard and sullen, Edith's face was so determined in its expression as to be stern. Mrs. Allen lamented feebly and indefinitely, Laura only appeared more settled in her apathy, and, like Zell and Edith, was utterly silent through the forlorn meal.

When it was over, Zell went up to her room and Edith followed her. Zell had not spoken to her sister since the thunder peal had suddenly checked her bitter words. Edith dreaded the alienation she saw in Zell's face, and felt wronged by it, knowing that she had only acted as truest friend and protector. But in order still to shield her sister she must secure her confidence, or else the danger averted the past evening would threaten as grimly as ever. She also realized how essential Zell's help would be in the struggle for bread on which they must enter, and wished to obtain her hearty co-operation in some plan of work. She saw that labor now was inevitable, and must be commenced immediately. From Laura little was to be hoped. She seemed so lacking in mental and physical force since their troubles began, that it appeared as if nothing could arouse her. She threatened soon to become an invalid like her mother. The thought of help from the latter did not even occur to her.

Edith had not slept, and as the chaos and bitterness of the past evening's experience passed away, her practical mind began to concentrate itself on the problem of support. Her disappointment had not been so severe as that of Zell, by any means, and so she was in a condition to rally much sooner. She had never much more than liked Elliot, and now the very thought of him was sickening, and though labor and want might be hard indeed, and regret for all they had lost keen, still she was spared the bitterer pain of a hopeless love.

But it was just this that Zell feared, and though she repeated to herself óver and over again Van Dam's last words, "I will never give you up," she feared that he would, or what would be equally painful, she would be compelled to give him up, for she could not disguise from herself that her confidence had been shaken.

But sincere love is slow to believe evil of its object. If Van Dam had shown preference for another, Zell's jealousy and anger would have known no bounds, but this he had never done, and she could not bring herself to believe that the man whom she had known since childhood, who had always treated her with uniform kindness and most flattering attention, who had partaken of their hospitality so often and intimately that he almost seemed like one of the family, meditated the basest evil against her.

"Gus Elliot is capable of any meanness, but Edith was mistaken about my friend. And yet Edith has so insulted him that I fear he will never come to the house again," she said with deep resentment. "If I had declined a private marriage, I am sure he would have married me openly."

Therefore when Edith entered their little room Zell's face was averted, and there was every evidence of estrangement. Edith meant to be kind and considerate, and patiently show the reasons for her action.

She sat down and took her sister's cold, impassive hand, saying:

"Zell, did I not help you dress in this very place last evening? Did I not wait against my judgment till Mr. Van Dam came? These things prove to you that I would not put a straw between you and a true lover. Surely we have trouble enough without adding the bitter one of division and estrangement. If we don't stand by each other now what will become of us?"

"What right had you to misjudge Mr. Van Dam by such a mean little scamp as Gus Elliot? Why did you not give him a chance to explain himself?"

"O Zell, Zell, how can you be so blinded? Did he not ask you to go away with him in the night—to elope, and then submit to a secret marriage in New York?"

"Well, he told me there were good reasons that made such a course necessary at present."

"Are you George Allen's daughter, that you could even listen to such a proposal? When you lived on Fifth Avenue would he have dared to even faintly suggest such a thing? Can he be a true lover who insults you to begin with, and, in view of your misfortunes, instead of showing manly delicacy and desire to shield, demands not only hard but indecent conditions? Even if he purposed to marry you, what right has he to require of you such indelicate action as would make your name a byword and hissing among all your old acquaintances, and a lasting stain to your family? They would not receive you with respect again, though some might tolerate you and point you out as the girl so desperate for a husband that she submitted to the grossest indignity to get one."

Zell hung her head in shame and anger under Edith's inexorable logic, but the anger was now turning against Van Dam. Edith continued:

"A lady should be sought and won. It is for her to set the place and time of the wedding, and dictate the conditions. It is for her to say who shall be present and who absent, and woman, to whom a spotless name is everything, has the right, which even savage tribes recognize, to shield herself from the faintest imputation of immodesty by compelling her suitor to comply with the established custom and etiquette which are her safeguards. The daughter of a poor laborer would demand all this as a matter of course, and shall the beautiful Zell Allen, who has had scores of admirers, have all this reversed in her case, and be compelled to skulk away from the home in which she should be openly married, to hunt up a man at night who has made the pitiful promise that he will marry her somewhere at some time or other, on condition that no one shall know it till he is ready? Mark it well, the man who so insults a lady and all her family never means to marry her, or else he is so coarse and brutal in all his instincts that no decent woman ought to marry him."

"Say no more," said Zell, in a low tone, "I fear you are right, though I would rather die than believe it. Oh, Edith, Edith!" she cried in sudden passionate grief. "My heart is broken. I loved him so! I could have been so happy!"

Edith took her in her arms and they cried together. At last Zell said languidly:

"What can we do?"

"We must go to work like other poor people. If we had only done so at first and saved every dollar we had left, we should not now be in our present deeply embarrassed condition. And yet, Zell, if you, with your vigor and strength, will only stand by me, and help your best, we will see bright days yet. There must be some way by which two girls can make a livelihood here in Pushton as elsewhere. We have at least a shelter, and I have great hopes of the garden."

"I don't like a garden. I fear I couldn't do much there. And it seems like man's work too. I fear I shall be too wretched and ignorant to do anything."

"Not at all. Youth, health, and time, against all the troubles of the world." (This was the best creed poor Edith then had.) "Now," she continued, encouragingly, "you like housework. Of course we must dismiss our servants, and if you did the work of the house with Laura, so that I had all my time for something else, it would be a great saving and help."

"Oh, dear! oh, dear! that we should ever come to this!" said Zell despairingly.

"We have come to it, and must face the truth."

"Well, of course I'll try," said Zell with something of Laura's apathy. Then with a sudden burst of passion she clenched her little hands and cried:

"I hate him, the cold-hearted wretch, to treat his poor little Zell so shamefully!" and she paced up and down the room with inflamed eyes and cheeks. Then in equally sudden revulsion she threw herself down on the floor with her head in her sister's lap, and murmured, "God forgive me, I love him still—I love him with my whole heart," and sobbed till all her strength was gone.

Edith sighed deeply. "Can she ever be depended on?" she thought. At last she lifted the languid form on the bed, threw over her an afghan, and bathed her head with cologne till the poor child fell asleep.

Then she went down to Laura and her mother, to whom she explained more fully the events of last evening. Laura only muttered, "shameful," but Mrs. Allen whined, "She could not understand it. Girls didn't know how to manage any longer. There must be some misunderstanding, for no young men in the city could have meant to offer such an insult to an old and respectable family like theirs. She never heard of such a thing. If she could only have been present—"

"Hush, mother," said Edith almost sternly. "It's all

past now. I should gladly believe that when you were a young lady such poor villains were not in good society. Moreover, such offers are not made to young ladies living on the avenue. This is more properly a case for shooting than management. I have no patience to talk any more about it. We must now try to conform to our altered circumstances, and at least maintain our self-respect, and secure the comforts of life if possible. But we must now practice the closest economy. Laura, you will have to be mother's maid, for of course we can keep no servants. I have a little money left, and will pay your maid to-day and let her go."

"I don't see how I can get along without her," said Mrs. Allen helplessly.

"You must," said Edith firmly. "We have no money to pay her any longer, and your daughters will try to supply her place."

Mrs. Allen did not formally abdicate her natural position as head of the family, but in the hour of almost shipwreck Edith took the helm out of the feeble hands. Yet the young girl had little to guide her, no knowledge and experience worth mentioning, and the sea was rough and beset with dangers.

The maid had no regrets at departure, and went away with something of the satisfaction of a rat leaving a sinking ship. But with old Hannibal it was a different affair.

"You ain't gwine to send me away too, is you, Miss Edie?" said he, with the accent of dismay.

"My good old friend," said Edith feelingly, "the only friend I'm sure of in this great world full of people, I fear I must. We can't afford to pay you even half what you are worth any longer."

"I'se sure I doesn't eat sech a mighty lot," Hannibal sniffled out.

"Oh, I hope we shan't reach starvation point," said Edith, smiling in spite of her sore heart. "But, Hannibal, you are a valuable servant; besides, there are plenty

of rich upstarts who would give you anything you would
ask, just to have you come and give an old and aristocratic
air to their freshly-gilded mansions.''

"Miss Edie, you doesn't know nothin' 'tall about my
feelin's. What's money to ole Hannibal! I'se lived 'mong
de millionaires and knows all 'bout money. It only buys
half of 'em a heap of trouble and doesn't keep dar hearts
from gettin' sore. When Massa Allen was a livin', he paid
me big, and guv me all de money I wanted, and if he, at
last, lost my money which he keep, it's no mo'n he did wid
his own. And now, Miss Edie, I toted you and you'se sisters roun' on my shouler when you was babies, and I hain't
got nothin' left but you, no friends, no nothin'; and if you
send me away, it's like gwine out into de wilderness. What
'ud I do in some strange man's big house, when my heart's
here in de little house? My heart is all ole Hannibal has
left, if 'tis black, and if you send me away you break it.
I'd a heap rader stay here in Bushtown and starve to death
wid you alls, dan live in de grandest house on de avenue.''

"Oh, Hannibal," said Edith, putting her hand on the
old man's shoulder, and looking at him with her large eyes
dimmed with grateful tears, "you don't know how much
good you have done me. I have felt that there were none
to trust—not one, but you are as true as steel. Your heart
isn't black, as I told you before. It's whiter than mine.
Oh, that other men were like you!''

"Bress you, Miss Edie, I isn't a man, I'se only a
nigger.''

"You are my true and trusted friend," said Edith, "and
you shall be one of the family as long as you wish to stay
with us.''

"Now bress you, Miss Edie, you'se an angel for sayin'
dat. Don't be afeard, I'se good for sumpen yet, if I be
old. I once work for fear in de South; den I work for
money, and now I'se gwine to work for lub, and it 'pears
I can feel my ole jints limber up at de tought. It 'pears
like dat lub is de only ting dat can make one young agin.

Neber you fear, Miss Edie, we'll pull trough, and I'se see you a grand lady yet. A true lady you'se allers be, even if you went out to scrub.''

"Perhaps I'll have to, Hannibal. I know how to do that about as well as anything else that people are willing to pay for.''

CHAPTER XVII

THE CHANGES OF TWO SHORT MONTHS

A T the dinner-table it was reluctantly admitted to be
necessary that Edith should go to the city in the
morning and dispose of some of their jewelry. She
went by the early train, and the familiar aspects of Fourth
Avenue as she rode down town were as painful as the features of an old friend turned away from us in estrangement.
She kept her face closely veiled, hoping to meet no acquaintances, but some whom she knew unwittingly brushed against
her.   Her mother's last words were:

"Go to some store where we are not known to sell the
jewelry."

Edith's usually good judgment seemed to fail her in this
case, as generally happens when we listen to the suggestions
of false pride.   She went to a jeweller downtown who was
an utter stranger.   The man's face to whom she handed her
valuables for inspection did not suggest pure gold that had
passed through the refiner's fire, though he professed to
deal in that article.   An unknown lady, closely veiled,
offering such rich articles for sale, looked suspicious; but,
whether it was right or wrong, there was a chance for him
to make an extraordinary profit.   Giving a curious glance
at Edith, who began to have misgivings from the manner
and appearance of the man, he swept the little cases up and
took them to the back part of the store, on pretence of wishing to consult his partner.   He soon returned and said rather
harshly:

"I don't quite understand this matter, and we are not in

the habit of doing this kind of business. It may be all right that you should offer this jewelry, and it may not. If we take it, we must run the risk. We will give you"—offering scarcely half its value.

"I assure you it is all right," said Edith indignantly, at the same time with a sickening sensation of fear. "It all belongs to us, but we are compelled to part with it from sudden need."

"That is about the way they all talk," said the man coolly. "We will give you no more than I said."

"Then give me back my jewelry," said Edith, scarcely able to stand, through fear and shame.

"I don't know about that. Perhaps I ought to call in an officer any way and have the thing investigated. But I give you your choice, either to take this money, or go with a policeman before a justice and have the thing explained," and he laid the money before her.

She shuddered at the thought. Edith Allen in a police court, explaining why she was selling her jewelry, the gifts of her dead father, followed by a rabble in the street, her name in the papers, and she the town-talk and scandal of her old set on the avenue! How Gus Elliot and Van Dam would exult! All passed through her mind in one dreadful whirl. She snatched up the money and rushed out with one thought of escape, and for some time after had a shuddering apprehension of being pursued and arrested.

"Oh, if I had only gone to Tiffany's, where I am known!" she groaned. "It's all mother's work. Her advice is always fatal, and I will never follow it again. It seems as if everything and everybody were against me," and she plunged into the sheltering throng of Broadway, glad to be a mere unrecognized drop in its mighty tide.

But even as Edith passed out of the jeweller's store her eye rested for a moment on the face of a man whom she thought she had seen before, though she could not tell where, and the face haunted her, causing much uneasiness.

"Could he have seen and known me?" she queried most anxiously.

He had done both. He was no other than Tom Crowl, a clerk in the village at one of the lesser dry-goods stores, where the Allens had a small account. He was one of the mean loafers who were present at the bar-room scene, and had cheered, and then kicked Gus Elliot, and "laid for him" in the evening with the "boys." He was one of the upper graduates of Pushton street-corners, and having spent an idle, vicious boyhood, truant half the time from school, had now arrived at the dignity of clerk in a store, that thrived feebly on the scattering trade that filtered through and past Mr. Hard's larger establishment. He was one of the worst phases of the male gossip, and had the scent of a buzzard for the carrion of scandal. The Allens were now the uppermost theme of the village, for there seemed some mystery about them. Moreover, the rural dabblers in vice had a natural jealousy of the more accomplished rakes from the city, which took on something of the air of virtuous indignation against them. Of course the talk about Gus and Van Dam included the Allens; and if poor Edith could have heard the surmises about them in the select coterie of clerks that gathered after closing hours around Crowl, as the central fountain of gossip, she would have felt more bitterly than ever that the spirit of chivalry had utterly forsaken mankind.

When therefore young Crowl saw Edith get on the same train as himself, he determined to watch her, and startle, if possible, his small squad of admirers with a new proof of his right to lead as chief scandal-monger. The scene in the jewelry store thus became a brilliant stroke of fortune to him, though so severe a blow to Edith. (The number of people who are like wolves, that turn upon and devour one of their kind when wounded, is not small.) Crowl exultingly saw himself doubly the hero of the evening in the little room of the loft over the store, where poor Edith would be discussed that evening over a black bottle and sundry clay pipes.

As Edith returned up town toward the depot, the impulse to go and see her old home was very strong. She thought her veil sufficient protection to allow her to venture. Slowly and with heavy step she passed up the well-known street on the opposite side, and then crossed and passed down toward that door from which she had so often tripped in light-hearted gayety, or rolled away in a liveried carriage, the envied and courted daughter of a millionaire. And to-day she was selling her jewelry for bread—to-day she had narrowly, as she thought, escaped the police court —to-day she had no other prospect of support save her unskilled hands, and little more than two short months ago, that house was ablaze with light, resounding with mirth and music, and she and her sisters were known as among the wealthiest belles of the city. It was like a horrid dream. It seemed as if she might see old Hannibal opening the door, and Zell come tripping out, or Laura at the window of her room with a book, or the portly form of her father returning from business, indeed even herself, radiant with pride and pleasure, starting for an afternoon walk as of old. All seemed to look the same. Why was it not? Why could she not enter and be at home! Again she passed. A name on the door caught her eye. With a shudder of disgust and pain, she read—

"Uriah Fox."

"So the villain lives in the home of which he robbed us," she said bitterly. "The world seems made for such. Old Hannibal was right. God lumps the world, but the devil seems to look after his friends and prosper them."

She now hastened to the depot. The city had lost its attractions to her, in view of what she had seen and suffered that day, and though inclined to feel hard and resentful at her fate, she was sincerely thankful that she had a quiet home in the country from which at least the false-hearted and cruel could be kept away.

She saw during the day several faces that she knew, but none recognized her, and she realized how soon we are forgotten by our wide circle of friends, and how the world goes on just the same after we have vacated the large space we suppose we occupy.

She reached home in the twilight, weary and despondent. Her mother asked eagerly:

"Did you meet any one you knew?" as if this were the all-important question.

"Don't speak to me," said Edith impatiently. "I'm half dead with fatigue and trouble. Hannibal, please give me a cup of tea, and then I will go to bed."

"But, Edith," persisted Mrs. Allen querulously, "did you see any of our old set? I hope you didn't take the jewelry where you were known."

Edith's overtaxed nerves gave way, and she said sharply—

"No, I did not go where I was known, as I ought, and therefore have been robbed, and might have been in jail myself to-night. I will never follow your advice again. It has brought nothing but trouble and disaster. I have had enough of your silly pride and its results. What practical harm would it have done me, if I had met all the persons I know in the city? By going where I was not known I lost half my jewelry, and was insulted and threatened with great danger in the bargain. If I had gone to Tiffany's, or Ball and Black's, where I am known, I should have been treated politely and obtained the full value of what I offered. I can't even forgive myself for being such a fool. But I have done with your ridiculous false pride forever."

These were harsh words for a daughter to speak to her mother, under any provocation, and even Zell said:

"Edith, you ought to be ashamed of yourself to speak to mother so."

"I think so, too," said Laura. "I'm sure she meant everything for the best, and she took the course which is taken by the majority in like circumstances."

"All the worse for the majority then, if they fare anything as we have done. The division of labor in this family seems to be that I am to do all the work, and bear the brunt of everything, and the rest sit by and criticise, or make more trouble. You have all got to do something now or go hungry," and Edith swallowed her tea, and went frowningly away to her room. She was no saint, to begin with, and her overtaxed mind and body revenged themselves in nervous irritation. But her young and healthful nature soon found in sound sleep the needed restorative.

Mrs. Allen shed a few helpless tears, and Laura wearily watched the faint flicker on the hearth, for the night was chilly. Zell went into the dining-room and read for the twentieth time a letter received that day.

Unknown to Edith, the worst disaster yet had occurred in her absence. Zell had been to the village for the mail. She would not admit, even to herself, that she hoped for a letter from one who had acted so poor a part as her false lover, and yet, controlled so much more by her feelings and impulses than by either reason or principle, it was with a thrill of joy that she recognized the familiar handwriting. The next moment she dropped her veil to conceal her burning blush of shame. She hastened home with a wild tumult at heart.

"1 will read it, and see what he says for himself," she said, "and then will write a withering answer."

But as Van Dam's ardent words and plausible excuses burned themselves into her memory, her weak foolish heart relented, and she half believed he was wronged by Edith after all. The withering answer became a queer jumble of tender reproaches and pathetic appeals, and ended by saying that if he would marry her in her own home it all might be as secret as he desired, and she would wait his convenience for acknowledgment.

She also did another wrong and imprudent thing; for she told him to direct his reply to another office about a mile from Pushton, for she dreaded Edith's anger should her correspondence be discovered.

The wily, unscrupulous man gave one of his satanic leers as he read the letter.

"The game will soon be mine," he chuckled, and he wrote promptly in return:

"In your request and reproaches, I see the influence of another mind. Left to yourself you would not doubt me. And yet such is my love for you, I would comply with your request were it not for what passed that fatal evening. My feelings and honor as a man forbid my ever meeting your sister again till she has apologized. She never liked me, and always wronged me with doubts. Elliot acted like a fool and a villain, and I have nothing more to do with him. But your sister, in her anger and excitement, classed me with him. When you have been my loved and trusted wife for some length of time, I hope your family will do me justice. When you are here with me you will soon see why our marriage must be private for the present. You have known me since you were a child. I will be true to my word and will do exactly as I agreed. I will meet you any evening you wish on the down boat. Awaiting your reply with an anxiety which only the deepest love can inspire, I remain,

"Your slave, GUILLIAM VAN DAM."

Such was the false but plausible missive that was aimed as an arrow at poor little Zell. There was nothing in her training or education, and little in her character, to shield her. Moreover the increasing miseries of their situation were Van Dam's allies.

Edith rose the next morning greatly refreshed, and her naturally courageous nature rallied to meet the difficulties of their position. But in her strength, as was too often the case, she made too little allowance for the weakness of the others. She took the reins in her hand in a masterful and not merciful way, and dictated to the rest in a manner that they secretly resented.

The store wagon was a little earlier than usual that morning, and a note from Mr. Hard was handed in, stating that he had payments to make that day and would therefore request that his little account might be met. Two or three other persons brought up bills from the village, saying that for some reason or another the money was greatly needed. Tom Crowl's gossip was doing its legitimate work.

In the post-office Edith found all the other accounts against the family, with requests for payment, polite enough, but pressing.

She resolved to pay all she could, and went first to Mr. Hard's. That worthy citizen's eyes grew less stony as he saw half the amount of his bill on the counter. The rumor of Edith's visit to the city had reached even him, and he had his fears that collecting might involve some unpleasant business; but, however unpleasant it might be, Mr. Hard always collected.

"I hope our method of dealing has satisfied you, Miss Allen," he ventured politely.

"Oh, yes," said Edith dryly, "you have been very liberal and prompt with everything, especially your bill."

At this Mr. Hard's eyes grew quite pebbly, and he muttered something about its being the rule to settle monthly.

"Oh, certainly," said Edith, "and like most rules, no doubt, has many exceptions. Good-morning."

She also paid something on the other bills, and found that she had but a few dollars left. Though there was a certain sense of relief in the feeling that she now owed much less, still she looked with dismay on the small sum remaining. Where was more to come from? She had determined that she would not go to New York again to sell anything except in the direst extremity.

That evening Hannibal gave them a meagre supper, for Edith had told him of the absolute necessity of economy. There was a little grumbling over the fare. So Edith pushed her chair back, laid seven dollars on the table, saying:

"That's all the money I have in the world. Who's got any more?"

They raised ten dollars among them.

"Now," said Edith, "this is all we have. Where is more coming from?"

Helpless sighs and silence were her only answers.

"There is nothing clearer in the world," continued Edith, "than that we must earn money. What can we do?"

"I never thought I should have to work," said Laura piteously.

"But, my dear sister," said Edith earnestly, "isn't it

10—ROE—X

clear to you now that you must? You certainly don't expect me to earn enough to support you all. One pair of
hands can't do it, and it wouldn't be fair in the bargain.''

"Oh, certainly not," said Laura. "I will do anything
you say as well as I can, though, for the life of me, I don't
see what I can do."

"Nor I either," said Zell passionately. "I don't know
how to work. I never did anything useful in my life that
I know of. What right have parents to bring up girls in
this way, unless they make it a perfect certainty that they
will always be rich? Here we are as helpless as four children. We have not got enough to keep us from starving
more than a week at best. Just to think of it! Men are
speculating and risking all they have every day. Ever
since I was a child I have heard about the risks of business. I knew some people whose fathers failed, and they
went away, I don't know where, to suffer as we have perhaps, and yet girls are not taught to do a single thing by
which they can earn a penny if they need to. If anybody
will pay me for jabbering a little bad French and Italian,
and strumming a few operatic airs on the piano, I am at
their service. I think I also understand dressing, flirting,
and receiving compliments very well. I had a taste for
these things, and never had any special motive given me
for doing anything else. What becomes of all the girls thus
taught to be helpless, and then tossed out into the world to
sink or swim?"

"They find some self-sustaining work in it," said Edith.

"Not all of them, I guess," muttered Zell sullenly.

"Then they do worse, and had better starve," said Edith
sternly.

"You don't know anything about starving," retorted
Zell, bitterly. "I repeat, it's a burning shame to bring
girls up so that they don't know how to do anything, if
there's ever any possibility that they must. And it's a
worse shame that respect and encouragement are not given
to girls who earn a living. Mother says that if we become

working girls, not one of our old wealthy, fashionable set will have anything to do with us. What makes people act so silly? Any one of them on the avenue may be where we are in a year. I've no patience with the ways of the world. People don't help each other to be good, and don't help others up. Grown-up folks act like children. How parents can look forward to the barest chance of their children being poor, and bring them up as we were, I don't see. I'm no more fit to be poor than to be President."

Zell never before had said a word that reflected on her father, but in the light of events her criticism seemed so just that no one reproved her.

Mrs. Allen only sighed over her part of the implied blame. She had reached the hopeless stage of one lost in a foreign land, where the language is unknown and every sight and sound unfamiliar and bewildering. This weak fashionable woman, the costly product of an artificial luxurious life, seemed capable of being little better than a millstone around the necks of her children in this hour of their need. If there had been some innate strength and nobility in Mrs. Allen's character, it might have developed now into something worthy of respect under this sharp attrition of trouble, however perverted before. But where a precious stone will take lustre a pumice stone will crumble. There is a multitude of natures so weak to begin with that they need tonic treatment all through life. What must such become under the influence of enervating luxury, flattery, and uncurbed selfishness from childhood? Poor, faded, sighing, helpless Mrs. Allen, shivering before the trouble she had largely occasioned, is the answer.

Edith soon broke the forlorn silence that followed Zell's outburst by saying:

"All the blame doesn't rest on the parents. I might have improved my advantages far better. I might have so mastered the mere rudiments of an English education as to be able to teach little children, but I can scarcely remember a single thing now."

"I can remember one thing," interrupted Zell, who was fresh from her books, "that there was mighty little attention given to the rudiments, as you call them, in the fashionable schools to which I went. To give the outward airs and graces of a fine lady seemed their whole aim. Accomplishments, deportment were everything. The way I was hustled over the rudiments almost takes away my breath to remember, and I have as remote an idea of vulgar fractions as of how to do the vulgar work before us. I tell you the whole thing is a cruel farce. If girls are educated like butterflies, it ought to be made certain that they can live like butterflies."

"Well, then," continued Edith, "we ought to have perfected ourselves in some accomplishment. They are always in demand. See what some French and music teachers obtain."

"Nonsense," said Zell pettishly, "you know well enough that by the time we were sixteen our heads were so full of beaux, parties, and dress, that French and music were a bore. We went through the fashionable mills like the rest, and if father had continued worth a million or so, no one would have found fault with our education."

"We can't help the past now," said Edith after a moment, "but I am not so old yet but that I can choose some kind of work and so thoroughly master it that I can get the highest price paid for that form of labor. I wish it could be gardening, for I have no taste for the shut-up work of woman; sitting in a close room all day with a needle would be slow suicide to me."

"Gardening!" said Zell contemptuously. "You couldn't plow as well as that snuffy old fellow who scratched your garden about as deeply as a hen would have done it. A woman can't dig and hoe in the hot sun, that is, an American girl can't, and I don't think she ought."

"Nor I either," said Mrs. Allen, with some returning vitality. "The very idea is horrid."

"But plowing, digging, and hoeing are not all of gardening," said Edith with some irritation.

"I guess you would make a slim support by just snipping around among the rose-bushes," retorted Zell provokingly.

"That's always the way with you, Zell," said Edith sharply, "from one extreme to another. Well, what would you like to do?"

"If I had to work I would like housekeeping. That admits of great variety and activity. I wish I could open a summer boarding-house up here. Wouldn't I make it attractive!"

"Such black eyes and red cheeks certainly would—to the gentlemen," answered Edith satirically.

"They would be mere accessories. I think I could give to a boarding-house, that place of hash and harrowing discomfort, a dainty, homelike air. If father, when he risked a failure, had only put aside enough to set me up in a boarding-house, I should have been made."

"A boarding-house! What horror next?" sighed Mrs. Allen.

"Don't be alarmed, mother," said Zell bitterly. "We can scarcely start one of the forlornest hash species on ten dollars. I admit I would rather keep house for a good husband, and it seems to me I could soon learn to give him the perfection of a good home," and her eyes filled with wistful tears. Dashing them scornfully away, she added, "The idea of a woman loving a man, and letting his home be dependent on the cruel mercies of foreign servants! If it's a shame that girls are not taught to make a living if they need to, it's a worse shame that they are not taught to keep house. Half the brides I know of ought to have been arrested and imprisoned for obtaining property on false pretences. They had inveigled men into the vain expectation that they would make a home for them, when they no more knew how to make a home than a heaven. The best they can do is to go to one of those places so satirically called an 'intelligence office,' and import them into their elegant houses a small mob of quarrelsome, drunken,

dishonest foreigners, and then they and their husbands live
on such conditions as are permitted. I would be mistress
of my house, just as a man is master of his store or office,
and I would know thoroughly how work of all kinds was
done, and see that it was done thoroughly. If they wouldn't
do it, I'd discharge them. I am satisfied that our bad servants are the result of bad housekeepers more than anything
else."

"Poor little Zell!" said Edith, smiling sadly. "I hope
you will have a chance to put your theories into most happy
and successful practice."

"Little chance of it here in 'Bushtown,' as Hannibal
calls it," said Zell suddenly.

"Well," said Edith, in a kind of desperate tone, "we've
got to decide on something at once. I will suggest this.
Laura must take care of mother, and teach a few little children if she can get them. We will give up the parlor to her
at certain hours. I will put up a notice in the post-office
asking for such patronage, and perhaps we can put an advertisement in the Pushton Recorder, if it doesn't cost too
much. Zell, you must take the housekeeping mainly, for
which you have a taste, and help me with any sewing that
I can get. Hannibal will go into the garden and I will help
him there all I can. I shall go to the village to-morrow and
see if I can find anything to do that will bring in money."

There was a silent acquiescence in Edith's plan, for no
one had anything else to offer.

CHAPTER XVIII

IGNORANCE LOOKING FOR WORK

THE next day Edith went to the village, and frankly told Mr. Hard how they were situated, mentioning that the failure of their lawyer to sell the stock had suddenly placed them in this crippled condition.

Mr. Hard's eyes grew more pebbly as he listened. He ventured in a constrained voice as consolation:

"That he never had much faith in stocks—No, he had no employment for ladies in connection with his store. He simply bought and sold at a *small* advance. Miss Klip, the dressmaker, might have something."

To Miss Klip Edith went. Miss Klip, although an unprotected female, appeared to be a maiden that could take care of herself. One would scarcely venture to hinder her. Her cutting scissors seemed instinct with life, and one would get out of their way as naturally as from a railroad train. She gave Edith a sharp look through her spectacles and said abruptly in answer to her application:

"I thought you was rich."

"We were," said Edith sadly, "but we must work now and are willing to."

"What do you know about dressmaking and sewing?"

"Well, not a great deal, but I think you would find us very ready to learn."

"Oh, bless you, I can get all my work done by thorough hands, and at my own prices, too. Good-morning."

"But can you not tell me of some one who would be apt to have work?"

"There's Mrs. Glibe across the street. She has work sometimes. Most of the dressmakers around here are well trained, have machines, and go out by the day."

Edith's heart sank. What chance was there for her untaught hands among all these "trained workers."

She soon found that Mrs. Glibe was more inclined to talk (being as garrulous as Miss Klip was laconic) and to find out all about them than to help her to work. Making but little headway in Edith's confidence she at last said, "I give Rose Lacey all the work I have to spare and it isn't very much. The business is so cut up that none of us have much more than we can do except a short time in the busy season. Still, those of us who can give a nice fit and cut to advantage can make a good living after getting known. It takes time and training you know of course."

"But isn't there work of any kind that we can get in this place?" said Edith impatiently.

"Well, not that you'd be willing to do. Of course there's housecleaning and washing and some plain sewing, though that is mostly done on a machine. A good strong woman can always get day's work, except in winter, but you ain't one of that sort," she added, looking at Edith's delicate pink and white complexion and little white hands in which a scrubbing-brush would look incongruous.

"Isn't there any demand for fancy work?" asked Edith.

"Mighty little. People buy such things in the city. Money ain't so plenty in the country that people will spend much on that kind of thing. The ladies themselves make it at home and when they go out to tea."

"Oh, dear!" sighed Edith, as she plodded wearily homeward, "what can we do? Ignorance is as bad as crime."

Her main hope now for immediate necessities was that they might get some scholars. She had put up a notice in the post-office and an advertisement in the paper. She had also purchased some rudimentary school books, and the poor child, on her return home, soon distracted herself by a sudden plunge into vulgar fractions. She found herself so sadly rusty that she would have to study almost as hard as any of her pupils, were they obtained. Laura's bookish turn and better memory had kept her better informed. Edith soon threw aside grammars and arithmetics, saying to Laura:

"You must take care of the school, if we get one. It would take me too long to prepare on these things in our emergency."

Almost desperate from the feeling that there was nothing she could do, she took a hoe that was by no means light, and loosened the ground and cut off all the sprouting weeds around her strawberry-vines. The day was rather cool and cloudy, and she was surprised at the space she went over. She wore her broad-brimmed straw hat tied down over her face, and determined she would not look at the road, and would act as if it were not there, letting people think what they pleased. But a familiar rumble and rattle caused her to look shyly up after the wagon had passed, and she saw Arden Lacey gazing wonderingly back at her. She dropped her eyes instantly as if she had not seen him, and went on with her work. At last, thoroughly wearied, she went in and said half triumphantly, half defiantly:

"A woman can hoe. I've done it myself."

"A woman *can* ride a horse like a man," said Mrs. Allen, and this was all the home encouragement poor Edith received.

They had had but a light lunch at one o'clock, meaning to have a more substantial dinner at six. Hannibal was showing Zell and getting her started in her department. It was but a poor little dinner they had, and Zell said in place of dessert:

"Edith, we are most out of everything."

"And I can't get any work," said Edith despondingly. "People have got to know how to do things before anybody wants them, and we haven't time to learn."

"Ten dollars won't last long," said Zell recklessly.

"I will go down to the village and make further inqui-ries to-morrow," Edith continued in a weary tone. "It seems strange how people stand aloof from us. No one calls and everybody wants what we owe them right away. Are there not any good kind people in Pushton? I wish we had not offended the Laceys. They might have advised and helped us, but nothing would tempt me to go to them after treating them as we did."

There were plenty of good kind people in Pushton, but Mrs. Allen's "policy" had driven them away as far as pos-sible. By their course the Allens had placed themselves, in relation to all classes, in the most unapproachable posi-tion, and their "friends" from the city and Tom Crowl's gossip had made matters far worse. Poor Edith thought they were utterly ignored. She would have felt worse if she had known that every one was talking about them.

The next day Edith started on another unsuccessful ex-pedition to the village, and while she was gone, Zell went to the post-office to which she had told Van Dam to direct his reply. She found the plausible lie we have already placed before the reader.

At first she experienced a sensation of anger that he had not complied with her wish. It was a new experience to have gentlemen, especially Van Dam, so long her obsequi-ous slave, think of anything contrary to her wishes. She also feared that Edith might be right, and that Van Dam designed evil against her. She would not openly admit, even to herself, that this was his purpose, and yet Edith's words had been so clear and strong, and Van Dam's condi-tions placed her so entirely at his mercy, that she shrank from him and was fascinated at the same time.

But instead of indignantly casting the letter from her, she read it again and again. Her foolish heart pleaded for him.

"He couldn't be so false to me, so false to his written word," she said, and the letter was hidden away, and she passed into the dangerous stage of irresolution, where temptation is secretly dwelt upon. She hesitated, and, according to the proverb, the woman who does this is lost. Instead of indignantly casting temptation from her, she left her course open, to be decided somewhat by circumstances. She wilfully shut her eyes to the danger, and tried to believe, and did almost believe that her lover meant honestly by her.

And so the days passed, Edith vainly trying to find something to do, and working hard in her garden, which as yet brought no return. She was often very sad and despondent, and again very irritable. Laura's apathy only deepened, and she seemed like one not yet awakened from a dream of the past. Zell made some show of work, but after all left almost everything for Hannibal as before, and when Edith sharply chided her, she laughed recklessly and said:

"What's the use? If we are going to starve we might as well do so at once and have it over with."

"I won't starve," said Edith, almost fiercely. "There must be honest work somewhere in the world for one willing to do it, and I'm going to find it. At any rate, can raise food in my garden before long."

"I'm afraid we shall starve before your cabbages and carrots come to maturity, and we might as well as to try to live on such garbage. Supplies are running low, and, as you say, the money is nearly gone."

"Yes, and people won't trust us any more. Two or three declined to in the village to-day, and I felt too discouraged and ashamed to ask any further. For some reason people seem afraid of us. I see persons turn and look after me, and yet they avoid me. Two or three impudent clerks tried to make my acquaintance, but I snubbed them in such a way that they will let me alone hereafter. I wonder if any stories could have got around about us? Country towns are such places for gossip."

"Have you heard of any scholars?" said Laura languidly.

"No, not one," was Edith's despondent answer. "If nothing turns up before, I'll go to New York next Monday and sell some more things, and I'll go where I'm known this time."

Nothing turned up, and by Sunday they had nothing in the house save a little dry bread, which they ate moistened with wine and water. Mrs. Allen sighed and cried all day. Laura had the strange manner of one awaking up to something unrealized before. Restlessness began to take the place of apathy, and her eyes often sought the face of Edith in a questioning manner. Finding her alone in the garden, she said:

"Why, Edith, I'm hungry. I never remember being hungry before. Is it possible we have come to this?"

Edith burst into tears, and said brokenly:

"Come with me to the arbor."

"I'm sure I'm willing to do anything," said Laura piteously, "but I never realized we would come to this."

"Oh! how can the birds sing?" said Edith bitterly. "This beautiful spring weather, with its promise and hopefulness, seems a mockery. The sun is shining brightly, flowers are budding and blooming, and all the world seems so happy, but my heart aches as if it would burst. I'm hungry, too, and I know poor old Hannibal is faint, though he tries to keep up whenever I am around."

"But, Edith, if people knew how we are situated they would not let us want. Our old acquaintances in New York, or our relations even, though not very friendly, would surely help us."

"Oh, yes, I suppose so for a little while, but I can't bring myself to ask for charity, and no one would undertake to support us. What discourages me most is that I can't get work that will bring in money. Between people wishing to have nothing to do with us, on one hand, and my ignorance on the other, there seems no resource. Some of those whom we owe seem inclined to press us. I'm so afraid of losing this place and being out on the street. If I

could only get a chance somewhere, or get time to learn to
do something well!"

Then after a moment she asked suddenly, "Where's
Zell?"

"In her room, I think."

"I don't like Zell's manner," said Edith, after a brief
painful revery. "It's so hard and reckless. Something
seems to be on her mind. She has long fits of abstraction
as if she were thinking of something, or weighing some
plan. Could she have had any communication with that
villain Van Dam? Oh! that would be the bitterest drop
of all in our cup of sorrow. I would rather see her dead
than that."

"Oh, dear!" said Laura, "it seems as if I had been in a
trance and had just awakened. Why, Edith, I must do
something. It is not right to let you bear all these things
alone. But don't trouble about Zell, not one of George
Allen's daughters will sink to that."

CHAPTER XIX

A FALLING STAR

ZELL slept most of the day. She had reached that point where she did not want to think. On hearing Edith say that she would go to New York on Monday, a sudden and strong temptation assailed her. Impulsive, but not courageous, abounding in energy, but having little fortitude, she found the conditions of her country life growing unendurable. Van Dam seemed her only refuge, her only means of escape. She soon lost all hope of their sustaining themselves by work in Pushton. Her uncurbed nature could wait patiently for nothing, and as the long, idle days passed, she doubted, and then despaired, of any success from Edith's plans. She harbored Van Dam's temptation, and the consciousness of doing this hurt her womanly nature, and her hard, reckless tone and manner were the natural consequence. She said to herself, and tried to believe—

"He will marry me—he has promised again and again."

Still, there was the uneasy knowledge that she was placing herself and her reputation entirely at his mercy, and she long had known that Van Dam was no saint. It was this lurking knowledge, shut her eyes to it as she might, that acted on her nature like a petrifying influence.

And yet, Van Dam's temptation had more to contend with in her pride than in her moral nature. Everything in her education had tended to increase the former, and dwarf the latter. Her parents had taken her to the theatre far oftener than even to the fashionable church on the avenue.

From the latter she carried away more ideas about dress than about anything else. From a child she had been familiar with the French school of morals, as taught by the sensational drama in New York. Society, that will turn a poor girl out of doors the moment she sins, will take her at the most critical age of her unformed character, night after night, to witness plays in which the husband is made ridiculous, but the man who destroys purity and home-happiness is as splendid a villain as Milton's Satan. Mr. Allen himself had familiarized Zell's mind with just what she was tempted to do, by taking her to plays as poisonous to the soul as the malaria of the Campagna at Rome to the body. He, though dead, had a part in the present temptation of his child, and we unhesitatingly charge many parents with the absolute ruin of their children, by exposing them, and permitting them to be exposed, to influences that they know must be fatal. No guardian of a child can plead the densest stupidity for not knowing that French novels and plays are as demoralizing as the devil could wish them to be; and constantly to place young, passionate natures, just awakening in their uncurbed strength, under such influences, and expect them to remain as spotless as snow, is the most wretched absurdity of our day. Society brings fire to the tow, the brand to the powder, and then lifts its hand to hurl its anathema in case they ignite.

But Mr. Allen sinned even more grievously in permitting a man like Van Dam to haunt his home. If now one of the lambs of his flock suffered irretrievably, he would be as much to blame as a shepherd who daily saw the wolf within his fold. Mr. Allen was familiar with the stories about Van Dam, as multitudes of wealthy men are to-day with the character of well-dressed scoundrels who visit their daughters. Some of the worst villains in existence have the *entrée* into the "best society." It is pretty well known among men what they are, and fashionable mammas are not wholly in the dark. Therefore, every day, "angels that kept not their first estate" are falling from heaven. It may not be the open, disgraceful ruin that threatened poor Zell, but it is ruin nevertheless.

After all, it was the undermining, unhallowed influence of long association with Van Dam that now made Zell so weak in her first sharp stress of temptation. Crime was not awful and repulsive to her. There was little in her cunningly-perverted nature that revolted at it. She hesitated mainly on the ground of her pride, and in view of the consequences. And even these latter she in no sense realized, for the school in which she had been taught showed only the flowery opening of the path into sin, while its terrible retributions were kept hidden.

Therefore, as the miseries of her condition in the country increased, Zell's pride failed her, and she began to be willing to risk all to get away, and when she felt the pinch of hunger she became almost desperate. As we have said, on Edith's naming a day on which she would be absent on the forlorn mission that would only put off the day of utter want a little longer, the temptation took definite shape in Zell's mind to write at once to Van Dam, acceding to his shameful conditions.

But, to satisfy her conscience, which she could not stifle, and to provide some excuse for her action, and still more, to brace the hope she tried to cherish that he really meant truly by her, she wrote:

"If I will meet you at the boat Monday evening, will you surely marry me? Promise me on your sacred honor."

Van Dam muttered, with a low laugh, as he read the note:

"That's a rich joke, for her to accept such a proposition as mine, especially after all that has happened, and still prate of 'sacred honor.'"

But he unhesitatingly, promptly, and with many protestations assured her that he would, and at once prepared to carry out his part of the programme.

"What's the use of half-way lies?" he said, carelessly.

On Monday Edith again took the early train with the

valuables of which she designed to dispose. Zell had said indifferently:

"You may take anything I have left except my watch and chain."

But Laura had insisted on sending her watch, saying, "I really wish to do something, Edith. I've left all the burden on you too long."

Mrs. Allen sighed, and said, "Take anything you please."

So Edith carried away with her the means of fighting the wolf, hunger, from their doors a little longer. But if she had known that a more cruel enemy would despoil her home in her absence, she would rather have starved than gone.

Laura was reading to her mother when Zell put her head in at the door, saying:

"I am going for a short walk, and will be back soon."

She hastened to the office at which she had told Van Dam to address her, and found his reply. With feverish cheeks, and eyes in which glowed excitement rather than happiness, she read it as soon as she was alone on the road, and returned as quickly as possible. Her mind was in a wild tumult, but she would not allow herself one rational thought. She spent most of the day in her room preparing for her flight. But when she came down to see Hannibal about their meagre lunch, he said in some surprise and alarm:

"Oh, Miss Zell, how burnin' red your cheeks be! You'se got a ragin' feber, sure 'nuff. Go and lie right straight down, and I'se see to eberyting. I'se been to de willage and got some tea. A man guv it to me as a sample, and I told him we'se like our tea mighty strong, so you'se all hab a cup of tea to-day, and to-night Miss Edie'll come back wid a heap of money."

"Poor old Hannibal!" said Zell, with a sudden rush of tenderness. "I wish I were as good as you are."

"Lor bress you, Miss Zell, I isn't good. I'se kind of a heathen. But somehow I feels dat de Lord will bress me when I steals for you alls."

"Oh, Hannibal, I wish I was dead and out of the way! Then there would be one less to provide for."

"Dead and out of de way!" said Hannibal, half indignantly; "dat's jest how to get into de way. I'd be afeard of seein' your spook whenever I was alone. I had no comfort in New York arter Massa Allen died, and was mighty glad to get away even to Bushtown. And den Miss Edie and all would cry dar eyes out, and couldn't do nothin'. Folks is often more in de way arter dey's dead and gone dan when livin'. Seein' your sweet face around ebery day, honey, is a great help to ole Hannibal. It seems only yesterday it was a little baby face, and we was all pretty nigh crazy over you."

"I wish I had died then!" said Zell, passionately, and hurrying away.

"Poor chile, poor chile! she takes it mighty hard," said innocent Hannibal.

She kept her room during the afternoon, pleading that she did not feel well. It gave her pain to be with her mother and Laura, now that she purposed to leave them so abruptly, and she wished to see nothing that would shake her resolution to go as she had arranged. She wrote to Edith as follows:

"I am going, Edith, to meet Mr. Van Dam, as he told me. I cannot—I will not believe that he will prove false to me. I leave his letter, which I received to-day. Perhaps you never will forgive me at home; but whatever becomes of poor little Zell, she will not cease to love you all. I should only be a burden if I stayed. There will be one less to provide for, and I may be able to help you far more by going than staying. Don't follow me. I've made my venture, and chosen my lot.   ZELL."

As the long twilight was deepening, Hannibal, returning from the well with a pail of water, heard the gate-latch click, and, looking up, saw Zell hurrying out with hat and shawl on, and having the appearance of carrying something under her shawl. He felt a little surprise at first, but then Zell was so full of impulse, that he concluded:

"She's gwine to meet Miss Edie. We'se all a-lookin' and leanin' on Miss Edie, Lor bres her."

But Zell was going to perdition.

Little later the stage brought tired Edith home, but in better spirits than before, as she had realized a somewhat fair sum for what she had sold, and had been treated politely.

After taking off her things, she asked, "Where's Zell?"

"Lying down, I think," said Laura. "She complained of not feeling well this afternoon."

But Hannibal's anxious face in the door now caught her attention, and she joined him at once.

"Didn't you meet Miss Zell?" he asked in a whisper.

"Meet her? No," answered Edith, excitedly.

"Dat's quare. She went out with hat and shawl on a little while ago. P'raps she's come back, and gone upstairs again."

Trembling so she could hardly walk steadily, Edith hurried to her room, and there saw Zell's note. Tearing it open, she only read the first line, and then rushed down to her mother and Laura, sobbing:

"Zell's gone."

"Gone! Where?" they said, with dismayed faces.

Edith's only reply was to look suddenly at her watch, put on her hat, and dart out of the door. She saw that there were still ten minutes before the evening boat passed the Pushton landing, and remembered that it was sometimes delayed. There was a shorter road to the dock than the one through the village, and this she took, with flying feet, and a white but determined face. It would have been a terrible thing for Van Dam to have met her then. She seemed sustained by supernatural strength, and, walking and running by turns, made the mile and a half in an incredibly short space of time. As she reached the top of the hill above the landing, she saw the boat coming in to the dock. Though panting and almost spent, again she ran at the top of her speed. Half-way down she heard the plank ring out upon the wharf.

"Stop!" she called. But her parched lips uttered only a faint sound, like the cry of one in a dream.

A moment later, as she struggled desperately forward, there came, like the knell of hope, the command:

"All aboard!"

"Oh, wait, wait!" she again tried to call, but her tongue seemed paralyzed.

As she reached the commencement of the long dock, she saw the lines cast off. The great wheels gave a vigorous revolution, and the boat swept away.

She was too late. She staggered forward a few steps more, and then all her remaining strength went into one agonized cry:

"Zell!"

And she fell fainting on the dock.

Zell heard that cry, and recognized the voice. Taking her hand from Mr. Van Dam's arm, she covered her face in sudden remorseful weeping.

But it was too late.

She had left the shelter of home, and ventured out into the great pitiless world on nothing better than Van Dam's word. It was like walking a rotten plank out into the sea.

Zell was lost!

CHAPTER XX

DESOLATION

NOT only did Edith's bitter cry startle poor Zell, coming to her ear as a despairing recall from the battlements of heaven might have sounded to a falling angel, but Arden Lacey was as thoroughly aroused from his painful revery as if shaken by a giant hand. He had been down to meet the boat, with many others, and was sending off some little produce from their place. He had not noticed in the dusk the closely-veiled lady; indeed, he rarely noticed any one unless they spoke to him, and then gave but brief, surly attention. Only one had scanned Zell curiously, and that was Tom Crowl. With his quick eye for something wrong in human action, he was attracted by Zell's manner. He could not make out through her thick veil who she was, in the increasing darkness, but he saw that she was agitated, and that she looked eagerly for the coming of the boat, also landward, where the road came out on the dock, as if fearing or expecting something from that quarter. But when he saw her join Van Dam, he recognized his old bar-room acquaintance, and surmised that the lady was one of the Allen family. Possessing these links in the chain, he was ready for the next. Edith's presence and cry supplied this, and he chuckled exultantly:

"An elopement!" and ran in the direction of the sound.

But Arden was already at Edith's side, having reached her almost at a bound, and was gently lifting the unconscious girl, and regarding her with a tenderness only equalled by his helplessness and perplexity in not knowing what to do with her.

The first impulse of his great strength was to carry her directly to her home. But Edith was anything but ethereal, and long before he could have passed the mile and a half, he would have fainted under the burden, even though love nerved his arms. But while he stood in piteous irresolution, there came out from the crowd that had gathered round, a stout, middle-aged woman, who said, in a voice that not only betokened the utmost confidence in herself, but also the assurance that all the world had confidence in her:

"Here, give me the girl. What do you men-folks know about women?"

"I declare, it's Mrs. Groody from the hotel," ejaculated Tom Crowl, as this delightful drama (to him) went on from act to act.

"Standin' there and holdin' of her," continued Mrs. Groody, who was sometimes a little severe on both sexes, "won't bring her to, unless she fainted 'cause she wanted some one to hold her."

A general laugh greeted this implied satire, but Arden, between anger and desire to do something, was almost beside himself. He had the presence of mind to rush to the boat-house for a bucket of water, and when he arrived with it a man had also procured a lantern, which revealed to the curious onlookers who gathered round with craning necks the pale features of Edith Allen.

"By golly, but it's one of them Allen girls," said Tom Crowl, eagerly. "I see it all now. She's down to stop her sister, who's just run away with one of those city scamps that was up here awhile ago. I saw her join him and take his arm on the boat, but wasn't sure who she was then."

"Might know you was around, Tom Crowl," said Mrs. Groody. "There's never nothing wrong going on but you see it. You are worse than any old woman for gossip. Why don't you put on petticoats and go out to tea for a livin'?"

When the laugh ceased at Crowl's expense, he said:

"Don't you put on airs, Mrs. Groody; you are as glad to hear the news as any one. It's a pity you turned up and spoiled Mr. Lacey's part of the play, for, if this one is anything like her sister, she, perhaps, wanted to be held, as you—"

Tom's further utterance was effectually stopped by such a blow across his mouth, from Lacey's hand, as brought the blood profusely on the spot, and caused such disfigurement, for days after, that appropriate justice seemed visited on the offending region.

"Leave this dock," said Arden, sternly; "and if I trace any slander to you concerning this lady or myself, I will break every bone in your miserable body."

Crowl shrank off amid the jeers of the crowd, but on reaching a safe distance, said, "You will be sorry for this."

Arden paid no need to him, for Edith, under Mrs. Groody's treatment, gave signs of returning consciousness. She slowly opened her eyes, and turned them wonderingly around; then came a look of wild alarm, as she saw herself surrounded by strange bearded faces, that appeared both savage and grotesque in the flickering light of the lantern."

"O, Heaven! have mercy," she cried, faintly. "Where am I?"

"Among friends, I assure you, Miss Allen," said Arden, kneeling at her side.

"Mr. Lacey! and are you here?" said Edith, trying to rise. "You surely will protect me."

"Do not be afraid, Miss Allen. No one would harm you for the world; and Mrs. Groody is a good kind lady, and will see you safely home, I am sure."

Edith now became conscious that it was Mrs. Groody who was supporting her, and regained confidence, as she recognized the presence of a woman.

"Law bless you, child, you needn't be scared. You have only had a faint. I'll take care of you, as young Lacey says. Seems to me he's got wonderfully polite since last summer," she muttered to herself.

"But where am I?" asked Edith, with a bewildered air; "what has happened?"

"Oh, don't worry yourself; you'll soon be home and safe."

But the memory of it all suddenly came to Edith, and even by the lantern's light, Arden saw the sudden crimson pour into her face and neck. She gave one wild, depre- cating look around, and then buried her face in her hands as if to hide the look of scorn she expected to see on every face.

The first arrow aimed by Zell's great wrong already quivered in her heart.

"Don't you think you could walk a little now, just enough to get into the hack with me and go home?" asked the kind woman, in a soothing voice.

"Yes, yes," said Edith, eagerly; "let us get away at once." And with Mrs. Groody's and Arden's assistance, she was soon seated in the hack, and was glad to note that there was no other passenger. The ride was a comparatively silent one. Edith was too exhausted from her desperate struggle to reach the boat, and her heart was too bruised and sore, to permit on her part much more than monosyl- lables, in answer to Mrs. Groody's efforts at conversation. But as they stopped at the cottage her new friend said, cheerily:

"Don't take it so hard, my child; you ain't to blame. I'll stand by you if no one else will. It don't take me long to know a good honest girl when I see one, and I know you mean well. What's more, I've took a likin' to you, and I can be a pretty fair sort of friend if I do work for a livin'."

Mrs. Groody was good if not grammatical. She had broad shoulders, that had borne in their day many burdens—her own and others'. She had a strong, stout frame, in which thumped a large, kindly heart. She had long earned her bread by callings that brought her in contact with all classes, and had learned to know the world very thoroughly without becoming worldly or hardened. But she had a quick, sharp tongue, and could pay anybody off in his own coin with interest. Everybody soon found it to his advantage to keep on the right side of Mrs. Groody, and the old habitués of the hotel were as polite and deferential to her as if she were a duchess. She was one of those shrewd, strong, cheery people, who would make themselves snug, useful, and influential in a very short time, if set down anywhere on the face of the earth.

Such a woman readily surmised the nature of Edith's trouble, and knew well how deeply the shadow of Zell's disgrace would fall on the family. Edith's desperate effort to save her sister, her bitter humiliation and shrinking shame in view of the flight, all proved her to be worthy of respect and confidence herself. When Mrs. Groody saw that Edith lived in a little house, and was probably not in so high a social position as to resent her patronage, her big heart yearned in double sympathy over the poor girl, and she determined to help her in the struggle she knew to be before her; so she said, kindly:

"If you'll wait till a clumsy old body like me can get out, I'll see you safe into your home."

"Oh, no," said Edith, eagerly, following the strong instinct to keep a stranger from seeing herself, her mother, and Laura in the first hour of their shame. "You have been very kind, and I feel that I can never repay you."

"Bless you, child, I don't expect greenbacks for all I do. I want a little of the Lord's work to come to me, though I'm afraid I fell from grace long ago. But a body can't be pious in a hotel. There's so many aggravatin' people and things that you think swearin', if you darsn't say it out. But I'm a human sort of a heathen, after all, and I feel sorry for you. Now ain't there somethin' I can do for you?"

The driver stood with his lantern near the door, and its rays fell on Edith's pale face and large, tearful eyes, and she turned, and for the first time tried to see who this kind

woman was, that seemed to feel for her. Taking Mrs.
Groody's hands, she said, in a voice of tremulous pathos:

"God bless you for speaking to me at all. I didn't think
any one would again who knew. You ask if you can do
anything for me. If you'll only get me work, I'll bless
you every day of my life. No one on earth or in heaven
can help me, unless I get work. I'm almost desperate for
it, and I can't seem to find any that will bring us bread,
but I'll do any honest work, no matter what, and I'll take
whatever people are willing to give for it, till I can do
better." Edith spoke in a rapid manner, but in a tone that
went straight to the heart.

"Why, my poor child," said Mrs. Groody, wiping her
eyes, "you can't do work. You are pale as a ghost, and
you look like a delicate lady."

"What is there in this world for a delicate lady who has
no money but honest work?" asked Edith, in a tone that
was almost stern.

"I see that you are such a lady, and it seems that you
ought to find some lady-like work, if you must do it," said
Mrs. Groody, musingly.

"We have tried to get employment—almost any kind.
I can't think my sister would have taken her desperate
course if we could have obtained something to do. I know
she ought to have starved first. But we were not brought
up to work, and we can't do anything well enough to satisfy
people, and we haven't time to learn. Besides, before this
happened, for some reason people stood aloof from us, and
now it will be far worse. Oh, what shall we do? What
shall we do?" cried Edith, despairingly; and in her trouble
she seemed to turn her eyes away from Mrs. Groody, with
wild questioning of the future.

Her new acquaintance was sniffling and blowing her nose
in a manner that betokened serious internal commotion.
The driver, who would have hustled any ordinary passenger out quickly enough, waited Mrs. Groody's leisure
at a respectful distance. He knew her potential influence

at the hotel. At last the good woman found her voice, though it seemed a little husky:

"Lor' bless you, child! I ain't got a millstun for a heart, and if I had, you'd turn it into wax. If work's all you want, you shall have it. I'm housekeeper at the hotel. You come to me as soon as you are able, and we'll find something."

"Oh, thank you, thank you!" said Edith, fervidly.

"Is dat you, Miss Edie?" called Hannibal's anxious voice.

"Good-night, my dear," said Mrs. Groody, hastily. "Don't lose courage. I ain't on as good terms with the Lord as I ought to be. I seem too worried and busy to 'tend to religion; but I know enough about Him to be sure that He will take care of a poor child that wants to do right."

"I don't understand how God lets happen all that's happened to-day. The best I can believe is, that we are dealt with in a mass, and the poor human atoms are lost sight of. But I am indeed grateful for your kindness, and will come to-morrow and do anything I can. Good-by."

And the hack rumbled away, leaving her in the darkness, with Hannibal at the gate.

"Oh, Hannibal, Hannibal," was all that Edith could say.

"Is she done gone clean away?" asked Hannibal, in an awed whisper.

"Would to heaven she had never been born!" said Edith, bitterly. "Help me into the house, for I feel as if I should die."

Hannibal, trembling with fear himself, supported poor, exhausted Edith to a sofa, and then disappeared into the kitchen.

Mrs. Allen and Laura came and stood with white faces by Edith's languid, unnerved form.

There was no need of asking questions. She had returned alone, with her fresh young face looking old and drawn in its grief.

At last Mrs. Allen said, with bitter emphasis:

"She is no child of mine, from this day forth."

Then followed such a dreary silence that it might seem that Zell had died and was no more.

At last Hannibal bustled in, making a most desperate effort to keep up a poor show of courage and hope. He placed on a little table before Edith a steaming hot cup of tea, some toast, and wine, but the food was motioned away.

"It would choke me," said Edith.

Hannibal stood before her a moment, his quaint old visage working under the influence of emotion, almost beyond control. At last he managed to say:

"Miss Edie, we'se all a leanin' on you. We'se nothin' but vines a climbin' up de orange-bush. If you goes down, we all does. And now, Miss Edie, I'd swallow pison for you. Won't you take a cup o' tea for de sake of ole Hannibal? 'Cause your sweet face looks so pinched, honey, dat I feels dat my ole black heart's ready to bust;" and Hannibal, feeling that the limit of his restraint was reached, retreated precipitately to the kitchen.

The appeal, with its element of deep affection, was more needed by Edith in her half-paralyzed state than even the material refreshment. She sat up instantly, and drank the tea and wine, and ate a little of the toast. Then taking the cup and glass into the kitchen:

"There," she said, "see, I've drunk every drop. So don't worry about me any more, my poor old Hannibal, but go to bed, after your hard day's work."

But Hannibal would not venture out of his dark corner, but muttered, brokenly:

"Lor—bress—you—Miss Edie—you'se an angel—I'se be better soon—I'se got—de hiccups."

Edith thought it kindness to leave the old man to recover his self-control in his own time and way, so she said:

"Good-night, my faithful old friend. You're worth your weight in gold."

Meantime, Laura had helped Mrs. Allen to her room,

but now she came running down to Edith, with new trouble in her face, saying:

"Mother's crying so, I can't do anything with her."

At first Mrs. Allen's heart seemed hardened against her erring child, but on reaching her room she stood a few moments irresolutely, then went to a drawer, took out an old faded picture-case and opened it. From it Zell smiled out upon her, a little, dimpled baby. Then, as if by a sudden impulse rare to her, she pressed her lips against the unconscious face, and threw herself into her low chair, sobbing so violently that Laura became alarmed.

Even in that arid place, Mrs. Allen's heart, there appeared a little oasis of mother love, as this last and bitterest sorrow pierced its lowest depths. She might cast out from her affection the grown, sinning daughter, but not the baby that once slept upon her breast.

As Edith came and took her hand she said, brokenly:

"It seems—but yesterday—that she was—a wee black-eyed—little thing—in my arms—and your father—came—and looked at her—so proudly—tenderly—"

"Would to heaven she had died then!" said Edith, sternly.

"It would have been better if we had all died then," said Mrs. Allen drearily, and becoming quiet.

Edith's words fell like a chill upon her unwontedly stirred heart, and old habits of feeling and action resumed sway.

With Mrs. Allen's words ended the miserable day of Zell's flight. Hannibal's words were true. Zell, in her unnatural absence, would be more in the way—a heavier burden—than if she had become a helpless invalid upon their hands.

CHAPTER XXI

EDITH'S TRUE KNIGHT

THE next morning Edith was too ill to rise. She had become chilled after her extraordinary exertion of the previous evening, and a severe cold was the consequence; and this, with the nervous prostration of an over-taxed system, made her appear more seriously indisposed than she really was. For the sake of her mother and Laura, she wished to be present at the meagre little breakfast which her economy now permitted, but found it impossible; and later in the day her mind seemed disposed to wander.

Mrs. Allen and Laura were terror-stricken at this new trouble. As Hannibal had said, they were all leaning on Edith. They had lost confidence in themselves, and now hoped nothing from the outside world. They had scarcely the shadow of an expectation that Van Dam would marry Zell, and therefore they knew that worse than work would separate them from all old connections, and they had learned to hope nothing from the people of Pushton. Poor, feverish, wandering Edith seemed the only one who could keep them from falling into the abyss of utter want. They instinctively felt that total wreck was impossible as long as she kept her hand upon the helm; but now they had all the wild alarm of those who are drifting helplessly toward a reef, with a deep and stormy sea on either side of it. Thus to the natural anxiety of affection was added sickening fear.

Poor old Hannibal had no fear for himself. His devo-

tion to Edith reminded one of a faithful dog; it was so
strong, instinctive, unreasoning. He realized vaguely that
his whole existence depended on Edith's getting well, and
yet we doubt whether he thought of himself any more than
the Newfoundland, who watches beside the bed, and then
beside the grave of a loved master, till famine, that form of
pain which humanity cannot endure, robs him of life.

"We must have a physician immediately," said Laura,
with white lips.

"Oh, no," murmured Edith; "we can't afford it."

"We must," said Laura, with a sudden rush of tears.
"Everything depends on you."

Hannibal, who heard this brief dialogue, went silently
downstairs, and at once started in quest of Arden Lacey.

"If he is quar, he seemed kind o' human; and I'se
believe he'll help us now."

Arden was on the way to the barn, having just finished
a farmer's twelve o'clock dinner, when Hannibal entered
the yard. An angel of light could not have been more
welcome than this dusky messenger, for he came from the
centre of all light and hope to poor Arden. Then a feeling
of alarm took possession of him. Had anything happened
to Edith? He had seen her shrinking shame. Had it led
her to—and he shuddered at the thought his wild imagination suggested. It was almost a relief when Hannibal
said:

"Oh, Mr. Lacey, I'se sure from de way you acted when
we fust come, dat you can feel for people in trouble. Miss
Edie's berry sick, and I don't know whar to go for a doctor, and she won't have any; but she mus, and right away.
Den again, I oughter not leave, for dey's all nearly dead
with trouble and cryin'."

"You are a good, faithful fellow," said Arden, heartily.
"Go back and do all you can for Miss Edith, and I'll bring
a doctor myself, and much quicker too than you could."

Before Hannibal reached home, Arden galloped past
him, and the old man chuckled:

"De drunken Laceys' mighty good neighbors when dey's sober."

As may well be imagined, recent events, as far as he understood them, had stirred Arden's sensitive nature to the very depths. Hiding his feelings from all save his mother, and often from her; appearing to his neighbors stolid and sullen in the extreme, he was, in fact, in his whole being, like a morbidly-excited nerve. He did not shrink from the world because indifferent to it, but because it wounded him when he came in contact with it. He seemed so out of tune with society that it produced only jarring discord. His father's course brought him many real slights, and these he resented as we have seen, and he resented fancied slights quite as often, and thus he had cut himself off from the sympathies, and even the recognition, of nearly all.

But what human soul can dwell alone? The true hermit finds in communion with the Divine mind the perfection of companionship. But Arden knew not God. He had heard of Him all his life; but Jove and Thor were images more familiar to his mind than that of his Creator. He loved his mother and sister, but their life seemed a poor, shaded little nook, where they toiled and moped. And so, to satisfy the cravings of his lonely heart, he had created and peopled an unreal world of his own, in which he dwelt most of the time. As his interest in the real world ceased, his imagination more vividly portrayed the shadowy one, till at last, in the scenes of poetry and fiction, and the splendid panorama of history, he thought he might rest satisfied, and find all the society he needed in converse with those whom, by a refinement of spiritualism, he could summon to his side from any age or land. He secretly exulted in the still greater magic by which the unreal creatures of poetic thought would come at his volition, and he often smiled to think how royally attended was "old, drunken Lacey's" son, whom many of the neighbors thought scarcely better than the horses he drove.

Thus he lived under a spell of the past, in a world moon-lighted by sentiment and fancy, surrounded by his ideals of those about whom he read, and Shakespeare's vivid, life-like women were better known to him than any of the ladies of Pushton. But dreams cannot last in our material world, and ghosts vanish in the sunlight of fact. Woman's nature is as beautiful and fascinating now as when the master-hand of the world's greatest poet delineated it, and when living, breathing Edith Allen stepped suddenly among his shadows, seemingly so luminous, they vanished before her, as the stars pale into nothingness when the eastern sky is aglow with morning. Now, in all his horizon, she only shone, but the past seemed like night, and the present, day.

The circumstances under which he had met Edith had, in brief time, done more to acquaint him with her than years might have accomplished, and for the first time in his life he saw a superior girl with the distorting medium of his prejudice pushed aside. Therefore she was a sudden beauti-ful revelation to him, as vivid as unexpected. He did not believe any such being existed, and indeed there did not, if we consider into what he came to idealize Edith. But a better Edith really lived than the unnatural paragon that he pictured to himself, and the reality was capable of a vast improvement, though not in the direction that his morbid mind would have indicated.

The treatment of his sister, the sudden ceasing of all intercourse, and the appearance of Gus Elliot upon the scene, had cruelly wounded his fair ideal, but with a lover's faith and a poet's fancy he soon repaired the rav-ages of facts. He assured himself that Edith did not know the character of the men who visited her house.

Then came Crowl's gossip, the knowledge of her pov-erty, and her wretched errands to New York to dispose of the relics of the happy past. He gathered from such obser-vations as he could maintain without being suspected, by every crumb of gossip that he could pick up (for once he listened to gossip as if it were gospel), that they were in trouble, that Edith was looking for work, and that she was

so superior to the rest of the family that they now all de-
ferred to her and leaned upon her.   Then, to his deep satisfaction, he had seen Elliot, the morning after his scathing
repulse, going to the train, and looking forlorn and sadly
out of humor, and he was quite sure he had not been near
the little cottage since.   Arden needed but little fact upon
which to rear a wondrous superstructure, and here seemed
much, and all in Edith's favor, and he longed with an intensity beyond language to do something to help her.

Then came the tragedy of Zell's flight, Edith's heroic
and almost superhuman effort to save her, now followed by
her pathetic weakness and suffering, and no knight in the
romantic age of chivalry ever more wholly and loyally devoted himself to the high-born lady of his choice, than did
Arden to the poor sick girl at whom the finger of scorn
would now be generally pointed in Pushton.

To come back to our hero, galloping away on his old
farm horse to find a country doctor, may seem a short step
down from the sublime.   And so, perhaps, it may be to
those whose ideal of the sublime is only in outward and
material things.   But to those who look past these things
to the passionate human heart, the same in every age, it
will be evident that Arden was animated by the same spirit
with which he would have sought and fought the traditional
dragon.

Dr. Neak, a new-comer who was gaining some little
name for skill and success, and was making the most of it,
was at home; but on Arden's hurried application, ahemmed,
hesitated, colored a little, and at last said:

"Look here, Mr. —— (I beg your pardon, I've not the
pleasure of knowing your name), I'm a comparative stranger
in Pushton, and am just gaining some little reputation among
the better classes.   I would rather not compromise myself
by attendance upon that family.   If you can't get any one
else, and the girl is suffering, of course I'll try and go,
but—"

"Enough," interrupted Arden, starting up blazing with

wrath. "You should spell your name with an S. I want
a man as well as a physician," and, with a look of utter
contempt, he hastened away, leaving the medical man somewhat anxious, not about Edith, but whether he had taken
the best course in view of his growing reputation.

Arden next traced out Dr. Blunt, who readily promised
to come. He attended all alike, and charged roundly also.

"Business is business," was his motto. "People who
employ me must expect to pay. After all, I'm the cheap-
est man in the place, for I tell my patients the truth, and
cure them as quickly as possible."

Arden's urgency soon brought him to Edith's side, and
his practiced eye saw no serious cause for alarm, and having heard more fully the circumstances, he said:

"She will be well in a few days if she is kept very quiet,
and nothing new sets in. Of course she would be sick after
last night. One might as well put his hand in the fire and
not expect it to burn him, as to get very warm and then
cool off suddenly and not expect to be ill. Her pulse in-
dicates general depression of her system, and need of rest.
That's all."

After prescribing remedies and a tonic, he said, "Let
me know if I am needed again," and departed in rather ill-
humor.

Meeting Arden's anxious, questioning face at the gate,
he said gruffly:

"I thought from what you said the girl was dying.
Used up and a bad cold, that's all. Somewhat feverish
yourself, ain't you?" he added meaningly.

Though Arden colored under the doctor's satire, he was
chiefly conscious of a great relief that his idol was not in
danger. His only reply was the sullen, impassive expression he usually turned toward the world.

As the doctor rode away, Hannibal joined him, saying:

"Mr. Lacey, you'se a friend in need, and if you only
knowed what an angel you'se servin', you wouldn't look
so cross."

"Do I look cross?" asked Arden, his face becoming friendly in a moment. "Well, it wasn't with you, still less with Miss Edith; for even you cannot serve her more gladly than I will. That old doctor r'iled me a little, though I can forgive him, since he says she is not seriously ill."

"I'se glad you feels your privileges," said Hannibal, with some dignity. "I'se knowed Miss Edie eber since she was a baby, and when we lived on de avenue, de biggest and beautifullest in de city come to our house, but none of 'em could compare wid my young lady. I don't care what folks say, she's jes as good now, if she be poor, and her sister hab run away, poor chile. De world don't know all;" and old Hannibal shook his white head sadly and reproachfully.

This panegyric found strong echo in Arden's heart, but his habit of reticence and his sensitive shrinking from any display of feeling permitted him only to say, "I am sure every word you say is more than true, and you will do me a great favor when you let me know how I can serve Miss Edith."

Hannibal saw that he need waste no more ammunition on Arden, so he pulled out the prescriptions, and said:

"The doctor guv me dese, but, Lor bress you, my ole jints is stiff, and I'd be a week in gittin' down and back from de willage."

"That's enough," interrupted Arden. "You shall have the medicines in half an hour;" and he kept his word.

"He is quar," muttered Hannibal, looking after him. "Neber saw a man so 'bligin'. Folks say winegar ain't nothin' to him, but he seems sweet on Miss Edie, sure 'nuff. What 'ud he say, 'You'se do me great favor to tell me how I can serve Miss Edie'? I'se hope it'll last," chuckled Hannibal, retiring to his domain in the kitchen, " 'cause I'se gwine to do him a heap ob favors."

CHAPTER XXII

A MYSTERY

AT Arden's request his mother called in the evening, and also Mrs. Groody, from the hotel. Hannibal met them, and stated the doctor's orders. Mrs. Allen and Laura did not feel equal to facing any one. Though the old servant was excessively polite, the callers felt rather slighted that they saw no member of the family. They went away a little chilled in consequence, and contented themselves thereafter by sending a few delicacies and inquiring how Edith was.

"If you have any self-respect at all," said Rose Lacey to her mother, "you will not go there again till you are invited. It's rather too great a condescension for you to go at all, after what has happened."

Arden listened with a black look, and asked, rather sharply:

"Will you never learn to distinguish between Miss Edith and the others?"

"Yes," said Rose, dryly, "when she gives me a chance."

The doctor's view of Edith's case was correct. Her vigorous and elastic constitution soon rallied from the shock it had received. Hannibal had sent to the village for nutritious diet, which he knew so well how to prepare, and, after a few days, she was quite herself again. But with returning strength came also a sense of shame, anxiety, and a torturing dread of the future. The money accruing from her last sale of jewelry would not pay the debts resting on them now, and she could not hope to earn enough to pay the balance remain-

ing, in addition to their support. Her mother suggested
the mortgaging of her place. She had at first repelled the
idea, but at last entertained it reluctantly. There seemed
no other resource. It would put off the evil day of utter
want, and might give her time to learn something by which
she could compete with trained workers.

Then there was the garden. Might not that and the orchard, in time, help them out of their troubles?

As the long hours of her convalescence passed, she sat
at her window and scanned the little spot with a wistfulness
that might have been given to one of Eden-like proportions.
She was astonished to see how her strawberries had improved
since she hoed them, but noted in dismay that both they and
the rest of the garden were growing very weedy.

When the full knowledge of their poverty and danger
dawned upon her, she felt that it would not be right for
Malcom to come any more. At the same time she could
not explain things to him; so she sent a written request
through the mail for his bill, telling him not to come any
more. This action, following the evening when Gus Elliot
had surprised her in the garden, perplexed and rather net-
tled Malcom, who was, to use his own expression, "a bit
tetchy." Their money had grown so scarce that Edith
could not pay the bill, and she was ashamed to go to see
him till there was some prospect of her doing so. Thus
Malcom, though disposed to be very friendly, was lost to
her at this critical time, and her garden suffered accord-
ingly. She and Hannibal had done what they could, but
of late her illness, and the great accession of duties resting
on the old servant, had caused complete neglect in her little
plantation of fruit and vegetables. Thus, while all her
crops were growing well, the weeds were gaining on them,
and even Edith knew that the vigor of evil was in them,
and that, unchecked, they would soon make a tangled
swamp of that one little place of hope. She could not ask
Hannibal to work there now, for he was overburdened already. Laura seemed so feeble and crushed that her strength

was scarcely equal to taking care of her mother, and the few lighter duties of housework. Therefore, though the June sunshine rested on the little garden, and all nature seemed in the rapture of its early summer life, poor, practical Edith saw only the pestiferous weeds that threatened to destroy her one slender prospect of escape from environing difficulties. At last she turned away. To the sad and suffering, scenes most full of cheer and beauty often seem the most painful mockery.

She brooded over her affairs most of the day, dwelling specially on the suggestion of a mortgage. She felt extreme reluctance in perilling her home. Then again she said to herself, "It will at least give me time, and perhaps the place will be sold for debt, for we must live."

The next morning she slept late, her weary, overtaxed frame asserting its need. But she rose greatly refreshed, and it seemed that her strength had come back. With returning vigor hopefulness revived. She felt some cessation of the weary, aching sorrow at her heart. The world is phosphorescent to the eyes of youth, and even ingulfing waves of misfortune will sometimes gleam with sudden brightness.

The morning light also brought Edith a pleasant surprise, for, as she was dressing, her eyes eagerly sought the strawberry-bed. She had been thinking, "If I only continue to gain in this style, I shall soon be able myself to attack the weeds." Therefore, instead of a helpless look, such as she gave yesterday, her glance had something vengeful and threatening in it. But the moment she opened the lattice, so that she could see, an exclamation came from her lips, and she threw back the blinds, in order that there might be no mistake as to the wonder that startled her. What magic had transformed the little place since, in the twilight of the previous evening, she had given the last discouraged look in that direction? There was scarcely a weed to be seen in the strawberry-bed. They had not only been cut off, but raked away, and here and there she could see a berry reddening in the morning sun. In addition, some of her most important vegetables, and her prettiest flower border, had been cleaned and nicely dressed. A long row of Dan O'Rourk peas, that had commenced to sprawl on the ground, was now hedged in by brush; and, better still, thirty cedar poles stood tall and straight among her Lima beans, whose long slender shoots had been vainly feeling round for a support the last few days. Her first impulse was to clap her hands with delight and exclaim:

"How, in the name of wonder, could he do it all in a night! Oh, Malcom, you are a canny Scotchman, but you put the 'black art' to very white uses."

She dressed in excited haste, meaning to question Hannibal, but, as she left her room, Laura met her, and said, in a tone of the deepest despondency—

"Mother seems very ill. She has not felt like herself since that dreadful night, but we did not like to tell you, fearing it would put back your recovery."

The rift in the heavy clouds, through which the sun had gleamed for a moment, now closed, and a deeper gloom seemed to gather round them. In sudden revulsion Edith said, bitterly:

"Are we to be persecuted to the end? Cannot the heavy hand of misfortune be lifted a moment?"

She found her mother suffering from a low, nervous fever, and quite delirious.

Hannibal was at once despatched for the doctor, who, having examined Mrs. Allen's symptoms, shook his head, saying:

"Nothing but good nursing will bring her through this."

Edith's heart sank like lead. What prospect was there for work now, even if Mrs. Groody gave it to her, as she had promised? She saw nothing before her but the part of a weary watcher, for perhaps several weeks. She hesitated no longer, but resolved to mortgage her place at once. Her mother must have delicacies and good attendance, and she must have time to extricate herself from the difficulties into

which she had been brought by false steps at the beginning.
Therefore she told Hannibal to give her an early lunch,
after which she would walk to the village.

"You isn't able," said he earnestly.

"Oh, yes I am," she replied; "better able than to stay
at home and worry. I must have something settled, and
my mind at rest, even for a little while, or I shall go distracted." Then she added, "Did you see Malcom here early
this morning?"

"No, Miss Edie, he hasn't been here."

"Go look at the garden."

He returned with eyes dilated in wonder, and asked
quickly, "Miss Edie, when was all dat done?"

"Between dark last night and when I got up this morning. It seems like magic, don't it? But of course it is
Malcom's work. I only wish I could see him."

But Hannibal shook his head ominously and said with
emphasis, "Dat little Scotchman couldn't scratch around
like dat, even if de debil was arter him. 'Tain't his work."

"Why, whose else could it be?" asked Edith, sipping
a strong cup of coffee, with which she was fortifying herself
for the walk.

Hannibal only shook his head with a very troubled
expression, but at last he ventured:

"If 'tis a spook, I hope it won't do nothin' wuss to us."

Even across Edith's pale face a wan smile flitted at this
solution of the mystery, and she said:

"Why, Hannibal, you foolish old fellow! The idea of a
ghost hoeing a strawberry-bed and sticking in bean-poles!"

But Hannibal's superstitious nature was deeply stirred.
He had been under a severe strain himself of late, and the
succession of sorrows and strange experiences was telling
on him as well as on the others. He could not indulge in
a nervous fever, like Mrs. Allen, but he had reached that
stage when he could easily see visions, and tremble before
the slightest vestige of the supernatural. So he replied a
little doggedly:

"Spooks does a heap ob quar tings, Miss Edie. I'd tink it was Massa Allen, ony I knows dat he neber hab a hoe in his hand all his life. I doesn't like it. I'd radder hab de weeds."

"O Hannibal, Hannibal! I couldn't believe it of you. I'll go and see Malcom, just to satisfy you."

CHAPTER XXIII

A DANGEROUS STEP

EDITH took her deed, and went first to Mr. Hard. There were both coldness and curiosity in his manner, but he could gather little from Edith's face through her thick veil.

She had a painful shrinking from meeting people again after what had happened, and this was greatly increased by the curious and significant looks she saw turned toward her as soon as it was surmised who she was.

Mr. Hard promptly declined to lend any money. He "never did such things," he said.

"Where would I be apt to get it?" asked Edith, despondently.

"I scarcely know. Money is scarce, and people don't like to lend it on country mortgages, especially when there may be trouble. Lawyer Keen might give you some information."

To his office Edith went, with slow, heavy steps, and presented her case.

Mr. Keen was a red-faced, burly-looking man, hiding the traditional shrewdness of a village lawyer under a bluff, outspoken manner. He had a sort of good-nature, which, though not lending him to help others who were in trouble, kept him from trying to get them into more trouble, and he quite prided himself on this. He heard Edith partly through, and then interrupted her, saying:

"Couldn't think of it, miss. Widows, orphans, and

churches are institutions on which a fellow can never foreclose. I'll give you good advice, and won't charge you
anything for it. You had better keep out of debt."

"But I must have the money," said Edith.

"Then you have come to the wrong shop for it," replied
the lawyer, coolly. "Here's Crowl, now, he lends where
I wouldn't. He's got money of his own, while I invest
mainly for other people."

Edith's attention was thus directed to another red-faced
man, whom, thus far, she had scarcely noticed, though he
had been watching her with the closest scrutiny. He was
quite corpulent, past middle age, and not much taller than
herself. He was quite bald, and had what seemed a black
moustache, but Edith's quick eye noted that it was unskil-
fully dyed. There seemed a wide expanse in his heavy,
flabby cheeks, and the rather puggish nose appeared insig-
nificant between them. A slight tobacco stain in one corner of his mouth did not increase his attractions to Edith,
and she positively shrank from the expression of his small,
cunning black eyes. He was dressed both showily and
shabbily, and a great breastpin was like a blotch upon his
rumpled shirt-bosom.

"Let me see your deed, my dear," he said, with coarse
familiarity.

"My name is Miss Allen," replied Edith, with dignity.

The man paid little heed to her rebuke, but looked over
the deed with slow and microscopic scrutiny. At last he
said to Edith, whom nothing but dire necessity impelled to
have dealings with so disagreeable a person:

"Will you come with me to my office?"

Reluctantly she followed. At first she had a strong im-
pluse to have nothing to do with him, but then she thought,
"It makes no difference of whom I borrow the money, for
it must be paid in any case, and perhaps I can't get it anywhere else."

"Are you sure there is no other mortgage?" he
asked.

"Yes," replied Edith.

"How much do you want?"

"I will try to make four hundred answer."

"I suppose you know how hard it is to borrow money now," said Mr. Crowl, in a depressing manner, "especially in cases like this. I don't believe you'd get a dollar anywhere else in town. Even where everything is good and promising, we usually get a bonus on such a loan. The best I could do would be to let you have three hundred and sixty on such a mortgage."

"Then give me my deed. The security is good, and I'm not willing to pay more than seven per cent."

Old Crowl looked a moment at her resolute face, beautiful even in its pallor and pain, and a new thought seemed to strike him.

"Well, well," said he, with an awkward show of gallantry, "one can't do business with a pretty girl as with a man. You shall make your own terms."

"I wish to make no terms whatever," said Edith, frigidly. "I only expect what is right and just."

"And I'm the man that'll do what's right and just when appealed to by the fair unfortunate," said Mr. Crowl, with a wave of his hand.

Edith's only response to this sentiment was a frown, and an impatient tapping of the floor with her foot.

"Now, see how I trust you," he continued, filling out a check. "There is the money. I'll draw up the papers, and you may sign them at your leisure. Only just put your name to this receipt, which gives the nature of our transaction;" and, in a scrawling hand, he soon stated the case.

It was with strong misgivings that Edith took the money and gave her signature, but she did not see what else to do, and she was already very weary.

"You may call again the first time you are in the village, and by that time I'll have things fixed up. You see now what it is to have a friend in need."

Edith's only reply was a bow, and she hastened to the bank. The cashier looked curiously at her, and as he saw Crowl's check, smiled a little significant smile which she did not like; but, at her request, he placed the amount, and what was left from the second sale of jewelry, to her credit, and gave her a small check-book.

CHAPTER XXIV

SCORN AND KINDNESS

THOUGH her strength hardly seemed equal to it, she determined to go and see Malcom, for she felt very grateful to him. And yet the little time she had been in the village made her fear to speak to him or any one again, and she almost felt that she would like to shrink into some hidden place and die.

Quiet, respectable Pushton had been dreadfully scandalized by Zell's elopement with a man who by one brief visit had gained such bad notoriety. Those who had stood aloof, surmised, and doubted about the Allens before, now said, triumphantly, "I told you so." Good, kind, Christian people were deeply pained that such a thing could have happened; and it came to be the general opinion that the Allens were anything but an acquisition to the neighborhood.

"If they are going to bring that style of men here, the sooner they move away the better," was a frequent remark. All save the "baser sort" shrank from having much to do with them, and again Edith was insulted by the bold advances of some brazen clerks and shop-boys as she passed along. She also saw significant glances and whisperings, and once or twice detected a pointing finger.

With cheeks burning with shame and knees trembling with weakness, she reached Malcom's gate, to which she clung panting for a moment, and then passed in. The little man had his coat off, and, stooping in his strawberry-bed, he did look very small indeed. Edith approached quite near before he noticed her. He suddenly straightened himself up almost as a jumping-jack might, and gave her a

sharp, surprised look. He had heard the gossip in several
distorted forms, but what hurt him most was that she did
not come or send to him. But when he saw her standing
before him with her head bent down like a moss-rosebud
wilting in the sun, when he met her timid, deprecating
glance, his soft heart relented instantly, and coming toward
her he said:

"An' ha' ye coom to see ould Malcom at last? What
ha' I dune that I suld be sae forgotten?"

"You were not forgotten, Mr. McTrump. God knows
that I have too few friends to forget the best of them,"
answered Edith, in a voice of tremulous pathos.

After that Malcom was wax in her hands, and with
moistened eyes he stood gazing at her in undisguised
admiration.

"I have been through deep trouble, Mr. McTrump,"
continued she, "and perhaps you, like so many others, may
think me not fit to speak to you any more. Besides, I have
been very sick, and really ought not to be out to-day. Indeed I feel very weak. Isn't there some place where I could
sit down?"

"Now God forgie me for an uncoo Highlander," cried
Malcom, springing forward, "to think that I suld let ye
ston there, like a tall, white, swayin' calla lily, in the rough
wind. Take me arm till I support ye to the best room
o' me house."

Edith did take and cling to it with the feeling of one
ready to fall.

"Oh, Mr. McTrump, you are too kind," she murmured.

"Why suld I not be kind?" he said, heartily, "when I
see ye nipt by the wourld's unkindness? Why suld I not
be kind? Is the rose there to blame because a weed has
grown alongside? Ye could na help it that the wild bird
flitted, and I heerd how ye roon like a brave lassie to stop
her. But the evil wourld is quick to see the bad and slow
to see the gude." And Malcom escorted her like a "leddy
o' high degree" to his little parlor, and there she told him

and his wife all her trouble, and Malcom seemed afflicted with a sudden cold in his head. Then Mrs. McTrump bustled in and out in a breezy eagerness to make her comfortable.

"Ye're a stranger in our toon," she said, "and sae I was once mysel, an' I ken how ye feel."

"An' the Gude Book, which I hope ye read," added the gallant Malcom, "says hoo in entertainin' a stranger ye may ha' an angel aroond."

"Oh, Mr. McTrump," said Edith, with peony-like face, "Hannibal is the only one who calls me that, and he doesn't know any better."

"Why suld he know ony better?" responded Malcom quickly. "I ha' never seen an angel, na mair than I ha' seen a goolden harp, but I'm a thinkin' a modest bonny lassie like yoursel cooms as near to ane as anything can in this world."

"But, Mr. McTrump," said Edith, with a half-pathetic, half-comic face, "I am in such deep trouble that I shall soon grow old and wrinkled, so I shall not be an angel long."

"Na, na, dinna say that," said Malcom earnestly. "An ye will, ye may keepit the angel a-growin' within ye alway, though ye live as old as Methuselah. D'ye see this wee brown seed? There's a mornin'-glory vine hidden in it, as would daze your een at the peep o' day wi' its gay blossoms. An' ye see my ould gudewife there? Ah, she will daze the een o' the greatest o' the earth in the bright springtime o' the Resurrection; and though I'm a little mon here, it may be I'll see o'er the heads of soom up there."

"An ye had true humeelity ye'd be a-hopin' to get there, instead of expectin' to speir o'er the heads o' yer betters," said his wife in a rebuking tone.

"'A-hopin' to get there'!" said Malcom with some warmth. "Why suld I hope when 'I know that my Redeemer liveth'?"

Edith's eyes filled with wistful tears, for the quaint talk of these old people suggested a hope and faith that she

knew nothing of. But, in a low voice, she said, "Why
does God let his creatures suffer so much?"

"Bless your heart, puir child, He suffered mair than ony
on us," said Malcom tenderly. "But ye'll learn it a' soon.
He who fed the famishin' would bid ye eat noo. But wait
a bit till ye see what I'll bring ye."

In a moment he was back with a dainty basket of Tri-
omphe de Gand strawberries, and Edith uttered an exclamation of delight as she inhaled their delicious aroma.

"They are the first ripe the season, an' noo see what the
gudewife will do with them."

Soon their hulls were off, and, swimming in a saucer of
cream, they were added to the dainty little lunch that Mrs.
McTrump had prepared.

"Oh!" exclaimed Edith, drawing a long breath, "you
can't know how you ease my poor sore heart. I began to
think all the world was against me."

At this Malcom beat such a precipitate retreat that he
half stumbled over a chair, but outside the door he ventured to say:

"An ye coom out I'll cut ye a posy before ye go." But
Edith saw him rub his rough sleeve across his eyes as he
passed the window. His wife said, in a grave gentle tone:

"Would ye might learn to know Him who said, 'Be of
good cheer, I have overcome the wourld.'"

Edith shook her head sadly, and said, "I don't understand Him, and He seems far off."

"It's only seemin', me dear," said the old woman kindly,
"but, as Malcom says, ye'll learn it a' by and by."

Mrs. McTrump was one of those simple souls who never
presume to "talk religion" to any one. "I can ony venture
what I hope'll be a 'word in season' noo and then, as the
Maister gies me a chance," she would say to her husband.

Though she did not know it, she had spread before Edith
a Gospel feast, and her genuine, hearty sympathy was teaching more than eloquent sermons could have done, and already the grateful girl was questioning:

"What makes these people differ so from others ?"

With some dismay she saw how late it was growing, and hastened out to Malcom, who had cut an exquisite little bouquet for her, and had another basket of berries for her to take to her mother.

"Mr. McTrump," said Edith, "it's time we had a settlement; your kindness I never can repay, but I am able now to carry out my agreement."

"Don't bother me wi' that noo," said Malcom, rather testily. "I ha' no time to make oot your account in the height o' the season. Let it ston till I ha' time. An' ye might help me soomtimes make up posies for the grand folk at the hotel. But how does your garden sin ye dismissed ould Malcom ?"

"Oh, Mr. McTrump," said Edith, slyly, "do you know you almost scared old Hannibal out of his wits by the wonders you wrought last night or this morning in that same garden you inquire about so innocently. How can you work so fast and hard ?"

"The woonders I wrought! Indeed I've not been near the garden sin ye told me not to coom. Ye could hardly expect otherwise of a Scotchman."

"Who, then, could it be ?" said Edith, a little startled herself now, and she explained the mystery of the garden.

He was as nonplussed as herself, but, scratching his bushy head, he said, with a canny look, "I wud be glad if Hannibal's 'spook,' as he ca's it, would coom doon and hoe a bit for me," and Edith was so cheered and refreshed that she could even join him in the laugh.

They sent her away enveloped in the fragrance of strawberries and roses from the little basket she carried. But the more grateful aroma of human sympathy seemed to create a buoyant atmosphere around her; and she passed back through the village strengthened and armed against the cold or scornful looks of those who, knowing her to be "wounded," had not even the grace to pass by indifferently "on the other side."

CHAPTER XXV

A HORROR OF GREAT DARKNESS

BY the time Edith reached home the transient strength and transient brightening of the skies seemed to pass away. Her mother was no better and the poor girl saw too plainly the grisly spectres, care, want, and shame upon her hearth, to fear any good fairy that left such traces as she saw in her garden. But the mystery troubled her; she longed to know who it was. As she mused upon it on her way home, Arden Lacey suddenly occurred to her, and there was a glimmer of a smile and a faint increase of color on her pale face. But she did not suggest her suspicion to Hannibal, when he eagerly asked if it were Malcom.

"No, strange to say, it was not," said Edith. "Who could it have been?"

Hannibal's face fell, and he looked very solemn. "Sumpen awful's gwine to happen, Miss Edie," he said, in a sepulchral tone.

Edith broke into a sudden reckless laugh, and said, "I think something awful is happening about as fast as it can. But never mind, Hannibal, we'll watch to-night, and perhaps he will come again."

"Oh, Miss Edie, I'se hope you'll 'scuse me. I couldn't watch for a spook to save my life. I'se gwine to bed as soon as it's dark, and cover up my head till mornin'."

"Very well," said Edith, quietly. "I'm going to sit up with mother to-night, and if it comes again, I'll see it."

"De good Lord keep you safe, Miss Edie," said Hannibal, tremblingly. "You'se know I'd die for you in a minit;

but I'se couldn't watch for a spook nohow,'' and Hannibal
crept away, looking as if the very worst had now befallen
them.

Edith was too weary and sad even to smile at the absurd
superstition of her old servant, for with her practical, positive nature she could scarcely understand how even the
most ignorant could harbor such delusions. She said to
Laura, ''Let me sleep till nine o'clock, and then I will
watch till morning.''

Laura did not waken her till ten.

After Edith had shaken off her lethargy, she said, ''Why,
Laura, you look ready to faint!''

With a despairing little cry, Laura threw herself on the
floor, and buried her face in her sister's lap, sobbing:

''I am ready to faint—body and soul. Oh, Edie, Edie,
what shall we do? Oh, that I were sure death was an eternal sleep, as some say! How gladly I would close my eyes
to-night and never wish to open them again! My heart is
ashes, and my hope is dead. And yet I am afraid to die,
and more afraid to live. Ever since—Zell—went—the future
has been—a terror to me. Edith,'' she continued, after a
moment, in a low voice, that trembled and was full of dread,
''Zell has not written—the silence of the grave seems to
have swallowed her. *He has not married her!*'' and an
agony of grief convulsed Laura's slight frame.

Edith's eyes grew hard and tearless, and she said sternly,
''It were better the grave had swallowed her than such a
gulf of infamy.''

Laura suddenly became still, her sobs ceasing. Slowly
she raised such a white, terror-stricken face, that Edith was
startled. She had never seen her elder sister, once so stately
and proud, then so apathetic, moved like this.

''Edith,'' she said, in an awed whisper, ''what is there
before us? Zell's flight, like a flash of lightning, has revealed to me where we stand, and ever since I have brooded
over our situation, till it seems as if I shall go mad. There's
an awful gulf before us, and every day we are being pushed

nearer to it;'' and Laura's large blue eyes were dilated with
horror, as if she saw it.

"Mother is going to die," she continued, in a tone that
chilled Edith's soul. "Our money will soon be gone; we
then shall be driven away even from this poor shelter, out
upon the streets—to New York, or somewhere. Edith, Oh,
Edith, don't you see the gulf? What else is before us?"

"Honest work is before me," said Edith, almost fiercely.
"I will compel the world to give me a place entitled at least
to respect."

Laura shook her head despairingly. "You may struggle
back and up to where you are safe. You are good and strong.
But there are so many poor girls in the world like me, who
are not good and strong! Everything seems to combine to
push a helpless, friendless woman toward that gulf. Poor
rash, impulsive Zell saw it, and could not endure the slow,
remorseless pressure, as one might be driven over a preci-
pice, and one she loved seemed to stand ready to break the
fall. I understand her stony, reckless face now."

"Oh, Laura, hush!" said Edith, desperately.

"I must speak," she went on, in the same low voice, so
full of dread, "or my brain will burst. I have thought and
thought, and seen that awful gulf grow nearer and nearer,
till at times it seemed as if I should shriek with terror.
For two nights I have not slept. Oh! why were we not
taught something better than dressing and dancing, and
those hollow, superficial accomplishments that only mock
us now? Why were not my mind and body developed into
something like strength? I would gladly turn to the
coarsest drudgery, if I could only be safe. But after what
has happened no good people will have anything to do
with us, and I am a feeble, helpless creature, that can only
shrink and tremble as I am pushed nearer and nearer."

Edith seemed turning into stone, herself paralyzed by
Laura's despair. After a moment Laura continued, with
a perceptible shudder in her voice:

"There is no one to break my fall. Oh, that I was not

afraid to die! That seems the only resource to such as I.
If I could just end it all by becoming nothing—''

''Laura, Laura,'' cried Edith, starting up, ''cease your
wild mad words. You are sick and morbid. You are more
delirious than mother is. We can get work; there are good
people who will take care of us.''

''I have seen nothing that looks like it,'' said Laura, in
the same despairing tone. ''I have read of just such things,
and I see how it all must end.''

''Yes, that's just it,'' said Edith, impatiently. ''You
have read so many wild, unnatural stories of life that
you are ready to believe anything that is horrible. Listen:
I have over four hundred dollars in the bank.''

''How did you get it?'' asked Laura, quickly.

''I have followed mother's suggestion, and mortgaged
the place.''

Laura sank into a chair, and became so deathly white
that Edith thought she would faint. At last she gasped:

''Don't you see? Even you in your strength can't help
yourself. You are being pushed on, too. You said you
would not follow mother's advice again, because it always
led to trouble. You said, again and again, you would not
mortgage the place, and yet you have done it. Now it's
all clear. That mortgage will be foreclosed, and then we
shall be turned out, and then—'' and she covered her face
with her hands. ''Don't you see,'' she said, in a muffled
tone, ''the great black hand reaching out of the darkness
and pushing us down and nearer? Oh, that I wasn't afraid
to die!''

Edith was startled. Even her positive, healthful nature
began to yield to the contagion of Laura's morbid despair.
She felt that she must break the spell and be alone. By a
strong effort she tried to speak in her natural tone and with
confidence. She tried to comfort the desperate woman by
endearing epithets, as if she were a child. She spoke of
those simple restoratives which are so often and vainly pre-
scribed for mortal wounds, sleep and rest.

"Go to bed, poor child," she urged. "All will look differently in the sunlight to-morrow."

But Laura scarcely seemed to heed her. With weak, uncertain steps she drew near the bed, and turned the light on
her mother's thin, flushed face, and stood, with clasped
hands, looking wistfully at her.

"Yes, my dear," muttered Mrs. Allen in her delirium,
"both your father and myself would give our full approval
to your marriage with Mr. Goulden." The poor woman
made watching doubly hard to her daughters, since she
képt recalling to them the happy past in all its minutiæ.

Laura turned to Edith with a smile that was inexpressibly sad, and said, "What a mockery it all is! There
seems nothing real in this world but pain and danger. Oh,
that I was not afraid to die!"

"Laura, Laura! go to your rest," exclaimed Edith, "or
you will lose your reason. Come;" and she half carried
the poor creature to her room. "Now, leave the door
ajar," she said, "for if mother is worse I will call you."

Edith sat down to her weary task as a watcher, and
never before, in all the sad preceding weeks, had her heart
been so heavy, and so prophetic of evil. Laura's words
kept repeating themselves to her, and mingling with those
of her mother's delirium, thus strangely blending the past
and the present. Could it be true that they were helpless
in the hands of a cruel, remorseless fate, that was pushing
them down? Could it be true that all her struggles and
courage would be in vain, and that each day was only
bringing them nearer to the desperation of utter want?
She could not disguise from herself that Laura's dreadful
words had a show of reason, and that, perhaps, the mortgage she had given that day meant that they would soon be
without home or shelter in the great, pitiless world. But,
with set teeth and white face, she muttered:

"Death first."

Then, with a startled expression, she anxiously asked
herself: "Was that what Laura meant when she kept say-

ing, 'Oh, if I wasn't afraid to die!' " She went to her sister's door and listened. Laura's movements within seemed to satisfy her, and she returned to the sick-room and sat down again. Putting her hand upon her heart, she murmured:

"I am completely unnerved to-night. I don't understand myself;" and she looked almost as pale and despairing as Laura.

She was, in truth, in the midst of that "horror of great darkness" that comes to so many struggling souls in a world upon which the shadow of sin rests so heavily.

CHAPTER XXVI

FRIEND AND SAVIOUR

KNOWING of no other source of help than an earthly one, her thoughts reverted to the old Scotch people whom she had recently visited. Their sunlighted garden, and happy, homely life, their simple faith, seemed the best antidote for her present morbid tendencies.

"If the worst comes to the worst, I think they would take us in for a little while, till some way opened," she thought. "Oh that I had their belief in a better life! Then it wouldn't seem so dreadful to suffer in this one. Why have I never read the 'Gude Book,' as they call it? But I never seemed to understand it; still, I must say, that I never really tried to. Perhaps God is angry with us, and is punishing us for so forgetting Him. I would rather think that than to feel so forgotten and lost sight of. It seems as if God didn't see or care. It seems as if I could cling to the harshest father in the world, if he would only protect and help me. A God of wrath, that I have heard clergymen preach of, is not so dreadful to me as a God who forgets, and leaves His creatures to struggle alone. Our minister was so cold and philosophical, and presented a God that seemed so far off, that I felt there could never be anything between Him and me. He talked about a holy, infinite Being, who dwelt alone in unapproachable majesty; and I want some one to stoop down and love and help poor little me. He talked about a religion of purity and good works, and love to our fellow-men. I don't know how to work for myself, much less for others, and it seems as if nearly all my fellow-creatures hated and scorned me, and I am afraid of them; so I don't see what chance there is for such as we. If we had only remained rich, and lived on the avenue, such a religion wouldn't be so hard. It seems strange that the Bible should teach him and old Malcom so differently. But I suppose he is wiser, and understands it better. Perhaps it's the flowers that teach Malcom, for he always seems drawing lessons from them."

Then came the impulse to get the Bible and read it for herself. "The impulse!" whence did it come?

When Edith felt so orphaned and alone, forgotten even of God, then the Divine Father was nearest his child. When, in her bitter extremity, at this lonely midnight hour she realized her need and helplessness as never before, her great Elder Brother was waiting beside her.

The impulse was divine. The Spirit of God was leading her as He is seeking to lead so many. It only remained for her to follow these gentle impulses, not to be pushed into the black gulf that despairing Laura dreaded, but to be led into the deep peace of a loving faith.

She went down into the parlor to get the Bible that in her hands had revealed the falseness and baseness of Gus Elliot, and the thought flashed through her mind like a good omen, "This book stood between me and evil once before." She took it to the light and rapidly turned its pages, trying to find some clew, some place of hope, for she was sadly unfamiliar with it.

Was it her trembling fingers alone that turned the pages? No; He who inspired the guide she consulted guided her, for soon her eyes fell upon the sentence—

"Come unto me all ye that labor and are heavy laden, and I will give you rest."

The words came with such vivid power and meaning that she was startled, and looked around as if some one had spoken to her. They so perfectly met her need that it seemed they must be addressed directly to her..

"Who was it that said these words, and what right had

He to say them?" she queried eagerly, and keeping her finger on the passage as if it might be a clew out of some fatal labyrinth, she turned the leaves backward and read more of Him with the breathless interest that some poor burdened soul might have felt eighteen centuries ago in listening to a rumor of the great Prophet who had suddenly appeared with signs and wonders in Palestine. Then she turned and read again and again the sweet words that first arrested her attention. They seemed more luminous and hope-inspiring every moment, as their significance dawned upon her like the coming of day after night.

Her clear, positive mind could never take a vague, dubious impression of anything, and with a long-drawn breath she said, with the emphasis of perfect conviction:

"If He were a mere man, as I have been taught to believe, He had no right to say these words. It would be a bitter, wicked mockery for man or angel to speak them. Oh, can it be that it was God Himself in human guise? I could trust such a God."

With glowing cheeks and parted lips, she resumed her reading, and in her eyes was the growing light of a great hope.

The upper room of that poor little cottage was becoming a grand and sacred place. Heaven, that honors the deathless soul above all localities, was near. The God who was not in the vast and gold-incrusted temple on Mount Moriah sat in humble guise at "Jacob's well," and said to one of His poor guilty creatures: "I that speak unto thee am He." Cathedral domes and cross-tipped spires indicated the Divine presence on every hand in superstitious Rome, but it would seem that He was near only to a poor monk creeping up Pilate's staircase. Though the wealth of the world should combine to build a colossal church, filling it with every sacred emblem and symbol, and causing its fretted roof to resound with unceasing choral service, it would not be such a claim upon the great Father's heart as a weak, pitiful cry to Him from the least of His children. Though Edith knew it not, that Presence without which all temples are vain had come to her as freely, as closely, as truly as when it entered the cottage at Bethany, and Mary "sat at Jesus' feet and heard His word." Even to her, in this night of trouble, in this stony wilderness of care and fear, as to God's trembling servant of old, a ladder of light was let down from heaven, and on it her faith would climb up to the peace and rest that are above, and therefore undisturbed by the storms that rage on earth.

But it is God's way to make us free through truth. Christ, when on earth, did not deal with men's souls as with their bodies. The latter He touched into instantaneous cure; to the former He appealed with patient instruction and entreaty, revealing Himself by word and deed, and saying: In view of what I prove myself to be will you trust me? Will you follow me?

In words which, though spoken so long ago, are still the living utterances of the Spirit to every seeking soul, He was now speaking to Edith, and she listened with the wonder and hope that might have stirred the heart of some sorrowing maiden like herself, when His voice was accompanied by the musical chime of waves breaking on the shores of Galilee, or the rustle of winds through the gray olive leaves.

Edith came to the source of all truth with a mind as fresh and unprejudiced as that of one who saw and heard Jesus for the first time, as, in his mission journeys, he entered some little town of the Holy Land. She had never thought much about Him, and had no strong preconceived opinions. She was almost utterly ignorant of the creeds and symbols of men, and Christ was not to her, as He is to so many, the embodiment of a system and the incarnation of a doctrine— a vague, half-realized truth. When she thought of Him at all, it had been as a great, good man, the most famous religious teacher in the past, whose life had nobly "adorned a tale and pointed a moral." But this would not answer any more. "What could a man, dead and buried centuries ago, do for me now?" she asked, bitterly.

"I want one who can with right speak these words—

" 'Come unto me all ye that labor and are heavy laden, and I will give you rest.' "

And as, with finger still clinging to this passage, she read of miracle and parable, now trembling almost under the "Sermon on the Mount," now tearful under the tender story of the prodigal, the feeling came in upon her soul like the rising tide, "This was not mere man."

Then, with an awe she had never felt before, she followed him to Gethsemane, to the High Priest's palace, to Pilate's judgment-hall, and thence to Golgotha, and it seemed to her one long "Via Dolorosa." With white lips she murmured, with the centurion, "Truly this man was the Son of God."

She was reading the wonderful story for the first time in its true connection, and the Spirit of God was her guide and teacher. When she came to Mary "weeping without at the sepulchre," her own eyes were streaming, and it seemed as if she were weeping there herself.

But when Jesus said, in a tone perhaps never heard before or since in this world, "Mary," it seemed that to herself He was speaking, and her heart responded, "Rabboni—Master."

She started up and paced the little room, thrilling with excitement.

"How blind I have been!" she exclaimed—"how utterly blind! Here I have been struggling alone all these weary weeks, with scarcely hope for this world and none for the next, when I might have had *such* a friend and helper all the time. Can I be deceived? Can this sweet way of light out of our thick darkness be a delusion?"

She went to where her little Bible lay open at the passage, "Come unto me," and bowing her head upon it, pleaded as simply and sincerely as the Syro-Phœnician mother pleaded for her child in the very presence of the human Saviour—

"O Jesus, I am heavily laden. I labor under burdens greater than I can bear. Divine Saviour, help me."

In answer she expected some vague exaltation of soul, of an exquisite sense of peace, as the burden was rolled away.

There was nothing of the kind, but only an impulse to go to Laura. She was deeply disappointed. She seemed to have climbed such a lofty height that she might almost look into heaven and confirm her faith forever, and only a simple earthly duty was revealed to her. Her excited mind, that had been expanding with the divinest mysteries, was reacting into quietness, and the impression was so strong that she must go to Laura, that she thought her sister had been calling her, and she, in her intense preoccupation, had heard her as in a dream.

Still keeping the little Bible in her hand, she went to Laura's room. Through the partially open door she saw, with a sudden chill of fear, that the bed had not been slept in. Pushing the door open, she looked eagerly around with a strange dread growing upon her. Laura was writing at a table with her back toward the entrance. There was a strong odor of laudanum in the room, and a horrible thought blanched Edith's cheek. Stealing with noiseless tread across the intervening space, with hand pressed upon her heart to still its wild throbbings, she looked over her sister's shoulder, and followed the tracings of her pen with dilating eyes.

"Mother, Edith, farewell! When you read these sad words I shall be dead. I fear death—I cannot tell you how I fear it, but I fear more that dreadful gulf which daily grows nearer. I must die. There is no other resource for a poor, weak woman like me. If I were only strong—if I had only been taught something—but I am helpless. Do not be too hard upon poor little Zell. Her eyes were blinded by a false love; she did not see the black gulf as I see it. If God cares for what such poor forlorn creatures as I do, may He forgive. I have thought till my brain reels. I have tried to pray, but hardly knew what I was praying to. I don't understand God—He is far off. The world scorns us. There is none to help. There is no other remedy save the drug at my side, which will soon bring sleep which I hope will be dreamless. Farewell!

"Your poor, trembling, despairing   LAURA."

Every sentence was written with a sigh that seemed as if it might be the last that the burdened soul could give, and every line was blotted with tears.   Edith saw that the poor, thin face was pinched and wan with misery, and that the pallor of death had already blanched even her lips, and, with a shudder of horror, her eyes fell on a phial of lauda-num at Laura's left hand, from which she was partially turned away, in the act of writing.

With an ecstatic thrill of joy, she now understood how her prayer had been answered.   How could there have been rest—how could there have been peace—if this awful trag-edy had been consummated?

With one devout, grateful glance upward, she silently took away the fatal drug, and laid her Bible down in its place.

Laura finished her letter, leaned back, and murmured a long, trembling, "Farewell!" that was like a low, mournful vibration of an Æolian harp, when the night-breeze breathes upon it.   Then she pressed her right hand over her eyes, shuddered, and tremblingly put out her left for that which would end all.   But, instead of the phial which she had placed there but a little before, her hand rested upon a book.   Startled, she opened her eyes, and saw not the dreaded poison, but in golden letters that seemed luminous to her dazzled sight:

HOLY BIBLE.

Though all had lasted but a brief moment, Edith's power of self-control was gone.   Dashing the bottle on the floor, where it broke into many fragments, she threw herself on her sister's neck and sobbed:

"O Laura, Laura! your hand is on a better remedy.   It has saved me—it can save you.   It has shown me the Friend we need.   He sent me to you;" and she clung to her sister in a rapture of joy, murmuring, with every breath:

"Thanks, thanks, eternal gratitude!   I see how my prayer is answered now."

Laura, in her shattered condition, was too bewildered and feeble to do more than cling to Edith, with a blessed sense of being rescued from some great peril.   A horrid spell seemed broken, and for some reason, she knew not why, life and hope were still possible. A torrent of tears seemed to relieve her of the dreadful oppression that had so long rested on her, and at last she faltered:

"Who is this strange friend?"

"His name is Jesus—Saviour," said Edith, in a low, reverential tone.

"I don't quite understand," said Laura, hesitatingly. "I can only cling to you till I know Him."

"He knows you, Laura, and loves you. He has never forgotten us. It was we who forgot Him. He sent me to you, just in time. Now put your hand on this book, and promise me you will never think of such an awful thing again."

"I promise," said Laura, solemnly; "not if I am in my right mind. I don't understand myself. You seem to have awakened me from a fearful dream. I will do just what you tell me to."

"Oh, Laura, let us both try to do just what our Divine Friend tells us to do."

"Perhaps, through you, I shall learn to know Him. I can only cling to you to-night," said Laura, wearily. "I am so tired," and her eyes drooped as she spoke.

With a sense of security came a strong reaction in her overtaxed nature. Edith helped her to bed as if she were a child, and soon she was sleeping as peacefully as one.

CHAPTER XXVII

THE MYSTERY SOLVED

EDITH resumed her watching in her mother's room. The invalid was still dwelling on the past, and her delirium appeared to Edith a true emblem of her old, unreal life. Indeed, it seemed to her that she had never lived before. A quiet but divine exaltation filled her soul. She did not care to read any more, but just sat still and thought, and her spiritual light grew clearer and clearer.

Her faith was very simple, her knowledge very slight. She was scarcely in advance of a Hebrew maiden who might have been one of the mournful procession passing out of the gates of Nain, when a Stranger, unknown before, revealed Himself by turning death into life, sorrow into joy. The eye of her faith was fastened on the distinct, living, loving personality of our human yet Divine Friend, who no longer seemed afar off, but as near as to that other burdened one who touched the hem of His garment.

"He does not change, the Bible says," she thought. "He cannot change. Therefore He will help me, just as surely as He did the poor, suffering people among whom He lived."

It was but three o'clock, and yet the eastern sky was pale with dawn. At length her attention was gained by a faint but oft-repeated sound. It seemed to come from the direction of the garden, and at once the mystery that so oppressed poor Hannibal occurred to her. She rose, and

passed back to her own room, which overlooked the garden, and, through the lattice, in the faint morning twilight,
saw a tall, dusky figure, that looked much too substantial
to be any such shadowy being as the old negro surmised,
and the strokes of his hoe were too vigorous and noisy for
ghostly gardening.

"It must be Arden Lacey," thought Edith, "but I will
put this matter beyond all doubt. I don't like this night
work, either; though for different reasons than those of
poor Hannibal. We have suffered enough from scandal
already, and henceforth all connected with my life shall
be as open as the day. Then, if the world believes evil
of me, it will be because it likes it best."

These thoughts passed through her mind while she
hastily threw off her wrapper and dressed. Cautiously
opening the back-door, she looked again. The nearer
view and clearer light revealed to her Ardén Lacey. She
did not fear him, and at once determined to question him
as to the motive of his action. He was but a little way off,
and was tying up a grape-vine that had been neglected, his
back being toward her. Edith had great physical courage
and firmness naturally, and it seemed that on this morning
she could fear nothing, in the strength of her new-born
enthusiasm.

With noiseless step she reached his side, and asked,
almost sternly:

"Who are you, sir; and what does this action mean?"

Arden started violently, trembled like the leaves in the
morning wind, and turned slowly toward her, feeling more
guilty and alarmed than if he had been playing the part of
a burglar, instead of acting as her good genius.

"Why don't you answer?" she asked, in still more decided tones. "By what right are you doing this work?"

Edith had lost faith in men. She knew little of Arden,
and the thought flashed through her mind, "This may be
some new plot against us." Therefore her manner was
stern and almost threatening.

Poor Aden was startled out of all self-control. Edith's coming was so sudden and unexpected, and her pale face was so spirit-like, that for a moment he scarcely knew whether the constant object of his thoughts was really before him, or whether his strong imagination was only mocking him.

Edith mistook his agitation and hesitancy as evidences of guilt, and he so far recovered himself as to recognize her suspicions.

"I will be answered. You shall speak the truth," she said, imperiously. "By what right are you doing this work ?"

Then his own proud, passionate spirit flamed up, and looking her unblenchingly in the face, he replied:

"The right of my great love for you. Can I not serve my idol ?"

An expression of deep pain and repulsion came out upon Edith's face, and he saw it. The avowal of his love was so abrupt—indeed it was almost stern; and, coming thus from quite a stranger, who had little place even in her thoughts, it was so exceedingly painful that it was like a blow. And yet she hardly knew how to answer him, for she saw in his open, manly face, his respectful manner, that he meant no evil, however he might err through ignorance or feeling.

He seemed to wait for her to speak again, and his face, from being like the eastern sky, became very pale. From recent experience, and the teachings of the Patient One, Edith's heart was very tender toward anything that looked like suffering, and though she deemed Arden's feeling but the infatuation of a rude and ill-regulated mind, she could not be harsh, now that all suspicion of evil designs was banished. Therefore she said quietly, and almost kindly:

"You have done wrong, Mr. Lacey. Remember I have no father or brother to protect me. The world is too ready to take up evil reports, and your strange action might be misunderstood. All transactions with me must be like the sunlight."

With an expression of almost anguish, Arden bowed his head before her, and groaned:

"Forgive me; I did not think."

"I am sure you meant no harm," said Edith, with real kindness now in her tone. "You would not knowingly make the way harder for a poor girl that has too much already to struggle against. And now, good-by. I shall trust to your sense of honor, assured that you will treat me as you would wish your own sister dealt with;" and she vanished, leaving Arden so overwhelmed with contending emotions that he could scarcely make his way home.

An hour later Edith heard Hannibal's step downstairs, and she at once joined him. The old man had aged in a night, and his face had a more worn and hopeless look than had yet rested upon it. He trembled at the rustle of her dress, and called:

"Miss Edie, am dat you?"

"Yes, you foolish old fellow. I have seen your spook, and ordered it not to come here again unless I send you for it."

"Oh, Miss Edie!" gasped Hannibal.

"It's Arden Lacey."

Hannibal collapsed. He seemed to drop out of the realm of the supernatural to the solid ground of fact with a heavy thump.

He sank into a chair, regarding her first with a blank, vacant face, which gradually became illumined with a knowing grin. In a low, chuckling voice, he said:

"I jes declar to you I'se struck all of a heap. I jes done see whar de possum is dis minute. What an ole black fool I was, sure 'nuff. I tho't he'se de mos 'bligin man I eber seed afore," and he told her how Arden had served her in her illness.

She was divided between amusement and annoyance, the latter predominating. Hannibal concluded impressively:

"Miss Edie, it must be lub. Nothin' else dan dat which

so limbered up my ole jints could get any livin' man ober
as much ground as he hoed dat night."

"Hush, Hannibal," said Edith, with dignity; "and remember that this is a secret between ourselves. Moreover,
I wish you never to ask Mr. Lacey to do anything for us if it
can possibly be helped, and never without my knowledge."

"You knows well, Miss Edie, dat you'se only to speak
and it's done," said Hannibal, deprecatingly.

She gave him such a gentle, grateful look that the old
man was almost ready to get down on his knees before her.
Putting her hand on his shoulder, she said:

"What a good, faithful, old friend you are! You don't
know how much I love you, Hannibal;" and she returned
to her mother.

Hannibal rolled up his eyes and clasped his hands, as if
before his patron saint, saying, under his breath:

"De idee of her lubing ole black Hannibal! I could die
dis blessed minute," which was his way of saying, "*Nunc
dimittis.*"

Laura slept quietly till late in the afternoon, and wakened
as if to a new and better life. Her manner was almost child-
like. She had lost all confidence in herself, and seemed to
wish to be controlled by Edith in all things, as a little child
might be. But she was very feeble.

As the morning advanced Edith grew exceedingly weary.
Reaction from her strong excitement seemed to bear her
down in a weakness and lethargy that she could not resist,
and by ten o'clock she felt that she must have some relief.
It came from an unexpected source, for Hannibal appeared
with a face of portentous solemnity, saying that Mrs. Lacey
was downstairs, and that she wished to know if she could do
something to help.

The mother's quick eye saw that something had deeply
moved and was troubling her son. Indeed, for some time
past, she had seen that into his unreal world had come a
reality that was a source of both pain and pleasure, of fear
and hope. While she followed him every hour of the day

with an unutterable sympathy, she silently left him to open
his heart to her in his own time and manner. But her
tender, wistful manner told Arden that he was understood,
and he preferred this tacit sympathy to any spoken words.
But this morning the evidence of his mental distress was so
apparent that she went to him, placed her hands upon his
shoulders, and with her grave, earnest eyes looking straight
into his, asked:

"Arden, what can I do for you?"

"Mother," he said, in a low tone, "there are sickness and
deep trouble at our neighbors'. Will you go to them again?"

"Yes, my son," she replied, simply, "as soon as I can
get ready."

So she arranged matters to stay if needed, and thus in
Edith's extremity she appeared. In view of Arden's words,
Edith hardly knew how to receive her or what to do. But
when she saw the plain, grave woman sitting before her in
the simple dignity of patient sorrow, her course seemed
clear. She instinctively felt that she could trust this offered
friendliness, and that she needed it.

"I have heard that your mother has been sick as well as
yourself," Mrs. Lacey said kindly but quietly. "You look
very worn and weary, Miss Allen; and if I, as a neighbor,
can watch in your place for a while, I think you can trust
me to do so."

Tears sprang into Edith's eyes, and she said, with sudden
color coming into her pale face, "You take noble revenge
for the treatment you have received from us, and I gratefully submit to it. I must confess I have reached the limit
of my endurance; my sister is ill also, and yet mother needs
constant attention."

"Then I am very glad I came, and I have left things at
home so I can stay," and she laid aside her wraps with the
air of one who sees a duty plainly and intends to perform
it. Edith gave her the doctor's instructions a little incoherently in her utter exhaustion, but the experienced matron
understood all, and said:

"I think I know just what to do. Sleep till you are well rested."

Edith went to her room, and, with her face where the sweet June air could breathe directly upon it through the open window, sleep came with a welcome and refreshing balm that she had never known before. Her last thought was, "He will take care of me and mine."

She had left the door leading into the sick-room open, and Mrs. Lacey stepped in once and looked at her. The happy, trustful thought with which she had closed her eyes had left a faint smile upon her face, and given it a sweet spiritual beauty.

"She seems very different from what I supposed," murmured Mrs. Lacey. "She is very different from what people are imagining her. Perhaps Arden, poor boy, is nearer right than all of us. Oh, I hope she is good, whether he ever marries her or not, for this love will be the saving or ruining of him."

When Edith awoke it was dark, and she started up in dismay, for she had meant to sleep but an hour or two. Having hastily smoothed her hair, she went to the sick-room, and found Laura reclining on the sofa, and talking in the most friendly manner to Mrs. Lacey. Her mother's delirium continued, though it was more quiet, with snatches of sleep intervening, but she noticed no one as yet. Mrs. Lacey sat calmly in her chair, her sad, patient face making the very ideal of a watcher, and yet in spite of her plain exterior there was a refinement, an air of self-respect, that would impress the most casual observer. As soon as Laura saw Edith she rose as quickly as her feebleness permitted, and threw her arms around her sister, and there was an embrace whose warmth and meaning none but themselves, and the pitying eye of Him who saved, could understand. Then Edith turned and said, earnestly:

"Truly, Mrs. Lacey, I did not intend to trespass on your kindness in this manner. I hope you will forgive me."

"Nature knew what was best for you, Miss Allen, and ou have not incommoded me at all. I made my plans to tay till nine o'clock, and then Arden will come for me."

"Miss Edie," said Hannibal, in his loud whisper, "I'se ot some supper for you down here."

Why did Edith go to her room and make a little better oilet before going down? She hardly thought herself. It ras probably a feminine instinct. As she took her last sip f tea there was a timid knock at the door. "I will see him moment," she decided.

Hannibal, with a gravity that made poor Edith smile in er thoughts, admitted Arden Lacey. He was diffident but ot awkward, and the color deepened in his face, then left t very pale, as he saw Edith was present. Her pale cheek lso took the faintest tinge of pink, but she rose quietly, nd said:

"Please be seated, Mr. Lacey. I will tell your mother ou are here." Then, as Hannibal disappeared, she added arnestly, "I do appreciate your mother's kindness, and— ours also. At the same time, too deep a sense of obliga- ion is painful; you must not do so much for us. Please do ot misunderstand me."

Arden had something of his mother's quiet dignity, as e rose and held out to Edith a letter, saying:

"Will you please read that—you need not answer it— nd then perhaps you will understand me better."

Edith hesitated, and was reluctant.

"I may be doing wrong," continued he, earnestly and rith rising color. "I am not versed in the world's ways; ut is it not my right to explain the rash words I uttered his morning? My good name is dear to me also. Few care or it, but I would not have it utterly blurred in your eyes. Ve may be strangers after you have read it, if you choose, ut I entreat you to read it."

"You will not feel hurt if I afterward return it to you?" sked Edith, timidly.

"You may do with it what you please."

13—Roe—X

She then took the letter, and a moment later Mrs. Lacey appeared, and said:

"I will sit up to-morrow night, with your permission."

Edith took her hand, and replied, "Mrs. Lacey, you burden me with kindness."

"It is not my wish to burden, but to relieve you, Miss Allen. I think I can safely say, from our slight acquaintance, that in the case of sickness or trouble at a neighbor's, you would not spare yourself. We cease to be human when we leave the too heavily burdened to struggle alone."

Edith's eyes grew moist, and she said, simply, "I cannot refuse kindness offered in that spirit, and may God bless you for it. Good-night."

Arden's only parting was a grave, silent bow.

Edith was soon alone again, watching by her mother. With some natural curiosity, she opened the letter that was written by one so different from any man that she had ever known before. Its opening, at least, was reassuring.

"Miss Edith Allen—You need not fear that I shall offend again by either writing or speaking such rash words as those which so deeply pained you this morning. They would not have been spoken then, perhaps never, had I not been startled out of my self-control—had I not seen that you suspected me of evil. I was very unwise, and I sincerely ask your pardon. But I meant no wrong, and as you referred to my sister, I can say, before God, that I would shield you as I would shield her.

"I know little of the conventionalities of the world. I live but a hermit's life in it, and my letter may seem to you very foolish and romantic, still I know that my motives are not ignoble, and with this consciousness I venture.

"Reverencing and honoring you as I do, I cannot bear that you should think too meanly of me. The world regards me as a sullen, stolid, bearish creature, but I have almost ceased to care for its opinion. I have received from it nothing but coldness and scorn, and I pay my debt in like coin. But perhaps you can imagine why I cannot endure that you should regard me in like manner. I would not have you think my nature a stony, sterile place, when something tells me that it is like a garden that needs only sunlight of some kind. My life has been blighted by the wrong of another, who should have been my best helper. The knowledge and university culture for which I thirsted were denied me. And yet, believe me, only my mother's need— only the absolute necessity that she and my sister should have a daily protector—kept me from pushing out into the world, and trying to work my way

SHE LOOKED OVER HER SISTER'S SHOULDER WITH DILATING EYES.

What Can.

Page 286.

unaided to better things. Sacred duty has chained me down to a life that was outwardly most sordid and unhappy. My best solace has been my mother's love. But from varied, somewhat extensive, though perhaps not the wisest kind of reading, I came to dwell in a brave, beautiful, but shadowy world that I created out of books. I was becoming satisfied with it, not knowing any other. The real world mocked and hurt me on every side. It is so harsh and unjust that I hate it. I hate it infinitely more as I see its disposition to wound you, who have been so noble and heroic. In this dream of the past—in this unreal world of my own fancy—I was living when you came that rainy night. As I learned to know you somewhat, you seemed a beautiful revelation to me. I did not think there was such a woman in existence. My shadows vanished before you. With you living in the present, my dreams of the past ceased. I could not prevent your image from entering my lonely, empty heart, and taking its vacant throne, as if by divine right. How could I ? How can I drive you forth now, when my whole being is enslaved ?

"But forgive me. Though thought and feeling are beyond control, outward action is not. I hope never to lose a mastering grasp on the rein of deeds and words; and though I cannot understand how the feeling I have frankly avowed can ever change, I will try never, by look or sign, to pain you with it again.

"And yet, with a diffidence and fear equalled only by my sincerity and earnestness, I would venture to ask one great favor. You said this morning that you already had too much to struggle against. The future has its possibilities of further trouble and danger. Will you not let me be your humble, faithful friend, serving you loyally, devotedly, yet unobtrusively, and with all the delicate regard for your position which I am capable of showing, assured that I will gratefully accept any hints when I am wrong or presumptuous ? I would gladly serve you with your knowledge and consent. But serve you I must. I vowed it the night I lifted your unconscious form from the wharf, and gave you into Mrs. Groody's care. There need be no reply. You have only to treat me not as an utter stranger when we next meet. You have only to give me the joy of doing something for you when opportunity offers.

"ARDEN LACEY."

Edith's eyes filled with tears before she finished this most unexpected epistle. Though rather quaint and stately in its diction, the passion of a true, strong nature so permeated it all, that the coldest and shallowest would have been moved. And yet a half-smile played upon her face at the same time, like sunlight on drops of rain.

"Thank heaven!" she said, "I know of one more true man in the world, if he is a strange one. How different he is from what I thought! I don't believe there's another in this place who could have written such a letter. What would a New York society man, whose compliments are as extravagant as meaningless, think of it? Truly he doesn't know the world, and isn't like it. I supposed him an awkward, eccentric young countryman, that, from his very verdancy, would be difficult to manage, and he writes to me like a knight of olden time, only such language seems Quixotic in our day. The foolish fellow, to idealize poor, despised, faulty Edith Allen into one of the grand heroines of his interminable romances, and that after seeing me hoe my garden like a Dutch woman. If I wasn't so sad and he so earnest, I could laugh till my sides ached. There never was a more matter-of-fact creature than I am, and yet here am I enveloped in a halo of impossible virtues and graces. If I were what he thinks me, I shouldn't know myself. Well, well, I must treat him somewhat like a boy, for such he really is, ignorant of himself and all the world. When he comes to know me better, the Edith of his imagination will vanish like his other shadows, and he will have another revelation that I am an ordinary, flesh-and-blood girl."

With deepening color she continued: "So it was he who lifted me up that night. Well, I am glad it was one who pitied me, and not some coarse, unfeeling man. It seems strange how circumstances have brought him who shuns and is shunned by all, into such a queer relationship to me. But heaven forbid that I should give him lessons as to the selfish, matter-of-fact world. He will outgrow his morbidness and romantic chivalry with the certainty of years, and seeing more of me will banish his absurd delusions in regard to me. I need his friendship and help—indeed it seems as if they were sent to me. It can do him no harm, and it may give me a chance to do him good. If any man ever needed a sensible friend, he does."

Therefore Edith wrote him—

"It is very kind of you to offer friendship and help to one situated like myself, and I gratefully grant what you rather oddly call 'a favor.' At the same time, if you ever find such friendliness a pain or trouble to you in any way, I shall in no degree blame you for withdrawing it."

The "friendship" and "friendliness" were underscored, thus delicately hinting that this must be the only relation.

"There," she said, "all his chains will now be of his own forging, and I shall soon demolish the paragon he is dreaming over."

She laid both letters aside, and took down her Bible with a little sigh of satisfaction.

"His lonely, empty heart," she murmured; "ah, that is the trouble with all. He thinks to fill his with a vain dream of me, as others do with as vain a dream of something else. I trust I have learned of One here who can fill and satisfy mine;" and soon she was again deep in the wondrous story, so old, so new, so all-absorbing to those from whose spiritual eyes the scales of doubt and indifference have fallen. As she read she saw, not truths about Jesus, but *Him*, and at His feet her heart bowed in stronger faith and deeper love every moment.

She had not even thought whether she was a Christian or not. She had not even once put her finger on her spiritual pulse, to gauge the evidences of her faith. A system of theology would have been unintelligible to her. She could not have defined one doctrine so as to have satisfied a sound divine. She had not even read the greater part of the Bible, but, in her bitter extremity, the Spirit of God, employing the inspired guide, had brought her to Jesus, as the troubled and sinful were brought to Him of old. He had given her rest. He had helped her save her sister, and with childlike confidence she was just looking, lovingly and trustingly, into His divine face, and He was smiling away all her fear and pain. She seemed to feel sure that her mother would get well, that Laura would grow stronger, that they would all learn to know Him, and would be taken care of.

As she read this evening she came to that passage of exquisite pathos, where the purest, holiest manhood said to "a woman of the city, which was a sinner,"

"Thy sins are forgiven. Go in peace."

Instantly her thoughts reverted to Zell, and she was deeply moved. Could she be forgiven? Could she be saved? Was the God of the Bible—stern, afar off, as she had once imagined—more tender toward the erring than even their own human kindred? Could it be possible that, while she had been condemning, and almost hating Zell, Jesus had been loving her?

The feeling overpowered her. Closing the book, she leaned her head upon it, and, for the first time, sobbed and mourned for Zell with a great, yearning pity.

Every such pitiful tear, the world over, is a prayer to God. It mingles with those that flowed from His eyes as He wept over the doomed city that would not receive Him. It mingles with that crimson tide which flowed from His hands and feet when He prayed—

"Father, forgive them; for they know not what they do."

CHAPTER XXVIII

EDITH TELLS THE OLD, OLD STORY

MRS. ALLEN seemed better the next day, and Laura was able to watch while Edith slept. After tea Mrs. Lacey appeared, with the same subdued air of quiet self-respect and patient sorrow. She seemed to have settled down into that mournful calm which hopes little and fears little. She seemed to expect nothing better than to go forward, with such endurance as she might, into the deeper shadows of age, sickness, and death. She vaguely hoped that God would have mercy upon her at last, but how to love and trust Him she did not know. She hardly knew that it was expected, or possible. She associated religion with going to church, outward profession, and doing much good. The neighbors spoke of her and the family as "very irreligious," and she had about come to the conclusion that they were right. She never thought of taking credit to herself for her devotion to her children and patience with her husband. She loved the former, especially her son, with an intensity that one could hardly reconcile with her grave and silent ways. In regard to her husband, she tried to remember her first young girlish dream—the manly ideal of character that her fond heart had associated with the handsome young fellow who had singled her out among the many envious maidens in her native village.

"I will try to be true to what I thought he was," she said, with woman's pathetic constancy, "and be patient with what he is."

But the disappointment, as it slowly assumed dread certainty, broke her heart.

Edith began to have a fellow-feeling for her. "We both have not only our own burdens to carry, but the heavier burden of another," she thought. "I wonder if she has ever gone to Him for the 'rest.' I fear not, or she would not look so sad and hopeless."

Before they could go upstairs a hack from the hotel stopped at the door, and Mrs. Groody bustled cheerily in. Laura at the same time came down, saying that Mrs. Allen was asleep.

"Hannibal," said Edith, "you may sit on the stairs, and if she wakes, or makes any sound, let me know," and she took a seat near the door in order to hear.

"I've been worryin' about you every minute ever since I called, and you was too sick to see me," said Mrs. Groody, "but I've been so busy I couldn't get away. It takes an awful lot of work to get such a big house to rights, and the women cleanin', and the servants are so aggravatin', that I am just run off my legs lookin' after them. I don't see why people can't do what they're told, when they're told."

"I wish I were able to help you," said Edith. "Your promise of work has kept me up wonderfully. But before I half got my strength back mother became very ill, and, had it not been for Mrs. Lacey, I don't know what I should have done. It did seem as if she were sent here yesterday, for I could not have kept up another hour."

"You poor child," said Mrs. Groody, in a tone and manner overflowing with motherly kindness. "I just heard about it to-day from Arden, who was bringin' something up to the hotel, so I said, 'I'll drop everything to-night, and run down for a while.' So here I am, and now what can I do for you?" concluded the warm-hearted woman, whose invariable instinct was to put her sympathy into deeds.

"I told you that night," said Edith. "I think I could do a little sewing or mending even now if I had it here at home. But your kindness and remembrance do me more good than any words of mine can tell you. I thought no one would ever speak to us again," she continued in a low tone, and with rising color, "and I have had kind, helpful friends sent to me already."

Wistful mother-love shone in Mrs. Lacey's large blue eyes, but Mrs. Groody blew her nose like a trumpet, and said:

"Not speak to you, poor child! Though I ain't on very good terms with the Lord, I ain't a Pharisee, and after what I saw of you that night, I am proud to speak to you and do anything I can for you. It does seem too bad that poor young things like you two should be so burdened. I should think you had enough before without your mother gettin' sick. I don't understand the Lord, nohow. Seems to me He might scatter His afflictions as well as His favors a little more evenly. I've thought a good deal about what you said that night, 'We're dealt with in masses,' and poor bodies like you and me, and Mrs. Lacey there, that is, 'the human atoms,' as you called 'em, are lost sight of."

Tears sprang into Edith's eyes, and she said, earnestly, "I am sorry I ever said those words. They are not true. I should grieve very much if my rash, desperate words did you harm after all your kindness to me. I have learned better since I saw you, Mrs. Groody. We are not lost sight of. It seems to me the trouble is we lose sight of Him."

"Well, well, child, I'm glad to hear you talk in that way," said Mrs. Groody, despondently. "I'm dreadfully discouraged about it all. I know I fell from grace, though, one awfully hot summer, when everything went wrong, and I got on a regular rampage, and that's the reason perhaps. A she-bear that had lost her cubs wasn't nothin' to me. But I straightened things out at the hotel, though I came mighty near bein' sick, but I never could get straight myself after it. I knowed I ought to be more patient—I knowed it all the time. But human natur is human natur, and woman natur is worse yet sometimes. And when you've got on one hand a score to two of drinkin,' quarrelsome, thievin', and abominably lazy servants to manage, and on the other

two or three hundred fastidious people to please, and elegantly dressed ladies who can't manage their three or four
servants at home, dawdlin' up to you every hour in the
day, sayin' about the same as, Mrs. Groody, everything
ain't done in a minute—everything ain't just right. I'd
like to know where 'tis in this jumbled-up world—not
where they're housekeepers, I warrant you.

"Well, as I was telling you," continued Mrs. Groody,
with a weary sigh, "that summer was too much for me. I
got to be a very dragon. I hadn't time to read my Bible,
or pray, or go to church, or scarcely eat or sleep. I worked
Sundays and week days alike, and I got to be a sort of
heathen, and I've been one ever since," and a gloom seemed
to gather on her naturally open, cheery face, as if she feared
she might never be anything else.

Mrs. Lacey gave a deep, responsive sigh, showing that
her heavy heart was akin to all other burdened souls. But
direct, practical Edith said simply and gently:

"In other words, you were laboring and heavy laden."

"Couldn't have been more so, and lived," was Mrs.
Groody's emphatic answer.

"And the memory of it seems to have been a heavy burden on your conscience ever since, though I think you judge
yourself harshly," continued Edith.

"Not a bit," said Mrs. Groody sturdily, "I knowed better all the time."

"Well, be that as it may, I feel that I know very little
about these things yet. I'm sure I want to be guided rightly.
But what did our Lord mean when He said, 'Come unto Me,
all ye that labor and are heavy laden, and I will give you
rest' ?"

Mrs. Groody gave Edith a sort of surprised and startled
look. After a moment she said, "Bless you, child, how
plain you do put it! It's a very plain text when you think
of it, now, ain't it? I always tho't it meant kind o' good,
as all the Bible does."

"No, but He said them," urged Edith, earnestly. "It is

a distinct, plain invitation, and it must have a distinct, plain meaning.   I have learned to know that when you or Mrs. Lacey say a thing, you mean what you say, and so it is with all who are sincere and true.   Was He not sincere and true ?   If so, these plain words must have a plain meaning. He surely couldn't have meant them only for the few people who heard His voice at that time."

"Of course not," said Mrs. Groody, musingly, while poor Mrs. Lacey leaned forward with such an eager, hungry look in her poor, worn face, that Edith's heart yearned over her. Laura came and sat on the floor by her sister's chair, and leaning her elbow on Edith's knee, and her face on her hand, looked up with the wistful, trustful, child-like expression that had taken the place of her former stateliness and subsequent apathy.   Edith lost all thought of herself in her eagerness to tell the others of the Friend and Helper she had come to know.

"He must be God, or else He had no right to say to a great, troubled, sinning world, 'Come unto me.'   The idea of a million people going at once, with their sorrows and burdens, to one mere man, or an angel, or any finite creature !   And just think how many millions there are !   If the Bible is for all, this invitation is for all.   He couldn't have changed since then, could He ?   He can't be different in heaven from what He was on earth ?"

"No," said Mrs. Groody, quickly, "for the Bible says He is 'the same yesterday, to-day, and forever.' "

"I never read in that place," said Edith, simply.   "That makes it clearer and stronger than ever.   Please, don't think I am setting myself up as a religious teacher.   I know very little yet myself.   I am only seeking the light. But one thing is settled in my mind, and I like to have one thing settled before I go on to anything else.   This one thing seems the foundation of everything else, and it appears as if I could go on from it and learn all the rest.   I am satisfied that this Jesus is God, and that He said, 'Come unto me,' to poor, weak, overburdened Edith Allen.   I

went to Him, just as people in trouble used to, when He
first spoke these words. And oh, how He has helped me!"
continued Edith, with tears in her eyes, but with the glad
light of a great hope again shining through them. "The
world can never know all that He has done for us, and I
can't even think of Him without my heart quivering with
gratitude."

Laura had now buried her face in her sister's lap, and
was trembling like a leaf. Edith's words had a meaning to
her that they could not have for the others.

"And now," concluded Edith, "I was led to Him by
these words, 'Come unto me, all ye that labor and are
heavy laden, and I will give you rest.' I was in greater
darkness than I had ever been in before. My heart ached
as if it would burst. Difficulty and danger seemed on every
side, and I saw no way out. I knew the world had only
scorn for us, and I was so bowed down with shame and discouragement that I almost lost all hope. I had been to the
village, and the people looked and pointed at me, till I was
ready to drop in the street. But I went to Mr. McTrump's,
and he and his wife were so kind to me, and heartened me
up a little; and they spoke about the 'Gude Book,' as they
call it, in such a way as made me think of it in my deep
distress and fear, as I sat alone watching with mother. So
I found my neglected Bible, and, in some way, I seemed
guided to these words, 'Come unto me'; and then, for two
or three hours, I continued to read eagerly about Him, till
at last I felt that I could venture to go to Him. So, I just
bowed my head, on His own invitation; indeed, it seemed
like a tender call to a child that had been lost in the dark,
and was afraid, and I said, 'I am heavy laden, help me.'
And how wonderfully He did help me! He has been so
good, so near, ever since. My weary, hopeless heartache
is gone. I don't know what is before us. I can't see the
way out of our troubles. I don't know what has become
of our absent one," she said, in a low tone and with bowed
head, "but I can leave all to Him. He is God: He loves,

and He can and will take care of us. So you see I know very little about religion yet; just enough to trust and keep close to Him; and I feel sure that in time He will.teach me, through the Bible, or in some way, all I ought to know.''

"Bless the child, she's right, she's right," sobbed Mrs. Groody. "It was just so at first. He came right among people, and called all sorts to Him, and they came to Him just as they was, and stayed with Him, and He cured, and helped, and taught 'em, till, from being the worst, they became the best. That is the way that distressed, swearin', old fisherman Peter became one of the greatest and best men that ever lived; though it took a mighty lot of grace and patience to bring it about. Now I think of it, I think he fell from grace worse than I did that awfully hot summer. What an old fool I am! I've been readin' the Bible all my life, and never understood it before.''

"I think that if you had gone to Him that time when you were so troubled and overburdened He would have helped you," said Edith, gently.

"Yes, but there it is, you see," said Mrs. Groody, wiping her eyes and shaking her head despondently; "I didn't go."

"But you are heavy laden now. I can see it. You can go now," said Edith, earnestly.

"I'm afraid I've put it off too long," said Mrs. Groody, settling back into something of her old gloom. "I'm afraid I've sinned away my time.''

With a strange blending of pathos and reproach in her tone, Edith answered:

"Oh, how can *you*, with your big, kind heart, that yearned over a poor unknown girl that dreadful night when you brought me home—how can you think so poorly of your Saviour? Is your heart warmer—are your sympathies larger than His? Why, He died for us, and, when dying, prayed for those who crucified Him. Could you turn away a poor, sorrowing, burdened creature that came pleading to you for help? You know you couldn't. Learn from your own heart something of His. Listen, I haven't told you all. It seems as if I never could tell all about Him. But see how He feels about poor lost Zell, when I, her own sister, was almost hating her," and, reaching her hand to the table, she took her Bible and read Christ's words to "a woman of the city, which was a sinner."

At this Mrs. Groody broke down completely, and with clasped hands and streaming eyes, cried:

"I will go to Him; I will fear and doubt no more."

A trembling hand was now laid on Edith's shoulder, and, looking up, she saw Mrs. Lacey standing by her side with a face so white, so eager, so full of unutterable long-ing, that it might have made a Christian artist's ideal of a soul famishing for the "Bread of Life." In a low, timid, yet thrilling tone, she asked:

"Miss Allen, do you think He would receive such as me?"

"Yes, thus," cried Edith, as with a divine impulse and a great yearning pity she sprang up and threw her arms around Mrs. Lacey.

Hope dawned in the poor worn face like the morning. Belief in God's love and sympathy seemed to flow into her sad heart from the other human heart that was pressed against it. The spiritual electric circle was completed— Edith, with her hand of faith in God's, took the trembling, groping hand of another and placed it there also.

Two great tears gathered in Mrs. Lacey's eyes, and she bowed her head for a moment on Edith's shoulder, and murmured, "I'll try—I think I may venture to Him."

Hannibal now appeared at the door, saying, rather husk-ily and brokenly, considering his message:

"Miss Edie, you'se mudder's awake, an' 'd like some water."

"That's what we all have been wanting, 'water'—'the water of life,'" said Mrs. Groody, wiping her eyes, "and never was my parched old heart so refreshed before. I don't care how hot this summer is, or how aggravatin' things are, I feel as if I'd be helped through it. And, my dear, good-night. I come here to try to do you good, and you've done me more good than I ever thought could happen again. I'm goin' to kiss you—I can't help it. Good-by, and may the good Lord bless your sweet face;" and Mrs. Groody, like one of old, climbed up into her chariot, and "went on her way rejoicing."

In their close good-night embrace, Laura whispered, "I begin to understand it a little now, Edie, but I think I see everything only through your eyes, not my own."

"As old Malcom said to me the other day, so now I say to you, 'Ye'll learn it a' soon.' "

Edith soon retired to rest also, and Mrs. Lacey sat at Mrs. Allen's side, returning the sick woman's slights and scorn, somewhat as the patient God returns ours, by watching over her.

Her eyes, no longer cast down with the pathetic discouragement of the past, seemed looking far away upon some distant scene. She was following in her thoughts the steps of the Magi from the East to where, as yet far distant, the "Star of Bethlehem" glimmered with promise and hope.

CHAPTER XXIX

HANNIBAL LEARNS HOW HIS HEART CAN BE WHITE

WHEN Edith rose the next morning she found Laura only at her mother's bedside. Mrs. Lacey had gone home quite early, saying that she would soon come again. Mrs. Allen's delirium had passed away, leaving her exceedingly weak, but the doctor said, at his morning call:

"With quiet and good nursing she will slowly regain her usual health."

After he was gone, Laura said: "Taking care of mother will now be my work, Edie. I feel a good deal stronger. I'll doze in a chair during the day, and I am a light sleeper at night, so I don't think we shall need any more watchers. Poor Mrs. Lacey works hard at home, I am sure, and I don't want to trespass on her kindness any longer. So if Mrs. Groody sends you work you may give all your time to it."

And early after breakfast quite a bundle did come from the hotel, with a scrawl from the housekeeper: "You may mend this linen, my dear, and I'll send for it to-morrow night."

Edith's eyes sparkled at the sight of the work as they never had over the costliest gifts of jewelry. Sitting down in the airy parlor, no longer kept in state for possible callers, she put on her thimble, and, with a courage and heroism greater than those of many a knight drawing for the first time his ancestral sword, she took her needle and joined the vast army of sewing-women. Lowly was the position and work first assigned to her—only mending coarse linen. And yet it was with a thrill of gratitude and joy, and a stronger hope than she had yet experienced, that she sat down to the first real work for which she would be paid, and in her exultation she brandished her little needle at the spectres want and fear, as a soldier might his weapon.

Hannibal stood in the kitchen regarding her with moist eyes and features that twitched nervously.

"Oh, Miss Edie, I neber tho't you'd come to dat."

"It's one of the best things I've come to yet," said Edith, cheerily. "We shall be taken care of, Hannibal. Cheer up your faithful old heart. Brighter days are coming."

But, for some reason, Hannibal didn't cheer up, and he stood looking very wistfully at Edith. At last he commenced:

"It does my ole black heart good to hear you talk so, Miss Edie—"

"Why do you persist in calling your heart black? It's no such thing," interrupted Edith.

"Yes, 'tis, Miss Edie," said Hannibal, despondently, "I'se know 'tis. I'se black outside, and I allers kinder feel dat I'se more black inside. Neber felt jes right here yet, Miss Edie," said the old man, laying his hand on his breast. "I come de nighest to't de toder day when you said you lubbed me. Dat seemed to go down deep, but not quite to whar de trouble stays all de time.

"But, Miss Edie," continued he in a whisper, "I'se hope you'll forgive me, but I couldn't help listenin' to you last night. I neber heerd such talk afore. It seemed to broke my ole black heart all up, and made it feel like de big ribers down souf in de spring, when dey jes oberflow eberyting. I says to myself, dat's de Friend Miss Edie say she's gwine to tell me 'bout. And now, Miss Edie, would you mind tellin' me little 'bout Him? Cause if He's your Friend, I'd t'ink a heap of Him, too. Not dat I specs He's gwine to

bodder wid dis ole niggah, but den I'd jes like to hear 'bout
Him a little.''

Edith laid down her work, and turned her glorious dark
eyes, brimming over with sympathy, on the poor old fellow,
as he stood in the doorway fairly trembling with the excess
of his feeling.

"Come and sit down here by me," she said.

"Oh, Miss Edie, I'se isn't—"

"No words—come."

Hannibal crouched down on a divan near.

"What makes you think He wouldn't bother with you?"

"Well, I'se don't know 'zactly, Miss Edie. I'se only
Hannibal."

"Hannibal," said Edith, earnestly, "you are the best
man I know in all the world."

'Oh, Lor bless you, Miss Edie, how you talk! you'se jes
done gone crazy.''

"No I haven't. I never spoke in more sober earnest.
You are faithful and true, unselfish and patient, and abound
in the best material of which men are made. I admit," she
added, with a twinkle in her eye, "that one very common
element of manhood, as I have observed it, is dreadfully
lacking, that is conceit. I wish I were as good as you are,
Hannibal.''

"Oh, Miss Edie, don't talk dat way, you jes done discourages me. If you'd only say, Hannibal, you'se sick, but
I'se got a mighty powerful medicine for you; if you'd only
say, I know you isn't good; I know your ole heart is black,
but I know a way to make it white, I'd stoop down and kiss
de ground you walks on. Dere's sumpen wrong here, Miss
Edie," said he, laying his hand on his breast again, and
shaking his head, with a tear in the corner of each eye—
"I tells you dere's sumpen wrong. I don't know jes
what 'tis. My heart's like a baby a-cryin' for it doesn't
know what. Den it gits jes like a stun, as hard and as
heavy. I don't understan' my ole heart; I guess it's
kinder sick and wants a doctor, 'cause it don't work

right. But dere's one ting I does understan'. It 'pears dat it would be a good heaven 'nuff if I'se could allers be waitin' on you alls. But Massa Allen's gone; Miss Zell, poor chile, is gone; and I'se growin' ole, Miss Edie, I'se growin' ole. De wool is white, de jints are stiff, and de feet tired. Dey can't tote dis ole body roun' much longer. Where am I gwine, Miss Edie? What's gwine to become of ole Hannibal? I'se was allers afeard of de dark. If I could only find you in de toder world and wait on you, dat's all I ask, but I'se afeard I'll get lost, it seems such a big, empty place."

"Poor old Hannibal! Then you are 'heavy laden' too," said Edith, gently.

"Indeed I is, Miss Edie; 'pears as if I couldn't stan' it anoder minute. And when I heerd you talkin' about dat Friend last night, and tellin' how good He was to people, and He seemed to do you such a heap of good, I thought dat I would jes like to hear little 'bout Him."

"Wait till I get my Bible," said Edith.

"Bless you, Miss Edie, you'se needn't stop your work. You can jes tell me anyting dat come into you'se head."

"Then I wouldn't be like Him, Hannibal. He used to stop and give the kindest and most patient attention to every one that came to Him, and, as far as I can make out, the poorer they were, the more sinful and despised they seemed, the more attention He gave to them."

"Dat's mighty quar," said Hannibal, musingly; "not a bit like de big folks dat I'se seen."

"I don't understand it all myself yet, Hannibal. But the Bible tells me that He was God come down to earth to save the world. He says to the lost and sinful—to all who are poor and needy—in brief, to the heavy laden, 'Come unto me.' So I went to Him, Hannibal, and you can go just as well."

The old man's eyes glistened, but he said, doubtfully, "Yes, but den you'se Miss Edie, and I'se only black Hannibal. I wish we'd all lived when He was here. I might

have shine His boots, and done little tings for Him, so He'd
say, 'Poor ole Hannibal, you does as well as you knows
how. I'll 'member you, and you shan't go away in de
dark.' "

Edith smiled and cried at the same time over the quaint
pathos of the simple creature's words, but she said, earnestly, "You need not go away in the dark, for He said, 'I
am the light of the world,' and if you go to Him you will
always be in the light."

"I'd go in a minute," said Hannibal, eagerly, "if I only
know'd how, and wasn't afeard." Then, as if a sudden
thought struck him, he asked, "Miss Edie, did He eber hab
anyting to do wid a black man ?"

Edith was so unfamiliar with the Bible that she could
not recall any distinct case, but she said, with the earnestness of such full belief on her part, that it satisfied his child-
like mind, "I am sure He did, for all kinds of people—
people that no one else would touch or look at—came to
Him, or He went to them, and spoke so kindly to them and
forgave all their sins."

"Bress Him, Miss Edie, dat kinder sounds like what I
wants."

Edith thought a moment, and, with her quick, logical
mind, sought to construct a simple chain of truth that
would bring to the trusting nature she was trying to guide
the perfect assurance that Jesus' love and mercy embraced
him as truly as herself.

They made a beautiful picture that moment; she with
her hands, that had dropped all earthly tasks for the sake
of this divine work, clasped in her lap, her lustrous eyes
dewy with sympathy and feeling, looking far away into the
deep blue of the June sky, as if seeking some heavenly inspiration; and quaint old Hannibal, leaning forward in his
eagerness, and gazing upon her, as if his life depended upon
her next utterances.

It was a picture of the Divine Artist's own creation. He
had inspired the faith in one and the questioning unrest in

the other. He, with Edith's lips, as ever by human lips, was teaching the way of life. Glorious privilege, that our weak voices should be as the voice of God, telling the lost and wandering where lies the way to life and home! The angels leaned over the golden walls to watch that scene, while many a proud pageant passed unheeded.

"Hannibal," said Edith, after her momentary abstraction, "God made everything, didn't He?"

"Sartin."

"Then He made you, and you are one of His creatures, are you not?"

"Sartin I is, Miss Edie."

"Then see here what is in the Bible. Almost the last thing He said to His followers before He went up into heaven, was, 'Go ye into all the world and preach the gospel to every creature.' Gospel means 'good news,' and the good news was, that God had come down from heaven and become a man, so we wouldn't be afraid of Him, and that He would take away their sins and save all who would let Him. Now, remember, He didn't send His preachers to the white people, nor to the black people, but to all the world, to every creature alike, and so He meant you and me, Hannibal, and you as much as me. I am just as sure He will receive you as that He received me."

"Dat's 'nuff, Miss Edie. Ole Hannibal can go too. And I'se a-gwine, Miss Edie, I'se a-gwine right to Him. Dere's only one ting dat troubles me yet. What is I gwine to do wid my ole black heart? I know dere's sumpen wrong wid it. It's boddered me all my life."

"Oh, Hannibal," said Edith, eagerly, "I was reading something last night that I think will just suit you. I thought I would read a little in the Old Testament, and I turned to a place that I didn't understand very well, but I came to these words, and they made me think of you, for you are always talking about your 'old black heart.'" And she read:

"I will give them one heart, and I will put a new spirit

within you; and I will take the stony heart out of their flesh and will give them an heart of flesh.''

To Hannibal the words seemed a revelation from heaven. Standing before her, with streaming eyes, he said:

''Oh, Miss Edie, you'se been an angel of light to me. Dat was jes de berry message I wanted. I knowed my ole heart was nothin' but a black stun. De Lord couldn't do nothin' wid it but trow it away. But tanks be to His name, He says He'll give me a new one—a heart of flesh. Now I sees dat my heart can be white like yours, Miss Edie. Bress de Lord, I'se a-gwine, I'se a-comin','' and Hannibal vanished into the kitchen, feeling that he must be alone in the glad tumult of his emotions.

CHAPTER XXX

EDITH'S AND ARDEN'S FRIENDSHIP

A S Edith laid aside her work for a frugal dinner at one o'clock, she heard the sound of a hoe in her garden. The thought of Arden at once recurred to her, but looking out she saw old Malcom. Throwing a handkerchief over her head, she ran out to him, exclaiming:

"How good you are, Mr. McTrump, to come and help me when I know you are so very busy at home!"

"Weel, nothin' to boast on," replied Malcom; "I tho't that if ye had na one a-lookin' after the garden save Hannibal's 'spook,' ye'd have but a ghaistly crop. But I'm a-thinkin' there's mair than a ghaist been here."

"It was Arden Lacey," said Edith, frankly, but with deepening color. Malcom, in telling his wife about it, said, "She looked like the rose-bush, a' in bloom, that she was a-stonnin' beside."

Edith, seeing the mischievous twinkle in her little friend's eye, added hastily, "Both Mrs. Lacey and her son have been very kind to us in our sickness and trouble, as well as yourself. But, Mr. McTrump," she continued, anxious to change the subject, also eager to speak on the topic uppermost in her thoughts, "I think I am beginning to 'learn it a',' as you said, about that good Friend who suffered for us that we might not suffer. What you and your wife said to me the other day led me to read the 'Gude Book' after I got home. I don't feel as I did then. I think I can trust Him now."

Malcom dropped his hoe and came over into the path beside her.

"God be praised!" he said. "I gie ye the right hond o' fellowship an' welcome ye into the kirk o' the Lord. Ye noo belong to the household o' faith, an' God's true Israel, an' may His gude Spirit guide ye into all truth."

The little man spoke very earnestly, and with a certain dignity and authority that his small stature and rude working-dress could not diminish. A sudden feeling of solemnity and awe came over Edith, and she felt as if she were crossing the mystic threshold and entering the one true church consisting of all believers in Christ.

For a moment she reverently bowed her head, and a sweeter sense of security came over her, as if she were no longer an outsider, but had been received into the household.

Malcom, "a priest unto God" through his faith, officiated at the simple ceremony. The birds sang the choral service. The wind-shaken roses, blooming around her, with their sweet ordos, were the censers and incense, and the sun-lighted garden, the earliest sacred place of Bible history, where the first fair woman worshipped, was the hallowed ground of the initiatory rite.

"Why, Mr. McTrump, I feel almost as if I had joined the church," said Edith, after a moment.

"An' sae ye ha' afore God, an' I hope ere long ye'll' openly profess yer faith before men."

"Do you think I ought?" said Edith, thoughtfully.

"Of coorse I do, but the Gude Book'll teach a' aboot it. Ye canna gang far astray wi' that to guide ye."

"I would like to join the church that you belong to, Mr. McTrump, as soon as I feel that I am ready, for it was you and your good wife that turned my thoughts in the right direction. I was almost desperate with trouble and shame when I came to you that afternoon, and it was your speaking of the Bible and Jesus, and especially your kindness, that made me feel that there might be some hope and help in God."

The old man's eyes became so moist that he turned away

for a moment, but recovering himself after a little, he said:

"See, noo, our homely deeds and words can be like the seeds we drop into the mould. Look aroon once and see how green and grand the garden is, and a' from the wee brown seeds we planted the spring. Sae would the garden o' the Lord bloom and floorish if a' were droppin' a 'word in season' and a bit o' kindness here and there. But if I stay here an' preach to ye that need na preachin', these sins o' the garden, the weeds, will grow apace. Go you an' look in yer strawberry-bed."

With an exclamation of delight, Edith pounced upon a fair-sized red berry, the first she had picked from her own vines. Then glancing around, she saw one and another showing its red cheek through the green leaves, till with a little cry of exultation she said:

"Oh, Mr. McTrump, I'll get enough for mother and Laura."

"Aye, and enoof to moisten yer own red lips wi' too, I'm a-thinkin'. There'll be na crop the year wourth speakin' of; but next June 'twill puzzle ye to gither them. But ye a' can ha' a dainty saucer yoursels the season, when ye're a mind to stoop for them."

Edith soon had the pleasure of seeing her mother and Laura enjoying some, and, as Malcom said, there were plenty for her, and they tasted like the ambrosia of the gods. Varied experiences had so thoroughly engrossed her thoughts and time the past few days, that she had scarcely looked toward her garden. But with the delicious flavor of the strawberries lingering in her mouth, and with the consciousness that she enjoyed picking them much more than sewing, the thought of winning her bread by the culture of the ground grew in her favor.

"Oh, how much rather would I be out there with Malcom!" she sighed.

Glancing up from her work during the afternoon, she saw Arden Lacey on his way to the village. There was a strange mingling of hope and fear in his mind. His mo.

ther's manner had been such as to lead him to say when
alone with her after breakfast:

"I think your watching has done you good, mother, instead of wearying you too much, as I feared."

She had suddenly turned and placed both her hands on
his shoulders, saying:

"Arden, I hardly dare speak of it yet. It seems too
good to be true, but a hope is coming into my heart like
the dawn after night. She's worthy of your love, however
it may result, and if I find true what she told me last night
I shall have reason to bless her name forever; but I see
only a glimmer of light yet, and I rejoice with fear and
trembling." And she told him what had occurred.

He was deeply moved, but not for the same cause as his
mother. His desire and devotion went no further than
Edith. "Can she have read my letter?" he thought, and
he was consumed with anxiety for some expression of her
feeling toward him. Therefore he was glad that business
called him to the village that afternoon, but his steps were
slow as he approached the little cottage, and his eyes were
upon it as a pilgrim gazes at a shrine he long has sought.
He envied Malcom working in the garden, and felt that if
he could work there every day, it would be Adam's life before he fell. Then he caught a glimpse of Edith sewing at
the window, and he dropped his eyes instantly. He would
not be so afraid of a battery of a hundred guns as of that
poor sewing-girl (for such Edith now was), stitching away on
Mrs. Groody's coarse hotel linen. But Edith had noted his
timid, wistful looks, and calling Hannibal, said:

"Please give that note to Mr. Lacey. He is just passing
toward the village."

Hannibal, with the impressive dignity he had learned in
olden times, handed the missive to Arden, saying, "Miss
Edie told me to guv you dis 'scription."

If Hannibal had been Hebe he could not have been a
more welcome messenger.

Arden could not help his hand trembling as he took

the letter, but he managed to say, "I hope Miss Allen is well."

"Her health am berry much disproved," and Hannibal retired with a stately bow.

Arden quickened his steps, holding the missive in his hand. As soon as he was out of sight, he opened and devoured Edith's words. The light of a great joy dawned in his face, and made it look noble and beautiful, as indeed almost every human face appears when the light of a pure love falls upon it. Where most men would have murmured at the meagre return for their affection, he felt himself immeasurably rewarded and enriched, and it seemed as if he were walking on air the rest of the day. With a face set like a flint, he resolved to be true to the condition implied in the underscored word "friendship," and never to whisper of love to her again. But a richer experience was still in store for him. For, on his return, in the cool of the evening, Edith was in the garden picking currants. She saw him coming, and thought, "If he is ever to be a friend worth the name, I must break the ice of his absurd diffidence and formality. And the sooner he comes to know me as I am, the sooner he will find out that I am like other people, and he will have a new 'revelation' that will cure him of his infatuation. I would like him for a *friend* very much, not only because I need his help, but because one likes a little society now and then, and he seems so well educated, if he is 'quar,' as Hannibal says." So she startled poor Arden almost as much as if one of his Shakespearean heroines had called him in audible voice, by saying, as he came opposite her:

"Mr. Lacey, won't you come in a moment and tell me if it is time to pick my currants, and whether you think I could sell them in the village, or at the hotel?"

This address, so matter-of-fact in tone and character, seemed to him like the June twilight, containing, in some subtle manner, the essence of all that was beautiful and full of promise in his heart-history. He bowed and went toward the little gate to comply with her request, as Adam might if he had been created outside of Eden and Eve inside, and she had looked over a flowering hedge in the purple twilight and told him to come in. He was not going merely to look at currants and consider their marketable condition; he was entering openly upon the knightly service to which he had devoted himself. He was approaching his idol, which was not a heathen stock or stone, but a sweet little woman. In regard to the currants, he ventured dubiously—

"They might do for pies."

In regard to herself, his eyes said, in spite of his purpose to be merely friendly, that she was too good for the gods of Mount Olympus. He both amused and interested Edith, whose long familiarity with society and lack of any such feeling as swayed him made her quite at ease. With a twinkle in her eyes, she said:

"I have thought that perhaps Mrs. Groody could help me find sale for them at the hotel."

"I am going there to-morrow, and I will ask her for you, if you wish," said Arden, timidly.

"Thank you," replied Edith. "I shall be very much obliged to you if you will. You see, I wish to sell everything out of the garden that I can find a market for."

She was rather astonished at the effect of this mercenary speech, for there was a wonderful blending of sympathy and admiration in his face as he said:

"I am frequently going to the hotel and village, and if you will let me know what you have to dispose of, I can find out whether it is in demand, and carry it to market for you." He could not help adding, with a voice trembling with feeling, "Miss Allen, I am so glad you permit me to be of some help to you."

"Oh, dear!" thought Edith, "how can I make him understand what I really am?" She turned to him with an expression that was both perplexed and quizzical, and said:

"Mr. Lacey, I very frankly and gratefully accept your delicately offered friendship (emphasizing the last word), not only because of my need, but of yours also. If any one needs a sensible friend, I think you do. You truly must have lived a 'hermit's life in the world' to have such strange ideas of people. Let me tell you as a perfect certainty, that no such person exists as the Edith Allen that you have imagined. She is no more a reality than your other shadows, and the more you know of me, the sooner you will find it out. I am not in the least like a heroine in a romance. I live on the most substantial food rather than moonlight, and usually have an excellent appetite. I am the most practical matter-of-fact creature in existence, and you will find no one in this place more sharp on the question of dollars and cents. Indeed, I am continually in a most mercenary frame of mind, and this very moment here, in the romantic June twilight, if you ransacked history, poetry, and all the fine arts, you could not tell me anything half so beautiful, half so welcome, as how to make money in a fair, honorable way."

"There," thought she, "that will be another 'revelation' to him. If he don't jump over the garden fence in his haste to escape such a monster, I shall be glad."

But Arden's face only grew more grave and gentle as he looked down upon her, and he asked:

"Is it because you love the money itself, Miss Allen?"

"Well, no," said Edith, somewhat taken aback. "I can never earn enough to make it worth while to do that. Misers love to count their money," she added, with a little pathetic accent in her voice, "and I fear mine will go before I can count it."

"You wish me to think less of you, then, because you are bravely, and without thought of sparing yourself, trying to earn money to provide home-shelter and comfort for your feeble mother and sister. You wish me to think you commonplace because you have the heroism to do any kind of work, rather than be helpless and dependent. Pardon me, but for such a 'practical, matter-of-fact' lady, I do not think your logic is good."

Edith's vexation and perplexity only increased, and she said, earnestly, "But I wish you to understand that I am only Edith Allen, and as poor as poverty, nothing but a sewing-girl, and only hoping to arrive at the dignity of a gardener. The majority of the world thinks I am not even fit to speak to," she added, in a low tone.

Arden bowed his head, as if in reverence before her, and then said, firmly:

"And I wish you to understand that I am only Arden Lacey, with a sot for a father, and the scorn, contempt, and hatred of all the world as my heritage. I am a slipshod farmer. Our place is heavily mortgaged, and will eventually be sold away from us. It grows more weeds now than anything else; and it seems that nettles have been the principal crop that I have reaped all my life. Thus, you see, I am poorer than poverty, and am rich only in my mother, and, eventually, I hope," he added timidly, "in the possession of your friendship, Miss Allen; I shall try so sincerely and hard to deserve it."

With a frown, a laugh, and a shy look of sympathy at him, Edith said, "I don't see but you have got to find out your mistake for yourself. Time and facts cure many follies." But she found little encouragement in his incredulous smile."

The next moment she turned upon him so sharply that he was startled.

"I am a business woman," she said, "and conduct my affairs on business principles. You said, I think, you would help me find a market for the produce of my place?"

"Certainly," he replied.

"As certainly you must take fifteen per cent commission on all sales."

"Oh, Miss Allen," commenced Arden, "I couldn't—"

"There," said she, decisively, "you haven't the first idea of business. Not a thing can you touch unless you comply with my conditions. There is no sentiment, I assure you, connected with currants and cabbages."

"You may be certain, Miss Allen, that I would comply with any condition," said Arden, with the air of one who is cornered, "but let me suggest, since we are arranging this matter so strictly on business grounds, that ten per cent is all I should take. That is the regular commission, and is all I pay in sending produce to New York."

"Oh, I didn't know that," said the experienced and un-compromising woman of business, innocently. "Do you think that would pay you for your trouble?"

"I think it would," he replied, so demurely and yet with such a twinkle in his blue eyes, that now looked very different with the light of hope and happiness in them, that Edith turned away with a laugh.

But she said, with assumed sharpness, "See that you keep your accounts straight. I shall be a very dragon over your account-book."

Thus the ice was broken, and Edith and Arden became *friends*.

The future has now been quite clearly indicated to the reader, and, lest my story should grow wearisome as a "twice-told tale," we pass over several subsequent months with but a few words.

It was not a good fruit year, and Edith's place had been sadly neglected previous to her possession. Therefore, though Arden surprised himself in the sharp business traits he developed as Edith's salesman, the results were not very large. But still they greatly assisted her, and amounted to more than the earnings of her unskilled hands from other sources. She insisted on doing everything on business principles, and made Arden take his ten per cent, which was of real help to him in this way: he gave all the money to his mother, saying, "*I* couldn't spend it to save my life." Mrs. Lacey had many uses for every penny she could obtain.

Then Edith paid old Malcom by making up bouquets for sale at the hotel, and arranging baskets of flowers for parties there and elsewhere, and other lighter labors. Mrs. Groody continued to send her work; and thus during the summer and early fall she managed to make her garden and her labor provide for all family expenses, saving what was left of the four hundred, after paying all debts, for winter need. Moreover, she stored away in cellar and attic enough of the products of the garden to be of great help also.

Mrs. Allen did recover her usual health, and also her usual modes of thought and feeling. The mental and moral habits of a lifetime are not readily changed. Often and earnestly did Edith talk with her mother, but with few evidences of the result she longed to see.

Mrs. Allen's condition, in view of the truth, was the most hopeless one of all. She saw only her preconceived ideas, and not the truth itself. One day she said, with some irritation, to Edith, who was pleading with her:

"Do you think I am a heathen? Of course, I believe the Bible. Of course, I believe in Jesus Christ. I have been a member of the church ever since I was sixteen."

Edith sighed, and thought, "Only He who can satisfy her need can reveal it to her."

Poor Mrs. Allen! With the strange infatuation of a worldly mind, she was turning to the world, and it alone, for hope and solace. Untaught by the wretched experience of the past, she was led to enter upon a new and similar scheme for the aggrandizement of her family, as will be explained in another chapter.

Laura regained her strength somewhat, and was able to relieve Edith of the care of her mother and the lighter duties of the house. Her faith developed like that shy, delicate blossom called the "wind-flower," easily shaken, and yet with a certain hardiness and power to live and thrive in sterile places.

Edith and Mrs. Lacey were eventually received into the church that Malcom attended, and, after the simple service, they took dinner with the old Scotchman and his wife. Malcom seemed hardly "in the body" all day.

"My heart's a-bloom," he said, "wi' a' the sweet posies that God ever made blush when he looked at them the first time, an' ye seem the sweetest o' them a', Miss Edith. Ah, but the Gude Husbandman gathered a fair blossom the day."

"Now, Mr. McTrump," said Edith, reproachfully, but with a face like Malcom's posies, "you shouldn't give compliments on Sunday." For Arden and Rose were present also, and Edith thought, "Such foolish words will only increase his infatuation."

"Weel," said Malcom, scratching his head, in his perplexed effort at apology, "I wud na mak ye vain, nor hurt yer conscience, but it kind o' slippit out afore I could stop it."

In the laugh that followed Malcom's explanation Edith felt that matters had not been helped much, and she adroitly turned the conversation.

Public opinion, from being at first very bitter and scornful against the Allens, gradually began to soften. One after another, as they recognized Edith's patient, determined effort to do right, began to give her the credit and the respect to which she was entitled. Little acts and tokens of kindly feeling became more frequent, and were like glints of sunlight on her shadowed path. But the great majority felt that they could have no associations with such as the Allens, and completely ignored them.

In their relations with the church, Edith and Mrs. Lacey found increasing satisfaction. Many of its humble, and some of its more influential, members treated them with much kindness and sympathy, and they realized more and more that there are good, kind people in the world, if you look in the right way and right places for them. The Rev. Mr. Knox was a faithful preacher and pastor, and if his sermons were a little dry and doctrinal at times, they were as sound and sweet as a nut. Moreover, both Edith and Mrs. Lacey were sadly deficient in the doctrines, neither having ever had any religious instruction, and they listened with the grave, earnest interest of those desiring to be taught.

Mrs. Groody reconnected herself with her old church. "I want to go where I can shout 'Glory!'" she said.

Rose but faintly sympathized with her mother's feelings. Her restless, ambitious spirit turned longingly toward the world. Its attractions she could understand, but not those of faith. Through her father's evil habits, and Arden's poor farming, the pressure of poverty rested heavier and heavier on the family, and she had about resolved to go to New York and find employment in some store.

Arden rarely went to church, but read at home. He was somewhat sceptical in regard to the Bible, not that he had ever carefully examined either it or its evidences, but he had read much of the prevalent semi-infidelity, and was a little conceited over his independent thinking. Then, in a harsh, sweeping cynicism, he utterly detested church people, calling them the "holy sect of the Pharisees."

"But they are not all such," his mother would say.

"Oh, no," he would reply; "there are some sincere ones, of course; but I think they would be better out than in such a company of hypocrites."

But as he saw Edith's sincerity, and learned of her purpose to unite with the church, he kept these views more and more in the background; but he had too much respect for her and his mother's faith to go with them to what they regarded as a sacred place, from merely the personal motive of being near Edith.

One day Mrs. Lacey and Edith walked down to the evening prayer-meeting. Arden, who had business in the village, was to call for them at its close; as they were walking home, Edith suddenly asked him:

"Why don't you go to church?"

"I don't like the people I meet there."

"What have you against them?"

"Well, there is Mr. Hard. He is one of the 'lights and pillars'; and he would have sold the house over your head if you had not paid him. He can 'devour a widow's house' as well as they of olden time."

"That is not the question," said the practical Edith, earnestly. "What have you to do with Mr. Hard, or he with you? Does he propose—is he able to save you? The true question is, What have you got against Jesus Christ?"

"Well, really, Miss Edith, I can have nothing against Him. Both history and legend unite in presenting Him as one of the purest and noblest of men. But pardon me if I say in all honesty that I cannot quite accept your belief in regard to Him and the Bible in general. A man can hardly be a man without exercising the right of independent thought. I cannot take a book called the Bible for granted."

"But," asked, Edith keenly, "are you not taking other books for granted? Answer me truly, Mr. Lacey, have you carefully and patiently investigated this subject, not only on the side of your sceptical writers, but on God's side also? He has plenty of facts, as well as the infidels, and my rich, lasting, rational, spiritual experience is as much a fact as that stone there, and a good deal higher and better one, I think."

Arden was silent for some little time, and they could see in the moonlight that his face was very grave and thoughtful. At last he said, as if it had been wrung from him:

"Miss Allen, to be honest with you and myself, I have never given the subject such a fair examination." After a moment he continued, "Even if I became convinced that all were true, I might still remain at home, for I could find far more advantage in reading books, or the Bible itself, than from Mr. Knox's dry sermons."

"I think you are wrong," said Edith, gently but firmly. "Granting the premise you admitted a moment ago, that Christ was one of the purest and noblest of men, you surely, with your chivalric instincts, would say that such a man ought to be imitated."

"Yes," said Arden, "and He denounced the Pharisees."

"And He worshipped with them also," said Edith, quickly. "He went to the temple with the others. What was there to interest Him in the dreary forlorn little syna-

gogue at Nazareth ? and yet He was there with the regularity
of the Sabbath.   It was the best form of faith and worship
then existing, and He sustained it by every means in His
power, till He could give the people something better.
Suppose all the churches in this place were closed, not
one in a hundred would or could read the books you refer
to.   If your example were followed they would be closed.
As far as your example goes it tends to close them.   I have
heard Mr. Knox say, that wherever Christian worship and
the Christian Sabbath are not observed, society rapidly
deteriorates.   Is it not true ?''

They had stopped at Edith's gate.   Arden averted his
face for a moment, then turning toward Edith he gave her
his hand, saying:

"Yes, it is true, and a true, faithful friend you have
been to me to-night.   I admit myself vanquished.''

Edith gave his hand a cordial pressure, saying earnestly,
"You are not vanquished by the young ignorant girl,
Edith Allen, but by the truth that will yet vanquish the
world.''

After that Arden went regularly with them to church,
and tried to give sincere attention to the service, but his
uncurbed fancy was wandering to the ends of the earth
most of the time; or his thoughts were dwelling in rapt
attention on Edith.   She, after all, was the only object of
his faith and worship, though he had a growing intellectual
conviction that her faith was true.

And so the months passed into autumn, but with the
nicest sense of honor he refrained from word or deed that
would remind Edith that he was her lover.   She became
greatly attached to him, and he seemed almost like a brother
to her.   She found increasing pleasure in his society, for
Arden, after the restraint of his diffidence was banished,
could talk well, and he opened to her the rich treasures
of his reading, and with almost a poet's fancy and power
pictured to her the storied past.

To both herself and Mrs. Lacey, life grew sunnier and

sweeter. But they each had a heavy burden on their hearts, which they daily brought to the feet of the Compassionate One. They united in praying for Mrs. Lacey's husband, and for Zell; and their strong faith and love would take no denial. But, as Laura had said, the silence of the grave seemed to have swallowed lost Zell.

CHAPTER XXXI

ZELL

" AND the silence of the grave ought to swallow such as poor Zell had become," is, perhaps, the thought of some. All reference to her and her class should be suppressed.

We firmly say, No! If so, the New Testament must be suppressed. The Divine Teacher spoke plainly both of the sin and the sinner. He had scathing denunciation for the one, and compassion and mercy for the other. Shall we enforce His teachings against all other forms of evil, and not against this deadliest one of all—and that, too, in the laxity and wide demoralization of our age, when temptation lurks on every hand, and parents are often sleepless with just anxiety?

Evil is active, alluring, suggesting, insinuating itself when least expected, and many influences are at work, with the full approval of society, to poison forever all pure thoughts. And temptation is sure to come at first as an angel of light.

There is no safety save in solemn words of warning, the wholesome terror which knowledge inspires, the bracing of principle, and the ennobling of Christian faith. There are too many incarnate fiends who will take advantage of the innocence of ignorance.

Zell is not in her grave. She is sinning, but more sinned against. He who said to one like her, of old, "Her sins, which are many, are forgiven," loves her still, and Edith is praying for her. The grave cannot close over her yet.

But as we look upon this long-lost one, as she reclines

on a sofa in Van Dam's luxurious apartments, as we see her temples throbbing with pain, and that her cheeks are flushed and feverish, it would seem that the grave might soon hide her from a contemptuous and vindictive world.

Her head does ache sadly—it seems bursting with pain; but her heart aches with a bitterer anguish. Zell had too fine a nature to sin brutally and unfeelingly. Her betrayer's treachery wounded her more deeply than he could understand. Even her first strong love for him could not bridge the chasm of guilt to which he led her, and her passionate nature and remorse often caused her to turn upon him with such scathing reproaches that even he, in his hardihood, trembled.

Knowing how proud and high-strung she was, he feared to reveal his treachery in New York, a locality with which she was familiar; so he said that very important business called him at once to Boston, a city where he had few acquaintances. Zell reluctantly acquiesced in this further journey.

They jaunted about in the North and West through the summer and autumn, and now have but recently returned to New York.

With a wild terror she saw that his passion for her was waning. Therefore, her reproaches and threats became at times almost terrific, and again her servile entreaties were even more pitiable and dreadful, in view of what a true wife's position and right ought to be. He, wearying of her fierce and alternating moods, and selfishly thinking of his own ease and comfort, as was ever the case, had resolved to throw her off at the first opportunity.

But retribution for both was near. The smallpox was almost epidemic in the city: Zell's silk had swept against a beggar's infected rags, and fourteen days later appeared the fatal symptoms.

And truly she is weary and heart-sick this afternoon. She never remembered feeling so ill. The thought of death appalled her. She felt, as never before, that she wanted some one to love and take care of her.

Van Dam entered, and said, rather roughly:

"What's the matter?"

"I'm sick," said Zell, faintly.

He muttered an oath.

She arose from the sofa and tottered to his easy-chair, knelt, and clasped his knees.

"Guilliam," she pleaded, "I am very sick. I have a feeling that I shall die. Won't you marry me? Won't you take care of your poor little Zell, that loved you so well as to leave all for you? Perhaps I sha'n't burden you much longer, but, if I do get well, I will be your patient slave, if you will only marry me;" and the tears poured over the hot, feverish cheeks, that they could not cool.

His only reply was to ask, with some irritation:

"How do you feel?"

"Oh, my head aches, my bones ache, every part of my body aches, but my heart aches worst of all. You can ease that, Guilliam. In the name of God's mercy, won't you?"

A sudden thought caused the coward's face to grow white with fear. "I must have a doctor see you," was his only reply to her appeal, and he passed hastily out.

Zell felt that a blow would have been better than his indifference, and she crawled back to her couch. A little later, she was conscious that a physician was feeling her pulse, and examining her symptoms. After he was gone she had strength enough to take off her jewelry and rings—all, save one solitaire diamond, that her father had given her. The rest seemed to oppress her with their weight. She then threw herself on the bed.

She was next conscious that some one was lifting her up. She roused for a moment, and stared around. There were several strange faces.

"What do you want? What are you going to do with me?" she asked, in a thick voice, and in vague terror.

"I am sorry, miss," said one of the men, in an official tone; "but you have the smallpox, and we must take you to the hospital."

She gave one shriek of horror. A hand was placed over her mouth. She murmured faintly:

"Guilliam—help!" and then, under the effects of disease and fear, became partially unconscious; but her hand clenched, and with some instinct hard to understand, remained so, over the diamond ring that was her father's gift.

She was conscious of riding in something hard over the stony street, for the jolting hurt her cruelly. She was conscious of the sound of water, for she tried to throw herself into it, that it might cool her fever. She was conscious of reaching some place, and then she felt as if she had no rest for many days, and yet was not awake. But through it all she kept her hand closed on her father's gift. At times it seemed to her that some one was trying to take it off, but she instinctively struggled and cried out, and the hand was withdrawn.

At last one night she seemed to wake and come to herself. She opened her eyes and looked timidly around the dim ward. All was strange and unaccountable. She feared that she was in another world. But as she raised her hand to her head, as if to clear away the mist of uncertainty, a sparkle from the diamond caught her eye. For a long time she stared vacantly at it, with the weak, vague feeling that in some sense it might be a clew. Its faint lustre was like the glimmer of a star through a rift in the clouds to a lost traveller. Its familiar light and position remind him of home, and by its ray he guesses in what direction to move; so the crystallized light upon her finger threw its faint glimmer into the past, and by its help Zell's weak mind groped its way down from the hour it was given to the moment when she became partially unconscious in Van Dam's apartments. But the word smallpox was burned into her brain, and she surmised that she was in a hospital.

At last a woman passed. Zell feebly called her.

"What do you want?" said a rather gruff voice.

"I want to write a letter."

"You can't. It's against the rules."

"I must," pleaded Zell. "Oh, as you are a woman, and hope in God's mercy, don't refuse me."

"Can't break the rules," said the woman, and she was about to pass on.

"Stop!" said Zell, in a whisper. "See there," and she flashed the diamond upon her. "I'll give you that if you'll promise before God to send a letter for me. It would take you many months to earn the value of that."

The woman was a part of the city government, so she acted characteristically. She brought Zell writing materials and a bit of candle, saying:

"Be quick!"

With her poor, stiff, diseased hand, Zell wrote:

"GUILLIAM—You cannot know where I am. You cannot know what has happened. You could not be such a fiend as to cast me off and send me here to die—and die I shall. The edge of the grave seems crumbling under me as I write. If you have a spark of love for me, come and see me before I die. Oh, Guilliam, Guilliam! what a heaven of a home I would have made you, if you had only married me! It would have been my whole life to make you happy. I said bitter words to you—forgive them. We both have sinned—can God forgive us? I will not believe you know what has happened. You are grieving for me—looking for me. They took me away while you were gone. Come and see me before I die. Good-by. I'm writing in the dark—I'm dying in the dark—my soul is in the dark—I'm going away in the dark —where, O God, where?

"Your poor little   ZELL.
"SMALLPOX HOSPITAL (I don't know date)."

Poor, poor Zell! As in the case of a tempest-tossed one of old, "sun, moon, and stars" had long been hidden.

Almost fainting with weakness, she sealed and directed the letter, drew off the ring, pressed it to her lips, and then turned her eyes, unnaturally large and bright, on the woman waiting at her side, and said:

"Look at me! Promise me you will see that this letter is delivered. Remember, I am going to die. If you ever hope for an hour's peace, promise!"

"I promise," said the woman solemnly, for she was as superstitious as avaricious, and though she had no hesitancy in breaking the rules and taking a bribe, she would not have dared for her life to have risked treachery to a girl whom she believed dying.

Zell gave her the ring and the letter, and sank back for the time unconscious.

The woman had her means of communication with the city, and before many hours elapsed the letter was on its way.

Van Dam was in a state of nervous fear till the fourteen days passed, and then he felt that he was safe. He had his rooms thoroughly fumigated, and was reassured by his physicians saying daily: "There was not much danger of her giving you the disease in its first stage. She is probably dead by this time."

But the wheels of life seemed to grow heavier and more clogged every day. He was fast getting down to the dregs, and now almost every pleasure palled upon his jaded taste. At one time it seemed that Zell might so infuse her vigorous young life and vivacity into his waning years that his last days would be his best. And this might have been the case, if he had reformed his evil life and dealt with her as a true man. In her strong and exceptional love, considering their difference in age, there were great possibilities of good for both. But he had foully perverted the last best gift of his life, and even his blunted moral sense was awakening to the truth.

"Curse it all," he muttered, late one morning, "perhaps I had better have married her. I hoped so much from her, and she has been nothing but a source of trouble and danger. I wonder if she is dead."

He had been out very late the night before, and had played heavily, but not with his usual skill. He had kept muttering grim oaths against his luck, and drinking deeper and deeper till a friend had half forced him away. And now, much shaken by the night's debauch, depressed by his heavy losses, conscience, that crouches like a tiger in every bad man's soul, and waits to rush from its lair and rend, in the long hours—the long *eternity* of weakness and memory—already had its fangs in his guilty heart.

Long and bitterly he thought, with a frown resting like night on his heavy brow. The servant brought him a dainty breakfast, but he sullenly motioned it away. He had wronged his digestive powers so greatly the night before that even brandy was repugnant to him, and he leaned heavily and wearily back in his chair, a prey to remorse.

He was in just the right physical condition to take a contagious disease.

There was a knock at the door, and the servant entered, bringing him a letter, saying, "This was just left here for ye, sir."

"A dun," thought he, languidly, and he laid it unopened on the stand beside him.

It was; and from one whom he owed a reparation he could never make, though he paid with his life.

With his eyes closed, he still leaned back in a dull, painful lethargy. A faint, disagreeable odor gradually pervaded the room, and at last attracted his attention. The luxurious sybarite could not help the stings of conscience, the odor he might. He grew restless, and looked around.

Zell's letter caught his attention. "Might as well see who it's from," he muttered. Weakness, pain, and emotion had so changed Zell's familiar hand, that he did not recognize it.

But, as he opened and read, his eyes dilated with horror. It seemed like a dead hand grasping him out of the darkness. But a dreadful fascination compelled him to read every line, and re-read them, till they seemed burned into his memory. At last, by a desperate effort, he broke the strong spell her words had placed upon him, and, starting up, exclaimed:

"Go to her, in that pest-house! I would see her dead a thousand times first. I hope she is dead, for she is the torment of my life. What is it that smells so queer?"

His eyes again rested on the letter. A suspicion crossed

his mind. He carried the letter to his nose, and then started violently, uttering awful oaths.

"She has sent the contagion directly to me," he groaned, and he threw poor Zell's appeal on the grate. It burned with a faint, sickly odor. Then, as the day was raw and windy, a sudden gust down the chimney blew it all out into the room, and scattered it in ashes, like Zell's hopes, around his feet.

A superstitious horror that made his flesh creep and hair rise took possession of him, and hastily gathering a few necessary things, he rushed out into the chill air, and made his way to a large hotel. He wanted to be in a crowd. He wanted the hard, material world's noise and bustle around him. He wanted to hear men talking about gold and stocks, and the gossip of the town—anything that would make living on seem a natural, possible matter of course.

But men's voices sounded strange and unfamiliar, and the real world seemed like that which mocks us in our dreams. Mingling with all he saw and heard were ·Zell's despairing looks and Zell's despairing words. He wrapped himself in his great coat, he drank frequent and fiery potations, he hovered around the registers, but nothing could take away the chill at his heart. He tossed feverishly all night. His sudden exposure to the raw wind in his heated, excited condition caused a severe cold. But he would not give up. He dared not stay alone in his room, and so crept down to the public haunts of the hotel. But his flushed cheeks and strange manner attracted attention. As the days passed, he grew worse, and the proprietor of the house said:

"You are ill, you must go to bed."

But he would not. There was nothing that he seemed to dread so much as being alone. But the guests began to grow afraid of him. There was general and widespread fear of the smallpox in the city, and for some reason it began to be associated with his illness. As the suspicion was whispered around, all shrank from him. The proprietor had him examined at once by a physician. It was the fatal fourteenth day, and the dreaded symptoms were apparent.

"Have you no friends, no home to which you can go?" he was asked.

"No," he groaned, while the thought pierced his soul. "She would have made me one and taken care of me in it." But he pleaded, "For God's sake, don't send me away."

"I must," said the proprietor, frightened himself. "The law requires it, and your presence here would empty my house in an hour."

So, in the dusk, like poor Zell, he was smuggled down a back stairway, and sent to the "pest-house" also, he groaning and crying with terror all the way.

Zell did not die. Her vigorous constitution rallied, and she rapidly regained strength. But with strength and power of thought came the certainty to her mind of Van Dam's utter and final abandonment of her. She felt that all the world would now be against her, and that she would be driven from every safe and pleasant path. The thought of taking her shame to her home was a horror to her, and she felt sure that Edith would spurn her from the door. At first she wept bitterly and despairingly, and wished she had died. But gradually she grew hard, reckless, and cruel under her wrong, and her every thought of Van Dam was a curse.

The woman who helped her to write the letter greatly startled her one day by saying:

"There's a man in the men's ward who in his ravin' speaks of you."

"Could he, in just retribution, have been sent here also?" she thought. Pleading relationship, she was admitted to see him. He shuddered as he saw her advancing, with stony face and eyes in which glared relentless hate.

"Curse you!" he muttered, feebly, with his parched lips. "Go away, living or dead, I know not which you are; but I know it was through you I came here!"

Her only answer was a mocking smile.

The doctor came and examined his symptoms.

"Will he get well?" she asked, following him away a short distance.

"No," said the physician. "He will die."

Her cheek blanched for a moment; but from her eyes glowed a deadly gleam of satisfaction.

"What did he say?" whispered Van Dam.

"He says you will die," she answered, in a stony voice. "You see, I am better than you were. You would not come to me for even one poor moment. You left me to die alone; but I will stay and watch with you."

"Oh, go away!" groaned Van Dam.

"I couldn't be so heartless," she said, in a mocking tone. "You need dying consolation. I want to tell you, Guilliam, what was in my mind the night I left all for you. I did doubt you a little. That is where I sinned; but I shall only suffer for that through all eternity," she said, with a reckless laugh that chilled his soul. "But then, I hoped, I felt almost sure, you would marry me; and, oh, what a heaven of a home I purposed to make you! If you had only let even a magistrate say, 'I pronounce you man and wife," I would have been your patient slave. I would have kissed away even your headaches, and had you ten contagions, I would not have left you. I would have taken care of you and nursed you back to life."

"Go away!" groaned Van Dam, with more energy.

"Guilliam," she said, taking his hand, which shuddered at her touch, "we might have had a happy little home by this time. We might have learned to live a good life in this world and have prepared for a better one in the next. Little children might have put their soft arms around your neck, and with their innocent kisses banished the memory and the power of the evil past. Oh," she gasped, "how happy we might have been, and mother, Edith, and Laura would have smiled upon us. But what is now our condition?" she said, bitterly, her grip upon his hand becoming hard and fierce. "You have made me a tigress. I must cower and hide through life like a wild beast in a jungle. And you are dying and going to hell," she hissed in his ear, "and by and by, when I get to be an old ugly hag, I will come and torment you there forever and forever."

"Curse you, go away," shrieked the terror-stricken man.

An attendant hastened to the spot; Zell was standing at the foot of the cot, glaring at him.

"I thought you was a relation of his'n," said the man, roughly.

"So I am," said Zell, sternly. "As the one stung is related to the viper that stung him," and with a withering look she passed away.

That night Van Dam died.

In process of time Zell was turned adrift in the city. She applied vainly at stores and shops for a situation. She had no good clothes, and appearances were against her. She had a very little money in her portemonnaie when she was taken to the hospital. This was given to her on leaving, and she made it go as far as possible. At last she went to an intelligence office and sat among the others, who looked suspiciously at her. They instinctively felt that she was not of their sort.

"What can you do?" was the frequent question.

She did not know how to do a single thing, but thought that perhaps the position of waitress would be the easiest.

"Where are your references?"

It was her one thought and effort to conceal all reference to the past. At last the proprietor in pity sent her to a lady who had told him to supply her with a waitress; the place was in Brooklyn, and Zell was glad, for she had less fear there of seeing any one she knew.

The lady scolded bitterly about such an ignoramus being sent to her, but Zell seemed so patient and willing that she decided to try her. Zell gave her whole soul to the work, and though the place was a hard one, would have eventually learned to fill it. The family were a little surprised sometimes at her graceful movements, and the quick gleams of intelligence in her large eyes as some remark was made natu- rally beyond one in her sphere. One day they were trying to recall, while at the table, the name of a famous singer at the opera. Before she thought, the name was almost out of her lips. The poor girl tried to disguise herself by assuming, as well as she could, the stolid, stupid manner of those who usually blunder about our homes.

All might have gone well, and she have gained an hon- est livelihood, had not an unforeseen circumstance revealed her past life. Those who have done wrong are never safe. At the most unexpected time, and in the most unexpected way, their sin may stand out before all and blast them.

Zell's mistress had told her to make a little extra prepa- ration, for she expected a gentleman to dine that evening. With some growing pride and interest in her work, she had done her best, and even her mistress said:

"Jane" (her assumed name), "you are improving," and a gleam of something like hope and pleasure shot across the poor child's face. A passionate sigh came up from her heart—

"Oh, I will try to do right if the world will let me."

But imagine her terror as she saw an old crony of Van Dam's enter the room. The man recognized her in a mo- ment, and she saw that he did. She gave him an imploring glance, which he returned by one of cool contempt. Zell could hardly get through the meal, and her manner attracted attention. The cold-blooded fellow, whose soul was akin to that of his dead friend, was considerate enough to his hostess not to spoil her dinner or rob her of a waitress till it was over. But the moment they returned to the parlor he told who Zell was, and how she must have just come from the smallpox hospital.

The lady (?) was in a frenzy of rage and fear. She rushed down to where Zell was panting with weakness and emotion, exclaiming:

"You shameful hussy, how dare you come into a re-

15—ROE—X

spectable house, after your loathsome life and loathsome disease?''

"Hear me," pleaded Zell; "the doctor said there was no danger, and I want to do what is right."

"I don't believe a word you say. I wouldn't trust you a minute. How much you have stolen now it will be hard to tell, and I shouldn't wonder if we all had the smallpox. Leave the house instantly."

"Oh, please give me a chance," cried Zell, on her knees. "Indeed, I am honest. I'll work for you for nothing, if you will let me stay."

"Leave instantly, or I will call for a policeman."

"Then pay me my week's wages," sobbed Zell.

"I won't pay you a cent, you brazen creature. You didn't know how to do anything, and have been a torment ever since you came. I might have known there was something wrong. Now go, take your old, pest-infected rags out of my house, or I will have you sent to where you properly belong. Thank Heaven, I have found you out."

A sudden change came over Zell. She sprang up, and a scowl black as night darkened her face.

"What has Heaven to do with your sending a poor girl out into the night, I would like to know?" she asked, in a harsh, grating voice; "I wouldn't do it. Therefore, I am better than you are. Heaven has nothing to do with either you or me;" and she looked so dark and dangerous that her mistress was frightened, and ran up to the parlor, exclaiming:

"She's an awful creature. I'm afraid of her."

Then that manly being, her husband, towered up in his wrath, saying, majestically, "I guess I'm master in my own house yet."

He showed poor Zell the door. Her laugh rang out recklessly, as she called—

"Good-by. May the pleasant thought that you have sent one more soul to perdition lull you to sweet sleep."

But, for some reason, it did not. When they became

cool enough to think it over, they admitted that perhaps they had been a "little hasty."

They had a daughter of about Zell's age. It would be a little hard if any one should treat her so.

Zell had scarcely more than enough to pay her way to New York. It seemed that people ought to stretch out their hands to shield her, but they only jostled her in their haste. As she stood, with her bundle, in the ferry entrance on the New York side, undecided where to go, a man ran against her in his hurry.

"Get out of the way," he said, irritably.

She moved out one side into the darkness, and with a pallid face said:

"Yes, it has come to this. I must 'get out of the way' of all decent people. There is the river on one side. There are the streets on the other. Which shall it be?"

> "Oh! it was pitiful,
> Near a whole city full,"

that no hand was stretched to her aid.

She shuddered. "I can't, I dare not die yet. It must be a little easier here than there, where he is."

Her face became like stone. She went straight to a liquor saloon, and drank deep of that spirit that Shakespeare called "devil," in order to drown thought, fear, memory—every vestige of the woman.

Then—the depths of the gulf that Laura shrank from with a dread stronger than her love of life.

CHAPTER XXXII

EDITH BRINGS THE WANDERER HOME

MRS. LACEY and Arden, at last, in the stress of their poverty, gave their consent that Rose should go to the city and try to find employment in a store as a shop-girl. Mrs. Glibe, her dressmaking friend, went with her, and though they could obtain no situation the first day, one of Mrs. Glibe's acquaintances directed Rose where she could find a respectable boarding-house, from which, as her home, she could continue her inquiries. Leaving her there, Mrs. Glibe returned.

Rose, with a hope and courage not easily dampened, continued her search the next day, and for several days following. The fall trade had not fairly commenced, and there seemed no demand for more help. She had thirty dollars with which to start life, but a week of idleness took seven of this.

At last her fine appearance and sprightly manner induced the proprietor of a large establishment to put her in the place of a girl discharged that day, with the wages of six dollars a week.

"We give but three or four, as a general thing, to beginners," he said.

Rose was grateful for the place, and yet almost dismayed at the prospect before her. How could she live on six dollars? The bright-colored dreams of city life were fast melting away before the hard, and in some instances revolting, facts of her experience. She could have obtained situations in two or three instances at better wages, if she had assented to conditions that sent her hastily into the street with burning blushes and indignant tears. She knew the great city was full of wickedness, but this rude contact with it appalled her.

After finding what she had to live on, she exchanged her somewhat comfortable room, where she could have a fire, for a cold, cheerless attic closet in the same house. "As I learn the business, they will give more," she thought, and the idea of going home penniless, to be laughed at by Mrs. Glibe, Miss Klip, and others was almost as bitter a prospect to her proud spirit as being a burden to her impoverished family, and she resolved to submit to every hardship rather than do it. By taking the attic room she reduced her board to five dollars a week.

"You can't get it for less, unless you go to a very common sort of a place," said her landlady. "My house is respectable, and people must pay a little for that."

In view of this fact, Rose determined to stay, if possible, for she was realizing more every day how unsheltered and tempted she was.

Her fresh blond face, her breezy manner, and her wind-shaken curls made many turn to look after her. Like some others of her sex, perhaps she had no dislike for admiration, but in Rose's position it was often shown by looks, manner, and even words, that, however she resented them, followed and persecuted her.

As she grew to know her fellow-workers better, her heart sickened in disgust at the conversation and the evident life of many of them, and they often laughed immoderately at her greenness.

Alas for the fancied superiority of these knowing girls! They laughed at Rose because she was so much more like what God meant a woman should be than they. A weak-minded, shallow girl would have succumbed to their ridicule, and soon have become like them, but high-spirited Rose only despised them, and gradually sought out and found some companionship with those of the better sort in the large store. But there seemed so much hollowness and falsehood on every side that she hardly knew whom to trust.

Poor Rose was quite sick of making a career for herself alone in the city, and her money was getting very low. Shop life was hard on clothes, and she was compelled by the rules of the store to dress well, and was only too fond of dress herself. So, instead of getting money ahead, she at last was reduced to her wages as support, and nothing was said of their being raised, and she was advised to say nothing about any increase. Then she had a week's sickness, and this brought her in debt to her landlady.

Several times during her evening walks home Rose noticed a dark face and two vivid black eyes, that seemed watching her; but as soon as observed, the face vanished. It haunted her with its suggestion of some one seen before.

She went back to her work too soon after her illness, and had a relapse. Her respectable landlady was a woman of system and rules. From long experience, she foresaw that her poor lodger would grow only more and more deeply in her debt. Perhaps we can hardly blame her. It was by no easy effort that she made ends meet as it was. She had an application for Rose's little room from one who gave more prospect of being able to pay, so she quietly told the poor girl to vacate it. Rose pleaded to stay, but the woman was inexorable. She had passed through such scenes so often that they had become only one of the disagreeable phases of her business.

"Why, child," she said, "if I did not live up to my rule in this respect, I'd soon be out of house and home myself. You can leave your things here till you find some other place."

So poor Rose, weak through her sickness, more weak through terror, found herself out in the streets of the great city, utterly penniless. She was so unfamiliar with it that she did not know where to go, or to whom to apply. It was her purpose to find a cheaper boarding-house. She went down toward the meaner and poorer part of the city, and stopped at the low stoop of a house where there was a sign, ''Rooms to let.''

She was about to enter, when a hand was laid sharply on her arm, and some one said:

''Don't go there. Come with me, quick!''

''Who are you?'' asked Rose, startled and trembling.

''One who can help you now, whatever I am,'' was the answer. ''I know you well, and all about you. You are Rose Lacey, and you did live in Pushton. Come with me, quick, and I will take you to a Christian lady whom you can trust. Come.''

Rose, in her trouble and perplexity, concluded to follow her. They soon made their way to quite a respectable street, and rang the bell at the door of a plain, comfortable-appearing house.

A cheery, stout, middle-aged lady opened it. She looked at Rose's new friend, and reproachfully shook her finger at her, saying:

''Naughty Zell, why did you leave the Home?''

''Because I am possessed by a restless devil,'' was the strange answer. ''Besides, I can do more good in the streets than there. I have just saved her'' (pointing to Rose, who at once surmised that this was Zell Allen, though so changed that she would not have known her). ''Now,'' continued Zell, thrusting some money into Rose's hand, ''take this and go home at once. Tell her, Mrs. Ranger, that this city is no place for her.''

''If you have friends and a home to go to, it's the very best thing you can do,'' said the lady.

''But my friends are poor,'' sobbed Rose.

''No matter, go to them,'' said Zell, almost fiercely. ''I tell you there is no place for you here, unless you wish to go to perdition. Go home, where you are known. Scrub, delve, do anything rather than stay here. Your big brother can and will take care of you; though he does look so cross.''

"She is right, my child; you had better go at once," said the lady, decidedly.

"Who are you?" asked Rose of the latter speaker, with some curiosity.

"I am a city missionary," answered the lady, quietly, "and it is my business to help such poor girls as you are. I say to you from full knowledge, and in all sincerity, to go home is the very best thing that you can do."

"But why is there not a chance for a poor, well-meaning girl to earn an honest living in this great city?"

"Thousands are earning such a living, but there is not one chance in a hundred for you."

"Why?" asked Rose, hotly.

"Do you see all these houses? They are full of people," continued Mrs. Ranger, "and some of them contain many families. In these families there are thousands of girls who have a home, a shelter, and protectors here in the city. They have society in relatives and neighbors. They have no board to pay, and fathers and mothers, brothers and sisters, helping support them. They put all their earnings into a common fund, and it supports the family. Such girls can afford, and will work for two, three, four, and five dollars a week. All that they earn makes the burden so much less on the father, who otherwise would have supported them in idleness. Now, a homeless stranger in the city must pay board, and therefore they can't compete with those who live here. Wages are kept too low. Not one in a hundred, situated as you are, can earn enough to pay board and dress as they are required to in the fashionable stores. Have you been able?"

"No," groaned Rose. "I am in debt to my landlady now, and I had some money to start with."

"There it is," said Mrs. Ranger, sadly; "the same old story."

"But these stores ought to pay more," said Rose, indignantly.

"They will only pay for labor, as for everything else,

the market price, and that averages but six dollars a week,
and more are working for from three to five than for six.
As I told you, there are thousands of girls living in the
city glad to get a chance at any price."

Rose gave a weary, discouraged sigh and said, "I fear
you are right, I must go home. Indeed, after what has
happened I hardly dare stay."

"Go," said Zell, "as if you were leaving Sodom, and
don't look back." Then she asked, with a wistful, hungry
look, "Have you see any of—?" She stopped—she could
not speak the names of her kindred.

"Yes," said Rose, gently. (Yesterday she would have
stood coldly aloof from Zell. To-day she was very grateful
and full of sympathy.) "I know they are well. They were
all sick after—after you went away. But they got well
again, and (lowering her voice) Edith prays for you night
and day."

"Oh! oh!" sobbed Zell, "this is torment, this is to see
the heaven I cannot enter," and she dashed away.

"Poor child!" said Mrs. Ranger, "there's an angel in her
yet if I only knew how to bring it out. I may see her to-
morrow, and I may not for weeks. Take the money she left
with you, and here is some more. It may help her, to think
that she helped you. And now, my dear, let me see you
safely on your way home."

That night the stage left Rose at the poor dilapidated
little farmhouse, and in her mother's close embrace she felt
the blessedness of the home shelter, however poor, and the
protecting love of kindred, however plain.

"Arden is away," said the quiet woman of few words.
"He is home only twice a month. He has a job of cutting
and carting wood a good way from here. We are so poor
this winter he had to take this chance. Your father is doing
better. I hope for him, though with fear and trembling."

Then Rose told her mother her experience and how she
had been saved by Zell, and the poor woman clasped her
daughter to her breast again and again, and with streaming

eyes raised toward heaven, poured out her gratitude to God.

"Rose," said she, with a shudder, "if I had not prayed so for you night and day, perhaps you would not have found such friends in your time of need. Oh! let us both pray for that poor lost one, that she may be saved also."

From this day forth Rose began to pray the true prayer of pity, and then the true prayer of a personal faith. The rude, evil world had shown her her own and others' need, in a way that made her feel that she wanted the Heavenly Father's care.

In other respects she took up her life for a time where she had left it a few months before.

Edith was deeply moved at Rose's story, and Zell's wild, wayward steps were followed by prayers, as by a throng of reclaiming angels.

"I would go and bring her home in a moment, if I only knew where to find her," said Edith.

"Mrs. Ranger said she would write as soon as there was any chance of your doing so," said Rose.

About the middle of January a letter came to Edith as follows:

"MISS EDITH ALLEN—Your sister, Zell, is in Bellevue Hospital, Ward ——. Come quickly; she is very ill."

Edith took the earliest train, and was soon following an attendant, with eager steps, down the long ward. They came to a dark-eyed girl that was evidently dying, and Edith closed her eyes with a chill of fear. A second glance showed that it was not Zell, and a little further on she saw the face of her sister, but so changed! Oh! the havoc that sin and wretchedness had made in that beautiful creature during a few short months! She was in a state of unconscious, muttering delirium, and Edith showered kisses on the poor, parched lips; her tears fell like rain on the thin, flushed face. Zell suddenly cried, with the girlish voice of old:

"Hurrah, hurrah! books to the shades; no more teachers and tyrants for me."

She was living over the old life, with its old, fatal
tendencies.

Edith sat down, and sobbed as if her heart would break.
Unnoticed, a stout, elderly lady was regarding her with eyes
wet with sympathy. As Edith's grief subsided somewhat
she laid her hand on the poor girl's shoulder, saying:

"My child, I feel very sorry for you. For some reason
I can't pass on and leave you alone in your sorrow, though
we are total strangers. Your trouble gives you a sacred
claim upon me. What can I do for you?"

Edith looked up through her tears, and saw a kind,
motherly face, with a halo of gray curls around it. With
woman's intuition she trusted her instantly, and, with another rush of tears, said:

"This is—my—poor lost—sister. I've—just found her."

"Ah!" said the lady, significantly, "God pity you both."

"Were it not—for Him," sobbed Edith, with her hand
upon her aching heart, "I believe—I should die."

The lady sat down by her, and took her hand, saying,
"I will stay with you, dear, till you feel better."

Gradually and delicately she drew from Edith her story,
and her large heart yearned over the two girls in the sin-
cerest sympathy.

"I was not personally acquainted with your father and
mother, but I know well who they were," she said. "And
now, my child, you cannot remain here much longer; where
are you going to stay?"

"I haven't thought," said Edith, sadly.

"I have," replied the lady, heartily; "I am going to
take you home with me. We don't live very far away, and
you can come and see your sister as often as you choose,
within the limits of the rules."

"Oh!" exclaimed Edith, deprecatingly, "I am not fit—
I have no claim."

"My child," said the lady, gently, "don't you remember

what our Master said, 'I was a stranger and ye took me in'?
Is He not fit to enter my house? Has He no claim? In
taking you home I am taking Him home, and so I shall be
happy and honored in your presence. Moreover, my dear,
from what I have seen and heard, I am sure I shall love
you for your own sake."

Edith looked at her through grateful tears, and said, "It
has seemed to me that Jesus has been comforting me all the
time through your lips. How beautiful Christianity is, when
it is *lived* out. I will go to your house as if it were His."

Then she turned and pressed a loving kiss on Zell's unconscious face, but her wonder was past words when the
lady stooped down also, and kissed the "woman which was
a sinner." She seized her hand with both of hers and
faltered:

"You don't despise and shrink from her, then?"

"Despise her! no," said the noble woman. "I have
never been tempted as this poor child has. God does not
despise her. What am I?"

From that moment Edith could have kissed her feet, and
feeling that God had sent His angel to take care of her, she
followed the lady from the hospital. A plain but elegantly-
liveried carriage was waiting, and they were driven rapidly
to one of the stateliest palaces on Fifth Avenue. As they
crossed the marble threshold, the lady turned and said:

"Pardon me, my dear, my name is Mrs. Hart. This is
your home now as truly as mine while you are with us,"
and Edith was shown to a room replete with luxurious comfort, and told to rest till the six o'clock dinner.

With some timidity and fear she came down to meet the
others. As she entered she saw a portly man standing on
the rug before the glowing grate, with a shock of white
hair, and a genial, kindly face.

"My husband," said Mrs. Hart, "this is our new friend,
Miss Edith Allen. You knew her father well in business,
I am sure."

"Of course I did," said the old gentleman, taking Edith's

hand in both of his,"and a fine business man he was, too.
You are welcome to our home, Miss Edith. Look here,
mother,"he said, turning to his wife with a quizzical look,
and still keeping hold of Edith's hand, "you didn't bring
home an 'angel unawares' this time. I say, wife, you won't
be jealous if I take a kiss now, will you—a sort of scriptural
kiss, you know?" and he gave Edith a hearty smack that
broke the ice between them completely.

With a face like a peony, Edith said, earnestly, "I am
sure the real angels throng your home."

"Hope they do," said Mr. Hart, cheerily. "My old lady
there is the best one I have seen yet, but I am ready for all
the rest. Here come some of them," he added, as his daughters entered, and to each one he gave a hearty kiss, count-
ing, "one, two, three, four, five—now, 'all present or ac-
counted for?'"

"Yes," said his wife, laughing.

"Dinner, then," and after the young ladies had greeted
Edith most cordially, he gave her his arm, as if she had
been a duchess, and escorted her to the dining-room. After
being seated, they bowed their heads in quiet reverence,
and the old man, with the voice and manner of a child
speaking to a father, thanked God for His mercies, and in-
voked His blessing.

The table-talk was genial and wholesome, with now and
then a sparkle of wit, or a broad gleam of humor.

"My good wife there, Miss Edith," said Mr. Hart, with
a twinkle in his eye, "is a very sly old lady. If she does
wear spectacles, she sees with great discrimination, or else
the world is growing so full of interesting saints and sinners,
that I am quite in hopes of it. Every day she has a new
story about some very good person, or some very bad person becoming good. If you go on this way much longer,
mother, the millennium will commence before the doctors
of divinity are ready for it."

"My dear," said Mrs. Hart, with a comic aside to Edith,
"my husband has never got over being a boy. When he

will become old enough to sober down, I am sure I can't tell."

"What have I to sober me, with all these happy faces around, I should like to know?" was the hearty retort. "I am having a better time every day, and mean to go on so *ad infinitum.* You're a good one to talk about sobering down, when you laugh more than any of these youngsters."

"Well," said his wife, her substantial form quivering with merriment, "it's because you make me."

During the meal Edith had time to observe the young ladies more closely. They were fine-looking, and one or two of them really beautiful. Two of them were in early girlhood yet, and there was not a vestige of the vanity and affectation often seen in those of their position. They evidently had wide diversities of character, and faults, but there were the simplicity and sincerity about them which make the difference between a chaste piece of marble and a painted block of wood. She saw about her a house as rich and costly in its appointments as her own old home had been, but it was not so crowded or pronounced in its furnishing and decoration. There were fewer pictures, but finer ones; and in all matters of art, French taste was not prominent, as had been the case in her home.

The next day she sat by unconscious Zell as long as was permitted, and wrote fully to Laura.

The dark-eyed girl that seemed dying the day before was gone.

"Did she die?" she asked of an attendant.

"Yes."

"What did they do with her?"

"Buried her in Potter's Field."

Edith shuddered. "It would have been Zell's end," she thought, "if I hadn't found her, and she had died here alone."

That evening Mrs. Hart, as they all sat in her own private parlor, said to her daughters:

"Girls, away with you. I can't move a step without

stumbling over one of you. You are always crowding into my sanctum, as if there was not an inch of room for you anywhere else. Vanish. I want to talk to Edith.''

''It's your own fault that we crowd in here, mother,'' said the eldest. ''You are the loadstone that draws us.''

''I'll get a lot of stones to throw at you and drive you out with,'' said the old lady, with mock severity.

The youngest daughter precipitated herself on her mother's neck, exclaiming:

''Wouldn't that be fun, to see jolly old mother throwing stones at us. She would wrap them in eider-down first.''

''Scamper; the whole bevy of you,'' said the old lady, laughing; and Edith, with a sigh, contrasted this ''mother's room'' with the one which she and her sisters shunned as the place where their ''teeth were set on edge.''

''My dear,'' said Mrs. Hart, her face becoming grave and troubled, ''there is one thing in my Christian work that discourages me. We reclaim so few of the poor girls that have gone astray. I understand, from Mrs. Ranger, that your sister was at the Home, but that she left it. How can we accomplish more? We do everything we can for them.''

''I don't think earthly remedies can meet their case,'' said Edith, in a low tone.

''I agree with you,'' said Mrs. Hart, earnestly, ''but we do give them religious instruction.''

''I don't think religious instruction is sufficient,'' Edith answered. ''They need a Saviour.''

''But we do tell them about Jesus.''

''Not always in a way that they understand, I fear,'' said Edith, sadly. ''I have heard people tell about Him as they would about Socrates, or Moses, or Paul. We don't need facts about Him so much as Jesus Himself. In olden times people did not go to their sick and troubled friends and tell them that Jesus was in Capernaum, and that He was a great deliverer. They brought the poor, helpless creatures right to Him. They laid them right at the feet of a personal Saviour, and He helped them. Do we do this? I have thought a great deal about it," continued Edith, "and it seems to me that more associate the ideas of duty, restraint, and almost impossible effort with Him, than the ideas of help and sympathy. It was so with me, I know, at first."

"Perhaps you are right," said Mrs. Hart thoughtfully. "The poor creatures to whom I referred seemed more afraid of God than anything else."

"And yet, of all that ever lived, Jesus was the most tender toward them—the most ready to forgive and save. Believe me, Mrs. Hart, there was more gospel in the kiss you gave my sister—there was more of Jesus Christ in it, than in all the sermons ever written, and I am sure that if she had been conscious, it would have saved her. They must, as it were, *feel* the hand of love and power that lifted Peter out of the ingulfing waves. The idea of duty and sturdy self-restraint is perhaps too much emphasized, while they, poor things, are weak as water. They are so 'lost' that He must just 'seek and save' them, as He said—lift them up—keep them up almost in spite of themselves. Saved—that is the word, as the limp, helpless form is dragged out of danger. On account of my sister I have thought a good deal about this subject, and there seems to me to be no remedy for this class, save in the merciful, patient, personal Saviour. He had wonderful power over them when He was on earth, and He would have the same now, if His people could make them understand Him."

"I think few of us understand this personal Saviour ourselves as we ought," said Mrs. Hart, somewhat unveiling her own experience. "The Romish Church puts the Virgin, saints, penances, and I know not what, between the sinner and Jesus, and we put catechisms, doctrines, and a great mass of truth about them, between Him and us. I doubt whether many of us, like the beloved disciple, have leaned our heads on His heart of love, and felt its throbs. Too much of the time He seems in Heaven to me, not here."

"I never had much religious instruction," said Edith,

simply. "I found Him in the New Testament, as people of old found Him in Palestine, and I went to Him, just as I was, and He has been such a Friend and Helper. He lets me sit at His feet like Mary, and the words He spoke seem said directly to poor little me."

Wistful tears came into Mrs. Hart's eyes, and she kissed Edith, saying:

"I have been a Christian forty years, my child, but you are nearer to Him than I am. Stay close to His side. This talk has done me more good than I imagined possible."

"If I seem nearer," said Edith, gently, "isn't it, perhaps, because I am weaker than you are? His 'sheep follow' Him, but isn't there some place in the Bible about his 'carrying the lambs in His bosom'? I think we shall find at last that He was nearer to us all than we thought, and that His arm of love was around us all the time."

In a sudden, strong impulse, Mrs. Hart embraced Edith, and, looking upward, exclaimed:

"Truly 'Thou hast hid these things from the wise and prudent and hast revealed them unto babes.' As my husband said, I am entertaining a good angel."

The physician gave Edith great encouragement about Zell, and told her that in two weeks he thought she might be moved. The fever was taking a light form.

One evening, after listening to some superb music from Annie, the second daughter, between whom and Edith quite an affinity seemed to develop itself, the latter said:

"How finely you play! I think you are wonderful for an amateur."

"I am not an amateur," replied Annie, laughing. "Music is my profession."

"I don't understand," said Edith.

"Father has made me study music as a science," explained Annie. "I could teach it to-morrow. All of us girls are to have a profession. Ella, my eldest sister, is studying drawing and painting. Here is a portfolio of her sketches."

Even Edith's unskilled eyes could see that she had made great proficiency.

"Ella could teach drawing and coloring at once," continued Annie, "for she has studied the rules and principles very carefully, and given great attention to the rudiments of art, instead of having a teacher help her paint a few show pictures. But I know very little about it, for I haven't much taste that way. Father has us educated according to our tastes; that is, if we show a little talent for any one thing, he has us try to perfect ourselves in that one thing. Julia is the linguist, and can jabber French and German like natives. Father also insisted on our being taught the common English branches very thoroughly, and he says he could get us situations to teach within a month, if it were necessary."

Edith sighed deeply as she thought how superficial their education had been, but she said rather slyly to Annie, "But you are engaged. I think your husband will veto the music-teaching."

"Oh, well," said Annie, laughing, "Walter may fail, or get sick, or something may happen. So you see we shouldn't have to go to the poor-house. Besides, there's a sort of satisfaction in knowing one thing pretty well. But the half is not told you, and I suppose you will think father and mother queer people; indeed, most of our friends do. For mother has had a milliner come to the house, and a dressmaker, and a hair-dresser, and whatever we have any knack at she has made us learn well, some one thing, and some another. Wouldn't I like to dress your long hair! " continued the light-hearted girl. "I would make you so bewitching that you would break a dozen hearts in one evening. Then mother has taught us how to cook, and to make bread and cake and preserves, and Ella and I have to take turns in keeping house, and marketing, and keeping account of the living expenses. The rest of the girls are at school yet. Mother says she is not going to palm off any frauds in her daughters when they get married; and if we only turn out

half as good as she is, our husbands will be lucky men, if I
do say it; and if all of us don't get any, we can take care of
ourselves. Father has been holding you up as an example
of what a girl can do, if she has to make her own way in the
world.''

And the sprightly, but sensible, girl would have rattled
on indefinitely, had not Edith fled to her room in an uncontrollable rush of sorrow over the sad, sad, ''It might have
been.''

One afternoon Annie came into Edith's room, saying,
''I am going to dress your hair. Yes, I will—now don't
say a word, I want to. We expect two or three friends in
—one you'll be glad to see. No, I won't tell you who it is.
It's a surprise.'' And she flew at Edith's head, pulled out
the hairpins, and went to work with a dexterity and rapidity that did credit to her training. In a little while she
had crowned Edith with nature's most exquisite coronet.

A cloud of care seemed to rest on Mr. Hart's brow as
they entered the dining-room, but he banished it instantly,
and with the quaint, stately gallantry of the old school,
pretended to be deeply smitten with Edith's loveliness.
And so lovely she appeared that their eyes continually returned, and rested admiringly on her, till at last the blushing girl remonstrated:

''You all keep looking at me so that I feel as if I were
the dessert, and you were going to eat me up pretty soon.''

''I speak for the biggest bite,'' cried Mr. Hart, and they
laughed at her and petted her so that she said:

''I feel as if I had known you all ten years.''

But ever and anon, Edith saw traces of the cloud of care
that she had noticed at first. And so did Mrs. Hart, for she
said:

''You have been a little anxious about business lately.
Is there anything new ?''

''No,'' said Mr. Hart, who, in contrast to Mr. Allen,
talked business to his family; ''things are only growing a
little worse. There have been one or two bad failures to-

day. The worst of it all is, there seems a general lack of
confidence. No one knows what is going to happen. One
feels as if in a thunder-shower. The lightning may strike
him, and it may fall somewhere else. But don't worry,
good mother, I am as safe as a man can be. I have a
round million in my safe ready for an emergency."

The wife knew just where her husband stood that night.

At nine o'clock, Edith was talking earnestly with Mrs.
Ranger, whom she had expressed a wish to see. There
were a few other people present of the very highest social
standing, and intimate friends of the family, for her kind
entertainers would not expose her to any strange and un-
sympathetic eyes. Annie was flitting about, the very spirit
of innocent mischief and match-making, gloating over the
pleasure she expected to give Edith.

The bell rang, and a moment later she marshalled in Gus
Elliot, as handsome and exquisitely dressed as ever. He
was as much in the dark as to whom he should see as
Edith. Some one had told Annie of his former devoted-
ness to Edith, and so she innocently meant to do both a
kindness. Having a slight acquaintance with Elliot, as a
general society man, she invited him this evening to "meet
an old friend." He gladly accepted, feeling it a great honor
to visit at the Harts'.

He saw Edith a moment before she observed him, and
had time to note her exquisite beauty. But he turned pale
with fear and anxiety in regard to his reception.

Then she raised her eyes and saw him. The blood rushed
in a hot torrent to her face, and then left it in extreme pallor. Gus advanced with all the ease and grace that he
could command under the circumstances, and held out his
hand. "She cannot refer to the past here before them all,"
he thought.

But Edith rose slowly, and fixed her large eyes, that
glowed like coals of fire, sternly upon him, and put her
hand behind her back.

All held their breath in awe-struck expectation. She

seemed to see only him and the past, and to forget all the rest.

"No, sir," she said, in a low, deep voice, that curdled Gus's blood, "I cannot take your hand. I might in pity, if you were in the depths of poverty and trouble, as I have been, but not here and thus. Do you know where my sister is?"

"No," faltered Gus, his knees trembling under him.

"She is in Bellevue Hospital. A poor girl was carried thence to Potter's Field a day or two since. She might have been if I had not found her. And," continued Edith, with her face darkening like night, and her tone deepening till it sent a thrill of dread to the hearts of all present, "*in* Potter's Field *I* might now have been if I had listened to you."

Gus trembled before her in a way that plainly confirmed her words.

With a grand dignity she turned to Mrs. Hart, saying, "Please excuse my absence; I cannot breathe the same air with him," and she was about to sweep from the parlor like an incensed goddess, when Mr. Hart sprang up, his eyes blazing with anger, and putting his arm around Edith, said, sternly:

"I would shield this dear girl as my own daughter. Leave this house, and never cross my threshold again."

Gus slunk away without a word. As the guilty will be at last, he was "speechless." So, in a moment, when least expecting it, he fell from his heaven, which was society: for the news of his baseness spread like wildfire, and within a week every respectable door was closed against him.

Is it cynical to say that the well-known and widely-honored Mr. Hart, in closing his door, had influence as well as Gus's sin, in leading some to close theirs? Motives in society are a little mixed, sometimes.

Mr. Hart went down town the next morning, a little anxious, it is true, on general principles, but not in the least apprehensive of any disaster. "I may have to pay out a few hundred thousand," he thought, "but that won't trouble me."

But the bolt of financial suspicion was directed toward him; how, he could not tell. Within half an hour after opening, checks for twelve hundred thousand were presented at his counter. He telegraphed to his wife, "A run upon me." Later, "Danger!" Then came the words to the uptown palace, "Have suspended!" In the afternoon, "The storm will sweep me bare, but courage, God, and our right hands, will make a place and a way for us."

The business community sympathized deeply with Mr. Hart. Hard, cool men of Wall Street came in, and, with eyes moist with sympathy, wrung his hand. He stood up through the wild tumult, calm, dignified, heroic, because conscious of rectitude.

"The shrinkage in securities will be great, 1 fear," he said, "but I think my assets will cover all liabilities. We will give up everything."

When he came up home in the evening, he looked worn, and much older than in the morning, but his wife and daughters seemed to envelop him in an atmosphere of love and sympathy. They were so strong, cheerful, hopeful, that they infused their courage into him. Annie ran to the piano, and played as if inspired, saying to her father:

"Let every note tell you that we can take care of ourselves, and you and mother too, if necessary."

The words were prophetic. The strain had been too great on Mr. Hart. That night he had a stroke of paralysis and became helpless. But he had trained his daughters to be the very reverse of helpless, and they did take care of him with the most devoted love and skilled practical energy, making the weak, brief remnant of his life not a burden, but a peaceful evening after a glorious day. They all, except the youngest, soon found employment, for they brought superior skill and knowledge to the labor market, and such are ever in demand. Annie soon married happily, and her younger sisters eventually followed her example. But Ella, the eldest, remained single; and, though she never became eminent as an artist, did become a very useful and respected teacher of art, as studied in our schools for its refining influence.

To return to Edith, she felt for her kind friends almost as much as if she were one of the family.

"Do not feel that you must go away because of what has happened," said Mrs. Hart. "I am glad to have you with us, for you do us all good. Indeed, you seem one of us. Stay as long as you can, dear, and God help us both to bear our burdens."

"Dear, 'heavy-laden' Mrs. Hart," said Edith, "Jesus will bear the burdens for us, if we will let Him."

"Bless you, child, I am sure He sent you to me."

As Edith entered the ward that day, the attendant said, "She's herself, miss, at last."

Edith stole noiselessly to Zell's cot. She was sleeping. Edith sat down silently and watched for her waking. At last she opened her eyes and glanced fearfully around. Then she saw Edith, and instantly shrank and cowered as if expecting a blow.

"Zell," said Edith, taking the poor, thin hand, "Oh, Zell, don't you know me?"

"What are you going to do with me?" asked Zell, in a voice full of dread.

"Take you to my home—take you to my heart—take you deeper into my love than ever before."

"Edith," said Zell, almost cowering before her words as if they hurt her, "I am not fit to go home."

"Oh, Zell, darling," said Edith, tenderly, "God's love does not keep a debit and credit account with us, neither should we with each other. Can't you see that I love you?" and she showered kisses on her sister's now pallid face.

But Zell acted as if they were a source of pain to her, and she muttered, "You don't know, you can't know. Don't speak of God to me, I fear Him unspeakably."

"I do know all," said Edith, earnestly, "and I love you more fondly than ever I did before, and God knows and loves you more still."

"I tell you you don't know," said Zell, almost fiercely. "You can't know. If you did, you would spit on me and leave me forever. God knows, and He has doomed me to hell, Edith," she added, in a hoarse whisper. "I killed him—you know whom. And I promised that after I got old and ugly I would come and torment him forever. I must keep my promise."

Edith wept bitterly. This was worse than delirium. She saw that her sister's nature was so bruised and perverted, so warped, that she was almost insane. She slowly rallied back into physical strength, but her hectic cheek and slight cough indicated the commencement of consumption. Her mind remained in the same unnatural condition, and she kept saying to Edith, "You don't know anything about it at all. You can't know." She would not see Mrs. Hart, and agreed to go home with Edith only on condition that no one should see or speak with her outside the family.

At last the day of departure came. Mrs. Hart said, "You shall take her to the depot in my carriage. It will be among its last and best uses."

Edith kissed her kind friend good-by, saying, "God will send his chariot for you some day, and though you must leave this, your beautiful home, if you could only have a glimpse into the mansion preparing for you up there, anticipation would almost banish all thoughts of present loss."

"Well, dear," said Mrs. Hart, with a gleam of her old humor, "I hope your 'mansion' will be next door, for I shall want to see you often through all eternity."

Then Edith knelt before Mr. Hart's chair, and the old man's helpless hands were lifted upon her head, and he looked to heaven for the blessing he could not speak.

"Our ways diverge now, but they will all meet again. Home is near to you," she whispered in his ear as she kissed him good-by.

The old glad light shone in his eyes, the old cheery smile flitted across his lips, and thus she left him who had been the great, rich banker, serene, happy, and rich in a faith that could not be lost in any financial storm, or destroyed by disease, or enfeebled by age—she left him waiting as a little child to go home.

CHAPTER XXXIII

EDITH'S GREAT TEMPTATION

THOUGH even Mrs. Allen was tearful and kind in her greeting, and Laura warm and affectionate in the extreme, old Hannibal's welcome, so frank, genuine, and innocent, seemed to soften Zell more than any one's else.

"You poor, heavenly-minded old fool," she said, with an unwonted tear in her eye, "you don't know any better."

Then she seemed to settle down into a dreamy apathy; to sit moping around in shadowy places. She had a horror of meeting any one, even Mrs. Lacey and Rose, and would not go out till after night. Edith saw, more and more clearly, that she was almost insane in her shame and despair, and that she would be a terrible burden to them all if she remained in such a condition; but her love and patience did not fail. They would, had they not been daily fed from heavenly sources. "I must try to show her Jesus' love through mine," she thought.

Poor Edith, the great temptation of her life was soon to assail her. It was aimed at her weakest yet noblest side, her young enthusiasm and spirit of self-sacrifice for others. And yet, it was but the natural fruit of woman's helplessness and Mrs. Allen's policy of marrying one's way out of poverty and difficulty.

Simon Crowl had ostensibly made a very fair transaction with Edith, but Simon Crowl was a widower at the time, and on the lookout for a wife. He was a pretty sharp business man, Crowl was, or he wouldn't have become so rich in little Pushton, and he at once was satisfied that Edith, so beautiful, so sensible, would answer. Through the mortgage he might capture her, as it were, for even his vanity did not promise him much success in the ordinary ways of love-making. So the spider spun his web, and unconscious Edith was the poor little fly. During the summer he watched her closely, but from a distance. During the autumn and winter he commenced calling, ostensibly on Mrs. Allen, whom he at once managed to impress with the fact that he was very rich. Though he brushed up his best coat and manners, that delicate-nosed lady scented an air and manner very different from what she had been accustomed to, but she was half-dead with *ennui*, and, after all, there was something akin between worldly Mrs. Allen and worldly Mr. Crowl. Then, he was very rich. This had covered a multitude of sins on the avenue. But, in the miserable poverty of Pushton, it was a golden mantle of light. Mrs. Allen chafed at privation and want of delicacies with the increasing persistency of an utterly weak and selfish nature. She had no faith in Edith's plans, and no faith in woman's working, and the garden seemed the wildest dream of all. Her hard, narrow logic, constantly dinned into Edith's ears, discouraged her, and she began to doubt herself.

Mr. Crowl (timid lover) had in Edith's absence confirmed his previous hints, thrown out to Mrs. Allen as feelers, by making a definite proposition. In brief, he had offered to settle twenty-five thousand dollars on Edith the day she married him, and to take care of the rest of the family.

"I have made enough," he said majestically, "to live the rest of my life like a gentleman, and this offer is princely, if I say it myself. You can all ride in your carriage again." Then he added, with his little black eyes growing hard and cunning, "If your daughter won't accept my generosity, our relationship becomes merely one of business. Of course I shall foreclose. Money is scarce here, and I shall probably be able to buy in the place at half its worth. Seems to me," he concluded, looking at the case from his valuation of money, "there is not much room for choice here."

And Mr. Crowl had been princely—for him. Mrs. Allen thought so, too, and lent herself to the scheme with all the persistent energy that she could show in these matters. But, to do her justice, she really thought she was doing what was best for Edith and all of them. She was acting in accordance with her lifelong principle of providing for her family, in the one way she believed in and understood. But sincerity and singleness of purpose made her all the more dangerous as a tempter.

In one of Edith's most discouraged moods she broached the subject and explained Mr. Crowl's offer, for he, prudent man, had left it to her.

Edith started violently, and the project was so revolting to her that she fled from the room. But Mrs. Allen, with her small pertinacity, kept recurring to it at every opportunity. Though it may seem a little strange, her mother's action did not so shock Edith as some might expect; nor did the proposition seem so impossible as it might to some girls. She had all her life been accustomed, through her mother, to the idea of marrying for money, and we can get used to almost anything.

In March their money was very low. Going to Zell and taking care of her had involved much additional expense. She found out that her mother had already accepted and used in part a loan of fifty dollars from Mr. Crowl. Laura, from the long confinement of the winter, and from living on fare too coarse and lacking in nutrition for her delicate organization, was growing very feeble. Zell seemed in the first stages of consumption, and would soon be a sick, helpless burden. The chill of dread grew stronger at Edith's heart.

"Oh, can it be possible that I shall be driven to it!" she often groaned; and she now saw, as poor Laura said, "the black hand in the dark pushing her down." To her surprise her thoughts kept reverting to Arden Lacey.

"What will he think of me if I do this?" she thought, with intense bitterness. "He will tell me I was not worthy of his friendship, much less of his love—that I deceived him;" and the thought of Arden, after all, perhaps, had the most weight in restraining her from the fatal step. For then, to her perverted sense of duty, this marriage began to seem like an heroic self-sacrifice.

She had seen little of Arden since her return. He was kind and respectful as ever, outwardly, but she saw in his deep blue eyes that she was the divinity that he still worshipped with unfaltering devotion, and as she once smiled at the idea of being set up as an idol in his heart, she now began unspeakably to dread falling from her pedestal.

One dreary day, the last of March, when sleet and rain were pouring steadily down, and Laura was sick in her bed, and Zell moping with her hacking cough over the fire, with Hannibal in the kitchen, Mrs. Allen turned suddenly to Edith, and said:

"On some such day we shall all be turned into the street. You could save us, you could save yourself, by taking a kind, rich man for your lawful husband; but you won't."

Then Satan, who is always on hand when we are weakest, quoted Scripture to Edith as he had done once before. The words flashed into her mind, "He saved others, himself he cannot save."

In a wild moment of mingled enthusiasm and desperation, she sprang up before her mother, and said:

"If I can't pay the interest of the mortgage—if I can't take care of you all by some kind of work, I will marry him. But if you have a spark of love for me, save, economize, try to think of some other way."

Mrs. Allen smiled triumphantly, and tried in her gratitude to embrace her daughter, saying: "A kind husband will soon lift all burdens off your shoulders." The burden on the heart Mrs. Allen did not understand, but Edith fled from her to her own room.

In a little while her excitement and enthusiasm died

away, and life began to look gaunt and bare. Even her
Saviour's face seemed hidden, and she only saw an ugly
spectre in the future—Simon Crowl.

In vain she repeated to herself, "He sacrificed Himself
for others—so will I." The nature that He had given her
revolted at it all, and though she could not understand it,
she began to find a jarring discord between herself and all
things.

Mrs. Allen told Mr. Crowl of her success, and he looked
upon things as settled. He came to the house quite often,
but did not stay long or assume any familiarity with Edith.
He was a wary old spider; and under Mrs. Allen's hints,
behaved and looked very respectably. He certainly did
the best he could not to appear hideous to Edith, and
though she was very cold, she compelled herself to treat
him civilly.

Perhaps many might have considered Edith's chance a
very good one; but with an almost desperate energy she set
her mind at work to find some other way out of her painful
straits. Everything, however, seemed against her. Mr.
McTrump was sick with inflammatory rheumatism. Mrs.
Groody was away, and would not be back till the last of
May. On account of Arden she could not speak to Mrs.
Lacey. She tried in vain to get work, but at that season
there was nothing in Pushton which she could do. Farmers
were beginning to get out a little on their wet lands, and
various out-of-door activities to revive after the winter stag-
nation. Moreover, money was very scarce at that season of
the year. She at last turned to the garden as her only resource. She realized that she had scarcely money enough
to carry them through May. Could she get returns from
her garden in time? Could it be made to yield enough
to support them? With an almost desperate energy she
worked in it whenever the weather permitted through April,
and kept Hannibal at it also. Indeed, she had little mercy
on the old man, and he wondered at her. One day he
ventured:

"Miss Edie, you jes done kill us both," but his wonder increased as she muttered:

"Perhaps it would be the best thing for us both." Then, seeing his panic-stricken face, she added more kindly, "Hannibal, our money is getting low, and the garden is our only chance."

After that he worked patiently without a word and without a thought of sparing himself.

Edith insisted on the closest economy in the house, though she was too sensible to stint herself in food in view of her constant toil. But one day she detected Mrs. Allen, with her small cunning and her determination to carry her point, practicing a little wastefulness. Edith turned on her with such fierceness that she never dared to repeat the act. Indeed, Edith was becoming very much what she was before Zell ran away, only in addition there was something akin, at times, to Zell's own hardness and recklessness, and one day she said to Edith:

"What is the matter? You are becoming like me."

Edith fled to her room, and sobbed and cried and tried to pray till her strength was gone. The sweet trust and peace she had once enjoyed seemed like a past dream. She was learning by bitter experience that it can never be right to do wrong; and that a first false step, like a false premise, leads to sad conclusions.

She had insisted that her mother should not speak of the matter till it became absolutely necessary, therefore Laura, Zell, and none of her friends could understand her.

Arden was the most puzzled and pained of all, for she shrank from him with increasing dread. He was now back at his farm work, though he said to Edith one day despondently that he had no heart to work, for the mortgage on their place would probably be foreclosed in the fall. She longed to tell him how she was situated, but she saw he was unable to help her, and she dreaded to see the scorn come into his trusting, loving eyes; she could not endure his absolute confidence in her, and in his presence her heart ached as if it would break, so she shunned him till he grew very unhappy, and sighed:

"There's something wrong. She finds I am not congenial. I shall lose her friendship," and his aching heart also admitted, as never before, how dear it was to him.

Nature was awakening with the rapture of another spring; birds were coming back to old haunts with ecstatic songs; flowers budding into their brief but exquisite life, and the trees aglow with fragrant prophecies of fruit; but a winter of fear and doubt was chilling these two hearts into something far worse than nature's seeming death.

CHAPTER XXXIV

SAVED

EDITH'S efforts still to help Zell to better things were very pathetic, considering how unhappy and tempted she was herself. She did try, even when her own heart was breaking, to bring peace and hope to the poor creature, but she was taught how vain her efforts were, in her present mood, by Zell's saying, sharply:

"Physician, heal thyself."

Though Zell did not understand Edith, she saw that she was almost as unhappy as herself, and she had lost hope in everybody and everything. Though she had not admitted it, Edith's words and kindness at first had excited her wonder, and, perhaps, a faint glimmer of hope; but, as she saw her sister's face cloud with care, and darken with pain and fear, she said, bitterly:

"Why did she talk with me so? It was all a delusion. What is God doing for her any more than for me?"

But, in order to give Zell occupation, and something to think about besides herself, Edith had induced her to take charge of the flowers in the garden.

"They won't grow for me," Zell had said at first. "They will wither when I look at them, and white blossoms will turn black as I bend over them."

"Nonsense!" said Edith, with irritation; "won't you do anything to help me?"

"Oh, certainly," wearily answered Zell. "I will do the work just as you tell me. If they do die, it don't matter. We can eat or sell them." So Zell began to take care of the flowers, doing the work in a stealthy manner, and hiding when any one came.

The month of May was unusually warm, and Edith was glad, for it would hasten things forward. That upon which she now bent almost agonized effort and thought was the possibility of paying the interest on the mortgage by the middle of June, when it was due. All hope concentrated on her strawberries, as they would be the first crop worth mentioning that she could depend on from her place. She gave the plants the most careful attention. Not a weed was suffered to grow, and between the rows she placed carefully, with her own hands, leaves she raked up in the orchard, so that the ground might be kept moist and the fruit clean. Almost every hour of the day her eyes sought the strawberry-bed, as the source of her hope. If that failed her, no bleeding human sacrifice in all the cruel past could surpass in agony her fate.

The vines began to blossom with great promise, and at first she almost counted them in her eager expectation. Then the long rows looked like little banks of snow, and she exulted over the prospect. Laura was once about to pick one of the blossoms, but she stopped her almost fiercely. She would get up in the night, and stand gazing at the lines of white, as she could trace them in the darkness across the garden. So the days passed on till the last of May, and the blossoms grew scattering, but there were multitudes of little green berries, from the size of a pea to that of her thimble, and some of them began to have a white look. She so minutely watched them develop that she could have almost defined the progress day by day. Once Zell looked at her wonderingly, and said:

"Edith, you are crazy over that strawberry-bed. I believe you worship it."

For a time Edith's hopes daily rose higher as the vines gave finer promise, but during the last week of May a new and terrible source of danger revealed itself, a danger that she knew not how to cope with—drought.

It had not rained since the middle of May. She saw that many of her young and tender vegetables were wilting, but the strawberries, mulched with leaves, did not appear to mind it at first. Still she knew they would suffer soon, unless there was rain. Most anxiously she watched the skies. Their serenity mocked her when she was so clouded with care. Wild storms would be better than these balmy, sunny days.

The first of June came, the second, third, and fourth, and here and there a berry was turning red, but the vines were beginning to wilt. The suspense became so great she could hardly endure it. Her faith in God began to waver. Every breath almost was a prayer for rain, but the sunny days passed like mocking smiles.

"Is there a God?" she queried desperately. "Can I have been deceived in all my past happy experience?" She shuddered at the answer that the tempter suggested, and yet, like a drowning man, she still clung to her faith.

During the long evening, she and Hannibal sought to save the bed by carrying water from the well, but they could do so little, it only seemed to show them how utterly dependent they were on the natural rain from heaven; but the skies seemed laughing at her pain and fear. Moreover, she noticed that those they watered appeared injured rather than helped, as is ever the case where it is insufficiently done, and she saw that she must helplessly wait.

Arden Lacey had been away for a week, and, returning in the dusk of the evening, saw her at work watering, before she had come to this conclusion. His heart was hungry, even for the sight of her, and he longed for her to let him stop for a little chat as of old. So he said, timidly:

"Good-evening, Miss Allen, haven't you a word to welcome me back with?"

"Oh!" cried Edith, not heeding his salutation, "why don't it rain! I shall lose all my strawberries."

His voice jarred upon her heart, now too full, and she ran into the house to hide her feelings, and left him. Even the thought of him now, in her morbid state, began to pierce her like a sword.

"She thinks more of her paltry strawberry-bed than of me," muttered Arden, and he stalked angrily homeward. "What is the matter with Miss Allen?" he asked his mother abruptly. "I don't understand her."

"Nor I either," said Mrs. Lacey with a sigh.

The next morning was very warm, and Edith saw that the day would be hotter than any that preceded. A dry wind sprang up and it seemed worse than the sun. The vines began to wither early after the coolness of the night, and those she had watered suffered the most, and seemed to say to her mockingly:

"You can't do anything."

"Oh, heaven!" cried Edith, almost in despair, "there is a black hand pushing me down."

In an excited, feverish manner she roamed restlessly around and could settle down to nothing. She scanned the horizon for a cloud, as the shipwrecked might for a sail.

"Edie, what is the matter?" said Laura, putting her arms about her sister.

"It won't rain," said Edith, bursting into tears. "My home, my happiness, everything depends on rain, and look at these skies."

"But won't He send it?" asked Laura, gently.

"Why don't He, then?" said Edith, almost in irritation. Then, in a sudden passion of grief, she hid her face in her sister's lap, and sobbed, "Oh, Laura, Laura, I feel I am losing my faith in Him. Why does He treat me so?"

Here Laura's face grew troubled and fearful also. Her faith in Christ was so blended with her faith in Edith that she could not separate them in a moment. "I don't understand it, Edie," she faltered. "He seems to have taken care of me, and has been very kind since that—that night. But I don't understand your feeling so."

"Oh, oh, oh!" sobbed Edith, "I don't know what to

think—what to believe; and I fear I shall hurt your faith,"
and she shut herself up in her room, and looked despairingly
out to where the vines were drooping in the fierce heat.

"If they don't get help to-day, my hopes will wither like
their leaves," she said, with pallid lips.

As the sun declined in the west, she went out and stood
beside them, as one might by a dying friend. Her fresh
young face seemed almost growing aged and wrinkled under
the ordeal. She had prayed that afternoon, as never before
in her life, for help, and now, with a despairing gesture upward, she said:

"Look at that brazen sky!"

But the noise of the opening gate caused her to look
thither, and there was Arden entering, with a great barrel
on wheels, which was drawn by a horse. His heart, so
weak toward her, had relented during the day. "I vowed
to serve her, and I will," he thought. "I will be her slave,
if she will permit."

Edith did not understand at first, and he came toward
her so humbly, as if to ask a great favor, that it would
have been comic, had not his sincerity made it pathetic.

"Miss Allen," he said, "I saw you trying to water your
berries. Perhaps I can do it better, as I have here the
means of working on a larger scale."

Edith seized his hand and said, with tears:

"You are like an angel of light; how can I thank you
enough?"

Her manner puzzled him to-night quite as much as on
the previous occasion. "Why does she act as if her life
depended on these few berries?" he vainly asked himself.
"They can't be so poor as to be in utter want. I wish she
would speak frankly to me."

In her case, as in thousands of others, it would have been
so much better if she had.

Then Edith said, a little dubiously, "I hurt the vines
when I tried to water them."

"I know enough about gardening to understand that,"

said Arden, with a smile. "If the ground is not thoroughly soaked it does hurt them. But see," and he poured the water around the vines till the dry leaves swam in it. "That will last two days, and then I will water these again. I can go over half the bed thoroughly one night, and the other half the next night; and so we will keep them along till rain comes."

She looked at him as if he were a messenger come to release her from a dungeon, and murmured, in a low, sweet voice:

"Mr. Lacey, you are as kind as a brother to me."

A warm flush of pleasure mantled his face and neck, and he turned away to hide his feelings, but said:

"Miss Edith, this is nothing to what I would do for you."

She had it on her lips to tell him how she was situated, but he hastened away to fill his barrel at a neighboring pond. She watched him go to and fro in his rough, working garb, and he seemed to her the very flower of chivalry.

Her eyes grew lustrous with admiration, gratitude, hope, and—yes, *love*, for before the June twilight deepened into night it was revealed in the depths of her heart that she loved Arden Lacey, and that was the reason that she had kept away from him since she had made the hateful promise. She had thought it only friendship, now she knew that it was love, and that his scorn and anger would be the bitterest ingredient of all in her self-immolation.

For two long hours he went to and fro unweariedly, and then startled her by saying in the distance on his way home, "I will come again to-morrow evening," and was gone. He was afraid of himself, lest in his strong feeling he might break his implied promise not even to suggest his love, when she came to thank him, and so, in self-distrustfulness, he was beginning to shun her also.

An unspeakable burden of fear was lifted from her heart, and hope, sweet, warm, and rosy, kept her eyes waking, but rested her more than sleep. In the morning she saw that the watering had greatly revived one half of the bed, and that all through the hot day they did not wilt, while the unwatered part looked very sick.

Old Crowl also had seen the proceeding in the June twilight, and did not like it. "I must put a spoke in his wheel," he said. So the next afternoon he met Arden in the village, and blustered up to him, saying:

"Look here, young Lacey, what were you doing at the Allens' last night?"

"None of your business."

"Yes, it is my business, too, as you may find out to your cost. I am engaged to marry Miss Edith Allen, and guess it's my business who's hanging around there. I warn you to keep away." Mr. Crowl had put the case truly, and yet with characteristic cunning. He was positively engaged to Edith, though she was only conditionally engaged to him.

"It's an accursed lie," thundered Arden, livid with rage, "and I warn you to leave—you make me dangerous."

"Oh, ho; touches you close, does it? I am sorry for you, but it's true, nevertheless."

Arden looked as if he would rend him, but by a great effort he controlled himself, and in a low, meaning voice said:

"If you have lied to me this afternoon, woe be unto you," and he turned on his heel and walked straight to Edith, where she stood at work among her grapevines, breaking off some of the too thickly budding branches. He was beside her before she heard him, and the moment she looked into his white, stern face, she saw that something had happened.

"Miss Allen," he said, abruptly, "I heard a report about you this afternoon. I did not believe it; I could not; but it came so direct, that I give you a chance to refute it. Your word will be sufficient for me. It would be against all the world. Is there anything between you and Simon Crowl?"

Her confusion was painful, and for a moment she could not speak, but stood trembling before him.

In his passion, he seized her roughly by the arm and said, hoarsely, "In a word, yes or no?"

His manner offended her proud spirit, and she looked him angrily in the face and said, haughtily:

"Yes."

He recoiled from her as if he had been stung.

Her anger died away in a moment, and she leaned against the grape-trellis for support.

"Do you love him?" he faltered, his bronzed cheek blanching.

"No," she gasped.

The blood rushed furiously into his face, and he took an angry stride toward her. She cowered before him, but almost wished that he would strike her dead. In a voice hoarse with rage, he said:

"This, then, is the end of our friendship. This is the best that your religion has taught you. If not your pitiful faith, then has not your woman's nature told you that neither priest nor book can marry you to that coarse lump of earth?" and he turned on his heel and strode away.

His mother was frightened as she saw his face. "What has happened?" she said, starting up. He stared at her almost stupidly for a moment. Then he said, in a stony voice:

"The worst that ever can happen to me in this or any world. If the lightning had burned me to a cinder, I could not be more utterly bereft of all that tends to make a good man. Edith Allen has sold herself to old Crowl. Some priest is going through a farce they will call a marriage, and all the good people will say, 'How well she has done!' What a miserable delusion this religious business is! You had better give it up, mother, as I do, here and now."

"Hush, my son," said Mrs. Lacey, solemnly. "You have only seen Edith Allen. I have seen *Jesus Christ.*

"There is some mystery about this," she added, after a moment's painful thought. "I will go and see her at once."

He seized her hand, saying:

"Have I not been a good son to you?"

"Yes, Arden."

"Then by all I have ever been to you, and as you wish my love to continue, go not near her again."

"But, Arden—"

"Promise me," he said, sternly.

"Well," said the poor woman, with a deep sigh, "not without your permission."

From that time forth, Arden seemed as if made of stone.

After he was gone Edith walked with uncertain steps to the little arbor, and sat down as if stunned. She lost all idea of time. After it was dark, Hannibal called her in, and made her take a cup of tea. She then went mechanically to her room, but not to sleep. Arden's dreadful words kept repeating themselves over and over again.

"O God!" she exclaimed, in the darkness, "whither am I drifting? Must I be driven to this awful fate in order to provide for those dependent upon me? Cannot bountiful Nature feed us? Wilt Thou not, in mercy, send one drop of rain? O Jesus, where is Thy mercy?"

The next morning the skies were still cloudless, and she scowled darkly at the sunny dawn. Then, in sudden alternation of mood, she stretched her bare, white arms toward the little farmhouse, and sighed, in tones of tremulous pathos:

"Oh, Arden, Arden! I would rather die at your feet than live in a palace with him."

She sent down word that she was ill, and that she would not come down. Laura, Mrs. Allen, and even Zell, came to her, but she kissed them wearily, and sent them away. She saw that there was deep anxiety on all their faces. Pretty soon Hannibal came up with a cup of coffee.

"You must drink it, Miss Edie," he said, " 'cause we'se all a-leanin' on you."

Well-meaning words, but tending unconsciously to confirm her desperate purpose to sacrifice herself for them.

She lay with her face buried in the pillow all day. She

knew that their money was almost gone, that provisions were scanty in the house, and to her morbid mind bags of gold were piled up before her, and Simon Crowl, as an ugly spectre, was beckoning her toward them.

As she lay in a dull lethargy of pain in the afternoon, a heavy jar of thunder aroused her. She sprang up instantly, and ran out bare-headed to the little rise of ground behind the house, and there, in the west, was a great black cloud. The darker and nearer it grew, the more her face brightened. It was a strange thing to see that fair young girl looking toward the threatening storm with eager, glad expectancy, as if it were her lover. The heavy and continued roll of the thunder, like the approaching roar of battle, was sweeter to her than love's whispers. She saw with dilating eyes the trees on the distant mountain's brow toss and writhe in the tempest; she heard the fall of rain-drops on the foliage of the mountain's side as if they were the feet of an army coming to her rescue. A few large ones, mingled with hail, fell around her like scattering shots, and she put out her hands to catch them. The fierce gusts caught up her loosened hair and it streamed away behind her. There was a blinding flash, and the branches of a tall locust near came quivering down—she only smiled.

But dismay and trembling fear overwhelmed her as the shower passed on to the north. She could see it raining hard a mile away, but the drops ceased to fall around her. The deep reverberations rolled away in the distance, and in the west there was a long line of light. As the twilight deepened, the whole storm was below the horizon, only sending up angry flashes as it thundered on to parts unknown. With clasped hands and despairing eyes, Edith gazed after it, as the wrecked floating on a raft might watch a ship sail away, and leave them to perish on the wide ocean.

She walked slowly down to the little arbor, and leaned wearily back on the rustic seat. She saw night come on in breathless peace. Not a leaf stirred. She saw the moon rise over the eastern hills, as brightly and serenely as if its rays would not fall on one sad face.

Hannibal called, but she did not answer. Then he came out to her, and put the cup of tea to her lips, and made her drink it. She obeyed mechanically.

"Poor chile, poor chile," he murmured, "I wish ole Hannibal could die for you."

She lifted her face to him with such an expression that he hastened away to hide his tears. But she sat still, as if in a dream, and yet she felt that the crisis had come, and that before she left that place she must come to some decision. Reason would be dethroned if she lived much longer in such suspense and irresolution. And yet she sat still in a dreamy stupor, the reaction of her strong excitement. It seemed, in a certain sense, peaceful and painless, and she did not wish to goad herself out of it.

"It may be like the last sleep before execution," she thought, "therefore make the most of it," and her thoughts wandered at will.

A late robin came flying home to the arbor where the nest was, and having twittered out a little vesper-song, put its head under its wing, near his mate, which sat brooding in the nest over some little eggs, and the thought stole into her heart, "Will God take care of them and not me?" and she watched the peaceful sleep of the family over her head as if it were an emblem of faith.

Then a sudden breeze swept a spray of roses against her face, and their delicate perfume was like the "still small voice" of love, and the thought passed dreamily across Edith's mind, "Will God do so much for that little cluster of roses and yet do nothing for me?"

How near the Father was to His child! In this calm that followed her long passionate struggle, His mighty but gentle Spirit could make itself felt, and it stole into the poor girl's bruised heart with heavenly suggestion and healing power. The happy days when she followed Jesus and sat daily at His feet were recalled. Her sin was shown to her, not in anger, but in the loving reproachfulness of the Saviour's look upon faithless Peter, and a voice seemed to ask in her soul, "How could you turn away your trust from Him to anything else? How could you think it right to do so great a wrong? How could you so trample upon the womanly nature that He gave you as to think of marrying where neither love nor God would sanction?"

Jesus seemed to stand before her, and point up to the robins, saying, "I feed them. I fed the five thousand. I feed the world. I can feed you and yours. Trust me. Do right. In trying to save yourself you will destroy yourself."

With a divine impulse, she threw herself on the floor of the arbor, and cried:

"Jesus, I cast myself at Thy feet. I throw myself on Thy mercy. When I look the world around, away from Thee, I see only fear and torment. If I die, I will perish at Thy feet."

Was it the moonlight only that made the night luminous? No, for the glory of the Lord shone around, and the peace that "passeth all understanding" came flowing into her soul like a shining river. The ugly phantoms that had haunted her vanished. The "black hand that seemed pushing her down," became her Father's hand, shielding and sustaining.

She rose as calm and serene as the summer evening and went straight to Mrs. Allen's room and said:

"Mother, I will never marry Simon Crowl."

Her mother began to cry, and say piteously:

"Then we shall all be turned into the street."

"What the future will be I can't tell," said Edith, gently but firmly. "I will work for you, I will beg for you, I will starve with you, but I will never marry Simon Crowl, nor any other man that I do not love." And pressing a kiss on her mother's face, she went to her room, and soon was lost in the first refreshing sleep that she had had for a long time.

She was wakened toward morning by the sound of rain, and, starting up, heard its steady, copious downfall. In a sudden ecstasy of gratitude she sprang up, opened the blinds and looked out. The moon had gone down, and through the darkness the rain was falling heavily; she felt it upon her forehead, her bare neck and arms, and it seemed to her Heaven's own baptism into a new and stronger faith and a happier life.

CHAPTER XXXV

CLOSING SCENES

THE clouds were clearing away when Edith came down late the next morning, and all saw that the clouds had passed from her brow.

"Bress de Lord, Miss Edie, you'se yoursef again!" sad Hannibal, joyfully. "I neber see a shower do such a heap ob good afore."

"No," said Edith, sadly; "I was myself. I lost my Divine Friend and Helper, and I then became myself—poor, weak, faulty Edith Allen. But, thanks to His mercy, I have found Him again, and so hope to be the better self that He helped me to be before."

Zell looked at her with a sudden wonder, and went out and stayed among her flowers all day.

Laura came and put her arms around her neck, and said, "Oh, Edie, I am so glad! What you said set me to fearing and doubting; but I am sure we can trust Him."

Mrs. Allen sighed drearily, and said, "I don't understand it at all."

But old Hannibal slapped his hands in true Methodist style, exclaiming, "Dat's it! Trow away de ole heart! Get a new one! Bress de Lord!"

Edith went out into the garden, and saw that there were a great many berries ripe; then she hastened to the hotel, and said:

"Oh, Mrs. Groody, for Heaven's sake, won't you help me sell my strawberries up here?"

"Yes, my dear," was the hearty response; "both for

your sake and the strawberries, too. We get them from the city, and would much rather have fresh country ones."

Edith returned with her heart thrilling with hope, and set to work picking as if every berry was a ruby, and in a few hours she had six quarts of fragrant fruit. Malcom had lent her little baskets, and Hannibal took them up to the hotel, for Arden would not even look toward the little cottage any more. The old servant came back grinning with delight, and gave Edith a dollar and a half.

The next day ten quarts brought two dollars and a half. Then they began to ripen rapidly, the rain having greatly improved them, and Edith, with considerable help from the others, picked twenty, thirty, and fifty quarts a day. She employed a stout boy from the village, to help her, and, through him, she soon had quite a village trade also. He had a percentage on the sales, and, therefore, was very sharp in disposing of them.

How Edith gloated over her money! how, with more than miserly eyes, she counted it over every night, and pressed it to her lips!

In the complete absorption of the past few weeks Edith had not noticed the change going on in Zell. The poor creature was surprised and greatly pleased that the flowers grew so well for her. Every opening blossom was a new revelation, and their sweet perfume stole into her wounded heart like balm. The blue violets seemed like children's eyes peeping timidly at her; and the pansies looked so bright and saucy that she caught herself smiling back at them. The little black and brown seeds she planted came up so promptly that it seemed as if they wanted to see her as much as she did them.

"Isn't it queer," she said one day to herself, "that such pretty things can come out of such ugly little things." Nothing in nature seemed to turn away from her, any more than would nature's God. The dumb life around began to speak to her in many and varied voices, and she who fled from companionship with her own kind would sit and chirp and talk to the birds, as if they understood her. And they did seem to grow strangely familiar, and would almost eat crumbs out of her hand.

One day in June she said to Hannibal, who was working near, "Isn't it strange the flowers grow so well for me?"

"Why shouldn't dey grow for you, Miss Zell?" asked he, straightening his old back up.

"Good, innocent Hannibal, how indeed should you know anything about it?"

"Yes, I does know all 'bout it," said he, earnestly, and he came to her where she stood by a rosebush. "Does you see dis white rose?"

"Yes," said Zell, "it opened this morning. I've been watching it."

Poor Hannibal could not read print, but he seemed to understand this exquisite passage in nature's open book, for he put his black finger on the rose (which made it look whiter than before), and commenced expounding it as a preacher might his text. "Now look at it sharp, Miss Zell, 'cause it'll show you I does know all 'bout it. It's white, isn't it?"

"Yes," said Zell, eagerly, for Hannibal held the attention of his audience.

"Dat means pure, doesn't it?" continued he.

"Yes," said Zell, looking sadly down.

"And it's sweet, isn't it? Now dat means lub."

And Zell looked hopefully up.

"And now, dear chile," said he, giving her a little impressive nudge, "see whar de white rose come from—right up out of de brack, ugly ground."

Having concluded his argument and made his point, the simple orator began his application, and Zell was leaning toward him in her interest.

"De good Lord, he make it grow to show what He can do for us. Miss Zell," he said, in an awed whisper, "my ole heart was as brack as dat ground, but de blessed Jesus turn it as white as dis rose. Miss Edie, Lor' bless her, telled me 'bout Him, and I'se found it all true. Now, doesn't I know 'bout it? I knows dat de good Jesus can turn de brackest heart in de world jes like dis rose, make it white and pure, and fill it up wid de sweetness of lub. I knows all 'bout it."

He spoke with the power of absolute certainty and strong feeling, therefore his hearer was deeply moved.

"Hannibal," she said, coming close to him, and putting her hand on his shoulder, "do you think Jesus could turn my heart white?"

"Sartin, Miss Zell," answered he, stoutly. "Jes as easy as He make dis white rose grow."

"Would you mind asking Him? It seems to me I would rather pray out here among the flowers," she said, in low, tremulous tones.

So Hannibal concluded his simple, but most effective, service by kneeling down by his pulpit, the rosebush, and praying:

"Bressed Jesus, guv dis dear chile a new heart, 'cause she wants it, and you wants her to hab it. Make it pure and full of lub. You can do it, dear Jesus. You knows you can. Now, jes please do it. *Amen.*"

Zell's responsive "Amen" was like a note from an Æolian harp.

"Hannibal," said she, looking wistfully at him, "I think I feel better. I think I feel it growing white."

"Now jes look here, Miss Zell," said he, giving her a bit of pastoral counsel before going back to his work, "don't you keep lookin' at your heart, and seein' how it feels, or you'll get discouraged. See dis rose agin? It don't look at itself. It jes looks up at de sun. So you look straight at Jesus, and your heart grow whiter ebery day."

And Hannibal and the flower did gradually lead poor Zell to Him who "taketh away the sins of the world," and He said to her as to one of old, "Thy faith hath saved thee; go in peace."

On the evening of the 14th of June, Edith had more than

17—ROE—X

enough to pay the interest due on the 15th, and she was most anxious to have it settled. She was standing at the gate waiting for Hannibal to join her as escort, when she saw Arden Lacey coming toward her. He had not looked at her since that dreadful afternoon, and was now about to pass her without notice, though from his manner she saw he was conscious of her presence. He looked so worn and changed that her heart yearned toward him. A sudden thought occurred to her, and she said:

"Mr. Lacey."

He kept right on, and paid no heed to her.

There was a mingling of indignation and pathos in her voice when she spoke again.

"I appeal to you as a woman, and no matter what I am, if you are a true man, you will listen."

There was that in her tone and manner that reminded him of the dark rainy night when they first met.

He turned instantly, but he approached her with a cold, silent bow.

"I must go to the village to-night. I wish your protection," she said, in a voice she tried vainly to render steady.

He again bowed silently, and they walked to the village together without a word. Hannibal came out in time to see them disappear down the road, one on one side of it, and one on the other.

"Well now, dey's both quar," he said, scratching his white head with perplexity, "but one ting is mighty sartin, I'se glad my ole jints is saved dat tramp."

Edith stopped at the door of Mr. Crowl's office, and Arden, for the first time, spoke hastily:

"I can't go in there."

"I hope you are not afraid," said Edith, in a tone that made him step forward quick enough.

Mr. Crowl looked as if he could not believe his eyes, but Edith gave him no time to collect his wits, but by the following little speech quite overwhelmed both him and Arden, though with different emotions.

"There, sir, is the interest due on the mortgage. There is a slight explanation due you and also this gentleman here, who *was* my friend. There are four persons in our family dependent on me for support and shelter. We were all so poor and helpless that it seemed impossible to maintain ourselves in independence. You make a proposition through my mother, never to me, that might be called generous if it had not been coupled with certain threats of prompt foreclosure if not accepted. In an hour of weakness and for the sake of the others, I said to my mother, never to you, that if I could not pay the interest and could not support the family, I would marry you. But I did very wrong, and I became so unhappy and desperate in view of this partial promise, that I thought I should lose my reason. But in the hour of my greatest darkness, when I saw no way out of our difficulties, I was led to see how wrongly I had acted, and to resolve that under no possible circumstances would I marry you, nor any man to whom I could not give a true wife's love. Since that time I have been able honestly to earn the money there; and in a few days more I will pay you the fifty dollars that my mother borrowed of you. So please give me my receipt."

"And remember henceforth," said Arden, sternly, "that this lady has a protector."

Simon was sharp enough to see that he was beaten, so he signed the receipt and gave it to Edith without a word. They let his office and started homeward. When out of the village Arden said timidly:

"Can you forgive me, Miss Edith?"

"Can you forgive me?" answered she, even more humbly.

They stopped in the road and grasped each other's hands with a warmth more expressive than all words. Then they went on silently again. At the gate Edith said timidly:

"Won't you come in?"

"I dare not, Miss Allen," said Arden, gravely, and with a dash of bitterness in his voice. "I am a man of honor with all my faults, and I would keep the promise I made you in the letter I wrote one year ago. I must see very little of you," he continued, in a very heartsick tone, "but let me serve you just the same."

Edith's face seemed to possess more than human loveliness as it grew tender and gentle in the radiance of the full moon, and he looked at it with the hunger of a famished heart.

"But you made the promise to me, did you not?" she asked in a low tone.

"Certainly," said Arden.

"Then it seems to me that I have the right to absolve you from the promise," she continued in a still lower tone, and a face like a damask-rose in moonlight.

"Miss Allen—Edith—" said Arden, "oh, for Heaven's sake, be kind. Don't trifle with me."

Edith had restrained her feelings so long that she was ready to either laugh or cry, so with a peal of laughter, that rang out like a chime of silver bells, she said:

"Like the fat abbot in the story, I give you full absolution and plenary indulgence."

He seized her hand and carried it to his lips: "Edith," he pleaded, in a low, tremulous voice, "will you let me be your slave?"

"Not a bit of it," said she, sturdily. She added, looking shyly up at him, "What should I do with a slave?"

Arden was about to kneel at her feet, but she said:

"Nonsense! If you must get on your knees, come and kneel to my strawberry-bed—you ought to thank that, I can tell you." And so the matter-of-fact girl, who could not abide sentiment, got through a scene that she greatly dreaded.

They could see the berries reddening among the green leaves, and the night wind blowing across them was like a gale from Araby the Blest.

"Were it not for this strawberry-bed you would not have obtained absolution to-night. But, Arden," she added, seriously, "here is your way out of trouble, as well as mine. We are near good markets. Give up your poor, slipshod farming (I'm plain, you see) and raise fruit. I will supply you with vines. We will go into partnership. You show what a man can do, and I will show what a girl can do."

He took her hand and looked at her so fondly that she hid her face on his shoulder. He stroked her head and said, in a half-mirthful tone:

"Ah, Edie, Edie, woman once got man out of a garden, but you, I perceive, are destined to lead me into one; and any garden where you are will be Eden to me."

She looked up, with her face suddenly becoming grave and wistful, and said:

"Arden, God will walk in my garden in the cool of the day. You won't hide from Him, will you?"

"No," he answered, earnestly. "I now feel sure that, through my faith in you, I shall learn to have faith in Him."

CHAPTER XXXVI

LAST WORDS

EDITH did sustain the family on the products of her little place. And, more than that, the yield from her vines and orchard was so abundant that she aided Arden to meet the interest of the mortgage on the Lacey place, so that Mr. Crowl could not foreclose that autumn, as he intended. She so woke her dreamy lover up that he soon became a keen, masterful man of business, and, at her suggestion, at once commenced the culture of small fruits, she giving him a good start from her own place.

Rose took the situation of nurse with Judge Clifford's married daughter, having the care of two little children. She thus secured a pleasant, sheltered home, where she was treated with great kindness. Instead of running in debt, as in New York, she was able to save the greater part of her wages, and in two years had enough ahead to take time to learn the dressmakers' trade thoroughly, for which she had a taste. But a sensible young mechanic, who had long been attentive, at last persuaded her to make him a happy home.

Mrs. Lacey's prayers were effectual in the case of her husband, for, to the astonishment of the whole neighborhood, he reformed. Laura remained a pale home-blossom, sheltered by Edith's love.

With the blossoms she loved, Zell faded away in the autumn, but her death was like that of the flowers, in the full hope of the glad springtime of a new life. As her eyes closed and she breathed her last sigh out on Edith's bosom, old Hannibal sobbed—

"She's—a white rose—now—sure 'nuff."

Arden and Edith were married the following year, on the 14th of June, the anniversary of their engagement. Edith greatly shocked Mrs. Allen by having the ceremony performed in the garden.

"Why not?" she said. "God once married a couple there."

Mrs. Groody, Mr. and Mrs. McTrump, Mrs. Ranger, Mrs. Hart and her daughters, and quite a number of other friends were present.

Hannibal stood by the white rosebush, that was again in bloom, and tears of joy, mingling with those of sorrow, bedewed the sweet flowers.

And Malcom stood up, after the ceremony, and said, with a certain dignity that for a moment hushed and impressed all present:

"Tho' I'm a little mon, I sometimes ha' great tho'ts, an' I have learned to ken fra my gudewife there, an' this sweet blossom o' the Lord's, that woman can bring a' the wourld to God if she will. That's what she can do."

THE END